The Cut-Rate Kingdom

a novel by

Thomas Keneally

Allen Lane

Copyright © Thomas Keneally, 1980

Allen Lane
A Division of Penguin Books Ltd
536 King's Road, London SW10 OUH
Penguin Books Australia Ltd
487 Maroondah Highway, P.O. Box 257
Ringwood, Victoria, 3134, Australia
The Viking Press
40 West 23rd Street, New York, N.Y. 10010, U.S.A.

First published in Australia by Wildcat Press, Sydney, 1980
First published in book form by Penguin Books Australia, 1984

First published in the U.K., 1984

Typeset in Plantin by Dovatype

Made and printed in Australia by
The Dominion Press-Hedges & Bell, Victoria

All rights reserved. Except under the conditions described in the
Copyright Act 1968 and subsequent amendments, no part of this publication
may be reproduced, stored in a retrieval system, or transmitted in any
form or by any means, electronic, mechanical, photocopying, recording,
or otherwise, without the prior permission of the copyright owner.
Except in the United States of America, this book is sold subject to
the condition that it shall not, by way of trade or otherwise, be lent,
re-sold, hired out, or otherwise circulated without the publisher's
prior consent in any form of binding or cover other than that in which it
is published and without a similar condition including this condition
being imposed on the subsequent purchaser.

CIP

Keneally, Thomas, 1935-.
Cut-Rate Kingdom.

First published: Sydney: Wildcat Press, 1980.
ISBN 0 7139 1647 8.

I. Title.

A823'.3

Author's Note

There was a wartime prime minister of Australia, but he was not Mulhall, nor are Mulhall's character, affections and secrets in any way meant to reflect the character, affections and secrets of any prime minister of any era.

There was likewise a wartime general who had his command taken from him in Port Moresby, but he was not Masson, nor do Masson's character and extraordinary marriage reflect the character and private life of any Australian general.

For the sake of brevity in story-telling, some aspects of Australian party politics in the early '40s have been simplified. There is no Billy Hughes figure, not least because Hughes resists being a peripheral figure in other men's books. Paperboy Tyson and Mrs Masson never existed.

This therefore is no *roman-à-clef*, or, if it is, the author hopes the clues refer not to the privacies of any individual but to those that characterize the Australian soul.

Part One/Chapter One

What can you say of a city like this? Kings are not buried here. Nor have migrations of strangers bearing arms, trade samples and strange features come down to it through its circle of hills.

It had never seen Tartars nor – at the time of which I write – did it possess more Italians than were needed to run its fruit shops. It was and is not Budapest, it was and is not Chicago. It lacked a Latin Quarter, it was short of a Bowery. Even now, but more so then, should its dwellers ever get a taste for squalor, they have to seek it in their souls. Its suburbs remained spotless as hospital wards.

Its very name still lacks any gracious evocations for me. Its name rasps. I cannot put it on a page without first pausing. It does not convey the flow of a river (Paris) or the bulk of a fortress (London). Its name has the sound of, say, a disease of the joints. With apologies I mark its name down.

CANBERRA.

When spoken with the flat Australian 'a' – a sound which I, Paperboy Tyson, can manufacture as well as can any of my countrymen – it is a sump of sound, it is as a dried watercourse.

A few kilometres distant from it stands, in fact, a mesolithic lake called George. Bigger than Galilee, George rises from the secret cells of the earth and, in spite of his no-nonsense manly name, can be as fine and blue as a temporary gesture of faith

1

from a woman or child. Yet I use the word 'temporary' by good advice. For in the years the capital and I have co-existed. George has withdrawn himself back into the earth many times. And though no one knows what Canberra means in the tongue of the Aborigines, it resounds in me like the secret name of George, when he goes back into the earth and makes of his vast lake-bottom a bare and bitter pasture.

It may be worth saying that in the week before the Japanese took Singapore, and in a season of drought, George vanished into the soil once more. A Roman chronicler would have made a meal out of that. But our capital seemed too homely to be connected with great events in the sky and the earth. For one thing: less than a lifetime ago it did not exist as a capital at all but was instead sheep pastures, with a bush post office and a little stone church set in their midst. An earnest American observer visited the place at that period. There was snow on the distant hills and an astringent wind beating in his ears. He asked a farmer of the district whether he was not excited by the prospect of his nation's legislators, democratically elected, meeting in a parliament building right there in the spacious flats of the plain. The farmer is said not to have shown any national piety at all. 'As long as it doesn't put the cows off their feed,' he told the visitor.

When, in a sunny season in the '20s, the Pressmen and the politicians moved into that valley, they found a long, low, white Parliament House waiting for their occupation. In one of its two wings stood a gallery panelled in Australian hardwoods and upholstered in red plush where the House of Representatives sat. Walking through a plain, cream lobby called King Hall, where the umber portraits of the few past prime ministers of the nation hung lonesome below the high windows, you got to a gallery, panelled in Australian hardwoods and upholstered in red plush, where the Senate sat. Upstairs were the offices of the Representatives and the Senators and of the members of the Press Gallery. Stuck on the back were a library and a dining room and a parliamentary bar. The Aboriginal hills brooded on this plain, white, most plebeian of all parliaments.

I remember that when I went with Johnny Mulhall's retinue to see Franklin Delano R. in the spring of '44, we spotted an insurance building in New Brunswick, New Jersey, just like the House in Canberra of which Johnny Mulhall was monarch and which I occupied by his grace and favour.

We were travelling by army limousine at the time, to Washington down the New Jersey turnpike. I said, 'Hey Johnny, does that place down there on the left remind you of a House we both know?'

He looked and offered his full and sombre attention to the building I'd pointed out. After a while he turned his slow, wall-eyed grin on me. 'Well, I'll tell you this, Paper. If it does remind me of a House I know, it shows what a bloody good House that House is. What do you think people need more? A House that looks like a palace, or a House that takes after a bloody branch office?'

For Johnny's sake I will hereafter call the Parliament House in Canberra the Branch Office. And for the sake of sweet sound I'll call Canberra itself 'the capital,' 'the village' or any other sweet-sounding name.

I'm the only man who ever *lived* in the Branch Office. Yes, I worked there but I slept there, too. My dear Mrs Millie Burman could lie with me there, if she chose, in the full leisured manner, at peace on sheets. And when the Representatives and Senators were absent in their constituencies, in Kalgoorlie so far away, in East Sydney, in Queensland, in the Mallee, telling their lies, attending to their wives, bullying their local party machines, tending their farms, mending their fences and going to football games with carnations in their lapels, I was the lucky boy, the figure from juvenile literature, who stays behind in the empty school with the sinister schoolmaster at the end of term and finds out that he is a spy or a genius or just a good friend. In the Branch Office, only I had a bath. Only I bathed in it. Only I had my own water closet and only I slept there in the white corridors of the Press wing and woke to hear the curlews cawing from the red gums at this modest, strangely beloved, two-storey version of the Westminster system of democracy.

For only I, of all the members and Press who huddled there under that sky of intimidating azure, had suffered at the apogee of Australian myth. I alone of all of them had been savaged on that salmon-coloured morning, April 25, 1915. When that enamelled representative of the old world, Winston Churchill, demonstrated to antipodean boys why they should be forever suspicious of other races by landing me waist-deep off a beach on the Gallipoli peninsula and arranging for a Turkish trigger-man (you'll allow me this indulgence of blaming Winston directly; they were, after all, my legs) to shoot both my knee-caps inside out.

So, at such times as the week Singapore fell, I was in that House: an on-the-premises symbol of the ambiguities of helping and trusting any creatures of the northern hemisphere. Millie Burman's husband, Arthur, would have served as well but the same enfilading fire that crippled me took him in the throat. I was installed in the Branch Office on the same principle that unknown soldiers are given a modicum of real estate in which to lie in good parts of London, Paris, Washington. Though I might have been a memorial of war past, I was fortunate to be a sentient one, to be capable – as this record might show – of excursions, judgments, loyalties and passions. As well, I enjoyed my work.

I first met Millie when I called on her in the role of widow's comforter. The week Singapore fell I had – to my considerable joy – been her widow's comforter for twenty years. And she my comforter, support and most regular companion. As a girl she'd earned a living as a fashion buyer for a Sydney store and had moved to the infant capital early in its history, opening on credit her own fashion shop in the arcaded centre of the town. She avoided marrying me because she mistrusted her own power (I think) to battle on in her lonesome business once the giant fact of marriage intruded. She was, as you could guess, an old-fashioned girl. It was said she had the best boutique in the bush; for although the capital was a city by decree, its dimensions were those of a bush town. Yet in a miserable decade its populace earned well. Parliamentary wives came to Millie for ball gowns to wear in the Senate chamber at the opening of parliaments, or at cocktail parties slung by the nascent consular corps.

4

Once the openings and the balls and receptions ended, and the wives from far places went back to their children, a fair trade got going in racier dresses for parliamentary mistresses, while the Public Service fraus were always good customers. You can see that Millie had good commercial cause to keep her shop open and - the quaint economy of her soul requiring it - to remain a widow. If I ever asked her did my leglessness have something to do with it, she would laugh at me. The question of whether it did might in itself make a good story. It would not, however, be the love story in question.

In Johnny Mulhall's family the tale was told that one of his ancestors in some doomed Irish rebellion - 1798 or 1848 or whenever you like to take your pick - had eaten the liver of an English dragoon. None of the fury of this real or mythic act of political cannibalism showed up in Johnny Mulhall's eyes, neither the one with the squint nor the one he used to engage people. Not even the demands of wartime propaganda ever led a journalist to ascribe to Johnny's eyes the adjectives 'piercing' or 'penetrating'.

Look, then, at the photographs of Johnny beside General McLeod. McLeod's feral eyes were a godsend to journalists, who rushed to compare him to the nobler birds of prey. You could imagine generations of Highland, pre-American McLeods subsisting on the vitals of Anglo-Saxons. Whereas Johnny always had the look not of the fierce Celtic cannibal but of a drink-waiter who'd stumbled into an official area where the dignitaries were posing for the Press.

It was with the sideways slouch of a junior clerk or a copy boy that, on the night of Singapore's fall, he entered my room, not knocking before he did so. Perhaps that was the price I paid for my residence there. Perhaps I was furniture to him. If so, I was at least a respected item.

And, being furniture, I did not need to hide away the bottle of Scotch which sat on my desk, or the half-drunk glass of the stuff that waited atop a pile of *Smith's Weeklies* for my further

5

attention. My brain was tired. I had just sent off on the teleprinter some 5 000 words. First had been a report of Johnny's speech to the Representatives two hours before. It would be passed by the censor for the morning edition. Then I had despatched a feature worked up out of oddments I'd got from some of the young officers in the Department of the Army, the ones who were full of fury about the fall of Singapore Island and who blamed the British with a vehemence that once had characterized the young Paperboy Tyson. This piece had small chance with the censor. It might lie around in the paper's archives, however, and become History.

The third feature I had sent was one I had put together more for the good of my soul, I suppose, than any other reason. Rumours about the fall of the fortress had beset the House for days past. They brought to me a pungent sense of the grief of those women whose sons or boy-husbands faced captivity. So I had begun to investigate what conditions soldiers in the beaten garrison could expect during their internment. Would comfort parcels reach the prisoners? What powers did the Red Cross have in matters of the well-being of captives? It was not a usual Press Gallery article but I had some good sources in the Army Department, and a journalist must write something other than the cosmetic half-truths they push at him. I feared this piece, too, might be axed because it took – for the sake of grieving women – a moderate view of the jailors. By understanding the malice of Bushido, it might violate the National Security Act.

After such plentiful and barely useful work, I might want to drink until I felt the whisky radiance right down in the feet I had parted with some twenty-seven years past. I did not see why Johnny Mulhall's entry should inhibit my whisky arm, or why I should pay him the insult some in that House did of rushing liquor out of his sight whenever he entered any place where it was being openly drunk.

Likewise I did not rush out of sight the document a certain Major Jimmy Pointer had slipped me that afternoon. I did not see how I could use the thing in any journalistic way anyhow. For another demand of the Chief Publicity Censor was that all news reports should show that, even if the Allies were often guilty of bad luck, they had never been guilty of folly or disunity. The document on my table showed otherwise.

The good Major himself *knew* that the document was of no use to me as a newsman. Yet he felt the fall of fortress Singapore as such an intimate hurt that leaking it had been a sort of reflex easing of his soul.

Anyhow, Johnny Mulhall walked unseeing past the bottle, the pile of *Smith's Weeklies*, Jimmy Pointer's illicit document, and sat on my three-quarter bed by the window.

'Hot, Paper,' he commented.

I agreed that it was.

'If I wasn't a bloody proletarian,' he said, wiping his nose, 'if I was Hamish or one of those silvertails, I'd get a pool in at the Lodge.'

I said I thought he ought to get a pool installed.

'Never get away with it,' he said. 'There'd be cries of "Decadence!" from the Opposition. You know.'

He ran his finger along the patterned lines of the white coverlet and fell silent. Beyond the window the capital and its population matched him for stillness. I have implied that Canberra lacked a night-life, even on evenings when there was no historic emergency. Against the illimitable sky, its dalliances did not reverberate. And if public servants whispered desperate advice about the Japanese phenomenon to their trembling wives in the suburb of Reid this evening, no tide of whisperings lapped the white walls of the Branch Office.

Therefore, as Johnny Mulhall sat fingering the coverlet on my three-quarter bed, it was hard to believe in the national emergency, in the spectacular Asian advance. And you couldn't keep from hanging on to the idea that a country which could absorb all the noise of our dismay and leave no trace could absorb an invader just as well.

I believed, as I watched him, that Johnny suffered that same flatulence of unreality and terror I did. There was no recourse but to talk in normal terms, as if the world had not changed its nature.

'Not a bad job, Johnny,' I said. 'Cool, calm. Sympathy for the relatives . . . a statement of firm purpose. Not bad.'

He looked at me in that dismal, wall-eyed way. 'What?'

I repeated myself. 'I was saying nice job you did. This afternoon. Telling the House.'

'Oh,' he said, vapouring, as if I were a stranger, 'a man has to put the best interpretation on these things he can. You can't panic people.'

'But you've got to let them know what happened,' I said playing his game.

'That's it, that's it, Paper.'

Yawning, he began to test the bed. You would have thought it was his, and that I was keeping him up.

I said, 'What about my old mate Winston? What do you reckon Winston thinks about tonight?' I half yawned as I spoke, as if the man were habitual to us, as if he were just around the corridor in the House of Reps wing.

'It isn't night where he is. Not yet. He hasn't had to face the night yet. That bugger.' Johnny yawned again, full stretch of the mouth. 'He hasn't had to face the despair of the night, old Winnie.' He giggled a bit at the dramatic phrase, 'the despair of the night.'

'You're not in despair, Johnny,' I said, the way a mother might tell a child it's not scared of the doctor. All the time I'd known him I'd got this idea of his fragility. You didn't know which shock would split him asunder but you knew it would very likely be a random one.

'I'm not in despair, Paper. I'm just bloody angry.' But I couldn't see much anger in his grey, dispassionate face.

I picked up the document Jimmy Pointer had slipped me. I said, 'They just walked into that place. The Nips. As if they had right of inheritance.'

Johnny said, 'Sometimes I think they do. Anyhow . . .' Taking the paper he closed one eye, so that in his unfocused tiredness he could sight it better.

'It's just something I came by,' I told him.

He read it and looked up after a sentence, his manner exactly that of a man who's been given some poem to read and discovers after one line that he knows it by heart anyhow. It was a cable from Burton, the Australian Representative at Singapore. The date it bore was Christmas Day, 1941. It was therefore nearly three months old. It said: 'Deterioration of our position in Malaysia. Defence is assuming landslide proportions and in my firm belief is likely to cause a collapse in the whole system. Reinforcement of troops should not be in brigades but in divisions and to be of use they must arrive urgently . . . Anything that is not powerful, modern and immediate is futile . . . Plain fact is that without immediate air reinforcements Singapore must fall . . . Need for decision and action is a matter of hours not days.' And with similar declarations it went on to invoke the wills of distant statesmen and warn the planners that they had set up the conditions for chaos.

When he'd finished scanning it, Johnny stared at me without his usual smile. His jaw at last showed some colour, a touch of that liver-devouring ancestor.

'Why did you give me this?' he asked. 'Do you think I got this, read it, disbelieved it?' he was asking.

I began to apologize. I didn't know why I had pushed the damn thing at him.

Maybe I'd meant it to be a sort of conversational aid. But it wasn't a tactful thing to do to a friend, on the evening of a fiery day, when his blood cried for the clarifications of whisky or sleep, for a benign turn of the stars.

Johnny dropped the document. As an exercise to aid thought he took out his cigarette holder, fitted a 'deathstick' (as he called them) and lit it. The tentative lips drew on it as upon nourishment. There was an inexactness to this whole ritual. Sometimes he could spread it out for half an hour, the fitting of a cigarette to the holder, the lighting of it, and in that time use both as instruments of emphasis in an argument. It was as if he'd developed this whole rigmarole as an alternative to the rituals of booze, as a ceremony to numb the call of the liver.

Then his eyes moved along the wall to where a Robinson's map of Asia hung. It still had all the Asian colonies marked in; the events of the day had not made it change its colours or notations. According to it, Singapore still lay under its old

9

Britannic dominance. It was a lot to expect of a map but I couldn't stop from feeling that it should register one way or another that Asia was transformed, that tiffin was abrogated, that gin and muffins had been driven from that latitude.

His sight skidded over the map and then returned to me. For no more than a second, he grinned a grin almost as lopsided as his vision. 'One for your memoirs, is it, Paperboy?' he asked me, nodding at the document.

'That's right, Johnny.'

With his cigarette holder fixed between his soft lips, he stood and took the paper and limped across to my cabinet. 'Let me file the thing for you.'

It was not unknown for him, during his visits, to tidy up a bit; he didn't like me to go to the trouble of getting up on my crutches. Then, having done a few token exercises in house-keeping, he would in contradiction invite me to go strolling with him, or visit him in his lonesome Lodge. 'What'll it go under? L for leaks or D for disgruntled?'

'Come off it, Johnny. Put it under S for bloody Singapore. In fact, Singapore just about warrants a file of its own.'

'Oh, do you want me to label one for you?' he asked. There was no obvious irony; he was good at making sarcasm sound like a literal statement. His green, ill-focused eyes flickered across my face with fake shyness, fake innocence.

'All right, why don't you label one?' I told him, playing it – as they say – straight.

'I know how you hate those crutches,' he said. He smiled as if to himself. 'Old dig,' he said.

'Bloody hell,' I said, 'just drop the thing in S and sit down.'

He obeyed me, still limping. The old athlete. Once he had played for Brunswick, played that barbarous yet special Melbourne game that gives the natives of that city, even its atheists, their sense of God-ordained singularity. It had produced about the same damage to cartilage and tendons as less consecrated codes, though. Johnny Mulhall's limp was nothing but the universal old footballer's limp.

He muttered, 'I'm glad you've got that thing.' He gestured towards the filing cabinet, the cable from Burton, who tonight lay under capture. He said, 'If all the documents were to be published, they'd show that poor bloody Burton did his job all right.'

'And you too, Johnny,' I said.

'Got a game of snooker with Reg,' he said then. He had this driver called Reg Whelan, father of seven. Reg would leave his darlings asleep tonight in the invaders' shadow, while he went for the pink or black with Johnny Mulhall. Being both an Irish Catholic and an old-fashioned Labor man, Reg had that homely grittiness that John Mulhall remembered and was soothed by. Johnny himself had stopped being a believer at the age of sixteen. But it's been said to the point of boredom that once you have been a Catholic it affects even the kind of atheist you become, and Johnny was an infidel in the same style as Reg was a votary. I had seen them play together. As they sagely watched each other hit the cue-ball there was this tribal communality in the room; they had access to this particular code and it was as much a comfort to Johnny as the code he and I shared.

He crossed to the door, past my desk, past the bottle. Another safe passage for John Mulhall, boy trade unionist. He turned, coughing. 'There's a do at the Lodge, Sunday,' he said. 'Do you think Millie would like to come?'

'I do,' I said. 'Sight unseen.' For Millie would tell you frankly she took invitations to the Lodge with a childlike speed.

'Tell her to take a dress out of her own shop window.'

I said she would.

'It's for General Enright, the do is. I'd have asked poor bloody Burton if I could. It would have been handy to have him there. Someone who knows what's going on in *this* world.' With his cigarette holder he pointed towards the floor of my office. 'The one we have here.'

What I liked about Johnny was that unlike most princes, he didn't write people off. You got the impression that the onus of Burton and the 20 000 young prisoners dragged appropriately at his bowels. He looked pitiable. I nearly said, 'Have a few drinks and try to sleep.' I said, 'Try to sleep.'

'I think it's six o'clock,' he said. 'Sunday. The do.' He added, as if it were the clinching attraction, 'There'll be Americans there too.'

It was discovered some years later that while I counselled Johnny Mulhall towards rest, poor bloody Burton, hindered by arthritis, was digging his own grave on the front lawn of his bungalow in Siglap.

Chapter Two

If you had observed the guests crowding into the lobby of the Lodge that Sunday afternoon, you would have seen the women pause by the gilt-framed mirror to brush cinders from their shoulders, while officers of three armies, sighting down the breasts or along the shoulders of their uniforms, picked ashy fragments of leaf from badges of rank and campaign ribbons. In the hills beyond the capital, fires grew under a sharp west wind and the sky was fouled. The symbolism – wind, fire, black scraps of forest borne on the air – was such as could not be lost even on the soldiers and politicians of a callow capital. Millie Burman and I entered the place properly intimidated, sweating like navvies in our best, the taste of fire on our tongues.

The day before, the Japanese had bombed the northern town of Darwin.

A bit of a mêlée prevailed in the hallway. People formed in a line, waiting to pass through into the main parlour and be introduced to or be greeted by Johnny before being given a drink. Through an archway I could see Weeksie, the barman from the Branch Office, standing behind the long table stocked with liquors and beers; in his eyes, that deep and sullen contemplation which marks all waiters just before the rush begins.

Ahead of Millie and me in this line-up two officers of the US military mission shuffled along, heads bent to each other in shop talk. One of them was complaining that 'these jokers' had all their best fliers far away. Seventeen squadrons in goddamned Britain! Seventeen. Just bits and pieces left here. Someone called Chuck had told him the goddamned Hudsons up in Darwin didn't have bombs to fit the racks . . .

It did not escape him that Millie and I were avid listeners. He jiggled the collar of his dress uniform and switched on an even, well-teethed staff college smile. I think Millie and I were pretty disarmed. With whatever gangling grace we had picked up in childhood and youth we were pitted against the grand resources of American charm, which we could mock but never match. Johnny would not be able to manage a smile like that. When this smooth brigadier reached Johnny, he would be met by a smile which looked halfway like that of a man in pain.

'Hot, anyhow,' the officer said. 'Is it always this hot?'

Millie gave him a fuller answer than he wanted. 'No, not always,' she said. She began to pitch a tale of the Canberra climate, quoting seasonal temperatures, praising the capital's autumn and the spring. She spoke too much like a woman fulfilling a patriotic duty. I suppose she felt that if you lose a husband and the two legs of your lover to the defence of Australian seasonal averages, then you shouldn't let foreign career officers dismiss the continent as a mere furnace.

The American officers listened to Millie's small lecture with that omnivorous American politeness which Johnny Mulhall and all we poor hayseeds would come to know so well and mistrust, perhaps, not enough.

We pressed on into the reception room. Some five prime ministers, apart from Johnny, had lived in this anonymous villa of white stucco. Its furnishings looked ownerless, like furniture in a museum, and spoke of the transience of heads of government. It would have been interesting if its inhabitants had let their heads go. Two had been Irish Catholic, three had represented the Anglo-Saxon and Protestant tradition. Two had come up through trade unions, one had been a dazzling lawyer, one a failed army officer, another a mortgage-jobber from Queensland. You could see that each, for whatever reason, had hung back from marking his character on this studiedly characterless place. Old Joe Scanlon (1929-31) had nailed no Dublin Proclamation of 1916 to the kitchen walls, and Tony Hamish (1939-41) had placed no plaid of the clan Hamish on the stairwell. The furniture was tooled from the same Australian hardwoods as prevailed in the Branch Office and there were some antiques as well, French and English (no Asian), acquired lovelessly by a government procurement office, and looking it.

Among these passably superb items Johnny Mulhall stood, a man with no ideas about interior design. Over in Brighton in South Australia, in the small villa where he and his wife had lived – where Ada Mulhall herself still in fact resided – the family dining room suite was plain oak, the lounge suite was *petit-point* and the cat played merry hell with one of its arms. The Mulhall marriage bed had head and tail pieces with teak veneer panels which had split and separated in places. Johnny was as indifferent to the made-in-Ultimo furniture at home as he was to the staid, good things in the Lodge. He did not see them. They were but conditions of the space he rattled round in. Even Eddie Hoare, his Minister for Labour, recognized antiques. He saw them as the debris of that old history of the oppression of the masses. They were the wreckage of Europe that had washed up on our more-or-less innocent beaches. So that if Eddie Hoare had been prime minister he would have at least taken a posture towards the place. He would have disapproved of the Regency bookcases.

When we reached him, Johnny said, 'Nice dress, Millie.' Yet his gaze moved over her unseeingly. He had no eye for costume. Millie knew this. She smiled in that broad, yet private way of hers.

I was most aware of the yellow exhaustion of his features and the nerve beating and protesting in the corner of his mouth. I had an urge to offer condolences because the Japanese had raided in the north. It would be better to apologize to the corpses now being fitted for coffins under the iron roof of the Darwin School of Arts. But Johnny the public man would always have this astounding gift of making people believe in the private pain which large events brought him. People who would never meet him would always believe that he had made the Pacific War somehow interior to him. Its disasters were disasters personal to him, and so its triumphs would be personal to him and would bring him much benefit at the polls. At that time there had been no triumphs, and so we faced a John Mulhall who wore the aspect of a casualty of battle.

He took my elbow and said, 'Lots of copy, Paper.'

'Here, Johnny?' I looked around.

'Here,' he said.

'Enright?'

'Not so much Enright.'

General Enright stood further acros the reception room speaking to guests as pressure from behind swept them on past Johnny. He was Commander of the Allies in the Dutch East Indies. Since everyone knew it was going to be a short-lived campaign there, he had the unjustified problems of what a later age would call 'credibility.'

Johnny said, 'He didn't even want to come to his bloody party.'

My old northern hemisphere demon Winston had sent him down from Java, where he had been awaiting amphibious landings, to carry messages to Johnny. One message was that the British require l Johnny to send some 20 000 of his boys – his Depression children, his veterans presently at sea in the Indian Ocean, returning to their proper latitude – to the doomed city of Rangoon.

Millie said, 'Why ever would he be so ungracious?' She was, like all of us, very loyal and a touch parochial.

'You know, Millie,' he said. 'You can't always satisfy these blokes. Forgive the shop talk,' he urged her.

'I run a shop, too, Mr Mulhall,' said Millie.

'I know,' he said, 'I know you do.' And he stood chastised, so that what he said next was said with one eye on her and one on me, I being fixed by the astigmatic one. 'You wanted to talk about copy, Paper,' he falsely accused my. 'Everyone's known for weeks Singapore would go and that's brought all the generals racing home from the desert.' He meant no indigenous desert but the deserts of Egypt and Libya. 'You'd think gold had been discovered. They're funny buggers. They think the worse things

16

are going, the better the opportunity. Well, the big news is that the winner of the Generals' Gallop arrived yesterday and is here this evening.'

Millie and I followed the bearing of Johnny's lazy nod. Beyond the place where Enright spoke and found reason to laugh with the American mission, a tall sandy-haired general stood stooping, talking to Jimmy Pointer. Everyone spoke to Jimmy at these shows, either because they admired him for his great Pacific visions or so that they could make jokes about him afterwards. This general seemed to treat Jimmy with gravity. The man may have been older than forty but didn't look it. He had a lithe, taut, bloodless look.

'That's the one called Masson, isn't it?' I asked. I'd talked to him on the telephone once about the time of Sudetenland.

'That's him,' said Johnny.

I'd found out from someone that Masson's father had been a Huguenot lawyer who'd espoused Australia fifty years past as a cure for tuberculosis. Yet, as if the gritty Australian sunshine had gone into the fibre of the general's skin, he didn't look Gallic at all; he looked like the sort of lanky Presbyterian Scot a man got used to seeing in the officer corps.

I guessed that Masson stood in Johnny Mulhall's parlour this fire-rimmed evening, wearing the discreet advertisement of his reputation as a desert general, in the hope of getting his proper corner of the Pacific conflict, the same way that a speculator hopes for his corner of the boom. My contact with officers was what you'd call tangential but enough to learn something of their temperamental habits. They can seem tranquil as flies in amber while peace holds them fixed and orbitless. War renders them skittish; divides their minds between their present and their future. The brigadier works his brigade in the hope of a division and the general of a division wants a corps or a spacious zone of command. There is nothing like command itself to give the buggers a taste for it. The sedentary humility of the trooper, gunner, private, who spends an entire campaign or all a dreary war in the one section, is something generals must depend on but have no taste for imitating.

It turned out that Masson had reached Canberra before any

of the others through means fair, square and accidental. He had been flown home from Egypt, while his division rested, to make some representations or other to the War Cabinet. He would not have to return to the Middle East now. His division was already embarking at Suez and would steam home.

If Major-General Masson had come here for the usual reasons generals hang around princes, Mulhall, of course, made an unlikely prince. His childhood was, as I said, Melbourne Irish. His father had been an invalided railroad shunter. Johnny's short education had been in character: the Sisters of St Joseph had told him that the ironies of the secular world would make a monkey of him and the Christian Brothers of Ireland had slipped him the news that good Catholic men could adjust the inequities of the earth, inspired as they were by the Anglo-Saxon ruling class, by joining their local branch of the Australian Labor Party. He had worked in the union movement until he was near forty.

I doubt that up to the early 1930s he had met one professional officer. If he had been asked about them, he would have told you they were sons of the middle class, chosen and cosseted for Duntroon, so that if ever it were needed they could with a free conscience dismiss the lowly by firing over their heads and sending in the dragoons. His subscriptions to the local military journal began about the time Hitler won the Reichstag elections; by the time of the Ethiopian adventure he knew into what schools of thought the Staff Corps fell. Before Franco had won in Spain, he'd begun talking to generals of militia and making speeches in the House about how the continent could only be held by plenteous aircraft.

His socialist colleague Eddie Hoare had never let himself be side-tracked by world events and he looked on Johnny's concern for military strategy and the minds of soldiers as just part of Johnny's core-softness for 'proper' people. In the old tribal terms, Eddie was the black, blunt Celt of South Sydney and he saw Johnny as a lace-curtain job. 'His mother was just the same,' Eddie had told me once. 'When I met the bugger first he was still living at home with his people in Collingwood. Bloody pretentious! Arse out of the trousers but a manner like aristocracy in exile! Don't tell me Johnny's not his mother's boy.'

I asked Johnny if he'd talked to Masson yet. 'No,' said Johnny, tamping back a yawn. 'He hasn't been wheeled up to me.'

As he spoke we saw a woman approach the General's left hand. She appeared from the blind side of the hefty mass of Johnny's Minister for the Army. (I am not going to name many of his ministers, for each of their names has such potent and distracting evocations for the Australian native that they will only side-track this small memoir.) The Minister for the Army, then, had probably until that second been holding the girl behind his bulk with that strange bulge-eyed gaze of his. None of us had seen her enter the Lodge in the first place, so that she hove around the Minister's flank with the effect of an apparition.

'Who's that woman?' Johnny Mulhall asked. He looked sleepy, chin raised, eyes just about closed.

'I don't know,' I told him, as if I couldn't care less.

Millie could tell we were both pushing our indifference, pretending idle interest when in fact we were both absorbed by the glimpse of the girl. 'It's the wife,' said Millie, no fake dreaminess in her. 'Mrs Masson. I met her once.'

I don't think I'm having myself on when I say that even then I knew that Johnny's sighting of the girl was of a different order to mine. I might as well make a complete goat of myself or, to confound the animals, go the whole hog and say that I'm sure that at the time there was just about an audible resetting of . . . I don't know of what . . . of some emotional, aesthetic gear in Johnny. You can watch an anemone in a sea-gutter, all its fronds leaning with the current; and then the tide changes, the waters flow and the fronds are now seeking a new alignment, and the undersides of the filaments are showing upwards now and taking the light in a new way. As regards its functions, and the way it eats, sleeps and procreates, the anemone is still zoologically the same as five minutes back; but in the human sense, in the sense of the poet, the animal has changed utterly in aspect. I think Johnny's aspect changed for good when he saw Mrs Masson.

I am as bad as Johnny ever was at remembering what people wore on a particular occasion or observing what they are wearing at the present. I remember, though, that Mrs Masson wore that night a summer frock that had strawberries and green leaves on

19

it. It looked, I might say, like a garment put on to challenge the droughty land to bloom in the face of fire and to invoke George the lake to rise once more out of his hidden sources. Though she was so well-moulded, she carried her chin very high the way an obedient fourteen-year-old would whose parents have been nagging her about her posture. She wore a wide-brimmed, round crown straw hat on top of long brown hair. She had kept her complexion very English beneath it and similar hats. Most of the dozen or so other women in the parlour that evening were just back sun-kippered from their summer holidays down around Bateman's Bay. Beside these whom the sun had touched fairly heavily, she looked like a wanderer from a cocktail party in some more temperate latitude.

What I remember sharpest about her, though, was that when she walked there was – at least by the standards of '42 – a sort of unabashed fluency about the movement of her hips – not a sort of forced, provocative swing, a freedom that was just characteristic, that's all, but which I thought of straight off as 'unmarried.' Maybe she'd been too long separated from her desert-campaigning spouse. I think it more likely she was always like it.

I said, 'I've heard about her. They reckon she's very beautiful.' As if the data of beauty weren't there before me.

I could see the American career officers, the ones who'd got their meteorological lecture from Millie, watching her with the same openness they'd used to listen to my sweet widow. From the military staff of a certain General Brett, these officers had been on their way to the Philippines when the deterioration of that campaign had diverted them to Brisbane. You'd think that, having been saved from the murderous jungles of Bataan, they could have given up wife-coveting for a while.

Johnny bit his lower lip and squinted at the ceiling. 'She looks a bit independent-minded,' he said. 'Eh? Her own woman.' He grinned in a way that had a lot of boyish bar-room envy to it. There was something of the young alcoholic in the shy way his eyes, good and bad, slewed from the wonderful Mrs Masson to Millie to the ceiling to me. 'You know most people, Millie. Eh? You say you know her?'

'I met her at Randwick. The Spring Carnival. When was it? Last year, that's when it was.'

'Nice woman, is she?' he asked. There was, of course, some stupefaction in the question.

'We took to each other,' said Millie. She smiled a little, and I thought how generous the smile was. Most women would dislike someone like Mrs Masson on principle, the principle on which women who are uncertain or bitter about their beauty and their freedom always dislike the beautiful and the visibly free. Millie said, 'We had a good chat. Mind you, we got a little tiddly – it was a champagne lunch.'

'In wartime, Millie?' Johnny Mulhall said. 'Champagne? In wartime?'

Millie told us, 'She'd sort of been dragged along there. She said she was pleased she had me to talk to. And she seemed to be. Even though she's much better up on things than I am.'

Johnny did not seem to hear but grinned on in that hesitant way. I do not want to pretend that the Prime Minister even of a small nation was as backward and awkward as a boy. In fact Johnny's specialty was a sort of awkwardness, his strength was to look somewhat lost. He would look like that in caucus (or so I'm told); he would even bung on the tears. Yet in those first seconds of his sighting of Mrs Masson he was showing Millie and me an innocence that mightn't have been painful to him but caused us something close to pain.

I've noticed before that intense men from strict socialist boyhoods often grow up as the most simple-minded romantics. Apart from those Tories who had strong and generally narrow religious beliefs, the conservatives as a race were sexual bandits. They stayed at the licensed Hotel Canberra and introduced their partners in casual fornication through the lobbies or the kitchens or, by using a trey-bit as a screwdriver, through the wire screen windows of their rooms. The ideologues of the Labor Party stayed at the unlicensed Kurrajong Hotel. I don't want to paint them too pure – it's certain some of them ravened like the finest Tory ram. But in the lounge of the Kurrajong you heard social theory touted, whereas in the other place it seemed all wool prices, stocks and women. And in those unlicensed premises of

21

the Kurrajong you might sometimes find a Labor type which has recurred in the capital's short history; the man in his late forties or early fifties to whom love of some clerk or typist came as harsh, as demanding, as had the socialist vision of his boyhood. The more worldly brotherhood of the Hotel Canberra lounge had a crude phrase for it. They called it 'doing your nuts.' They made sure it didn't happen to them.

I refuse to descend to such terms in the case of John Mulhall. Yet Millie and I knew he had never seen anything like Mrs Masson. She wasn't the sort of girl who occurred in the earnest socialist families he'd grown up with in the poorer suburbs of Melbourne, in Collingwood, Coburg or Brunswick. He would have been unlikely to have seen anything like her since then. For in the '30s a Labor politician had no social stature and, even as Leader of the Opposition, Johnny used to travel round the country second class with his Press Secretary and stay with the less prosperous commercial travellers in economical hotels. And Canberra ... as I've said ... was no honeypot, no centre of fashion or of beauty.

Millie said, 'She's a bit of a fish out of water. She lives at Double Bay. But she went to Spain, she was telling me.'

'Spain,' said Johnny in a dazed way.

'With the Red Cross,' said Millie.

I said that Johnny must have lots of people to talk to. Millie and I would get a drink and let him do his stuff. 'No one's more important than you two,' he told us, but his eyes returned unwillingly from their consideration of Mrs Masson.

When we'd gone over to give Weeksie our orders, I looked back and watched Johnny for a second as he stood alone. Two junior departmental heads and their wives were approaching him from his wall-eyed left side, their faces set in the half-hopeful smile of those who are not fully sure of their right to draw near the monarch. '*His* wife ought to be here,' I said to Millie.

She threw me a concessive shrug. 'Doesn't stop most buggers,' she said, 'from looking at other women. Fact that their wives are around ...'

* * * *

Ada Mulhall stayed – for growing stretches of time that would almost justify a person in using the word 'separation' – over in the family home near Adelaide by the Southern Ocean, staring through her private eye at a sea which ran all the way to the ice-fringe of Antarctica. It was a house in which the ghost of their sixteen-year-old son was powerful. Six years past the boy had died of meningitis and, though Ada did not go in for that madness of keeping the house as a shrine for him, she had not thrown out his old text books and school football pictures and little trophies inscribed 'Kevin Mulhall, Best and Fairest 1935' seemed to populate every shelf.

The times I'd met her I'd found her far harder than Johnny to work out. Her mouth was as misleadingly soft as her husband's and it would have been easy to write her off as a fairly supine woman. Her face was handsome, broad, motherly but a dreaminess came easily into her eyes and a bewildered yet knowing smile to her lips. I don't know why she stayed over there in the low-slung bungalow amid the sand dunes. There were rumours that Johnny and Ada hadn't gone through what was then quaintly called 'the marriage act' since Kevin died of meningitis in 1936. I don't know if that is the truth, or why it should be the truth, and I would know as well as anyone but the parties themselves.

Others spoke of a fierce shyness that made her eschew the capital, set as it was like a dull and ill-formed gem in the heartland of a distant State, far from her son's grave. It takes a strong woman, though, to indulge her shyness in that measure; it takes strength of some sort to set your old man down alone amongst Canberra's nascent diplomatic corps and leave them to think him a bachelor.

Jimmy Pointer had once mentioned to me that Ada Mulhall was not even in the same military zone as Johnny. There were rumours that, when the Japanese came, calm-eyed Ada Mulhall would – together with the greater part of the land mass – be delivered up to them, that only the south-east corner of the continent would be fought for. Jimmy must have mentioned the curious possibility to others as well. For one day I heard drinkers in the parliamentary bar making low jokes about Johnny hoping the Japanese High Command would play a hand in his marital impasse. The jokes would've had more conviction if any of them had been sure what the marital impasse was.

Anyhow, they were both complicated people, the Mulhalls, and I still wonder if they *might* have been using the Japanese as part of what people would call these days 'the dynamics' of their marriage.

Eddie Hoare came up behind us as we stood together, sipping. 'Paper,' he said, 'Mrs Burman.' His brown eyes came to us magnified by the lenses of his spectacles. They were supposed to be weak eyes but they dominated us.

If he intended to grill us, Millie got in first. 'What's the news from Darwin, Eddie?' she asked.

He tossed his head a bit. 'You were with Johnny. He could have told you.'

'Didn't like to ask,' she said. 'These things upset him . . .'

'We're all able to feel pain, love,' Eddie told her with a little smile, but without much humour to it.

She waved her soft hand around in confusion.

'All right,' he promised her, pushing his anarchic Irish grin down into the corner of his mouth, 'I'll tell you all about Darwin, love. And you can watch my brows and warn me when the beads of blood break out.'

'That'll be the day!' said Millie.

'It began at ten o'clock this morning,' he said. 'Some ninety planes involved. They came in at 14 000 feet from the south-east . . . Have you ever been to Darwin, Millie?' he asked for no clear reason.

'No,' said Millie. 'I've never even been to Brisbane.'

'They killed about 250 people in the first sweep. Lots of the poor buggers they got were in air-raid shelters. So it goes to show. They got some poor bloody Chinks in Chinatown. The administrator lost his Abo maid – not exactly the Abo's war, is it? Soldiers started looting – yes, our decent Aussie boys. Then the Nips came back and did the air force station over. I believe there are airmen all over the mulga, hiding in the scrub.'

Millie and I stared at each other, for it was a larger disaster than the radio had told us.

We knew Eddie liked to deride the military as much as I did and wondered was he distorting the news.

'The wire services said there were fifteen dead,' I told him.

'Of course,' he said without blinking. 'Let me see now. What else won't you read in tomorrow's Press? Eight ships sunk, three beached. Eighteen planes wrecked on the ground. Maybe half a thousand dead . . . who can tell?' He turned to Millie and asked, 'Have you noticed any beaded gore on my forehead yet, love?'

'Not a drop, Mr Hoare,' said Millie.

He began to shake his head. 'Bugger it, Millie,' he said. 'No one's got a corner on mourning. Let me place the tragedy in its context. Do you two know how many deaths there have been in mines in this State since 1918? Go to any country town and ask. No one knows. What sort of memorial is there to miners? On what day do Heads of State lay down floral tributes to coal cutters?'

'Oh Gord!' said Millie.

'But,' he said, 'this means more to the newspaper proprietors, to your own boss, Paper. They can denounce the massacre in Darwin since it was not performed by shareholders or advertisers . . .'

'Fair go, Eddie,' I said. 'This is an invasion.'

'I'm glad you realize it, Paper. This is an invasion, old dig. We have a foreign army in Brisbane. And foreign officers in here, drinking some stuff Weeksie got from the officers' mess at Duntroon. It's called bourbon and they pronounce it, ignorant buggers (pardon me, Millie!) they pronounce it burbin.'

'You mean the Americans?' said Millie, who saw them as saviours. 'The Americans? Invaders?'

'Exactly, Millie. Look at it from this aspect. They cut off the Japanese oil by means of embargo. They invited the conflict . . .'

'You say the Japanese didn't!' asked Millie on a high note.

'They invited it, too. What I mean, Millie, is who caused the Second Punic War?'

'I don't have the faintest clue,' said Millie, proud to be free of the mental burden of historical analogies.

'The answer is, both sets of the bastards did. The Romans did and the Carthaginians did. Because they had a notion they both needed exclusive use of the sea. For trade, my love. For *trade*.'

Millie was beginning to colour and get really angry. 'The Marx Brothers,' she said. 'Harpo and Karl and Eddie!'

His little jokes grated in that week when Asia changed. But now, when you look back at some of the things Eddie said, they have the same value as prophecies – it was in part his unfortunate manner of delivering his opinions that made us resist them.

When he left us, I looked for Johnny again. I never knew any other figure who had the power to make people check on him at public functions – even at ones called by himself – just to see that he was not left alone and awkward. As if he were the cack-handed boy and the party had been called to bring him out of himself.

He was not alone. He stood with his square-faced Minister for External Affairs (who himself had a grandiose and tragic future, which is another story). He stood also with Mrs Masson, and he and the Minister and Mrs Masson all listened to the General. In fact the woman's interest seemed equal to that of the two politicians, even though she may have already heard everything the General had to say.

Millie liked to drift, which was hard on my left stump and my armpits.

I think she'd always had a secret taste for Tony Hamish. It went hand in hand with her expressed dislike of him. In the days he'd been Prime Minister, he'd once or twice visited Millie's boutique with his wife. I think that when he fell from power you could detect a sneaking sympathy in Millie, even though he was no sincere friend or even acquaintance. He was said to be good at parties, he was always boss wit at table. So Millie thought he'd be easy to find tonight, would be somewhere in the centre of the floor. In fact we found him in near hiding. He stood beyond a potted palm, his large nose and flat brow emerging in profile from the far side of the heavy gilt frame of a landscape.

It was uncharacteristic of him to make use of the shelter of foliage and picture frames in this place which, until only six months before, he and his lean wife had occupied. His usual manner in the Lodge was that of a landlord visiting a short-term tenant. And a short-term tenant was exactly what Johnny Mulhall always looked like.

Tony had been talking with yet another of Johnny's cabinet ministers. We said good evening and how did they do, and Tony frowned and looked remote and the cabinet minister took the chance to break loose from him and, as he walked away, gave little shakes of his head. There'd been some sort of dispute between them and we had therefore delivered Labor and Tory from each other.

I said, 'If you're busy, Tony . . .'

He decided it was time to smile and turn delightful and he left the shelter of the gilt frame, though not entirely that of the pot plant. 'Always a delight to see Millie,' he said, in that way that implied they had a swag of secrets between them I was excluded from. 'Can't say the same about you, Paper, you bloody old Press lackey.'

The latter compliment creaked in Tony's mouth. He'd never been easy with that sort of unbuttoned friendly insult but I believe that a supporter of his had told him that one of the reasons the independents in the House had voted against him, giving power to Johnny, was his lack of the gift of easy camaraderie. So what he was doing now was practising his geniality. It gave me a moment's happy fantasy to imagine him trying his pally insults out on General Hyakutake, whose Seventeenth Army was said (by experts like Jimmy Pointer) to have been rostered to take our gangling, vacant continent.

He began to look sober then, tucking in the corners of his even mouth. 'What I was wondering,' he said, 'was who invited Madam Red?'

'Invited who?' I said.

His breath flapped his lips in a strange way. He rumbled. 'The Red whore,' he said. Across the fronds of the pot plant, he took a glance at the group listening to General Masson. Then he muttered, 'Saving your presence, Millie.'

Millie bobbed her head, a taut, grudging assent. But she didn't know him well enough to pin his ears back, if that's what she had in mind.

'Millie knows her,' I told him. 'And says she drinks champagne just like a Tony Hamish supporter.'

Through his fixed lips he laughed, and it was like groaning. 'The bombo, Paper, sweet wine, that's no test. All the buggers like that. Some socialists I know liked it all too well in their early years.'

His movements got all at once more flamboyant. He flung his hand out and held it in place in a genuine King's Counsel gesture. 'Dick Masson's a decent enough chap, I'll admit that. But the Lodge represents something, surely. An invitation here ought to be a reward for some sort of service. I'm serious, Paper. When I was here an invitation to the Lodge . . . and I say this knowing you'll probably mention it to John Mulhall; in fact, I hope you do . . . an invitation to the Lodge well, I'll tell you this, anyone who'd been secretary of the League for Peace and Freedom – *she* wouldn't have been invited no matter who – to whom, I should say – to whom she was married. Johnny could just as well invite Masson round to the Parliament and they'd have a better talk than they'll have here.'

Millie was bewildered. I could see in her frown the suspicion that Hamish might be reflecting on us, too, for we had never – in his pontificate – been invited here. I was used to the Hamish manner and knew I could get away with making a deprecating noise. I made one. I said, 'The lady doesn't like Franco, eh?'

'Use your imagination,' said Tony.

Millie was able to speak now. 'She told me, last year. She's an air-raid warden . . .'

Tony said, 'All the comrades are willing to be air-raid wardens now that Holy Mother Russia is involved.'

'But why would she marry a soldier then?' Millie persisted. She knew enough politics to understand that girls who disliked Franco didn't usually marry staff officers.

'There are women, Millie,' he said, instructing her, 'who get a thrill out of associating with men of a different political kidney.

However, I believe that when they first married she wasn't so bad. Of course even now she's playing at it. Masson ought to give her a good beating. It's possible to admire a sincere Red ... but the Double Bay variety... !' He looked at his watch and thought a while, pushing his tongue against his upper lip, as if he were wondering was it safe to leave cover. He said then, 'I've got to speak to Enright before I go. John Mulhall is spending so much time with Masson that you'd think *he* was the most important person in the room.'

So he said goodbye to us both, stepped away, stopped, settled himself as an actor does in the flies in the seconds before an appearance, then walked out of that obscure corner he'd been sharing with us and, in the face of the sublime red peril, called noisy greetings to Enright.

Again I don't know if it's hindsight but it seems to me that Enright stood in the room that night like a sort of token being, rather than a real force. He and Johnny had had an argument earlier in the night over troops for Java and Rangoon. He had been in our capital some twenty-four hours and would fly away again tomorrow morning to his headquarters in what was in those days called Batavia. Tonight he did not talk at length to other people, he nodded as they told him things. He stood there like the ghost of empire – no, not that; he *was* the ghost of empire. A distinguished man, of course. A good stylist, he was writing a biography of his commanding officer in the first war even then, even in the week Asia was transmuted.

Now Tony Hamish walked up to him and for the first time that night the General found himself in earnest conversation. Tony stood a little higher than him, shoulder turned in, right hand caressingly held close to the General's elbow. They looked like men getting together at a late hour to put together between them some great imperial strategy to match that of the adroit Nips.

Tony had a Britannic bias. He did not understand, he never would, that the old show was over in Asia. Once he had complained that the further a place was from Westminster, the more parlous were Winston's strategic judgments about it. Yet in spite of such outbursts, I'm sure that the night he spoke to Enright, the wide brown land was, in the atlas of his emotions, still moored somewhere off Beachy Head.

From our corner it was clear that in spite of the transmuted Pacific, in the presence of Enright the British ghost and in the face of Masson's analysis, Johnny's good eye kept being dragged towards Mrs Pam Masson's strawberry dress, to her mildly frowning face, to her wide eyes unimpaired by booze or the harsh sun, to the well-ordered body beneath the fabric. I suppose it's true that I watched Johnny watching her because I was aroused myself. It was an unreal arousal, though, at least for me. It was like the arousal that occurs between the cripple in the stalls and Ginger Rogers on the screen. In saying 'cripple', though, I'm probably putting on side. If I'd come whole through Anzac Day, I would still not have been as ambitious a man as Johnny. It was Johnny who got the idea of taking the Pacific War into his fibres as an owned reality, a weird bird for his particular nest. And it was Johnny who got that same sort of idea about Pam Masson.

Johnny allowed the party to go on some three hours. Once General Enright had left, to get in a night's sleep before he went back to his biography and to his disastrous front, the evening got a kick along, as a wake does once the corpse is under the sod. Then, towards nine, everyone seemed to receive the host's message that the evening had ended, that it would not develop further, that there would be no unexpected songs. A collective departure set in and Millie and I rushed our drinks to join it. I was just refitting my crutches into the hollows of my arms when Jim Cowan, Johnny's Press Secretary, found us in our corner. He said that Johnny wanted to go on talking with Masson, and wondered could we two stay on and entertain Masson's wife?

We both hurried to say yes. We were flattered at being asked to perform this service of State. For the first time that evening we found chairs. I eased into one and Millie propped the crutches against the wall. The chair I'd found was up against the big square window and even by turning my head a little – which I was doing anyhow, working my shoulder blades and armpits so that they'd forget the bite of the crutch-pads – I could see the guests leaving, bunching together on the gravel paths, waiting for their cars, squinting at the sky in an instinctive desire for rain clouds. Jimmy Pointer stood by that window staring out at them, too. Beneath his beautifully brushed brown hair, his blue eyes judged them. He must also have been invited to wait back, to be a conversational partner for Mrs Masson. A sweet enough duty for a soldier.

'Just take a look at them, Paper,' Jimmy invited me, the way people always do when a large window puts them at a distance from a party of others. I didn't look at them at any length, I was still working out the cricks in my shoulders the better to enjoy Mrs Masson's company. I noticed, though, in taking an obedient quick look, that there was a terrible tenebrous redness in the night sky above the garden.

'There's Tony Hamish brushing cinders off Enright's epaulets and the Minister for the Army doing the same bloody thing for the Yanks. The question is, who'll brush the cinders off Tony, though, off the Minister? We're a race of bloody servants, Paper, and it gives me the shits, bloody hell it does. We're a race of . . . of bloody ostlers, that's what we are. A former prime minister of this Commonwealth and a member of the Cabinet behaving like a pair of bloody theatrical dressers, Paper, a pair of poncy window-dressers. That Yank, that *top* Yank, is a mere bloody staff brigadier. Yet, dear chap, he cops a cabinet minister for a valet!'

'They're just being polite, Jimmy,' I grunted, working away with my buttocks and my elbows to impose some of my temperamental subtleties on this nameless, unowned chair. 'Foreigners aren't used to having ash fall out of the sky. The Minister's just being polite to guests. We're not *all* rude buggers.'

'Guests!' said Jimmy, and he turned his broad, immaculately shaven face to me and laughed. 'If we treat them as guests, Paper – Jesus, old friend! – we'll lose it all for good and ever. We'll be the same old colony again, Paper. New management, same old business . . .'

And he came out with more of the same. Though it might sound like Eddie Hoare's line of argument, in fact Jimmy

Pointer held a simple, mystical idea of Australia as a child of the south, as Asia's permanent European resident, referee, missionary and wise brother. In this vision the Americans were gate-crashers, demons of expedience. By an irony it was a phrase once used by an American President in another context which best described the sort of feelings Pointer had about this burning summer nation in which we stood and sat around holding the dregs of our drinks and waiting to meet Mrs Masson. The phrase was 'manifest destiny.'

'They'll be brushing the shoulder straps of another race in a month or two,' I muttered, and terror washed through my body like a tide of the blood and I reached out and took Millie's hand.

My fit passed on into Millie, in fact. She gave a hearty shudder. 'Horrible,' she said, as if to herself. She had read somewhere that the Japanese cut off the breasts of the women they misused. The censor would have been very pleased to pass stories like that, stories that marshalled the nation's women more or less by the pits of their wombs.

Johnny and Mrs Masson took us by surprise. They arrived while our attention was somehow beyond the window still, with the fires, the decamping guest and the alien threat.

Johnny said with his soft smile he believed Millie had already met Mrs Masson. 'Dick and I are going to have a talk for a while,' he said. 'You'll pour the drinks, will you, Jimmy?' For Weeksie was packing up with that doggedness of a man who's worked his award hours and has a right to go home to his family.

I looked up at the woman and was introduced. In our dry little sump of government, the English lushness of her skin was all the more notable but I noticed the humour, the near irony in her eyes as well. 'I'm Tyson the hack,' I told her. 'They call me Paper. Do you mind if I don't stand up, Mrs Masson.'

'Paper is one of the most powerful men in the whole Commonwealth,' said Johnny. There was all his normal gawky, crook-shouldered bashfulness there; at least three-quarters of it wasn't a performance and it would have telegraphed to a woman like Pam Masson exactly where he came from and all his inner Melbourne ignorance of her. 'I ask Paper to these corroborees,' he said, 'because I'm scared if I don't, he and his boss will point the bone at me.'

He waited to watch us a while, as if he hoped we'd catalyse before his eyes. Then he nodded his head in a jerky way, said 'Well!' and left the reception room to go up the hall to his office.

At first we talked about the fires. Jimmy Pointer said 'the garrison' of the capital was being mobilized to fight them. I thought it was a bit fancy to call the few battalions of militia thereabout 'a garrison' but the word served Jimmy's grandiloquent style. I said I'd heard that an old Abo in Bungendore had stretched his hand back into the future of his cranium and beheld a deluge above the smouldering hills. I said they ought to put him on the staff, to keep Jimmy company. As the only two hopeful men in the country. Millie gave a striving laugh at that, Mrs Masson grinned into her shallow gin and Jimmy's face was still clouded over with ideas like 'garrison' and 'Pacific destiny.'

I could tell that Jimmy and Mrs Masson knew each other. It was not surprising, since they were both Sydneysiders. Yet in spite of their familiarity none of us started feeling easy with each other until we got on to the subject of General Starkey.

If you go into any Australian town you'll find a thoroughfare – avenue, drive, street – named after old Starkey. But the age when his name would be favoured by municipalities was still in the future.

In the year I'm writing about, Starkey was Masson's generalissimo in the deserts. An earthy but influential journal called *Smith's Weekly* was pushing an editorial campaign to have him moved and Masson's name was sometimes raised as a replacement. In spite of military censors, poisonous stories about Starkey came back across the equator to ordinary people in Australia. The families of soldiers would tell you Starkey operated his headquarters from a brothel in the Buka: then in contradiction they would complain that, unlike every other campaigner, he was allowed to have his wife with him in Cairo.

I think I started the subject off that night by asking Mrs Masson if her husband had seen the old chap lately.

Mrs Masson put together a brief little smile and her lips, this furnace-blast evening, shone with moisture. She said, 'General Starkey has leg ulcers again.'

'I heard that,' Jimmy Pointer murmured. 'If he gets leg ulcers in the desert, how much more in the jungle .. !'

Jimmy couldn't see an old man with bandages on his legs as the Charles Martel of the tropic war. Maybe he could see someone else because his eyes were near closed, as if visualizing a face.

Mrs Masson considered the knuckles of her right hand, rubbed at them with the thumb of her left. 'Dick admires him,' she murmured, as if informing Jimmy Pointer but also allowing us, Millie and me, to overhear. 'But he's never really respected him since last year.'

'Last year?' said Jimmy. He frowned; he was keen for more.

'Well, after the evacuation from a certain Aegean locality . . .' She didn't say the word 'Greece' and it seemed this was not so much from coyness but because she suspected the raw name could hurt people. 'Dick was sleeping under an olive tree just outside . . . I've forgotten the name of the place . . . Mandra, that's the place . . . that's where Starkey found him and ordered him to leave. He keeps saying he wishes he'd never left that olive tree.'

Jimmy Pointer rubbed his hands, a little like an undertaker. 'It's a dreadful thing,' he said, 'to be asked to leave a whole brigade behind. Young men, old men, fellows you know . . .'

'He was under orders, of course,' Mrs Masson said. 'But he still debates whether he should have disobeyed them.'

I said, 'Starkey got his own son out, didn't he? He couldn't get his own son out and leave his generals behind.'

The woman considered me but did not deal with my statement. She said – again it seemed to be for Pointer's information – 'He kept going back to it this afternoon. On the way in the car from Goulburn.

It was getting too much for me. Millie could tell it. I saw her caution me with a wave of a forefinger in front of her lips. I wanted to remark that Masson's inner debates about Greece hadn't stopped him turning up here to report, to see what was offering.

Jimmy said, 'I know how he goes on sometimes.'

'I think he's concerned,' she said, 'the Press will begin hammering the whole story.'

'No,' I told her, closing my eyes. 'Censorship's too heavy.'

She said, 'Well, you'd know. But they got on to Starkey, didn't they?'

I could tell that she wasn't the average ambitious wife. She gave too much away in ordinary talk. She didn't push the merits of her husband or, if she did, she was ignorant of what merits generals ought to have.

I said, 'If I were him, I'd take it easy. Look, Napoleon got himself evacuated from Egypt. And there's little record he ever bored Josephine on the subject.'

She laughed at that, as did Millie, so grateful - behind her sweet complexion - that I hadn't pulled a scene.

'I've talked too long about my husband anyhow,' Pamela Masson said then.

Jimmy looked at his left hand, turning it over in the light from the standard lamp. 'It's fair talk for a night like this,' he murmured. 'Talk of generals, you know. It's fair talk.'

'No,' she said, 'let's ask Mrs Burman where she gets silk from these days.'

Major Pointer held up his hand. 'Not *haute* bloody *couture*! Not on a night like this. Of course, no offence, Millie.'

'None,' said Millie. She seemed to have been forced into saying it all night.

'A more political topic,' Jimmy insisted, turning to me. 'Mrs Masson collects sheepskins for Stalin . . .'

'Not for Stalin,' she said. 'Politicians never seem to be in need of gifts of clothing. My committee sends sheepskins to the partisans.' She was smiling broadly, as if inviting us to comment as wryly as we liked.

Jimmy said, 'Does the average squatter like to think of his sheepskins going to keep a Bolshevik warm?'

'The average squatter isn't as narrow-minded as you. He understands that cold isn't an ideological quantity.'

Jimmy whistled at this deft reply.

Mrs Masson said, 'Dick doesn't like me mentioning the sheepskins. So let's just go back to the question of where the silk will come from now.'

And we did talk for half an hour about where the rubber, the silk, the quinine would come from in the next year, now that Asia had reverted to its ancient inaccessibility.

The north wind grew noisier and butted the eaves and threw gravel at the windows. Red dust seemed to infiltrate the room and slow the blades of the big overhead fans. It had turned into an impossible hour. All at once there was sweat on Pam Masson's throat.

Some time after eleven o'clock, Johnny Mulhall came back in with the General. Johnny blinked a little and grinned like someone who is unaffrighted by any turn the world might have taken during the time he'd talked with Dick Masson. The General himself stood smiling faintly, looking very cool and comfortable in his light Cairo uniform.

Johnny said, 'Hope we didn't keep you waiting.' You'd have thought that they'd been talking racehorses, he and the General, the way he said it.

We were all free to go now. Jimmy Pointer, in view of his status as the army's visionary, had his own car and driver and went first. Millie and I tumbled into her small Austin.

As we slowly drove around the gravelled circle in front of the Lodge, we could see Johnny and the Massons on the steps. Above their heads the stars were swamped by the crimson echo of the fires.

Chapter Three

Friend to friend, I didn't see Johnny again for the bigger slice of a week. I saw the public Johnny, though, when he talked to the Press on Monday night. He seemed to be in a lively mood, and as he spoke to us he moved his hands as if on a diaphanous map of the Pacific hung between him and us. 'Java,' he'd say, amassing a handful of Canberra's thick summer air and moulding it on the unseen map into the shape of a threatened spice isle. 'Timor,' he'd say, locating that Portuguese island with a more delicate pushing action, involving his fingertips.

In the first days he was in power, his Press briefings had been pretty melancholy. You could see in his face the effects of finding out from experts, from generals and bureaucrats who should have known, that the holy continent could not be kept. On those nights he spoke with all his sharp, pulpit orator's inflections, yet you felt the leaden drag of events in your stomach as in his.

This Monday night he was entertaining. I wondered had the sight of Mrs Masson made the difference. At this reach of time, I am sure it had.

Johnny liked the Press. He'd edited the Labor paper in Adelaide and described himself as an 'old journo.' On the nights he was feeling well, I think he liked to startle his old colleagues with the range of his comprehension of the war - the wide war and its organic segment, the Pacific War. As Eddie Hoare would have quickly said, strange sport for an old socialist. Johnny could tell you about the broad aspects of strategy one second – how the Japanese advance in the northern Solomons threatened our line of communication with the United States – and the next come down to encyclopaedic minutiae. He'd tell us, as an example, that the militia at Kieta on Bougainville numbered twenty-five men and was commanded by an electrician from Kyabram in Victoria.

Some time during that week, Johnny went to Sydney on the morning train from Goulburn, and most of the Cabinet and the leaders of the Opposition went with him. They were to appear on a platform in Martin Place in the exercise known as a war loan rally. My newspaper carried two pictures of the event. One is of a rain-drenched square, for it had begun to rain that Tuesday and had soused all the bush fires in Eastern Command. This wide lens photograph is of a modest scene – a quadrilateral of umbrellas, a few companies of militia, some Greeks in white-pleated skirts who had somehow got to Martin Place from last year's Cretan débâcle. Some American sailors; some maidens in the national costumes of oppressed nations, raindrops glittering on their veils. A newsreel cameraman stands atop a Buick, blocking for at least one-third of the crowd their view of the low, covered rostrum where the political leaders sit. A scratch military band is cramped hard up against the Buick under the rostrum. There is a piano there with a tarpaulin slung over it, but the rain is falling on the ivories and the militiaman pianist stares sideways at them, estimating the damage.

The second photograph contradicts the church fête atmosphere of drenched flags, flopping amplifier wires, restless umbrellas. It is taken from within the rostrum. Johnny's mouth is open, his profile is strong, his arms flung as wide as a pontiff's. None of the politicians under that tarpaulin roof seems to be amazed by this un-Australian posture, this prophetic stance, this taking of the people to him, this compelling of them. Tony Hamish seems placid, an ear cocked as if to catch the sound of the rain on the roof.

The reference to 'arms flung as wide as a pontiff's' is not accidental. In his speech Johnny not only called on people to invest.

38

He also asked for 'spiritual renewal,' he called on every Australian to 'examine his conscience' (a phrase with dangerous overtones of his convent school education) and to go to his tasks 'armed with a new conscience.' It is risky in this country to invoke conscience, for people will not believe that politicians are endowed with such an organ. And no one should have been able to appeal to the Protestant majority in terms that were so close to being Irish Catholic. But it seemed that when Johnny finished talking, the damp crowd cheered, the soldiers smiled and editorialists – as soon as reports of Johnny's speech reached their offices – began leafing through their dictionaries of praises.

Back from chivvying the national conscience in Martin Place, he came to my room again, signifying his weariness by throwing his Stetson at a chair and missing by a mile. There wasn't any trace in him, at that hour of the night, of the certitude of the public Johnny. He seemed just another tired accountant, home from the mail order department.

Even more than I could sense, he was being threatened. Winston, that shaman of the strategic gesture, had got the Admiralty to divert Johnny's transports (Johnny's boys inside them) towards Burma, in the belief that God would justify those who did not give up subcontinents without serious immolations of young men. Then he had tried to compel Johnny into consenting retrospectively to this perilous change of course, bludgeoning him with the idea that the President of the Washington circle, 'on whom (said Winnie) you are largely dependent,' would be turned away by Johnny's refusal. It was the sort of menace to which prime ministers of small nations customarily gave way.

All I could sense was that Johnny was being hectored from the direction of two great capitals, that he was standing up to both of them, but that there was an appropriate cost to his system. I think I could tell, too, that what he most feared was that the Depression children who filled the transports would be sunk at sea anyhow, even without the interference of Winnie, and that he, Johnny Mulhall, would become all at once a great murderer.

So I knew at least by vague feel the demands by which Johnny lived, and when he asked me all at once about the Massons, I thought the question must have something to do with matters of command, with coming battles. I had just about forgotten the enchantments of the previous Sunday night.

He said, 'Listen, Paper, Dick Masson's gone down to Melbourne.'

'Staff work,' I said.

'That's right.' Contemplatively he shut one eye. 'His wife's stayed on here,' he said.

He listened to me say it was a bit strange, because they'd been apart all that time in the past few years.

'Does Millie know what's going on?' he asked me.

The idea of Millie as an informant made me blink. 'She hasn't told me anything.'

'Why don't you ask her? A woman in her position . . . Millie's . . . they often hear these things.'

As soon as Johnny left, I called Millie at her house. I still thought I was performing a national service. I knew that among the generals was a party who wanted Starkey deposed and that this party hoped for Masson. Johnny must have been told how fat Starkey had got eating French, Greek and Levantine cuisine, must have known how widely Starkey expended himself on the women of the Middle East. He'd know, too, that Masson was sober, clever, not a womanizer. Masson's blemish, though, was that his wife didn't want to go to Melbourne with him, would rather stay on for a few days holiday in a somnolent capital, as if she were convalescing from the reunion.

I've said Millie didn't go in for scandal but her shop was something like a modest clearing house for information. What the women of Canberra said while they fingered the dress racks and robed themselves in the fitting rooms was often astray in detail but right in substantial form. When I called her Millie was drowsy at first but warmed to the subject.

'Everyone says the marriage is one in name,' she told me. 'Soldiers have to be careful about getting divorced; it bars their chances of promotion.'

'How do you know all this?' I asked her. I was surprised by the authoritative way she spoke of generals as a race and the Massons in particular.

'I've had a friend of the Massons in the shop.'

'Ah!'

'They look so good together. So handsome . . .'

'What's that got to do with it?' I snarled. 'A marriage isn't a boxed bloody set of figurines.'

'I suppose,' she said, 'they'll stay married until the war ends. Why do you want to know?'

I told her Johnny had asked. That I thought it had something to do with what she'd mentioned earlier. Chances of promotion. She got worried then. She knew the limitations of information you picked up in a dress shop.

'Don't believe *me*,' she said, 'This is all just stuff I hear in the fitting room. You'd better ask Jimmy Pointer.'

I couldn't find Jimmy until the next morning. Over the line I could hear the rain battering on the tin roof in the corner of the barracks which had been assigned to his nebulous one-man mystification act.

Hearing me out, Jimmy gave a know-all laugh, a real superior Phillip Street job. 'Definitely a dry relationship, Paper. Since Christmas '37, I'd say. Soon after she came home from Spain.'

For some reason I was appalled that he could put a date to the cessation of the marriage. 'That's a lot to say, Jimmy, that they haven't had a bash . . .'

'Well, there might be accidents. In the past week maybe. But I spoke to him in November '39 – he's an old friend, you know. It'd all been off two years then.'

When I thanked him, he said, 'I've already divined the cause for your inquiry, old dig. John Mulhall's taken a fancy. Isn't that so?'

Straight off I knew it was the truth. I'd known from the start, of course, that you don't pick up intelligence of State among the dress racks but you can find out something certain there about a woman and her husband. I felt offended. Yesterday Johnny had made an austerity speech. Yet there wasn't any margin of austerity in Mrs Masson.

'I'll let the girl know,' Jimmy said. 'He's too bloody shy on that level.'

I advised him not to take over. Did he think he was some kind of engineer? 'National welfare, mate. Had to happen. Johnny needs some of the old medicine. Every bugger does . . .'

I started to argue. I said he was supposed to be intelligent and here he was talking like a bloody matchmaking old aunt. Johnny wasn't that reckless, I said. What if Dick Masson was made commander-in-chief? Then you'd have a classic triangular mess-up. And so on.

'Dick Masson won't be commander-in-chief,' Jimmy told me flat.

'Oh, do you know that? The War bloody Cabinet doesn't know it yet but you know it.'

'Starkey will stay as commander-in-chief. Masson will be given a corps. He'll go north somewhere to defend us from the deadly Nip. It's exactly what he wants. Mrs Masson will stay on in Sydney as an air-raid warden.'

I was just going to reproach him for his flippancy when his voice grew lawyerish and solemn. 'Listen, Paper. I would like Johnny to be with us when this war is over.' It seemed that Johnny counted as part of whatever tapestry Jimmy was weaving in his tin hut. 'He hasn't got a wife to speak of . . .'

'I saw a woman once,' I said, heaping on the irony, 'who claimed to be his missus. I don't think she's dead yet.'

'Ho, ho,' said Jimmy.

'Have you ever met her? Ada Mulhall?'

'No,' he said.

I could believe that. He was the sort of person she was terrified of, the sort of self-sure talker who drove her to put on the stupid grimace she wore whenever she was in Canberra.

I remembered the time I'd spoken to her, over there in Adelaide. That was '37, too, the year when – if Jimmy could be believed – the Masson marriage vanished. Ada and I sat together on a screened-in verandah of Chez Mulhall looking at the Southern Ocean sweep in on a beach peopled by mothers and kids in big sunhats and unemployed mug-lairs in woollen bathing trunks – boys who were probably now, in 1942, in the troop convoys in the Indian Ocean. The longer I sat, the more long silences there were. I got the idea, as she looked out at the boys on the sand, that it was the absence of her son Kevin that gave the scene its meaning for her – that is, that it was his ghost among the waves that took her attention.

Just the same, I found out – sitting there with her on her own front porch – how sharp her mind was. She told me her father had been one of those literate Irishmen, a stationmaster in Queensland, whose idea of a good Sunday was to get his wife and kids around the fire in the sharpest winter, or behind a screen of damp hessian bags on a summer afternoon, and read them chapters from Tunncliffe's *The Problem of Poverty*, from Frank Harris's *The Pit or Octopus*, from Ensor's *Modern Socialism*, and from other matter likely to turn a tender girl into her daddy's darling Fabian. She had always read much more, understood much more than the facile wives of departmental heads who thought she was dense.

At this limit of time I think we were both pretty sinister – Jimmy with his idea that he could pull the strings of subtle people, me with my jealousy for Mrs Mulhall and for my friendship with Johnny. I suppose I was cringing from the old problem that friendship is the hard work of years but obsession descends from the sky in a second and changes everything.

I'd left it until late in the afternoon to call Johnny's office. I told him what Millie had said and the provisos Millie had made. I told him about Jimmy Pointer – that Jimmy Pointer had said it was known among acquaintances of the pair that the marriage was done for. Then, still holding to the idea that Johnny wanted to know about the Massons for reasons of policy and decision, I said, 'So all the pundits agree the marriage has had it. You know me, Johnny, I don't like bloody generals. But the experts say it didn't seem to do his performance in the desert any damage.'

'No, that's right,' Johnny said in a sort of daze. He thought a long time and he seemed to be putting the datum of the Masson's dead marriage up against the other news that had come in that day – that three ships taking supplies to Manila Bay had been sunk, that the Japanese had Sumatra and Enright had given up Java, taking his part-finished biography with him to India.

When he spoke again I could tell he was playing at being casual, for it didn't sound like the genuine casual John Mulhall. He said, 'Paper, I've got a favour I want to ask you. Do you think Millie would mind bunging on a meal? Just a small dinner party, I thought, before Mrs Masson leaves. Just you and Millie and Mrs Masson, and I'd be honoured if Millie'd invite me, too.'

'When?'

'Well, what about tomorrow night? I'll have to let Jim Cowan know where I am. Most of what happens in the world happens during our night, Paper. It might explain why we're such dazed buggers. But tomorrow night, we may be lucky.'

'I hope so, Johnny,' I told him without sincerity. But I could tell what these requests were costing him, that his body would be clenched in his office chair. He said, 'Could you make it clear to Mrs Masson that she ought to be there. That the request comes from . . .' he laughed '. . . the highest quarter.'

'Millie will do her best,' I said. Then I was silent. I knew it sounded to him like some sort of judgment but I couldn't think of anything to say.

'Paper,' he muttered, in a routed sort of way. 'A man has to see what sort of woman she is. Tell Millie I'm grateful. Listen, I'd better clear this line.'

When he'd hung up I could imagine him seated in the other wing of our humble Parliament, the cables and memoranda of woe perched on his desk, while he took a second or two to squint at the wall and tell himself, I've done it now, I've done the uncharacteristic thing. I'm working on the pursuit of a really unlikely woman.

When he turned up at Millie's door it was already after nine. We'd been sitting around making talk with Mrs Masson for an hour already in Millie's sitting room. Beyond an archway, a set table awaited the Prime Minister. German cut-glass cruets which Millie had inherited from her mother stood in the midst of the silverware and a faint musk of flyspray filled the house. Out in the cattle pastures that surrounded the gauche capital, a last plague of late summer bushflies was hatching. But Millie didn't mean to let any of them into the house.

Pam Masson was easy to talk to. If there was any awkwardness between us, it was the idea of Johnny turning up at any time that caused it. She was – as I expected – English. Her father had been a professor of philosophy who'd got the chair at Sydney in 1931. Her childhood had been a pretty eccentric one. The old man had permitted her sister and her to wander in and out of his study, had allowed them access to his books, had given them a lesson now and then in Latin or Greek and then expected them – as she said – to take it on from there. He at no time sent them to a conventional school, boarding or day, State or private.

When she was twelve he had sent her to work for three months on a farm in Oxfordshire. Likewise her younger sister when she turned twelve. When they reached fourteen he got them work as waitresses for six months, then brought them back home again and got them started on Descartes and Spinoza.

I don't remember if she gave her history in year-by-year order while we waited in the flyspray-scented evening for the arrival of Johnny. I don't think so. Then or later, however, I found out that in the Sydney of the '30s she'd worked for relief organizations, first for the seemly ones run by polite people on the basis that the poor are always with us, then on more political committees. I suppose she must have been at least still half-way polite when she married Masson.

We wanted to know about Spain. She told us that at the invitation of an aunt – her dotty old man's sister – she'd joined an English medical party despatched to Spain with some sort of Red Cross backing to run a hospital under the Loyalist administration. Her father had died while she was gone and her mother and sister had transported the corpse out of the hot summer term of Sydney University back to the mists of Highgate Cemetery. 'I got home to find I was alone in Australia,' she told us. I could believe in that 'alone.' I wondered how – in view of her Spanish excursion – she got on with the wives of other officers. I wondered how she got on with Masson himself.

When she talked about the Siege of Madrid, in which she'd taken part as a sort of ward attendant, she said bitter things about both sides. I stoked her with questions, so I could define what sort of political creature she was. The executions performed by Loyalists in the name of ideological purity shocked her as much as did the savagery of Franco's Moors. She'd had an outsider's childhood and her politics suited it. Tony Hamish would call her Red, Bolsheviks would call her a soft-headed socialist, socialists would call her an anarchist and all of them would be wrong. She was what her old man's education had made her, too bright and too primitive to belong to a party.

I'd gauged all this by the time Millie let in the Prime Minister. Coming in, Johnny didn't look like a picture of a sensual adventurer. His face was grey, the creases around his jaw line seemed to reach up his cheeks as far as the ears.

'You look exhausted, Johnny,' I told him, as if I was annoyed by it. 'You ought to get some pills.'

He just said, 'Mrs Masson,' and nodded and grinned towards her. 'Let's all sit down, except maybe Millie. I've got a special task for Millie.'

Another one? I thought.

'A cup of strong tea, Millie my love.'

He folded himself into one of Millie's loungechairs. He began chatting. It was hard to tell if he was talking to me or to her, or even to her by way of me. 'Didn't get any sleep last night. Foolish really. Anyhow I went for a walk up Red Hill. There was a drover up there, sleeping beside his wagon. Or at least his missus was sleeping. She was inside the wagon. But he was awake like me. I would've thought that drovers didn't have much trouble dropping off. He said he goes hunting sometimes when he gets desperate. Anyhow we got the fire going and had a cuppa. Ah, thank you, Millie. Wouldn't be a bad life that. Travelling the country with a flock of sheep. A good horse. Good solid missus sloping along behind the wagon. There are worse lives.' In one gulp he three-quarters emptied the cup.

I looked at Pam Masson. I tried to fit her to the role of drover's wife. She said, 'You *ought* to take pills, Mr Mulhall.'

I said, 'I didn't think you'd believe in pills. Someone like you. Who grew up sort of . . . naturally.'

'I've never taken an aspirin,' she told me, then turned to Johnny. 'But you have to remember, Mr Mulhall, that your rest isn't a private thing. It's something you owe to the country . . .'

Millie raised her eyebrows, amused at this girl who was lecturing Johnny on the duties of sleep.

'You know old Ion Idriess,' said Johnny, ignoring all the talk of medication, 'and all that chat about the People's Army and guerilla forces and so on. Well, a bloke like that drover would make a good guerilla. He's the sort of person who'd give an occupying power most trouble, if it ever came to that.' He said it lightly; you'd have thought he could tolerate the idea of invasion. 'I mean, blokes like that are so Australian, they don't even know it.'

He finished the rest of the cup and reached it out to Millie to be refilled. When he got it back, he thrust his head against the cushions and spoke mainly to the ceiling. 'Anyhow, we can sleep tonight well enough. The convoy, Mrs Masson . . . your husband's division . . . it's in Colombo. God is good, Paper. Eh?'

He always said 'God is good.' Like most fallen Catholics he was an atheist. But he kept saying God, I think, because he hated to talk of luck. He thought it debased destiny to use a word like that.

We ate lamb then, with a bottle of Murray River claret for Millie and Pamela Masson and me. Johnny drank tea all through the meal. His thirst seemed immense.

'Have you tried herb tea?' Pam Masson asked him.

'No,' he said. He laughed. 'Herb tea. That's very English. They murder rich old dowagers with herb tea. In murder mysteries. You know.'

'It wouldn't keep you awake as much,' she suggested.

He winked at me. 'Doesn't have the same kick though. Does it, Paper?'

He was trying to throw up a sort of defence, a sort of matey, manly insouciance shared between him and me. Raunchy tannin versus the English pallor of herb tea. That he even tried such a lame, stupid thing shows you how far in he was. And I? Even though enchanted, even with a pint of Murray mud aboard, I kept thinking of the shy wife, getting angry with her because of her terror of the capital. Only now and then pitying her.

When the meal was over Millie cleared up, refusing Pam Masson's *pro forma* offers of help, disappearing into her kitchen. Even through the brick wall I could feel Millie willing me also to leave the room. In my flashy, independent way I laboured upright, quickly and without needing help, and made off for the lavatory. In leaving them alone I felt I had been forced into casting a vote for the alliance. When I reached the hall, Millie stood in her kitchen door, out of their line of sight, gesturing me to join her. I entered the kitchen, where she was unloading one of her cakes on to a plate. She said, 'Well?'

'I don't know.'

'Well, he can't spend the whole war roaming all over Red Hill, talking to bloody drovers.'

She took more tea and the cake into them after an interval she considered to be appropriate – one not just by the kitchen clock but by some clock she had in her head. 'Half a pound of butter, six eggs. People won't be allowed to make cakes like this much longer,' I overheard her say as she placed it between them.

I went and rejoined them. They looked familiar to each other now. Johnny had taken off his coat, undone the top button on his vest, taken the expanders off the sleeves of his shirt. I got the idea, as well, that there was a sort of cautious understanding between them, as if they'd promised to watch and consider each other for a while. I was not surprised when Johnny called his car to the door at eleven-thirty and Mrs Masson, kissing Millie with a direct warmth, took off in a borrowed Ford in the direction of Duntroon, where she was staying with some friends on a small farm. Both Millie and I knew somehow the distinct directions Johnny and Pam Masson had taken were not blinds, that they would not be meeting at an agreed third point.

I stayed in the open door, balancing the pleasure I felt in Mrs Masson against the resentment. 'Poor bloody Johnny,' I told Millie. 'You can see how buggered he is. He wouldn't be able to mount steps tonight.'

'Yes,' she said, as if it was I who'd failed the two of them.

'You always think of the crudities of the situation, don't you?'

She punched my shoulder and the crutch jarred against my side. It felt like genuine anger but I'm sure a proportion of it was aimed at Johnny for co-opting her as hostess and – as in my case – at Ada Mulhall for being absent.

Chapter Four

Far be it from me to descend to documentation. Nonetheless I think the first night John Mulhall and Pam Masson spent together was towards the end of that month, at the Australia Hotel in Sydney. It happened that Millie and I were also on the premises, in rooms that frankly adjoined each other, but on a different floor from the one where Johnny and Mrs Masson occupied two separate rooms at opposite ends of the hallway.

Millie and I had reasons – in what you'd call our own right – for being there. I'd come to town on a job for the Office of Information. Millie, on a buying trip to the fashion houses, had made an occasion of it by booking herself into a flash hotel. But there was a sense in which we were wedding guests, too. In the evening we'd eaten in a private room with Johnny, his Press Secretary, Jim Cowan, and Mrs Masson. While the convoys were far out in the Indian Ocean, Johnny had gone on missing most of his sleep. Now the returning ships were strung out along the south-east coast and rest and love – you could tell – were about to have their season.

There had been no liquor at the meal. We drank tea and water. Jim Cowan, in his good suit and smooth face, looked a plausible companion for Mrs Masson. Johnny and the girl had got more companionate since their evening at Millie's and she began teasing Johnny on why he hadn't said anything about Spain at the time and tried to nip fascism in its earliest buds. Johnny made shy apologies for his party's laxity in the matter of Franco. 'It's the Catholics in the Party Executive,' he muttered. 'They don't want to offend the Pope and I can't afford to offend them.'

She shrugged, made a mouth and stared at me with her large shadowy eyes. 'Then I can't see much use for Party Executives,' she murmured.

As well as the favour of dining with Johnny, Millie and I also were invited to join him on a headland at dawn. We retired to our room(s) with a bottle of Scotch I'd managed to get and I cosseted thereby my tea-laden bladder and the small discomfort I felt over the Mulhall and Masson business.

We were woken before dawn by a soldier. I sat on a toilet seat, shaved myself and felt leaden. Millie dressed herself with great speed in a violet summer frock.

In the foyer, Mrs Masson sat in an armchair speaking to some officers. Across the room Johnny occupied a black plush sofa with Eddie Hoare. A silver teapot sat before the two politicians; there were two stained and well-used cups. Both men were teetotal and the nation's boozers, me among them, took it as a bad portent.

'Going out to the South Head circus, Eddie?' I called.

I just didn't think it was likely. This would be a military event and Eddie spoke only glancingly of military things, as when he said that if the Government meant to conscript labour and the militia, it should also conscript wealth. And as when he frightened the conservative Press by saying, one summer's day in the Branch Office, that the Government ought to stop paying interest on war loans.

In fact, there had been pressure, editorial and subtle (to name two distinct types), for Johnny to drop Eddie from the Cabinet. But Johnny kept saying Eddie was so good with the unions, especially with the miners. 'They trust him from the bottom of their black lungs,' said Johnny with an unaccustomed cynicism.

Anyhow, 'Going to the circus, Eddie?' I called.

'No fear, Paper,' he said. He'd got up and was dragging on an old oilskin raincoat. 'Going up the Hunter.'

'Saying good-day to the miners,' I suggested.

'No other bugger will.' He got a crumpled handkerchief from the pocket of his raincoat and blew his nose in his typical clarion-of-conscience way. With that attended to, he began to grin. 'Johnny himself is going to come up for a visit soon. When all the glamour events are over.'

Johnny shook his head. 'You talk like a bloody parson, Eddie. Coal's a fact of life, like death and taxes. But you really make a bloody meal of it.'

'All right,' said Eddie, smoothing his ratty raincoat, 'I'll tell them to go easy on production.'

He left with an easy half grin on his face. As he went down the front stairs, three generals – one of them American – and a small crush of staff officers passed him on their way indoors. I clenched my shoulders as usual. My old antipathies to generals as a race ran in me, though I got more accustomed to them by the day.

Johnny went and met this group and united it to the one to which Pam Masson belonged, introducing her as if she were a shy girl of whom they should take special care. Then we all went out on to the front steps of the hotel and Johnny squinted at the thunderous sky above Pitt Street and at the filament of lightning high above the opposing buildings. I heard him mutter. 'Send her down, Hughie,' addressing the perverse god of antipodean weather.

By the time the Buicks drew up one by one, I felt smothered by the military presence. 'What's the matter?' Millie asked, noticing my darting eyes.

'Nothing, nothing,' I told her in a hurry. And then I mouthed it. 'F. . .ing generals!'

Johnny got into the first car with the most important of the breed. A swarm of the buggers took to the second. The third car, I was pleased to find, was for Millie and Pam Masson and me. We had to share it with a brigadier and a colonel but they took subordinate places, sitting facing us on the dicky seats.

Early in the journey they asked Pam Masson questions about her distinguished husband but somehow I was comforted to find that she dismissed them pretty quickly. As we reached the Cross, I felt easy enough to nudge Millie and point to the few harlots, quite pretty, quite young, on the corners in the grey light, perhaps expecting a dawn rush, perhaps expecting nothing. Millie gave a little 'tch tch' noise and then, in the strait-laced presence of the khaki and the red tabs, began to laugh silently. Pam Masson herself saw the laugh and she began to smile, too, allying herself with us, laying her head back against the plush and exposing her long neck to the austere gaze of the brigadier. By these means her straw hat was disarranged and she sat readjusting it, lifting her arms above her head. She looked like an artless girl instead of a woman who'd nursed for seven months in the Siege of Madrid and seen the anarchists dragged forth to the firing squads.

Under our flippant influence, the officers began to behave more and more like people on the way to a State funeral.

'The ground's uneven here, sir,' a young and over-kindly artillery officer told me, edging me towards the tip of the cliff.

'Please don't hold my elbow,' I told him, 'it destroys my balance.'

By the light of dawn the party had gathered on a flat slab of sandstone. Chairs had been placed for any who needed them but I had not been allowed to make my way to one unassisted. Everyone else stood. A few cabinet ministers had got there before Johnny's squad and were already squinting out to sea through binoculars. Before us the ocean turned light violet and broke in soft violet surf against the rock-clad walls beneath us. On both sides of us and on the cliffs below stood coastal gun emplacements and we could smell the early tea being brewed. I could see the tannin addicts, Johnny Mulhall himself among them, crinkling their noses at that fragrance. Behind us, the drivers of the limousines unloaded picnic baskets into a tent with its side rolled up, I made a dismal bet with myself that not a drop of wine had been included among the delights therein.

The heads of storm clouds which Johnny had invoked in Pitt Street were now travelling away to the east – it looked as if Eddie Hoare would not need his ragged oilskin – and beneath the clouds the sun rose. The great hazy salt sea radiance lit everyone's face. A file of gunners came tramping down the rocks to relieve the night crews on the cannons. The aggressive beating of their heels on stone brought my whisky tiredness on again and I huddled deeper in the chair. But all around me generals and politicians congratulated each other on what a beautiful day it would be.

Then, descending from nowhere, Mrs Masson sat down at my side. She'd taken off the light coat she'd been wearing in the Buick. I could see now that she wore one of those patriotic dresses – the pockets and the turn-ups made out of patch material – into which the magazines were urging women. I noticed her sturdy legs as she tucked them under her chair.

She mightn't have had such limbs I reflected, if her father hadn't put her on a farm at the age of puberty.

She grinned at the ascendent sun. I had a little pork-pie hat, its brim not adequate for the blazing sunrise. I squinted and watched Mrs Masson's eyes, level and unblinking in the shadow of her big black straw hat. All this early morning perfection annoyed me.

She said, 'I'm glad he asked you two along.'

I smiled and shook my head. 'Love,' I said, 'however you look at it, Millie and I are bloody courtiers, acting under orders.'

My ungraciousness made her laugh. 'Are you always so aggressive in the mornings, Paper?'

'I had an aunt,' I said, 'who was always feeling imaginary grievances. Lived forty miles up the Tweed with a weak husband. The isolation made her worse. My mother always told me I took after her. You know. Do you know anyone who's brought along booze?'

'No,' she said. 'No, I could ask some of the dignitaries . . .'

'Don't bother, I'm just being discourteous.' I looked at her again, at least sideways, and then I started to grunt with unwilling laughter. 'You can tell who's against it, can't you?'

'Against it?'

'Against you. As a mate for Johnny. You can tell I've got doubts. Without any disrespect to your bloody fine person, Mrs Masson.'

She said, 'I can't do much for your doubts, Paper.'

'I think of his missus . . .'

'So do I,' she told me. She got some colour in her cheeks, a few freckles surfaced for an instant out of the deeps of her complexion. 'For God's sake,' she said, 'will you be so kind as to look at me. Do you think I'm working on Johnny for something? Do you think I want to be the wife of a generalissimo? Is that what you think I'm aiming for?'

I looked away. Her clear-eyed conviction that she was an honest girl was just about as hard to look at as was the sunrise.

'Listen, love, all I know is that it's a respectable excuse for adultery. It always has been, hasn't it? . . . No offence, honest to Christ, no offence.'

'Honest to Christ,' she said, transfixing me with a smile.

'A respectable excuse,' I persisted, 'that you're doing your old man's career some good . . .'

I noticed another flush of red across her throat but it didn't take. 'Have you ever known John Mulhall to be so simple-minded?' she asked.

'He's never had anyone like you.'

'Like me? I'm a woman. Never had a woman?'

'You're not the average of the species, Mrs Masson. Look, you're an object of bloody desire. I'm sorry if I'm offensive. Most women are companions. But you're an object of bloody desire.'

'What a thoroughly simple fellow you are,' she said, getting really offended now.

'So is Johnny. He can deal with a phenomenon like Japan. Like bloody Winston Churchill. He's equipped. It's you he's not equipped for.'

'For God's sake. I'm just a girl. Paper, just a girl.'

But I wouldn't admit her to membership of that honest tribe: I stayed perverse, I stayed defensive.

An adjutant, swagger-stick tight into his armpit, was bringing round a tray of tea set with Stafford china teacups and silver spoons, a silver sugar bowl and tongs. It was quite a sight to see him advancing over the rose-coloured barbarous sandstone with the salmon light of morning transmuting his shoulder pips.

'Here comes breakfast, Paper,' Mrs Masson whispered to me.

'If you'll eat it at my side I promise to behave just like an average person.'

Johnny, of course, took the tea but waved away the white-aproned army cook who offered him a plate of ham and eggs. He kept looking into the radiant haze through field glasses and then he'd lower them and fiddle with cigarettes and holder, without lighting up though, and then he would again raise the glasses. Both Mrs Masson and I were watching him as I took a cup of tea and a few hot scones. Mrs Masson leaned forward with an elbow on her crossed legs. She waved all the food away as Johnny had, in spite of her half-promise to eat with me, and so she kept a fast with him. I could see she wanted to get up and walk through the screen of officers around Johnny and to take his arm, telling him not to be anxious; that ships could not with ease be seen against that golden radiance out there in the Pacific.

She said to me, 'They got two ships last week, so I believe.'

'That's right,' I told her.

'A trawler off Evans Head. Then they got a cargo ship off Smoky Cape.' She shivered in her sky blue dress. 'I believe it's a shark ground up there.'

I had heard about it. The submarine had risen from the water and shelled the freighter. It was full of butter for the Americans in North Queensland. Forty seamen had taken to the water yet only two had reached the beach. The lighthouse keeper at the Cape had made a frenzied statement by telephone to the Press that the sea was a red froth in which fins and butterboxes and terrified sailors were to be seen. The censor had, of course, suppressed the statement as bad for the already timorous national soul.

For a second Mrs Masson and I sort of trembled in unison, remembering that beneath the rose-tinted placidity of those off-Sydney waters moved populations of the shark. Sharks bulked in the dreams of Sydneysiders; to all their sweet beaches, the shark was a corollary. I knew that from the times I'd stood legless on the promenade and arrested the populace by the very sight of me, until I felt I should call to them, 'No, it wasn't any mindless beast. This is the fruit of planning. Intelligent creatures arranged these stumps.'

For some reason, all this shark talk reminded her of Johnny. She said, 'You know him, Paper.'

'A bit,' I admitted.

'Does he still believe all that terrible Irish stuff?'

'What?'

She lowered her eyes and her voice. 'This morning,' she said, 'he woke up early and stood at the window.'

'Well?' I said. I was short about it. I wondered why she was already making me privy to little bedroom secrets.

'He was pushing those beads through his fingers, those beads old nuns wear on their belts. And his lips were moving quickly. You know the sort of thing. You see it in Ireland . . .' She looked straight at me again. I could see the beads distressed her, were an index of Johnny's distress.

I said, 'An old nun in Brisbane sends them to him. Rosaries, medals, all sorts of stuff.'

'My father,' she said. 'His tolerance didn't extend to that sort of thing.' She was telling me that neither did hers.

I said, 'Well, it should have.'

She kept so silent that I began to laugh. 'You're a pretty narrow-minded girl, aren't you? You're dead set against rosaries and aspirin.'

'I'm sorry,' she told me, 'and don't mention it to anyone . . .'

Shrugging, I implied it was her look-out if she trusted me.

'. . . But I can't understand,' she went on, 'anyone in this world . . . the way it is . . . standing in a window, pushing beads through his fingers.'

I shook my head. It came to me for the first time in my life that God and events might be touched by incantations when they're muttered by insomniac boys like Johnny at a window in the first light. I didn't utter this idea; I didn't want her to write me off, too.

'If it soothes him,' I said, 'who's to argue?'

'It's irrational,' she said. 'And it's alien.'

I told her, 'Not alien to Johnny. It's his boyhood. Jesus, we all go back to it for comfort.'

'Don't misunderstand me,' she murmured. 'But what can you do for a man who's as distressed as that?'

'You can wait,' I suggested, 'for his boats to come in.'

From where we sat, Johnny seemed to have edged to the brink of the cliff. We saw one of the officers approach him and recommend that he look out on a particular bearing to the south-east. I saw Johnny accept the recommendation, nod, then lay down his glasses and begin to accept congratulations. Seeing Pam Masson beside me, he sent an aide to fetch her. I surprised myself by rising and going with her and she adjusted her pace to mine.

'Paper, Mrs Masson,' Johnny called. 'They're visible.'

Through the glasses I was handed I could see two masts off to the south-south-east. Millie appeared at my side, and perhaps to make up for having been engrossed in Mrs Masson I handed the glasses to her. After a while she crooned like a mother or at least an aunt. 'There are soldiers everywhere,' she said. 'Even up the masts.' She laughed at their boyish enterprise.

Everyone on the clifftop began beaming and looking in a questioning way at each other, wondering what gesture was the proper one for this hour. I knew, of course, in my whisky head exactly what the proper gesture was. Orderlies should now run along the clifftops pouring Great Western. I knew equally that it would not happen.

Johnny came up and patted my shoulder. 'Good on you, Johnny,' I said. 'Now you've got no bloody excuse for insomnia.'

But the staff officers who laughed and lit cigarettes were still anxious, for this ship or that could still be sunk in sight of the continent's old sandstone coast.

An expert announced that the first mast was the *Aquitania*, the second the *Queen Mary*. But there were others, too. Homecoming boys hung like gibbons from every masthead. Within half an hour I could see them with my own eyes. A sight smudged by tears, because the hope and bull energy which had moved them up to every height and foothold on the super-structure of the liners reminded me of young Archie Burman and then, of course, of my own sighting of the continent from the deck of the hospital ship *Hygeia*, some eras past.

When we made our way back over the uneven stones towards the limousine, Johnny appeared at my side. He yawned, shook his head, smiled. 'Dick Masson's boys,' he murmured. 'Every one of them a professional. It's not the whole show, Paper. But a bloody good omen, eh? Eh?' And then he looked away again to join his ministers and generals.

It seemed, as we were driven back through the eastern suburbs, that Mrs Masson had got over her concern for Johnny's tribal habits with rosary beads. The elation of those cargoes of young men touched us, made us all pleasant travelling companions. And somehow people knew about our passage. They stood at the gates of bungalows along Old South Head Road, they stood at the edges of footpaths, in front of sandbagged milk bars, women in house-frocks, men in their vests and watch chains – arrested in dressing for work by the unpublished news which was nonetheless travelling faster than semaphore. Maybe Sydney people were sensitive to the arrival of ships, having begun their history waiting for them. I could not explain it myself. I did not quite know the medium by which popular ecstasy travelled down Old South Head Road and William Street into the heart of the city.

Chapter Five

A week later Johnny saw away to America one of his ministers, whose name (again) is evocative and who is therefore a story in his own right. The minister and his wife climbed into a Catalina flying boat afloat at Rose Bay and took off, island hopping towards San Francisco.

Some cruel bugger in the Press Gallery said, 'They should have sent you, Paper. You and Franklin could have had wheelchair races and you could've sweetened him up by letting him win.'

The gibe showed that everyone knew the herein un-named minister's task was to convince America's wheelchaired monolith that Johnny, who had lived and bathed in the Pacific all his life, knew more of it than did Winston, to whom it was but a map.

I felt at the time the departure of this particular minister left Canberra unbalanced, left a gap in its small circle of talents. The balance was redressed, however, damn quick and, as they say, in spades. The minister's plane must have been no more than halfway to Suva Harbour when General Donald McLeod's B-17 dropped on to Batchelor Field in the north. To stretch the image: if the continent were in danger of slipping under by the bows, General McLeod's ponderous descent righted it.

General McLeod had escaped from General Homma and the

Philippines. At Batchelor Field, they carried his son off the plane on a mattress, for the boy had been ill all the way from Del Monte in the Philippines. Although distressed for his son, General McLeod showed at once his firm sense of his own importance to the future of Western culture by awarding the entire flight crew Silver Stars, there in the Northern Territory scrub.

He had begun as he intended to proceed.

The story is that the party flew to Alice Springs then, by which time the boy was so ill that General McLeod decided that everyone had to continue the rest of the way south by train. The weekly train, however, had just left. A special had to be called up from Adelaide. While it chuffed north, across creek beds subject to flood, the hotel was plagued by flies. Mrs McLeod, contemplating a forkload of steak before placing it in her mouth, saw it seized upon instantly by a tribe of insects. It is said she cried out, 'I pity the women who have to live in this country.'

But her husband could tell this country was not a disaster. He could sniff out how it could be used. 'Rubbish, my dear,' he said. 'Flies never hurt a soul.'

They made good time to Adelaide and then on to Melbourne where – as Donald McLeod had assured his wife – Mrs McLeod found the Hamish Hotel at least as flyless as their lost penthouse in Manila, now occupied by General Masaharu Homma himself.

The House was in session. So Johnny wasn't able to go down to Melbourne to greet the man. In any case it was essential, in the symbolic sense, that Donald McLeod come to the capital.

He travelled all the way up from Melbourne by limousine. I saw him bound up the steps of Parliament House – there weren't so many, they were no awesome barrier. But how much the more spryly did Donald McLeod bounce up them, like a laird entering his inheritance. Seeing him do it, I mistrusted him immediately, for he looked as if he had just left a zone of battle – his garrison hat with the padding taken out, his windcheater open at the top button to show a shirt collar on which four stars shone; all of it said, 'I have battled to the limits of this fabric.' And, in view of my prejudices, I did not believe it. For in the

61

Philippines he had abandoned a garrison. And having been, for short periods of my life, a member of garrisons, I was determined not to forgive him.

When Johnny put on a dinner for him at the Lodge, I did not attend. I sent my young bureau assistant in my place. He took Millie as his companion and after it was all over Millie came back to me and rhapsodized about McLeod.

'And Johnny?' I asked Millie, as we sat together drinking Scotch in my office near midnight.

'Well, you know Johnny,' she told me. 'Very commanding.' She spread her arms wide to imitate the public Johnny, the Johnny of the rostrum. 'Very eloquent. You know . . .'

'I'm sure,' I said. There was some real disappointment in me that she didn't see through the event.

'I was there,' she insisted. She frowned so quickly, so intensely, that a few flakes of powder fell from her forehead to the breast of her good violet dress. 'I heard what he said.'

'And I can bloody guess what you heard.' I mimicked Johnny's solid accent, his emphatic delivery. *'General McLeod has come here as a result of my own most urgent representations to his government in Washington.'*

Millie looked away. 'You remind me of Jimmy Pointer and you know what I think of him.'

'McLeod came here because he had nowhere else to go. Oh, Chile, maybe. The South Pole. . .'

'I despise you when you're like Pointer. . .'

'The bastard dropped down out of the monsoon like an interloper. Johnny wasn't so much as told he was coming.'

'Oh, the gospel according to Pointer again.'

'Pam Masson there?' I asked, as if it were the next step in an argument, though it wasn't.

'With your friend,' she told me. She meant Jimmy, of course.

I nodded and nodded about that, as if it did clinch something. 'Put you off your tucker, did he?'

'Reminded me of you.'

'He knows. McLeod shot through, buggered off, left his boys. But Johnny - who didn't just get in from the bush either - says,

62

"I begged him to be here." That's damn generous of Johnny, to risk taking that odium . . .'

'Odium? there wasn't any odium. Everyone cheered.'

'. . . And it's cunning as hell. It just shows you about politicians. The truth isn't in the beggars. Even when they're your best mate.'

She went on shaking her head, wanting to be left alone with the conviction that she had beheld two giants sparking off each other. Yet I wouldn't stop harrying her for Johnny's prevarications. 'Did your general mention the chaps in Bataan? Or are they written off?'

'He said something. The usual things. What would you expect?'

'I would expect the bastard to weep into his Queensland pineapple and his bloody Bega ice-cream.'

'This is childish,' called Millie. 'You ought to be grateful. Everyone is. So grateful!'

I snorted at that.

She said, 'We've all suffered, you know. You're not the only one. I don't hear other old Diggers carry on like you. At least you're still alive.'

'I must be a cynic,' I said.

'This is impossible. Do you want your glass filled before I go?'

'As you imply, I'm not a bloody corpse.'

'Good night,' she said, getting up and shaking her head over me again. I could hear her high heels retreating down the Press Gallery corridor. I grabbed for my crutches, heaving up, nearly pitching brow-first against the sharp corner of my desk. Regaining balance I managed to make my way to the door and call out to her. 'You ought to remember your husband, Mrs Burman,' I yelled. 'He was a private and no one prevailed on him to attend government dinners.'

I couldn't see it but I could hear that she was just about at the top of the Senate steps. 'How can you be so bloody simpleminded?' I called after her.

Of course, even now, I don't know what I was arguing about more - the light the general threw on Johnny Mulhall or the business of Mrs Masson. Johnny had taken an untypical woman in the past two weeks and then gone on to treat the arrival of a Republican general as the second coming. Such a rate of change in a man over fifty might have been to the nation's benefit. But it gave me distress and seemed more dangerous both to Mulhall and to the essential Tyson than any invasion risk.

Chapter Six

No one shared my perverse view of the McLeod dinner apart from Jimmy Pointer, who had a professional duty to look askance at these affairs. The dinner and the speeches had been such a success, in fact, that in their wake it was announced that McLeod and Johnny would attend a country race meeting, a plebeian event alien to both their temperaments. The meeting chosen was the annual Gold Cup at Bungendore, over there beyond George's sun-cracked lake bottom.

I remember that the afternoon I saw the timetable for this visit to Bungendore I got the impression that a new and exacting idea of time had entered the country with McLeod. An exact hour (written as 14.15 hrs) was set for the departure from Canberra. Arrival at Bungendore was nominated as 15.02 hrs. A marshalling time of three minutes was allowed before the dignitaries entered the course at 15.05 hrs. They would then have at their disposal a neat thirty minutes before post time. There was even a notation for the time of the cup presentation by the Honourable the Leader of the Opposition, Tony Hamish, which showed that the man who drew up the timetable either had no idea of bush race meetings or else believed that time was at last in charge.

A quarter of an hour after the cup was handed to the winning owner, the visitors would return to their limousines and so to the capital. In this way they would signify that they were busy salvaging the nation yet were not enemies of Saturday joy. Press from all the capitals and from the United States would be present and McLeod would be seen taking in, with his mysterious blue eyes, authentic Australian life.

It was, as the timetable also told us, less than an hour from our manufactured capital to the township of Bungendore. Millie and I travelled in the convoy and shared a car with Jimmy Pointer and Pam Masson. We were driven out through the burnt and already green-sprouting forests and then south along the dusty littoral of the phantom lake. Mrs Masson had been sportive last time we shared a car with her. But today she kept her face blank and looked out the window for long periods, like a woman who just couldn't see enough of red dust and ghost gums. By various signals, the rest of us could tell her remoteness had nothing to do with us.

Most of the way to the races, Jimmy Pointer whinged about the phenomenon of McLeod, as he was free to. I knew better than to join in. I could see the tightness of Millie's lips. 'It's like a bloody Roman carnival,' said Jimmy. 'They've already deified him and now they're taking him to bless the bloody horses.'

Of course in Jimmy's little tin-roofed laboratory it was axiomatic that McLeod, however necessary, was the gatecrasher, the final danger, the intruding ally who would still be there when the enemy was defeated. And so, the final enemy.

'You know,' Jimmy persisted, 'I was talking to an American intelligence officer – who shall remain nameless – and from him I learned something which puts a strange light on McLeod's qualifications. I mean his qualifications to undergo this process of canonization that he's been enjoying both in our callow nation and in the mighty States.'

I could see Millie tossing her head and so could Jimmy. It . amused him.

'This gentleman tells me that from the interrogation of Japanese captured during a certain counter-attack at the Agno River, it is quite clear that there are but two . . . repeat *two*, Paper, old dig . . . Japanese divisions involved in the Philippines. A mere 55 000 Japanese imperial souls, my old friend. Now you may

66

have noticed that McLeod has been placed in the pantheon on the grounds that he brilliantly immobilized a quarter of a million Japanese who would otherwise have been thrown into areas . . . this very latitude . . . or any other where there was a supply of babies to bayonet, women to ravish and ears to cut off. But what if the truth was that McLeod himself had been immobilized by a smaller force? What would you think then, Millie?'

'I'd think,' said Millie, 'that there are always small men willing to knock down greater.'

'Oh, I plead guilty to being a little man,' said Jimmy with such graveside solemnity it made even me laugh. Mrs Masson turned her face towards us and smiled: the way adults with love affairs to fret over, or worries about money, smile at children shouting in a sandpit.

I asked Jimmy would it be possible to talk to this officer he'd mentioned.

'Sent home I'm afraid,' said Jimmy. 'A brawl with McLeod's chief-of-staff . . .'

'There you are,' said Millie. Her long mouth settled in lines of awesome contentment and it was the Major's turn to laugh.

The somnolent bungalows of Bungendore appeared at last through the brown dust our convoy was raising. Only a Greek café in all the town was open. The Greek came out from under his awning to watch us pass. He had no customers but would stay open all afternoon, prodigal with his time, for that was his concept of commerce.

Every other citizen of the hamlet of Bungendore was at the race course.

'We're here,' said Pam Masson, making a contribution as we drew up. Jimmy helped her out of the car and then he helped Millie and they all waited to help me. We stumbled forth into an area where a militia company was drawn up beneath the palisades of corrugated iron which screened off the course proper. From within the enclosure, gum trees grew up over the fence and shed leaves on the slouch hats of the soldiers. At a late-blooming box brush just beside the turnstile, bees kept their ancient commerce with the blossoms. As the dust settled a sublime afternoon was revealed and the beery blather of the race crowd could be heard within the grounds. I looked at my watch. It was, as the timetable had predicted, 15.02 hrs.

The official party – Johnny, McLeod and his dark pretty wife, their little boy, pale and querulous, and all the rest of us, doubters, devotees, friends of kings and generals – massed at the entrance of the funnel of militia, waiting for some protocol expert to stage-manage us. But no one seemed to volunteer for the job.

In the hiatus, Johnny looked around with that slight and almost permanent full-lipped grin of his and yelled to me, 'Heard anything for the Cup, Paper?'

I called out, with the usual provisos, the name of a horse I'd heard from someone in the Press Gallery. I noticed Johnny looked at Mrs Masson and grinned or grimaced at her. But beneath that same big black hat she'd worn on South Head, her eyes were considering the ground at her feet. I thought it was just as well the thing seemed to be breaking up. Johnny couldn't expect to go very far with a girl who was shocked by such tribal realities as rosary beads and the Franco boys in the Victorian Executive. Then, the way birds will suddenly form a migratory V, we did something of the same and teemed down the alley of troops, with the Eastern Command Band, white-jacketed, rushing through *The Star Spangled Banner* and *The Road to Gundagai*. Beside Millie and me, Jimmy Pointer murmured, 'Well, I suppose that's the sort of *Te Deum* they play at bush race meetings. Should Jesus Christ drop in.'

He strode ahead, craning his neck. Millie said to me, 'Pam Masson's upset at being given escorts all the time. Especially old boyfriends of hers.'

'It's more than that,' I said, like what they call 'an authoritative source.'

'No,' said Millie, her own voice taking on that sighing knowingness of the insider. 'She told me herself.'

'What does she want? Does she want to sit beside Johnny?'

'No. She wants to attend these things on her own.'

'Is she a bloody suffragette or something?'

68

'Well . . . she thinks that way.'

After an accolade, Johnny and the McLeods were led to some reserved seats in the small decrepit stand where Tony Hamish stood up to greet them. Millie and I wandered among the rails bookmakers, wanting to form a modest syndicate, unable to agree. At last Millie saw, across the paddock, a squatter she knew and she went off to ask him if he had the name we wanted, the horse that would come home.

'Paper, Paper!' I heard a voice roaring as I waited. Swinging on my crutches I saw Clarrie Doig bearing towards me. As he rucked his way through the crowd he unbuttoned his shirt and dragged at the waist of his trousers, exposing old scar tissue from a time in the Concord Repat when we'd occupied neighbouring beds and both undergone surgery. Over a decade, wherever we met, he flashed his old scar as if it were a passport. 'Thereyar, thereyar Paper,' he yelled, reaching me. 'Never knew I bloody had it.'

I was then supposed to unbutton myself, even though my scars were lower than his and exposure of them was closer to being something that would frighten the horses.

He was a farmer, beef and wheat. I could never see him without feeling the closeness of my dead father. There was in both of them the same desperate, grinning hope – hope of a downpour, a race track killing, a season of high yield, a year's mercy from the bank. So all Clarrie's eccentricities were poignant to me and when I laughed at him I seemed always a hair's breadth from tears.

Clarrie also had that passion for bush horseflesh that had marked my old man. He went to all the race meetings and sat on race committees. Though baggy-gutted now, he had as a light horseman ridden to Damascus behind Lawrence and, in a knock-about way, the horse was holy to him and all its possible uses were matters of fascination. Yet I knew from what he'd whispered to me at bush race meetings that he wasn't beyond nobbling or pulling thoroughbreds, or at least mixing with richer and stronger people who did.

'Often thought I'd come and see you,' he told me. 'Up there

in the Parliament. This Mulhall bloke. Mate of yours, isn't he?' He lowered his voice. 'What's this about him abolishing the bloody nags?'

It had been talked about in Cabinet, I told Clarrie. The Wednesday before, I said, Johnny Mulhall had been trying to call army headquarters in Melbourne. He hadn't been able to get through and so had called the exchange. They'd told him that he was sixty-third in the queue, that most of the calls ahead of him were betting calls.

'Gordstruth,' Clarrie whispered. He took out a tin of weed; the hams of his thumbs ground the flake tobacco and arranged it on a cigarette paper. It was a little ritual of grief.

I said, 'One thing, Clarrie. Midweek racing's had it.' I sounded impatient. I *was* impatient in a filial sort of way. They put up with anything, Clarrie and my old man. They sold their produce cheap, they waited on the ravening word of a bank. Then John Mulhall thought of cancelling Wednesday race meetings and *that* made them think of storming the Senate stairs.

Clarrie cupped the cigarette in his meaty hand and lit it. 'No Wednesday doctor? I'd shoot the missus without that. Isn't bloody Mulhall interested in nags? Doesn't he ever have a punt?'

'He bets on football. Sometimes.'

'Football? Jesus! I voted for the bastard!' He inhaled, closed his eyes against the smoke and smiled, a sort of clay-red mandarin. 'Doesn't matter. For once I've got the bastards beat.' His head began jerking. He wanted me to follow him. I saw Millie was still occupied with the squatter and that gave me a pretext to go with him, to tag along, all at once a seven-year-old again, accompanying the big bloke among the adult mysteries of the farm, the agricultural show, the race track.

I followed him behind the stand. Against the wall of a shed sat a gristly little Aborigine wearing a big hat, white silk riding britches and dusty riding boots. His upper half displayed no man's colours but was wrapped up in a sports coat. His wide thunderous eyes fell on me as I advanced.

'This's Spider,' said Clarrie. 'Comes from Trangie. Ugly as a hat full of arseholes but a bloody good bush rider. Spider, say g'day to Mr Tyson. Speak up big and he'll get you in his paper.'

'G'day,' said Spider.

'Got a stallion in the Cup,' Clarrie hissed in my ear. 'Name of Captain's Flat. All the summer we been nursing him along, giving him a run like, but not letting the odds shorten on him too much.'

'He's in the Cup?'

Spider winked.

I started to laugh but again the tears I mentioned earlier, the filial tears, fell behind the laughter. 'Pulling him, Clarrie? Setting him up for a killing? The bloody world's falling to pieces and you've spent the summer setting up a stallion?'

'Ask Spider,' Clarrie advised. 'Ask Spider if the old Captain's going to do it.'

'He good, Spider?'

The Aboriginal jockey laid his head back against the door frame and stroked his chin. 'A goer, Mr Paper,' he murmured. 'Greased f. . .in' lightnin'.'

Clarrie and I laughed together. Spider just looked at us with an ancient composure. 'Got 65 quid on him at 16s,' Clarrie murmured. 'You can still get 10s with the rails bookies. Got some powerful mates with money on him, too. The other jocks've been looked after. You know . . .'

I said, sputtering away, 'You've got Tony Hamish, Leader of the Federal bloody Opposition, handing over the prize for a race that's fixed. You've got a Yankee general and a prime minister looking on.' My laughter redoubled and there were real tears now. The solemnity of the day had been subverted, the digits on the timetable mocked, the invader's time-worship vitiated. All by my father's ghost.

'Look at it my way,' Clarrie invited me. 'The expenses I've got. Sending both the girls to the Sisters of Mercy in Parramatta. Could send 'em to Bungendore Public I suppose. But I want 'em to turn out like bloody ladies . . .'

'Of course, of course,' I said, laughing, nodding, weeping. For I knew how things had gone for him these past two decades, since his return from Damascus.

I could tell that to him it seemed a reasonable adjustment to fix a race if you could and to get the Prime Minister along to consecrate the transfer of wealth. 'You got money on it, Spider?' I asked the Aborigine who still rested by the wall, a case of chronic composure.

'Would've, Mr Paper. Ain't got none to put on nags but.'

'He's a bloody spendthrift,' Clarrie told me. 'Every penny on booze and lubras. I put 10 quid on it for him.'

'You're a white man, Clarrie,' the jockey told him and winked a sombre eye at me. Then he returned his gaze to the knees of his britches and lost himself in the weave of the fabric.

Millie had had no joy from the squatter but I returned to her full of certitude. Together we rushed to the rails bookmakers and found the stallion was still at good odds. When she didn't get the money out of her purse willingly enough I burrowed in with my hand, making light promises. If the thing didn't come home, I'd repay her investment myself.

'There's no need for that,' she told me, as if I had impugned her honour as a fellow speculator.

Oh Clarrie, I was singing in my heart, you'll be able to keep your girls at the good Sisters in Parramatta until they're polished bright. And afford a few frugal comforts of your own. And amaze the bastards from the bank. And have a cup and a photograph to hang over your fireplace.

It was near post time, when we were down on the rails watching the full-chested horses and the scrawny jockeys drifting past towards the start, that Jimmy Pointer found us. I had just called out to Spider as he passed in Clarrie's good Catholic colours, the Virgin blue and the Erin green. Millie, wiser, had kept her frowning peace.

Jimmy said, 'Johnny sent me looking for you.' He looked like an outsider here among the picnic crowd in his tailored uniform and with his thinking-man's pallor.

'One of the committee men slipped him the word. The goer happens to be a mare from Goulburn called Miss Chance.' He gurgled and shook his head. 'High matters of State,' he said.

Millie reacted at once. She cried, 'Oh hell! Certainties!' and ran decisively towards the rails bookmakers to cover our earlier investment. I levered my way against the crowd looking for

Clarrie Doig. Millie was successful in her enterprise but not I in mine.

It is an old story and I shall not bore the reader as if it were a classic of the turf. Both Captain's Flat and Miss Chance started in a mediocre way but were what they call 'handily placed' at the one mile. Miss Chance seemed boxed in on the rails, as if the other jockeys did not really intend parting and allowing her a triumphant run. At the 1½ miles, Captain's Flat was placed third on the neck of some plough horse from Yass and Miss Chance still ran hampered on the rails some ten places behind the leader. 'Jesus,' I said to Millie, 'it almost looks legal.'

Three furlongs out, the stallion seemed to be drawing nicely level with the second-placed horse and the Judas goat in first was, as they also say, 'flagging badly.' Miss Chance checked then and, for a second, I thought it not inevitable that she would win. But it was simply that her jockey had dragged her wide and as soon as she began her run all the crowd could tell what would happen, for she moved not with the contingent qualities of horseflesh, but like a scheduled train. She beat Captain's Flat by three lengths.

Looking up to the stands, I saw Johnny and McLeod rise to applaud the mare into the saddling paddock. Then I turned to watch the beaten stallion, how Spider rode it in, his knees up to the level of his chin as if to make himself less of a target. Yet there was no apology in the way he sat his mount. He seemed to say, believe me a mere jockey if you want and make me wear the colours of alien gods. But the dingo is my totem . . . He seemed to be saying, tough cheese, Clarrie Doig. But I can tell who belongs in the winner's circle. And who doesn't.

I saw Miss Chance's owners, a grazier and his wife, quite credible owners of a cup winner, strolling into the circle. Seeing them move with such an assumption of success, I wriggled my shoulders and worked my way right up to the fence of the saddling enclosure. People made way for me.

'Shame, Spider!' I called. 'Bloody shame!' The bastard had betrayed the ancient, doomed paternity that resided in Clarrie Doig.

Some people stared at me, a few laughed. But Millie had caught up. 'Ssh, Maurice,' she ordered me. The fine skin of her arms, above the elbow, had gone pink. 'Don't you dare embarrass me!'

Tony Hamish was himself already descending the stand, his long benign features set in a grin. The Press photographed him. Johnny and the General stayed where they were. I noticed for the first time the place Pam Masson occupied up there. She spoke to the man beside her, a general who was McLeod's operations officer, a man of maybe forty years, blond, even featured, with an ironic mouth. Neither he nor Mrs Masson watched the saddling paddock. She spoke, he spoke, and both their heads went back and they laughed in unison, their mouths raised to the iron roof.

From the crowd at the base of the steps a man's voice cried out, 'Are the boys in Corregidor at the races today, Donald?' But no one in the stand seemed to hear it. Only in the crowd did a scuffle begin and some defender of McLeod, cursing foully, threw a punch.

Turning my eyes back to the enclosure, I could see Clarrie Doig's bleak face on the far side of the paddock. The corners of his mouth cut deep. He dodged beneath the railings and prowled up to Spider's stirrup. I can remember cringing. No one there could understand him or forgive him. But there were photographers who might decide to snap him. And so his besotted, grieving face would enter history.

Clarrie wrenched the jockey's boot out of the stirrup and began hauling on it. The abuse he was roaring was exactly what you'd expect. 'You black ingrate bastard! I treated you like one of the bloody family . . .'

I couldn't watch but of course I took glimpses. No matter how Clarrie hauled, little Spider hardly moved on that light saddle and was not only hard to tear down but worse – he sat pat there, his eyes fixed sideways on the group of winners. There was no envy in his eyes and, as I said, no remorse. And the US Army Press photographers who danced round the mare and its connections made so much noise that hardly anyone noticed Clarrie's peripheral fury.

In half a minute the Bungendore constabulary dragged Clarrie away from his jockey and though military police turned up they were told it was just Clarrie Doig chucking a fit, that it had no political meaning. I saw them talking sensibly to him, letting go of his arm experimentally, watching him to see if they must again grapple with him. But he stood like an unstrung puppet and was no further threat to the peace. I watched Spider unsaddle the stallion with wondrous neutral movements of his thin black hands. Going into the committee room to weigh in, he did not even glance up at the gentry in the stands.

I struggled towards Clarrie, Millie following, angry, sure I was exposing her to ridicule.

Clarrie saw me. 'It just goes to bloody show,' he said. He shook his head but didn't want to speak further and staggered away towards the committee room.

I turned to Millie and asked her to give me any notes she had on her. There was, of course, an argument. 'Clarie should have known he couldn't fix a race,' she said, with all that economic harshness of a small shopkeeper. 'Couldn't fix a tap, let alone a race.'

'Some bastard fixed it,' I said. 'Jesus, Millie, you're so *laissez-faire* I bet you vote for bloody Tony Hamish.'

Perhaps to prove her political bona fides she handed me the money she had in a wad.

I found Major Jimmy Pointer and talked him into speaking to the same committee man who'd put Johnny Mulhall and General McLeod right. I saw Jimmy whispering in the ear of a middle-aged squatter in the shade of a stand and the committee man whispering into Jimmy's. Then Jimmy came and whispered into mine. 'He reckons Billie Posh at 9-2,' he told me. 'But he can't be absolutely sure.'

I found a rails bookmaker and got a better price than that: 11-2, odds that gave me a sense of value for money. Not that it mattered, it could be but a gesture. I left the ticket at the committee room to be handed to Clarrie Doig.

It was time to go then. Millie was depressed – Clarrie Doig and I had soured the afternoon for her – she knew that the conjunction of McLeod and the horse should produce events more portentous and exhilarating then the ruin of a Catholic cow-cocky and a crass voice from the St Leger reminding a general of his lost army.

The official party was leaving. A wind had come up from the west and a dust of pollen fell on the lapels of Johnny Mulhall's suit, yet seemed to leave McLeod alone. Mrs McLeod and her boy had already taken to their car but McLeod himself stood talking with his chief-of-staff and, although Johnny was near them, he looked almost excluded and stood fingering that long cigarette holder of his in the way a man examines an artefact of some other tribe. Stuck there, half in and half out of the General's ambience, he waved to us and we both went up to join him.

I said in a low voice, 'Thank you, Mr Prime Minister. For putting us right concerning the nag.'

He said, 'Journo's pay isn't that grand, Paper, that you can throw it away on non-certainties.'

He was distracted by a woman's laugh, we all were, and looking up we saw it was Mrs Masson laughing at a joke of that officer with whom she'd shared the afternoon. They stared at each other's faces, both taking some sort of clannish amusement out of this crass bush derby, neither of them taking account of the ground they advanced upon.

I have to say there was nothing pointed in her behaviour, any more than there was in Spider's. But there was a terrible rightness to their walking together under that sharp late summer sun. They didn't belong to the same universe as Clarrie Doig. Their combined beauty compelled everyone, maybe even McLeod. For a few seconds – an era in matters like these – Johnny's smile sat immobile and piteous and his eyes turned away and locked on some indefinite focus over towards the Goulburn Road. Then he caught on that Millie and I were observing him. 'All right,' he told us, 'we'd better go home.' He looked around for his driver.

'She's just bloody asserting herself,' I would have told him if Millie hadn't been there. 'But forget her. She's not appropriate.' There was a rule that operated in those days, though, that you didn't give a friend woman-advice in front of women, even Millie.

We found that only Jimmy Pointer, blessedly sleepy, shared the limousine with us on the way back to Canberra. 'Milady Masson's travelling with the Yankee general,' he told me. But he knew what it meant, that it wasn't any true defection, and therefore it didn't seem to worry him.

I heard on the radio that night that Billy Posh ran a close fifth. The news appeared to me not as a fit punishment for petty crime but as the defeat of old antipodean virtues. The timetable, that is, had won the day.

Chapter Seven

I got the news of the army appointments on Good Friday. I had been working in my office in the almost abandoned Parliament when a source in Melbourne rang them through to me. I had had the feeling all that day that Johnny's austerity speeches and the fear of an alien race had had little influence on this festival and that the remainder of the nation was determinedly on holiday. Most soldiers had leave, munitions factories stood empty in the strong Easter sun, the Show attracted crowds in Sydney, the Press still spent three pages on the Easter Race Carnival and the family feasts of Sunday were under preparation.

When my source called through I knew that there were some people working in Melbourne. He told me General Starkey had been appointed to command all land forces under the supreme South-West Pacific godhead of Donald McLeod. Dick Masson had been promoted and given a corps. It was all as Jimmy Pointer had predicted.

My source also told me that some of the Masson supporters down there were what he called 'ropeable'. They were getting together behind closed doors and saying there must be a secret arrangement between Starkey and Mulhall, that Starkey must have something on Mulhall.

'Bloody nonsense,' I said. But the idea that it *was* now possible for people to have something on Johnny alarmed me.

A friendship – I suppose it was part respect and part conspiracy – had got going between Millie and Mrs Masson on my blind side, without my taking much notice of it. All at once there it was, set up and sealed by the fact that Pam Masson, on an Easter jaunt to the capital, hadn't chosen to stay with her friends out Duntroon way but had instead moved in to Millie's place in the suburb of Reid. The arrangement made Millie an accomplice and I knew, if I wasn't an accomplice already, it made me one, too.

It was natural enough for me to ring Millie's place with the news, I suppose, and it was partly in the function of neutral newsgiver that I gave the operator her number. But I also half-hoped that Starkey's appointment might shock Mrs Masson loose from Johnny, that I could do that service for Johnny and Mrs Mulhall, that I could thereby be delivered from my moral discomfort.

'Oh,' said Millie, when I got through to her. 'We were sitting out under the camphor laurel. Reading.' The drowsiness of the day was in her voice. She'd resented having to answer the phone. I told her I had news for Pam Masson. But Millie was a long time fetching her guest.

When the girl did arrive, the first thing I told her was the fact of Starkey's appointment. I could hear on the line no spasm of soured ambition. She said, 'I'd heard it would be Starkey. I mean, he's not really so old. And they can't sack him on the grounds of lack of previous success. Now can they?'

So, the drum on Starkey having failed to disenchant her, I told her about her husband's corps. She said, 'Good. It's what he wanted.' She didn't sound very intense about it, just pleased at a friend's success. 'He'll do very well,' she said. 'Very well.' And that was it. Except, 'I must telephone him,' she said.

'Take you hours to get through.' I told her. I was disappointed and yet delighted that she'd evaded my trap.

'That doesn't matter. Poor old Dick. He might even allow himself a little claret tonight.'

'You think he'll be happy?' I asked her.

'Of course. Wouldn't you be?'

'Don't ask me, love. I was a bloody private before my accident.'

She said, 'He's happy to wait for bigger things still. He's only a boy, as generals go.'

'You *must* be disappointed,' I accused her.

'Disappointed? Why in the name of God would I be disappointed, Paper? I'll tell you what, I dread the day, Dick will want me to do all those interviews – the woman behind our generalissimo! Telling lies about how I sit at home crocheting.' She said, not unkindly. 'I have the damned Press calling me already.'

I said, 'Come off it. You could've done interviews. It wouldn't have mattered anyway. No one knows about you and Johnny...'

'Perhaps we can't expect to escape comment for ever ... A person begins to understand that ...'

She thanked me and gave the phone back to Millie. It was Millie who came on furious. 'What are they doing, those politicians?' she asked me. 'Giving an old libertine an appointment like that? Because Starkey *is* an old libertine.'

'He's not as old as McLeod.' I told her, hitting her in a soft area.

'He's led a dirtier life than McLeod,' she said. 'McLeod hasn't had Arab girlfriends ...' Millie was too fair-minded to believe a single rumour but she was more susceptible to a series of them. 'His health,' she said, 'will go within a month.'

'In that case,' I said, 'Dick Masson will succeed him.' And, in a lowered voice, 'What does she really think?'

Millie groaned. 'She doesn't have any straight-up-and-down ambitions for her men,' she told me at last.

'Johnny's her man,' I said. 'It's a bit superfluous for her to have ambitions for Johnny.'

Millie said, 'Her politics worry me. For Johnny's sake. She mightn't be a Red but she sits on committees with the buggers. She could land him in real trouble ... I mean with the Press ... with his own crowd ...'

Millie had all the average Labor stalwart's genial fear of Marxism. She'd approved Tony Hamish's outlawing of the Communist Party and even Johnny, saddled with a party of a thousand Millies, was waiting for the fall of Stalingrad before rescinding Hamish's edict against the Reds.

'I can't work her out,' said Millie. 'She doesn't look like a *genuine* sympathizer.'

'What does a sympathizer look like?' I asked. As if I knew the answer.

There was a silence. It seemed a formative one and then I knew what was being formed in it. Millie was reaching towards asking Mrs Masson to stay somewhere else in the capital. I said, 'You want her to leave you alone?'

Millie groaned again. 'Yes. No. She's a wonderful girl.'

'Yes,' I said.

'Oh,' Millie laughed. 'We *are* impressed.'

'We're caught, Millie,' I said. She sighed and on the still line we shared our mutual distress and gratitude.

Chapter Eight

I'm indebted to Jim Cowan, Johnny's Press Secretary, everyone's favourite gentleman, for some details of a weekend Johnny spent in Adelaide about this time. It was, in fact, the first weekend he had visited Ada since the affair with Mrs Masson was initiated. Jim remembered it as a constrained and melancholy two days.

The beaches opposite Ada Mulhall's bungalow were empty now except for the more fanatic all-seasons swimmers. The autumn waves beat like a pulse and the cottage's double-brick locked in the unspectacular but uncrackable secret of the Mulhall marriage.

Jim, of course, knew about Mrs Masson. It must have been an irksome weekend for him. He told me that Johnny was very attentive to Ada during those two windy autumn days but that he slept a great deal. Then they had had a debate for two hours on the Sunday morning about her coming to Canberra and Johnny said that if she would not do that, she ought at least to get a flat in Sydney. She gave her slow familial grin, so much like Johnny's, and kept on refusing. I'm sure that Johnny, influenced by the loneliness of the Southern Ocean just there across the street and spurred by diverse guilt, was pretty sincere in arguing that she should come.

I think it was that weekend also that Millie took me a few

miles out of the gumnut capital to a birthday party for one of her customers. The subject of the celebration was a squatter's wife, she and her husband both descendants of the nineteenth century families who'd made pastures of this primeval valley. The homestead we approached in the dusk matched the low hills too well to be called a mansion. Its stone walls looked like transmutations of the evening sunlight. But by Tyson standards a mansion was what it was. The front of the house was the family's first stone bungalow, built about 1850, I suppose, on the income from the first fleeces grown here and shipped out to a weaving world. Later wool clips had gone into a two-storey wing of limestone with nice fluted Victorian chimneys and ornate wooden valance boards around the eaves. I felt a flush of pleasure as soon as I saw it, even though in the car I had whinged to Millie about having to spend an evening with polo-playing graziers and remittance men.

In defiance of the Japanese High Command, all the lights of this delightful house were burning. Millie and I climbed the stairs and found the front parlour. There was a crowd inside – craggy squatters in good houndstooth coats and trousers that looked a little pegged, as if the wearers might at any time take to horse. There were quantities of tall well-turned-out officers and pretty women in autumn gowns, some of the latter originating from Chez Millie.

I'd had two Scotches and was talking quite companionably to the host, and Millie was whispering satirically in my ear, 'Be careful, you look as though you're just about enjoying yourself,' when Jimmy Pointer – dressed in a brown civilian suit – came through the ruck towards us. He had at his elbow an English girl from the High Commissioner's and, as if she'd been trained for the exercise, she drew Millie into talk while Jimmy dragged me off a few paces.

'Paper,' Jimmy said. The broad soft-featured face was wrapped in a frown which I thought theatrical, full of all that false emotion that marks an address to the jury. 'There's a lavatory out the back in the other wing.' He got very precise about where it was. He said, 'I'd be grateful if you'd meet me there in twenty minutes.'

I began to laugh.

He said, 'If the door's locked, knock.'

'Is this a proposition, eh?' I asked him.

He winked at me but without smiling. 'If anything's going to be buggered, old friend, it will be this fair, sunburnt land of ours.'

I knew I would come. He was such a good source. At the time he'd nominated I followed his instructions, passing the kitchens full of catering staff, and reached the lavatory at last. A sign on its door proclaimed it but the door itself was locked from the inside. I knocked, squinting either way in the empty corridor, and the door was opened. I stepped through it to the sort of lavatory you generally saw only in pubs, a urinal with a stainless steel splash-barrier and an enclosed sit-down water chest.

Jimmy was leaning against the frame of the window. He said without smiling, 'The role of the privy in the history of intrigue! I'm glad you came.'

I asked him if we could leave the door open. I didn't want to get a reputation as Canberra's legless sodomite. He said no, he didn't want it left ajar. So I entered the cubicle instead and shut its door.

I suspended myself on my two rubber-tipped crutches, undid my belt and unbuttoned myself. In public I might be the sulky cripple, sometimes adopting a wilful clumsiness, only sometimes being nifty. But in the privacy of a water closet I was always pretty adroit.

Outside, Jimmy Pointer was talking. 'I'm not sure I'm so happy with your attitude, Paper, old dig. I am taking no small risk, as you must know. But the best you can manage is to be bloody frivolous. I think you should come out.'

I wouldn't be moved. 'I can hear you perfectly. I've managed without mischance to put down on the bowl and I'm all ears, my dear James.'

He was silent for a time. Then without warning he said, 'What do you think abour Moresby?'

He was speaking of course, of the port called Moresby in New Guinea. Theories on that tropic place abounded in Canberra but before I could speak up with any theory of my own, he went on. 'I think it's the key. But McLeod doesn't understand that. McLeod's ignorant in these matters – the Yanks in general are ignorant about the Pacific and don't want to be told. You know Masson? Yes, I know you know Masson. Dick's appalled by the ignorance of McLeod's staff. They're baffled, they're shell-shocked, they can't even read the maps.'

He told me of a meeting Masson had had with some of the Americans in Melbourne. The general (yes, *the general*, Jimmy emphasized) with whom Masson was conferring took from his pocket a small, schoolchildish map of the continent and pointed to its north-west corner. 'What would you do if the Japanese landed here at Broome and advanced on Alice Springs?' the American asked. Dick Masson had explained there was no surface water in the thousand miles between Broome and Alice Springs, that the surface was unnegotiable and that he would send in the Salvage Corps to retrieve the bones.

'And this sort of question comes from a man who is advising McLeod.' There was a pause. 'Are you listening, Paper?' Jimmy asked, alarmed by some reverberations from my cubicle.

'Of course.'

'I do bloody hope so,' he said. 'Dick Masson believes that this continent must be defended at Moresby. McLeod doesn't know what in the hell to do. McLeod doesn't understand.'

Jimmy expatiated on the confusion of those military planners, even among the Australians, who believed that Moresby must fall, that its fall could not be argued with and that the holy continent of Johnny Mulhall and Jimmy Pointer could be defended only from within its own boundaries.

'It happens' Jimmy said, 'that there's a great massing of Japanese troop ships and so on. At Rabaul. McLeod hasn't told any journalists about it because he thinks it would be bad for the Australian peace of soul. This convoy . . . there's no doubt that its destination is Moresby. Oh, for God's sake, come out of there, Paper! I can't run a conspiracy through a shit-house door.'

He would not say anything more until I obeyed him. I had gone in frolicsome but I came out sober enough. I began to scrub my hands and he leaned close to me over the basin.

'I have all the details,' he said. 'All the intelligence reports.

He took an envelope from the breast pocket of his brown suit. But I did not reach for it, even after I had finished towelling myself. I knew why I was being enlisted. I would pass the stuff to my boss, who would then write a fervent editorial about Moresby and within two weeks the port would be more strongly fortified and manned. But perhaps the place was untenable, anyhow, and to increase the numbers of the garrison was to increase the number of victims. I didn't know. But Singapore had gone, almost as if – like the *Titanic* – it had been destined to. What chance did little tropic municipalities like Moresby have?

I said, 'I don't know, Jimmy. It's a big responsibility . . .'

He did not object when I opened the envelope and began to read the pages inside. It was more or less what he'd promised. I could see how the contents would create public alarm and certain pressures of State. 'Of course.' I said, 'I'm a great believer in the public's access to information.'

Jimmy had the grace not to smirk. 'Of course you are, Paper. That's why I approached you.'

I re-read the pages. It was to a nicety the sort of material for which my boss kept me on the payroll, in spite of my Mulhallian bias. I said, 'Have you got a map or anything?' As if an atlas could instruct me somehow in my puzzlement.

He said, 'It's a question of whether you think Masson's judgment is better than McLeod's.' Then he smiled. 'It's a question, too, of whether you think I'm a buffoon or a clever eccentric.'

With panic rising, I considered the envelope for another thirty seconds. Then I put it in my pocket, finding it easy all at once to believe that Jimmy and Masson had the true view of the crisis. Jimmy said that one of us should go back to the parlour first and the other wait three minutes before moving. This time I did not think him theatrical; he went first and I waited my full three minutes, compelled to exactitude by the nature of the documents.

Two mornings later the news Jimmy had slipped me in a squatter's lavatory became headlines. To get the story past the censor my editor had stuck the tag ALLIED HQ AUSTRALIA on to the dateline, and so within a few days the story appeared in the Chicago *Tribune*, the *New York Times* and the San Francisco *Examiner*.

I see now that I was a blundering infant and that perhaps Jimmy Pointer was, too. I read in biographies of McLeod that the chiefs-of-staff in Washington gave the General some grief over this illicit despatch. They complained that the material was too detailed to have been drawn from reconnaissance alone and that therefore the enemy would be justified in believing that his codes had been broken, as was the case. The papers Jimmy Pointer had shown me by the wash basin therefore hid refinements at which Jimmy and I could not have guessed. Yet I still believe that John Mulhall's antipodes and new society, a country as much of the mind as of the map, was guaranteed by our actions there amid all that inane country plumbing.

On the obverse side, Jimmy's leaking of documents would lead to a peculiar censorship. Donald McLeod went from his insurance building in Collins Street to an Advisory War Council meeting at Victoria Barracks and asked to be given sole power over all communiqués. Censors were to rinse all material in his clear blue gaze. And Colonel Gustav Zimmer, the General's Press Officer, would approve all words that were spoken concerning our hemisphere. I go into these ramifications only because they were to influence the Massons, Mulhall and your humble servant.

It was the first day of winter. A needling rain had fallen in the morning. By noon a sun of subtle radiance shone in the sky, where lumps of cloud scattered towards Goulburn on the first piercing wind of 1942. In the illimitable alps to the south (according to Canberra radio) fresh snow had fallen.

This also had been the last day of that parliamentary session. The westerners, who had so far to travel, had already left and were aboard the Melbourne Express. Certain north Queenslanders were waiting cheerily on Goulburn's iron-filigreed station for the Sydney train. It would take them two days to return to their threatened Capricornian electorates.

Some Labor senators from New South Wales had shouted me lunch that day and, after Question Time in the Reps, I'd waited on in the Press Gallery, hoping for a soothing, digestive debate. The House was now, as I'd expected, nearly empty. A bare quorum occupied the benches. On the government front bench sat John Mulhall, the Minister for the Army and Eddie Hoare, the latter glaring away across the table through heavy-lensed spectacles. Tony Hamish seemed full of composure, even though he was speaking at some social dinner in Sydney that very night and must have been hoping for an early end to the business of the House. He stared back at Eddie in the mocking Hamish manner. In and between those two burned the House flames of ideological hate.

The debate in progress concerned the provisions of the Women's Employment, Wages and Compensation Act, 1942. I sat for a while, half asleep, in the steep-canted gallery. I saw one of Johnny's other ministers enter, make a negligent obeisance towards the Speaker and hand Johnny and his Army Minister some typed sheets. Johnny read his page slowly, his eyelids coming nearly closed as if the message filled him with somnolence. Then he got up, one shoulder rising before the other. The Speaker recognized him, he asked leave to speak and was given it.

Though he moved like a farmer, his voice was always pulpit-sharp. But with a sort of cardiac flutter in it today that reminded me he'd had warnings from physicians about his heart. He said that there was a communiqué from McLeod, there in his hand, which told of a vast naval engagement under way in the South-West Pacific. He knew the conflict was a vital one but had no news of how it was developing. He then said that there were young boys dying somewhere so that the continent could retain its body and its soul and that therefore men and women in Australia should subject themselves to the same stern discipline as that which prevailed in the battle zone.

It was a characteristic Mulhall speech and, as I retell it, it has an undistinguished sound. Yet it roused that slightly-manned House. They stood up and clapped, as if the effort and the turmoil of both fleets were connected with the tremors of Johnny's questionable heart. The applauders included Tony Hamish, on his feet, pale, doing some little homage to the event.

Even as I rang the speech through to Sydney, I had this urge to see Millie at her dress shop. It's easy to suppose now that to me on that quiet Friday her boutique signified what was at risk. But I didn't see that then. I just called a cab and went straight there. The shops of the capital stood together, promenades of faintly Spanish design. They were a blockhouse in the bare midst of the plain; perhaps the most defensible structure in the whole defenceless capital.

Given that my motives for coming were certain instincts to do with the precious nature of women, I was pleased to find that Millie had two women on the premises, one in the fitting room, the other wearing a violet winter suit, frowning, fingertips on shoulders, turning in front of a man-sized mirror. I did not know her name but her movements composed me, had an honesty and an eternal instinctive sameness about them, like the eternal instinctive sameness of the movements of cats.

'You can always take up the sleeves,' said Millie. 'Take up the hem, yes, yes.' Her eyes were glimmering with the potentialities of the sale but she left the woman in violet, who needed that mysterious small time to weigh and ponder and to do her sums, and approached me, using the cover of a rack of frocks to flash me a secret smile.

I asked her, 'Are you all right, Millie, eh?' It sounded as if I'd been told by some third person that she'd had an accident.

She put her hand up to shield her mouth. 'Nearly 22 quid in the till,' she whispered. I smiled at that. Millie was holding off a circle of perils with a full till.

I told her what Johnny had said in the House and she nodded, but studied my own face for symptoms of the news. She said, 'Mmm!' like a mother examining a rash. Then she excused herself and went and closed the sale of the violet suit to the tall woman by the mirror. On Fridays and Saturdays she had a girl in who could box and tie up things for customers, and the tall woman went into the second cubicle and passed the violet jacket and the skirt out to the girl. Before returning to me, Millie asked the client in the first cubicle if she were all right, and the client inquired in a breathy voice if Millie had any elastic – there'd been an accident with her lingerie. Millie fetched her some elastic and scissors and then came back to me. All this oblivious behaviour of women dazzled me and settled my animal panic.

Millie gave me instructions, just as if she knew I operated in a daze. 'Pam's out in the other room. Drinking tea. Why don't you go out there and sit with her? I'll come out when I've sent these two along. Go on. Go on.'

I obeyed her. I edged by her two customers, now emerged from the fitting rooms, one with that mysterious purchaser's complacency on her lips, the other frowning, still not suited and angry over whatever accident had befallen her smalls. Neither looked at me and I thought that a good omen. The invader would have a job getting their attention.

The access to Millie's back room was through a screen door. Beyond was a limited space, a storeroom, a place where stock was received and ticketed. In one corner stood a table and a mobile tray with an electric jug and teapot and four cups. There were also three chairs crowded in.

When I went in, Pam Masson looked up from her chair. In front of her a cup of black tea steamed. She had a book open and a pencil in her hand, and at her elbow a small mantel radio was plugged in, switched on and turned right down. I could hear enough to tell that she'd tuned in the broadcast from the Branch Office and I could hear Eddie Hoare defending his industrial policies amidst a sea of interjections. The House, which had been nearly empty when I left, sounded full in transmission.

The girl was wrapped in an immense red cardigan, so large it may have been lent her by a friend or taken out of Millie's stock. She smiled up at me as if she knew exactly why I'd come. She looked very young in that too-big garment, her eyes seemed immense. I saw in her the twelve-year-old kid, exiled all at once from her old man's study to some muddy English farm.

'Heard about it,' she said, nodding at the radio set. 'Sit down, Paper. Could I pour you some tea?'

She frowned at me while I sat, giving me no aid. There was none of Millie's till-happiness in her, none of that clothes-absorption I'd been grateful to see in the women outside. She said, 'He sounds quite magnificent, doesn't he?'

'Yeah,' I said. 'He's got a presence all right.'

'Yes,' she said. 'He conveys confidence to the population.' She laughed. 'To everyone except himself.'

'Rosaries again?' I asked.

'No, no,' she said, chopping me off. I wasn't to expect any private news. 'I think he believes it's inevitable.'

'What?'

'The whole disaster,' she said. 'Invasion. The works.'

'Well,' I asked, 'what about yourself? What do you believe?'

Shivering inside the cardigan and narrowing her eyes, she did not answer. Then she held up the book she'd been reading; held up, too, the pencil she'd been using to mark it. 'By a coincidence, Paper,' she said. The title was *Japanese Things*, by Basil Hall Chamberlain. 'Extraordinary people. Extraordinary.'

She began to read to me:

How sweet Japanese woman is! All the possibilities of the race for goodness seem to be concentrated in her. It shakes one's faith in some Occidental doctrines. If this be the result of suppression and oppression, then suppression and oppression are not altogether bad. On the other hand, how diamond-hard the character of the American woman becomes under the idolatry of which she is the object. In the eternal order of things, which is the higher being – the childish, confiding, sweet Japanese girl or the superb, calculating, penetrating Occidental Circe of our more artificial society, with her enormous power for evil and her limited capacity for good?

She looked up at me, one eyebrow raised. From the mantel radio I could hear Tony Hamish interjecting and Eddie Hoare replying that the only experience the Honourable Member had had of the Australian working female was in the dining rooms of silvertail houses in Toorak and Vaucluse, and only then in the second when she interrupted his renowned anecdotes by placing his sausage and mash in front of him. This laboured attack attracted the slow jeers it deserved.

I hadn't thought of the connection between this afternoon's

news and the talks Jimmy Pointer and I had had in the squatter's lav. Now it was Pam Masson who made the link.

She said, 'It must be *that* convoy. The one from Rabaul. You know. The one written up in the Press this week. And our friends and allies have run into it.'

Until then, without knowing it, I had thought of Jimmy Pointer's convoy as something dreamed up under his tin roof or in Masson's office in Melbourne. I was amazed. I slapped my upper leg. 'Of course,' I said. 'Of course.' Jimmy and I, two fools by the urinals, we had touched that convoy, given the Western world an attitude towards it. 'Hell,' I said. 'I didn't even think.'

She poured me a cup, leaned over to a little ice chest Millie had there and fetched me the jug of milk from it. I had begun to grow suspicious. I said, 'Your husband tells you things, doesn't he? When you see him? Can't help himself, can he?'

'He tells me nothing,' she told me, concentrating on pouring the milk. 'Not straight out, anyhow. I don't deny you can always gather a certain amount without even wanting to.'

'If he can't help letting things out,' I said, 'it's because he's still keen.'

'Keen?'

'On you. Still – you know – in love.'

She groaned and shook her head. 'No, it's not love. It's more like a friendship between first cousins.'

Once I had the word 'love' out of my mouth – a pretty extravagant performance by my standards – I found I was off in an obsessed direction. I got her wrist with my hands. My short nails scored her skin. 'Jesus, *I* want you, Mrs Masson,' I told her. Of course I had not revealed that even to myself before. I was shocked with myself. But she wasn't shocked. She nodded a while. Any damage I'd done or was doing to the flesh of her wrist didn't seem to worry her much. Her left hand reached my face and ran along my jaw. The fingers made some real effort to define me. I said, 'I need a shave.' She made a soothing noise with the front of her lips. The hand reached my brow and surveyed it. Then she withdrew it altogether.

Somehow, through those pressures of face and hand, I was reconciled to the whole business of her and Johnny and, of course, drawn closer into it. But more so, we understood the balance of impulse between the two of us and it amazed me to identify for the first time her possible jealousy of me as Johnny's father-confessor – or whatever post at court it was that I had.

Soon Millie got rid of her customer with the withered elastic and she came in, the sane and sweet creature who knew what incantations to offer to customers. I was grateful to see her. The three of us sat drinking tea and listening for bulletins until closing time. But nothing further was disclosed.

Chapter Nine

We went to sleep without knowing. Some time after midnight, I opened my eyes in the dark. I knew at once that the rattling of the wire screen in Millie's bedroom window was caused by an intruder; that not even the wind off Mount Ainslie could be as rhythmic as that. At first I associated the noise with the dominant Asians of the dream from which I'd awoken. I reached out and made such a clutch for Millie's shoulder that she, too, sat up and would have in turn, given the nature of her own dreams, woken a third party if one had been available.

I was nearer the noise and without thinking of it I swung my legs towards the edge of the bed, fumbled on my false left leg, found my crutches by the bedside chair and so got to the window. By the three-quarter moon I could see Johnny out there, standing among Millie's rhododenron bushes, wearing his chief-accountant-style Akubra, having to clamp it in place with his fist. I eased the window up a few inches while Millie, off to my right in the dark, hissed at me. 'Who is it, Maurice? *Maur-ice!*'

'Johnny,' I said, as an answer to her and also to encourage the visitor to speak.

'Mind if I come in, Paper?' he asked. He wavered on his feet. I wondered if bad news had driven him back to his old vices.

'Through the bloody window?'

He flapped a dismissive hand. 'Front door'll do. Went to your office. Couldn't find you there. Guessed where you'd be.' He yawned and then he smiled at me.

Millie went to the front door to let him in and by the time she had I'd pulled the drapes in the sitting room and was waiting for him with the lights turned on. He staggered in, sat in a chair, grinned at me again, palely, like a patient who wants to reassure his visitors. Then he seemed to doze for half a minute. Opening his eyes, he said, 'Didn't want to alarm anyone at this hour, hammering on the front door.'

'You scared the bejesus out of us anyhow,' I told him.

'It's all right,' said Millie. For that hour of the morning, she seemed loyal and compliant.

He said, 'Millie, would you mind rousing Pamela? Would you mind that?'

Millie frowned a bit at me but left to do it.

I could tell it wasn't liquor that gave him his wobbles, his pallor. It was the dizziness of his insomnia. 'Johnny,' I said, 'don't you sleep at all?' We laughed together. Though I knew he had final news, it was against the rules to ask until the women came in.

A fashion I didn't approve of – women wearing men's pyjamas – had just hit the antipodes. Mrs Masson came in in a heavy flannel pyjama suit that bunched at her waist. With all its volume, it made her seem smaller than she was. I kept watching Johnny but saw her obliquely.

She looked something like a refugee and I saw Johnny get up and take her elbow. 'Sit down, sit down, Pamela. You too, Millie.' Both women were themselves smiling and shaking their heads, for he was like a favourite uncle come home from the sea. But they obeyed him. He touched Pam Masson's shoulder to stress that she ought to be still, that she was the centre of the event, and then he came and sat down himself.

'I got Don's communiqué an hour ago,' he told us. 'Don McLeod's.' Even I was struck by the habitude with which he uttered the name, as if he were talking of some old friend from the Melbourne Socialist Club or from inside the party machine.

'And?' said Pamela Masson.

He told us everything. There had been an invasion force on

its way to Port Moresby, he said. Transports and escorts and a striking force to cover it. Both had been turned back in an astounding battle where no ship fired at any other ship. 'Aircraft only, Paper,' he said, turning to me for a second. Perhaps thinking that I – as a former campaigner in a more antique war than this – would be stimulated by the fact as he himself seemed to be. In the mid '30s, when he'd first got his itch for the capitalist sport of military strategy, he had pushed in speeches the primacy of the plane, speeches which Tony Hamish and other veterans of the Melbourne University Regiment had dismissed as if the idea of air-fleets had a Marxist taint to it.

He might have turned to me for the reference to aircraft. But most of the time he looked from Millie to Pam Masson and his manner of doing it confused me for a while, set me searching for precedents in the deportment of men I'd known in the past, not so much politicians but ordinary men, men perhaps like my father. And it came to me that his tone and his manners were exactly those of a man who brings home a really preposterous gift, diamonds no less, pearls from the bed of Timor, something that will stun not just his woman but the neighbour women too. That was it. He was making free of the gift of the three-day sea battle, he was landing it in front of Pam Masson, and that he should feel free to do that is something which even at this distance of time seems both frightful and yet endearing. It was clear he felt entitled to bestow the victory like this. All the tax of those ideas which he'd brought with him out of his boyhood, and which he'd paid over to the conflict, entitled him. Seeing him grinning all squinty-eyed at Mrs Masson, I felt the sting of tears on my eyelids. But I felt scared for him too. Didn't he know more of the world? Didn't he know you can't trade with the war like that, open your secret cache to it, turn over your glittering contents and expect to get glittering contents back?

In my amazement, I looked at Mrs Masson to gauge whether she saw all this, or whether she did not dare see it. To gauge if she was flattered, if she was appalled, if she saw him just as a man in the know who'd called in as early as he could with what qualified in that season as good news. But there were few signs from her. Her eyes were open to the limit but not necessarily

96

in any amazement, just for the sake of letting in the substantial news of the hour.

'You ought to be very happy with this,' she told him, as if in doubt that he *would* be happy. She shivered in her pyjamas. 'And the British,' she said. 'It ought to make them more biddable.'

Johnny had now settled himself more deeply in his seat, had sighed well satisfied, undone all the buttons on his coat and taken out his cigarette holder. The gift-giving – if that was what it had been – was over and Millie and I were free now to offer our congratulations from the sideline.

After a while, when his cigarette was lit and he'd drawn on it to the limit of his lungs, choking on the smoke, he began to talk again. 'Of course,' he said, 'the communiqué mentions a terrible carnage. Ten ships sunk, five disabled. Deliverance wears two faces, see, as it always does. I don't have to tell any of you that.'

'Oh, John,' said Mrs Masson, 'it'd be ridiculous for you to think too much of that side of it.'

'Is there any tea, Millie?' Johnny asked.

Millie danced up, the least stunned, the most stimulated of the lot of us. Johnny himself had gone to sleep before she reached the door. Mrs Masson went up to him, touched the crown of his head and smoothed his hair down; then returned to her chair and sat, chin in hand, considering him. Once she glanced at me, as if inviting a second opinion, but she said nothing and neither did I. Perhaps the extent of the gift he'd brought frightened her.

Outside, the capital slept its prosaic sleep in a storm of falling leaves and Johnny's driver, Reg Whelan, huddled in the government Buick and wondered whether he might see the mother of his six kids that night.

By this time the Branch Office had taken on a more anonymous look. Its windows were sandbagged. A brick screening wall was being built, not over its white façade, where it would look like a confession of official fright, but around the back. For every

97

inhabitant of the place there was an appropriate slit trench or hole in the rose gardens and on the parliamentary lawns.

When the sirens roared on the morning of the practice, every native of the place – barmen, librarians, ushers, clerks, typists, scribes, aides and members – had his shelter to make for. In the corridors, wardens harried the population out into the open and so into their appropriate holes. But I would not let them harry me. Therefore I was among the last to drag down the stairs of the House. Above my head, infants in Mitchell bombers flew low over the roof, measuring it in their unmarred brains for the silent explosions of this fake bomb run.

The organizers of the ritual had got the Cabinet as far as the lip of their proper trench but had been unable to make them enter it. I could see Johnny standing behind a rose bush, squinting up at the wings above us. Under the great blunt racket of the engines, he noticed the sharp click-clack of my crutches on the pavement. We nodded to each other and he moved away from his colleagues, looking sheepish, remembering perhaps the evening he'd made the grandiose gift. He rounded a bush, where some game yellow rose hung on, and stood in front of me.

'We should be dead.' I yelled, pointing at the aircraft. 'If it was Nips . . .'

He reached out and took my elbow. It was a confidential gesture. I wondered if my fellow journalists in their slit trench would see it and misjudge it. Another bomber, a succubus half as big as the Branch Office, so low it seemed to rise out of the parliamentary chimneys, prevented him speaking for a time.

'Some of that stuff I told you last week,' he said as the bombers wheeled above the War Memorial to return on a second sweep, 'about that business in the Coral Sea. A bloke like you, a fellow who deals in fact . . . you've probably heard that some of the . . . what you'd call . . . the *statistics* were a bit off . . .'

'That's all right,' I told him, lightly, as if he was just a functionary amending an earlier statement, as if the incident in Millie's sitting room hadn't been so strange and intimate and indivisible. 'I had heard a whisper, Johnny. You know . . . from certain sources. That your friend McLeod overstated things a bit. Gilded the lily. You know.'

Johnny closed his eyes. 'The details of it . . . whether ten ships were sunk or not . . . they don't alter the event,' he said.

'Did you ask him, Johnny? Did you ask him how he came to think ten ships had been sunk?'

Johnny's hand rocked my elbow a little. Through a fabric I could feel the extent of the palm and the fingers. 'Well, early reports, Paper . . . early reports are always optimistic. And the General said to me, "You know, your fellows were pestering me for a communiqué".' He looked away, he nodded to himself, like a man saying, 'And fair enough too!'

I said, 'Well, the papers were happy with the inexact news.' No one would be any the wiser until the conflict ended and the wreckage and the bones of the young were transmuted into history.

'That's right,' said Johnny. 'All too happy. And so was I. All too happy.'

But the longer Johnny spoke, defending the General amid the noise of engines, the less forgiving I grew. 'Well,' I said, 'he turned it into a beauty, didn't he? A bloody work of fiction. Didn't he?'

Johnny tried to laugh my awkwardness away. 'Your old Digger prejudices are coming up,' he said. 'He didn't *write* the communiqué, you know.'

'But he wanted to be first with the news,' I screamed as the airmen repeated their tricks right above our heads. 'He thought – I bet he thought – *if the communiqué has my name at the end of it, people will think it was a personal ruddy victory.* And all those magazines . . . you know, *Harpers* and all that crowd, they'll be pushing him for Republican candidate all over again. That's what it means, Johnny. It's not just because a few poor bloody colonials wanted news of the battle.'

Though I was talking so hotly against McLeod, I think we could both tell he wasn't the subject. There was a question Johnny wanted asked and answered – even though it would take him at the base of a heart that had already been declared weak by the doctors. 'Don't you think McLeod has corrupted the gift you gave your love? At that sweet hour? In that exultant night? At the core of a saved nation?' That was the question.

Of course, I did not ask it. I was an old-fashioned friend who didn't have the necessary talents, and there were some bones I could not cut too close to.

Instead, I asked, 'Does he know you're using him? You know, does he know all this work of his imagination . . . ten ships sunk . . . all that stuff . . . does he know you've got socialist plans for this place, once he's saved it with his communiqués?'

'We're happy with the arrangement, Paper,' said Johnny. 'We understand each other.'

I couldn't understand I'd lost track of him since that night he'd brought the news to Millie's bedroom window. It was as if I couldn't read him now. The world gets more and more complex to a man and makes him more and more so, until its complexity kills him off. I suspected that the falsehoods in McLeod's communiqué had been a step in the complicating of John Mulhall. I make the banal remark with apology, for Johnny had come through the '30s as something like a simple apparatus.

He said to me, 'I complained, you know, Paper. I sent a note to Colonel Zimmer.'

'Zimmer?'

'He's Public Relations Officer. General McLeod has such a thing.' He touched the side of his nose the way street traders do when they get conspiratorial with clients.

'That,' I said, 'is like complaining to bloody Seutonius because Nero burned Rome.'

A month later, when the battle of Midway was fought, Johnny was absent in Melbourne, and Pam Masson was in her lonely house at Double Bay above the harbour in Sydney. I was therefore not in a position to tell whether he brought Midway to her as a diadem. But I knew by instinct that it could not have the same reverberations for him as had that earlier, misreported fracas.

Part Two/Chapter One

The lift to the penthouse operated from a corner of Lennon's Hotel where the public were not permitted. The door was guarded by two soldiers with automatic rifles, who asked for and inspected my Press pass with that sweet American politeness that other English-speakers mock but cannot reproduce.

One of the guards took me up in the lift, the weapon in his hands looking complex and powerful, an icon of the great American manufactury. By contrast the ancient lift was slow, you could hear the cables sigh. When the door opened on the top floor, the soldier pointed out on which further door I should knock. The General wasn't home yet from his headquarters up the road (he told me), but Mrs McLeod said I should come in without waiting.

The General's door was opened to me by a Chinese woman in a high-collared gown. I could see, behind her, a beautiful little boy with black hair. I knew from the press release Colonel Zimmer had handed me that the child was four years old. It was a vulnerable face, a slightly indulged one, and I supposed that Chinese nannies weren't very harsh on little Westerners.

I introduced myself to the nanny and was of course admitted. I said something dismissive to the child, 'G'day, Tiger' or something like it, and hoped that would be all I'd have to outlay on him, for somehow his large eyes, his features which would be

101

feminine even in manhood, filled me with as much disquiet as would a cripple's. He didn't answer me, of course, but I could tell he expected my comradeship.

The Chinese woman had also been explained in Zimmer's briefing. She had accompanied the McLeods on their long flight from Mindanao and her English, in which she asked if I would take a drink, sounded Latin rather than Asian. The little boy went on watching me seat myself by the tall windows of the penthouse. I saw that look on his face, the expectancy augmented, as if I might just turn out to be a clown or a magician his old man had hired for a party. I looked away from him outwards at the last light of Brisbane bleeding away across the façade of the city, across the cathedral steps, across the ornamental flourishes of that race of anonymous Victorian architects from the British Colonial Office who gave the city its official buildings.

The little boy had followed me across the room and balked five paces off. 'What did you do with your legs?' he asked me.

I thought of doing the normal uncle-some thing of telling the poor child I'd been half-eaten by a circus animal or had sold them to a butcher when I was hard up. But I could tell that no one else teased him like that, that he would have no precedents by which he could put together an expression of mocking disbelief. In any case, according to Zimmer, the poor little sod had undergone a fierce migration. They had feared for his life, he'd been so ceaselessly travel sick in the torpedo boats and in the high, dry, noisy turbulence of the B-17 that had brought the family to this continent. Dehydration, Zimmer said. The poor little bugger had sloughed a layer of skin while recovering.

The sweet Chinese nanny, bringing my drink, started hushing him and saying, 'Don't be rude, Mr Dougal.'

I said, 'They were both shot off in a battle.'

'Was it Corregidor?' he asked, grinning and short of breath. For he hoped this was going to be a veterans' reunion. 'Were you in hospital in the tunnel?'

The Chinese nanny chuckled and placed a hand on his shoulder.

102

'No, it was another . . . it was a war when your daddy was a young general.'

'My name's Paperboy anyhow.'

'Mine is Sergeant,' he said, extending his small ivory hand.

The Chinese lady said softly, 'The soldiers in the Malinta Tunnel used to call him Sergeant. Then they tried to promote him Second Lieutenant but he wouldn't have it, nossir!'

'How did you like it in the tunnel, Sergeant?' I asked him.

'I had a birthday party. I turned four. General Hill gave me a Japanese flag and it had blood on it. I got a wooden truck, too. Colonel White gave me a cigarette holder.'

'A toy,' said the loving nanny. 'A toy one. So he can take off his father, you know.'

Across the room, beyond a settee, a door opened and a thin pretty woman with her son's features walked towards my chair, speaking in a voice of crystalline Yankee sweetness. 'Please don't you even try to get up, Mr Tyson, sir. I've heard a great deal about you from our dear friend, John Mulhall, and only the peculiarity of our situation here has prevented us meeting you before now.'

'The peculiarity of my situation, too, Mrs McLeod,' I said, smiling but still perverse. The mother and son both smiled back at me with their apparent innocence and like an echo of each other. I concluded that the Sergeant's pixie features derived from his fine-drawn mother rather than from his basilisk old man.

As soon as I saw her I thought of Scott Fitzgerald. I had read *The Great Gatsby* only the year before and found the women therein so removed from my experience that the book was like a romance of some ancient and eccentric court. As she talked now, Mrs McLeod gave the book a fleshly dimension and could have been – with her easy, mannered grace, her cool prettiness which just about had on it the glow of well-mulched accumulations of family money – Nick Carradine's girlfriend.

There were reasons why you didn't see many women like Mrs McLeod in Australia. The immigrant with the shame of a steerage passage glowing beneath the make-up was not quite submerged beneath the skin of many Australian 'society' ladies. I got no sense from them of the refining power of Puritan money as I did from Scott Fitzgerald's women and now from Mrs McLeod.

'I suppose I'll have a gimlet,' she told the Chinese nanny and she sat down to wait for it, hands in lap. And, hands in lap, the Sergeant sat beside her like an echo.

As the nanny had, she talked about the boy, sometimes looking at him and swapping smiles with him, sometimes as if he weren't there. The child frowned faintly to himself, weighing the question of his own strange life atop an alien city, as if it were the fate of another person.

'Dougal got very pale in the tunnel,' the mother told me. 'We could only safely go out for an evening stroll about seven at night, when the Japanese gunners called a halt. The cocktail hour, we used to call it. The air was so bad down there in the tunnel and, of course, Mr Tyson, there was the inevitable malodorousness. I don't think I knew until then . . . I suppose you'd know – John Mulhall tells us you're an old soldier . . . that wounds themselves have a certain stench . . .'

There was a few seconds' pallor under her eyes. It was as if she was confessing that loving a general brought its condign punishments and that the blind ghosts of private soldiers soured the marital fire, made the marriage bed uneasy. I could not stop a sort of flush of sympathy from rising in me. It wasn't her fault she loved a Caesar.

'Of course there was no one of Dougal's age. Here at least he can sometimes go down to that park on the other side of the road. The manager has a five-year-old boy. Ah Min takes him and Colonel White and – unfortunately – there have to be certain escorts . . .'

The child and I surveyed each other for a second. Our brains were full of the grand dizziness of the razzle-dazzle. I found that I wished I had brought him a gift and that I hadn't became a sudden regret with me that itched away all evening.

A man wearing a lieutenant-colonel's insignia on his shirt collar and an apron on top of his uniform appeared in another doorway. We were introduced. It was the Colonel White of

104

whom she'd spoken, a staff officer who had been sidetracked to take care of the wife and the hothouse child. He nodded at me, pleasant but preoccupied. 'Missy Ah,' he said to the nanny, 'didn't you get any bean curd?'

Missy Ah said, 'The man said his machine got broken, colonel, sir.' It seemed she went by staff car twice a week to a grocery run by one of Brisbane's Chinese residents.

'Oh, shoot!' the Colonel said.

'Only bean curd machine in town,' Ah Min intoned.

'Does it wreck your menu, Whitie?' Mrs McLeod asked him, so resonant, so sweet and amused and concerned.

'We'll make do,' said the Colonel. He winked at young Dougal, did some genial semaphoring towards me and closed the door again.

Five minutes later, the General came home.

Missy Ah handed him a drink she had prepared without my noticing from the platoon of bottles on the sideboard. I wondered what it was. Perhaps I could mention it in my copy – 'Likes to relax with one . . .' whatever it was, bourbon or Canadian whisky. I didn't have an eye for their respective tintings.

The boy paled with the excitement of his father's homecoming. He was jumping, jumping towards his old man's omniscient blue eyes. In his photographs, the General struck the pose of a gorgon; you registered him as a visitation rather than an individual. But here, in the penthouse, the unconditional broadness of his smile reduced him to the status of family man. You remembered he was sixty-two. You wondered if his hair, more consistently black than yours, showed the effects of a dye, whether his tall unseamed brow was the reward for a clean life or just a bit of congenital luck, and whether his inhumanly even teeth were the fruit of that same Yankee technology that had put the strange elegant sheen on his shirt or the automatic in the hands of his guard.

With his free hand, McLeod held in the air a brown paper parcel, which he twisted a few times to make his son's excitement the sweeter.

'Oh, Donald,' said Mrs McLeod, 'that's two days in a row!'

'Well,' said McLeod, raising his jaw in a mock combativeness, 'Calder saw it in a shop window at lunchtime and thought, that's just the thing for the Sergeant.'

He put the parcel in Dougal's hands, while the women both made their reproving and unheeded noises. Opened, the thing proved to be a sturdy toy ambulance that clanged as it rolled. The Sergeant seemed transported and I found myself a member of the family, laughing in unison with his parents and Missy Ah as he pushed it on a hectic emergency run among the table legs and chairs.

Then Mrs McLeod stood and offered her cheekline to the General's lips and the kiss went down softly on to her fine-pored skin. In that second I thought, I'm party to all this family intimacy, the sweetness of it will bear me away if I let it. I thought, a toy, a kiss. What am *I* rostered for?

I chose to counter first. As he crossed the room towards me, I shot myself upright. I also extended my right hand before he could, meaning perhaps to show that soldiers exist by the tolerance of the citizen. He came on, his eyes now hawkish enough to make me feel puny. An ageing private's quick reflexes left him feeling indifferent.

He said what his wife had, that he'd heard so much about me from John Mulhall. I nodded and grinned. But I could not find it credible that when Johnny sat down with the General in some secret and guarded room and considered how flights of B-17s might be diverted to Townsville, they spent much time on the question of Paperboy Tyson.

'Whitie making dinner?' McLeod asked his wife over his shoulder.

'Yes, general,' said his wife.

He told me, as if it might be an item for my exclusive article, 'Colonel White is very gifted in Filipino cuisine . . . We should use the study, I think.'

Following him across the floor, I felt that all that was most obvious about me – my honourable crippledom, my fraternity with Johnny Mulhall – was about to be fed into the McLeod-aggrandizing machine.

* * * *

Its servant, Colonel Zimmer, was a little olive, shrivelled man who behaved like an impresario in a motion picture. (Which was, of course, the only kind of impresario I'd ever laid eyes on.) When offering me the job, he'd spoken as if he'd been attracted by my raw talent and my special characteristics and meant to take me to the top. In fact he used the phrase to indicate where I could take what I wrote – I could expect serialization in one of the great American journals. 'And that's only first print rights – it's not like your local rags here, who take the whole damn copyright.' He told me that what I wrote would be subject to 'the normal limits of censorship' – that is, subject to his blue pencil. 'But I won't be peremptory. We can *consult* on the article.'

'It won't be a partisan job,' I'd told him. 'If you want me to tell you straight, I consider every general suspect until it's proved otherwise.'

This had tickled Zimmer. He laughed as if he'd always known I was a character and this bore out his expectations. He had come out then with a nice little aphorism. 'Truth is the only partisan we seek, Mr Tyson. Just the same, there's one area in which I'd seek your co-operation. None of us thinks it does any good to say anything about the boys on Corregidor.'

'But there's no problem with censorship,' I had protested.

Zimmer had shaken his head. 'It isn't as if they aren't always in his thoughts. But it isn't even good journalism to raise them.' He had whispered, 'It only makes him clam up.'

I had muttered some sort of undertaking but had approached the interview knowing I had in my pocket a weapon I could use if it were needed.

I had this idea that I was risking my soul in writing for McLeod. I don't know why – it was no better or worse than writing for my boss. But doubts about my salvation made me stumble on the carpet and the General looked around, concerned, permitting me, however, the small exercise of dignity involved in righting myself and following him into the study.

It was a little room. It had one mahogany desk, two chairs,

but neither books nor papers. On the desk were a tobacco humidor and a corn-cob pipe.

'Please sit, Mr Tyson,' he said, sitting himself and gauging me as he filled the pipe with shag from the humidor. 'I've heard two things about you. That you're John Mulhall's confidant. And that you aren't enamoured of the military.'

I laughed at that, I was a little abashed. I hoped he would laugh, too. But he went on surveying me. Tranquil, exuding much smoke, he spoke through his teeth. 'One thing I would like to emerge from this article . . . and in a funny way, coming from you, it will have more credence than it would coming from one of my fellow countrymen. It is simply that I don't covet the presidency. If we could convey that, it would assist our supply situation . . . if you catch my drift. I would be grateful if you wrote that down now. That as a soldier, I assure you I don't wish to seek the presidency while ever I am engaged on this crusade.'

Colouring, I stared at him. His eyes were level. The bugger wanted me to take dictation. 'Does not seek the presidency while ever engaged in this crusade,' I wrote in shorthand. But for the sake of my independence I underlined the word *crusade*. It was a word that came as obsessively to McLeod's lips as 'just society' came to Johnny's. It was one of his proprietary words. Underscoring it gave me a fake sense of having his measure, being on to him; of engaging in an equal contest.

The first part of the interview went as I'd expected. He stated the needs of his theatre. He hoped that base political rivalries in the United States would not prevent the military necessities of the South-West Pacific from being met. He said he had been impressed by Johnny. When he and Mrs McLeod came down out of the sky he hadn't known what sort of man he would be dealing with. He had found a friend, a visionary. Without Johnny the crusade was unimaginable.

I asked him about Johnny's politics, *vis-à-vis* his own. Wasn't he aware that the stated platform of Johnny's Party was the nationalization of all means of production, communication and exchange?

There was a little curving of his lips around the stem of the corn-cob. 'I won't say Mr Mulhall's party doesn't mean what it says . . . I won't say that . . . I *will* say that in the matter of this threat to democracy, it has done as much as any conservative party could have. That's what I'll say.'

'So Johnny doesn't strike you as a true Labor man?' I asked him.

He took the pipe from between his teeth. 'Mr Tyson,' he said. 'John Mulhall is your friend and mine. We don't want to get him into trouble with his narrow-minded rank and file.'

'All right,' I said, bending over my pad, consulting my notes.

'We could talk about coalminers,' he suggested. 'And long-shoremen. And the fifth column. All these wildcat strikes. A dozen ammunition ships banked up in Brisbane. Waiting on the good will of the waterfront workers . . .'

I said, 'There's no fifth column, general.'

'You'd say not?'

'It's just the perversity of the natives. You have to understand, there's a different attitude to work here . . .'

'But you'd think they'd listen to someone like John Mulhall. You'd think they'd listen to that Eddie Hoare. There's someone.' He whistled. 'Boy! A socialist! You'd think they'd trust their own.'

'It's the tradition of convictism,' I said, reaching for an historic and harmless cause rather than a present subversive one. 'Trust no boss. No boss at all.'

'That's all past,' he told me.

'Do you think the *Mayflower* is past?' I asked him, thinking of his *Mayflower* wife.

'Anyhow, I don't want to disparage the Australians,' he said. 'In any case, the censor wouldn't permit it. It is necessary that the people of this nation be shown to be at least as gallant as those of Russia.' He grinned at that. 'And so they are. They are very high in my affections.'

I nodded. I knew that great proconsuls had to talk like that. With his wife and wide-eyed son, with the nanny and the cooking colonel, he suffered exile in a tower in a hayseed city. He was Drusus on a hill in barbarous Germania, smiling on the natives while waiting for winter to end. It would have been naïve to expect any other attitude.

But even so, I was not prepared for his next extravagance. 'You see,' he told me, nodding his head, a father, a teacher, 'I consider this nation an immense aircraft carrier – I know I'm borrowing an image from a service other than the one I represent. But this continent is the deck for my B-17s. It also has the resounding benefit of being a granary. I consider John Mulhall my executive, the best a commander ever had. That's why it distresses me when some of the crew cause trouble or delay. The crew in general . . .' He looked upward, weighed them in a cupped hand, '. . . are first class people to have aboard.'

'Sort of USN Australia?' I asked him.

That did bring a wide grin. 'If you wish,' he said.

I had an image of the nation, equipped with half-a-dozen comic funnels, shunting around a Disney ocean. I could tell the picture was copy but it shamed me somewhat. A potent impulse of uncertain value, a tribal meanness, a colonial pride, began to rise in me.

I said, 'A last question. The garrison you left behind. Perhaps you'd like to say something. You know, general. For the comfort of relatives.'

For a while his two lips brushed each other. Dry from the tobacco, they sounded like the considered rubbing of two hands. His eyes became abominably gentle. From his chair, where he'd been stoking the pipe, he got up, walked to the draped window, pulled a curtain aside, considered the profile of the blackened city, returned to his chair, returned his pipe to his dry lips, letting it drag down the corner of his mouth. It seemed to me, maybe without foundation, that he was considering hitting me and, in my perverse mood, the chance of that exalted me.

He said, 'I know you don't ask out of any malice, Paper.'

I turned my eyes away, confused at being credited with good faith like that.

He said, 'They have seared the names of Corregidor, Topside and Malinta Tunnel into the national soul . . .' His voice petered out; he raised his eyes like a man who's heard his wife calling him in another room.

Neither the old journo nor the young private of whom I was composed felt any triumph. There was no sense in harrying him.

110

No censor would permit me to say that a general faltered over the question of a lost army.

Within ten seconds anyhow he retrieved his aura and began to look again like the impermeable opportunist he was. Command had passed back to him and he finished off the interview in quick time. He seemed happy to let me speak of young Dougal and admit to Dougal's predilection for the rank of Sergeant. The wife, the Asian nanny, the frugal household, the staff colonel improvising in the kitchen, they would all get a guernsey in my article.

He joined his hands, one atop the other, and made a sideways cutting gesture with them. 'That's it, then,' he said.

I made much play of closing my notebook.

He said, 'I ask this as a friend of Johnny's. He's seeing a woman, isn't that so?'

I wondered were we now getting down to true purposes. 'General,' I said, turning in my seat, 'I can't say.'

'I believe he's seeing a woman. I don't think many know. I don't think Starkey knows, for example, and I don't mean to tell him. But we have an officer who's close to Dick Masson . . .' He waved the corn-cob. 'I . . . I'm broad-minded,' he said. 'But it happens more often than you think that a general might offer his wife to a politician, that's all. I've seen it . . . not that Masson would be likely to . . .'

'No,' I said. 'No. Not Masson . . . as far as I know.'

He puffed a while longer. 'No. Well, in that case . . . the General's the one to feel sorry for.'

We emerged to the devoted gaze of Mrs McLeod and of the Sergeant, whose eyes were rolling with fatigue. The faces of the women looked pale now, as if Donald McLeod had taken, through no fault of his own, just because of his substance, some of their oxygen.

Unsatisfied with the interview, I went back to my room on one of the humbler levels of Lennon's. I suppose I'd gone into the penthouse half hoping to be carried away by the casual floodtide of McLeod's charm. That would have put me at one with Millie and John Mulhall. Instead, I suffered the comedown of finding him so liable to falter.

I lay on my bed, in full dress, which included my false leg. I was beginning to unbutton my shirt and trousers at a slow rate, dozing in between, when one of the elderly staff came belting at my door. He told me General Masson was waiting in the lounge downstairs and wondered whether he could see me. At first it seemed like a dream continuation of my interview with McLeod. The old porter waited at the door until I'd scratched myself, buttoned up and risen. Then he escorted me downstairs in the lift that eked from floor to floor at a gracious banana-land rate.

We located Dick Masson in a private corner of the lounge. I noticed his light civilian suit that he'd probably got off a Greek tailor at Alexandria; it didn't look like traditional Queensland tailoring. He stood up as I got close to his chair. He looked very straight, very blond, the lines of his jaw just starting to crease into mid-forties jowls. The faded African tan he'd had when I first met him had been enriched by a Queensland sun. I knew that he commanded, under McLeod's more remote hand, that Queensland coastline of cow-cockies, banana farmers, sugarcane croppers.

'You shouldn't be troubled here, gentlemen,' the old man told us. 'Most of the American gents go somewhere else on Saturday nights.'

Masson, leaning towards me, poured me Scotch. I didn't quite like the unconvivial way he was doing it; he reminded me of a policeman priming an informant. 'My headquarters are up in the Esk area,' he told me, to explain why he'd turned up. 'We're living under canvas the whole week. I try to get down here to the Brisbane Club for a hot tub every Saturday.'

We drank and settled back, stiffly at ease. Johnny and Pam Masson had made true ease between us impossible and at the moment I was angry with them on that account.

'I heard you were up here, Tyson,' he said. 'I must say that last stuff you placed for us had wonderful results. I believe I can raise other matters with you and, if they're misunderstood, that's just unfortunate.' He tapped a big knuckle three times against the flange of the whisky tray. '... I don't come to you like a pathetic victim, you see. I don't come to you like a poor bloody cuckold.'

'No, no, no,' I assured him, frowning stiffly and making soothing motions with my free hand.

He looked away at the wall. I saw his parched lips and got an impression of saplessness. 'He should have chosen some other woman,' he told me. 'Her ... you know, her attachments ... mean little to me. But it isn't very responsible of him to pick a general's wife ...'

I laughed, not very loud, but all his talk about *choosing* seemed to apply to a stranger, a man who chose women by the week or month or year. 'He doesn't *pick* people. You've seen him ... He knows damn all about women.' I shook my head. 'You can't talk about him *choosing* a woman.'

'All right then,' the General said. 'It's not responsible of him to *respond* to one. Listen, Tyson ...'

I interrupted him and told him to call me Paper like everyone else. This invitation made him smile, a shy, analytic smile, as if he was a researcher and – like a lab animal – I'd answered to an exact stimulus. He said, 'My worry is this. I can imagine a man like Mulhall appointing Starkey just to show ... I mean, to himself more than to anyone ... that he hadn't been influenced by Pamela.'

I said, 'But we all battle along under disabilities. You know. Johnny himself. Half his party whingeing because he isn't a socialist. And the Press – my master included – whingeing because he is ...'

'He's top of the heap, though,' said Masson. It was a blunt statement of ambition. He knew it was. He wanted me to get the news of his painstaking ambition through to Johnny. He said, 'I don't want to be promoted for false reasons. Worse still, I don't want to miss a chance for false ones. That's what I wanted to relay to you, Tyson.'

I said, 'My bloody soubriquet is a hint that politicians treat me with familiarity. That doesn't mean I run messages for people.'

I suppose there was bush righteousness in my anger, some

113

simple Methodist shock. Because the cool man who sat in front of me seemed unworried by how many times Johnny had had his wife. There was no loss of professional standing for him in that. What exercised him was that the estimable stallion of his ambition should get a fair run.

He filled up his own glass but now left me to top mine – he wasn't going to fawn. 'I'm sorry if you feel demeaned,' he told me. 'But it's more complex than I've said, Tyson . . . I mean, Paper.'

He asked me had I heard from any of my sources that the Japanese were now trying for Port Moresby overland, dragging everything they needed – food, mortars, the diverse tools of war – on their backs, up towards a pass two miles or more high. They were to be admired in a way, he said. I suggested that the native labour on the Japanese side of Papua must be suffering harsh employment. Masson said there was no doubt of that, yet Japanese initiative was still to be respected. And Starkey, dissatisfied with what was happening up there, had decided to send Masson himself.

'I thought you'd be pleased about that,' I told him.

'Of course I'm pleased. Except that . . . I'll be general in the first battle.'

I shook my head. I didn't understand the phrase.

'Well,' he explained, 'the general in the first battle is the man who takes command when the other side is at flood tide. And when his own resources of men and supplies are not even ready . . . You know how it is, Tyson, you're an old soldier, I believe . . .'

'I'm closer,' I said, red-ragging, 'to the poor buggers who become the *corpses* of the first battle . . .'

'Oh, yes,' he told me, shaking his head, 'that's part of it all right.'

'Tell us some more about this general in the first battle,' I suggested.

'It's worse if you're fighting on what we'll call a domestic front – I don't mean with Pamela – I mean, in a place that's close to the national front door, in a place that's accessible to politicians. A person merely has to look at the history of the American Civil War – all the generals sacked one by one . . . well, at least *they* were well supplied. I wonder if I'll be well supplied, Paper. And I certainly wonder about the politicians. Have some more of that stuff, by the way.'

He pointed again to the Scotch bottle, and I was surprised to see that during our awkward conference I'd drunk some two-thirds of it, minus the modicum he himself was still sipping.

He went on, 'I'm explaining all this for your benefit, Paper. There isn't any need for you to talk to Mulhall about any of it. I'm sure he understands my position exactly. He's got a strange understanding of these things, considering he's a politician, especially considering the *sort* of politician he is . . . but the general in the first battle normally ends up the subject of a demand that he be sacrificed. Either he's too wary or too reckless of lives. He is blamed for all administrative fiascos. Anyhow, when that demand comes in my case, and I know it will come, I want Mulhall to be capable of making a simple judgment, that's all. That's why someone just ought to say to him, leave that woman alone!'

I shook my head. I didn't like these great national tasks people lumbered me with. 'Say I did?' I asked him. 'He might end up pretty narked at you.'

Masson dropped his hand to the tray and began making apportioning motions with his fingers, dividing up the argument between us. 'I don't mind him sacking me because he doesn't like me,' he said. 'I don't want him sacking me because he's guilty.'

'Guilt, guilt?' I growled, as if John Mulhall were a stranger to it. Whereas the nuns and the Socialist League of Victoria had peppered up his conscience since babyhood.

Masson slapped his hands together – a concluding gesture. He stood up and buttoned his coat, reached across and pressed a bell for his Homburg. 'I'm no moralist, Tyson . . . Paper. It's fair enough for a general or a politician to go to bed with someone he fancies – everyone else does. But people shouldn't admit women into the mechanisms they use for decisions. It's bad for everyone. In my book it's the final sin, the worst of all. I think you feel the same way, Tyson, otherwise you might not be so much on the defensive for that man.'

I watched him while he waited for the porter to bring him his hat. He looked more like a stage aristocrat than a visitor from a tented camp at Esk.

I said, 'How in the hell did you come to marry her?'

He thought for a while. 'I'd never met anyone like her. There *is* no one like her. Also . . . I'm impetuous sometimes.'

It was hard to believe. But it must have been the truth, it was the only explanation that worked. He smiled at me. 'I'm not rash in the field. I'm not hidebound, either. I think the field's my medium. Hence . . . it's goodbye to all this.'

With an opened hand, palm up, he indicated the room, the bottle, me. The old porter came with his hat and he went away, perhaps to another appointment. Maybe he had a Brisbane girl to visit but I got this idea of him as a military eunuch, as much so as Starkey was a military satyr. Probably he found messes and the quiet but unrelenting maleness of the Brisbane Club just up his alley.

When he'd gone I sat on feeling that by now familiar rancour against Johnny. Even in a cut-rate kingdom the myths of kingship are fulfilled and Johnny had set up, in his oblique, wall-eyed manner, a fair model of the king-general-general's wife fable. There were even the procuring serfs, Millie and myself, who might suffer in the end for their part in the king's dark intentions. There was the king's forgotten wife. There was a symbolic fortress, Moresby, which, should it be yielded up – with its airstrip and port facilities – by the general, would deliver the fair maid of civilization (and the buxomer girls of north Queensland) to the barbarians.

I got up, struck a revolving chair with my fist, thinking of Johnny and his grinning possession of the girl.

I was embarrassed to see that the old man was watching me. He got a curt goodnight from me as I tottered off and gave me one back.

He could tell that, unlike Masson, I was no gentleman.

Chapter Two

I'd scarcely got back to the scrub capital, seen rare snow on Mount Ainslie, arranged myself into my chair and rubbed the soreness from my legs when Johnny turned up in my office, wandered around it sideways and asked me to go to Melbourne with him.

'Why?' I wanted to know.

He grinned and inclined one shoulder towards me, as if he was confessing he needed company. He said, 'There's a rumour Hamish is having trouble in his local branch . . . Surely your boss would think that's worth a first-class return to Melbourne.'

'We've got a bureau down there,' I said. 'They could look into it.'

He said, 'None of them are princes of their profession, Paper. Not canny, that lot. The way you are.' It wasn't until he was leaving the office that he said, 'We could visit the Grants.'

The Grants were three sisters I'd known once in Melbourne. He'd known them, too, better than I ever had, good Ruskin class girls, handmaidens of the Victorian Socialist League. Though I felt nothing like the urgency to behold them that I felt to behold Millie, I ended up catching the Albury train with Johnny that same evening. It wasn't so much any electoral troubles Tony Hamish might have been having that got me aboard, either. It was the chance to talk to Johnny about Masson.

I shared a twin berth with Jim Cowan, who cleaned his teeth in the little sink, propped his feet for a while on the metal foot-warmer, climbed into the top bunk and went to sleep. I love railways with all the passion of a country boy who grows up in a village far beyond hearing of a train whistle. But I could not enjoy the honest sensualities of railway travel that night.

I squatted on the little dicky seat by the wash basin, took a drag from my flask and watched, through a little gap in the blackout paint on the window, the numb silhouettes of the pastures roll by. Johnny knocked on the door of our apartment, came in, looked up at the upper berth, grinning, and said, 'He must have led a blameless bloody youth, that Jimmy, the way the bugger sleeps.'

He sat on the edge of my bunk as I told him about Masson. He was in his shirt sleeves, the cloth rucked up around expanding metal armbands. In his usual meticulous way, he fingered the holder with the lit cigarette in it. When I told him, he leaned back across my bunk and Jim Cowan's upper berth threw a shadow over his eyes. 'So he's worried, eh? About how I make my decisions?' He sprang forward then, he was on the edge of the cot. 'The bugger's got where he is because of my decisions . . . others' decisions, too. He's commanding a bloody corps, Paper, which is what he deserved and what he's got. He can't complain about that decision.'

I said, 'The malicious . . . I'm just trying to anticipate what the malicious would say. About direct or indirect influence from Pamela. You know.'

'Huh!' he said. He waved his cigarette. He would not see it, that people would make the linkages, jump from clue to clue. 'I've got many friends, Paper,' he said, almost boastful. 'I've got you. Does anyone say you influence me?'

I said, 'You're not . . . far gone on *me*.' A term such as 'in love' would have been too much, would have expanded and clogged the debate. 'Far gone' was bad enough.

He got very quiet, his eyes enlarged and even the crooked one focused on me. I heard the jingling of the water jug in its bracket over my head. I had an urge to get up to it and put a wad of paper between the glass and the metal frame, the way my father used to do when travelling. I wasn't happy with Johnny's eyes on me; a quiet man's anger isn't comfortable to face.

In something like a whisper, he said, 'Hasn't bloody Masson heard about original sin? Does he think everyone else's decision . . . you know, Starkey's, all the other members of the War Cabinet . . . does he think their decisions are fine and unalloyed and straightforward. Does he think everyone's decision except mine is bloody impeccable?'

I shrugged. I didn't know how Masson's thinking stood on the matter of original sin. Johnny took a deep drag on his cigarette, forgetting to breathe out the smoke he'd taken in. Coughing, he began to grimace at me through the tobacco tears. 'Ada!' he said without warning.

'Yes?' I said.

'I'd rather tell her myself than have somebody write her an anonymous letter.'

'Yes.'

'She's got no one to fall back on over there. Of course it's the only bloody thing that'd bring her to Canberra, you know. She hates the place so much . . .'

The way his eyes, remote again now, flickered over my face, I feared for a second he would charge me with the job of telling her.

He raised a hand and prodded the base of the upper berth. 'Good old Jimmy Cowan,' he said, as if nominating one of the earth's few constants.

'Here!' Johnny called, patting the driver's shoulder. His crooked eyes were darting. He crushed out the cigarette he'd been smoking and stowed the holder in his side-pocket, careless of stains and of any black seepage which might come from the device.

The house we had stopped in front of was a narrow brick terrace in Coburg. A little grace-note – a jaunty blue on its wrought-iron fence – was all that marked it off from its neighbours. But faced with it, Johnny was actually smacking his lips, taking in wide gasps of air as he dismounted from the back seat of the car and, with an absent flourish of his hand, helped me out.

I watched a child drag a butter-box on wheels beneath the cold streaky sky and heard from an open door across the street the ABC's race commentator ranting out the running in the Improvers' Welter from Flemington. Saturday afternoon in Melbourne and even in its threatened state, even in its exhilarating stature as a Japanese imperial target, it emitted from its bitumen, it fumed forth from its chimneys an insidious mist of ennui.

But Johnny was fairly hopping, dancing in the gateway of the three Grant girls. What made me less joyous was that they might all have been Ada's sisters. Each of them must have, during one or other of the Sunday afternoon socialist corroborees at the Gaiety Theatre, seen herself as potentially John Mulhall's wife. John Mulhall may well have considered each of them in the same light before choosing Ada. As his Catholic cousins were scheduled by circumstance to marry girls from the Children of Mary at St Francis' Church, across the road from the theatre, Johnny could not avoid the option of Ada or the Grants or someone like any and all of them. No more could they avoid the option of him or someone like him. They all therefore felt a sort of ownership over Johnny.

Yet the man rang now at the door of these possible wives as lightly as a free boy, as if none of the connections had been changed. And having rung he began to sniff strenuously, the way an animal does, to pick up the house musk he remembered from other visits.

It was Dimp Grant, one of the three sisters, who opened the door. She couldn't be identified straight off, though, for I remembered her as a square-faced, fairly husky girl, with athletic calf muscles. She was very thin now, her nose had grown sharp from illness and her cheekbones pushed at the blue tissue of her skin.

Seeing Johnny first, she began to shake her head. Her tremors could have meant anything – that she was verifying his features, that she was regretting the parallel wastage of both their faces or that the shaking was a symptom of her disease. I think that then, even then, on the way into the house, I got the idea that the other two sisters, who were less gentle, less passive than Dimp, had sent her out to lead him in to be measured and judged.

Dimp greeted me next but the shaking of her head now didn't seem so full of portents. As I stumped down the hall behind Johnny I could hear the voices of the others from the kitchen. I was already sorry I'd come to Melbourne. The morning had been a failure. The supposed threat to Tony Hamish's seat had been investigated and was not worth more than a par. A New Guard businessman from Toorak had fetched together a handful of party men who despised Tony Hamish for going so soft on Johnny. This backyard revolt had been transmuted by rumour to the extent that I had travelled all night by train to cover it.

Dimp opened the kitchen door a small space but held on to the handle so that only a sliver of light showed from within. She said, 'Mah's in a bad mood, Johnny. Don't take her seriously.'

Once we pushed inside the room the second sister, Penny, danced up, looking sturdy enough to have answered the front door, and kissed Johnny and held him for a few seconds. The oldest one, the unmarried girl they'd misnamed Mah, stayed solid in her chair, her wide back up against the dresser, surveying if not judging the way her sisters fussed Johnny into his seat. I remembered that the times we'd met I had always fought Mah. She was more witty, ironic and earthy than the other two and she was as unyielding as any girl ever raised on such scriptures as Jevons's *The State in Relation to Labour*. She had a broad whimsical smile, I knew that from the past, but she wasn't showing it now.

I got closer to her and spoke to her under cover of the noise the other sisters were making. 'Don't you stand up any more, Mah,' I asked, 'for prime ministers of small nations?'

'It's a long time since you were here, Paper,' she told me, slapping a seat at her side. 'Sit down.'

'Is it safe, Mah? I can't get away as quick as other blokes.'

'I guarantee your safety, Paper. Of course you're an honest old bugger. You live in sin with your milliner, hiding nothing. I call that honest.'

I looked at her. She had that sort of knowing limpidity in her eye. She'd heard about Johnny and Pamela, as McLeod had, but her news could only have come from a different source. It's frightening when knowledge gets diverse, instead of being fixed among one species; when the socialists and the generals both know. With my false leg, I levered myself sideways and leaned close to her massive head. 'Who told you?' I asked.

'Artie Thorn,' she said.

'Oh, yes,' I said. 'Artie.'

Artie Thorn was one of the old push. This kitchen sat in his electorate. Last year the Catholics in the Victorian Executive had thrown him out of the Labor Party on disciplinary grounds but he still voted with Johnny's government. Artie was what you'd call heavy weather; he liked to think he was Johnny's conscience on the back-bench. But it was the Grant girls who were the sort of kitchen goddesses of Johnny's conscience. And they'd been tipped off by Artie.

Even as a girl, Mah – who perhaps already knew she frightened boys away – used to sit here, thick in the hips already, already a presence, already in the position of a sentry over the cups and saucers, fixed hard up under the crinkly brown glass face of the kitchen dresser while her lighter, softer sisters passed sandwiches to the blokes.

It was in here that I'd first met Johnny. That had been Good Friday, 1926.

The kitchen had been crowded all that day. I can't remember why. I can remember, though, that Good Friday was a dismal business in Melbourne then and you needed to go to an agnostic kitchen to find any joy. Johnny was about forty at the time, a back-bencher in the South Australian State House, over in Melbourne on party business. When he walked in that day, everyone there grinned and called out except Mah and me. That was because he was a stranger to me.

But Mah had reasons of her own for keeping quiet.

She said aloud, 'Here we have him, then. The representative of a hanging government!'

122

I didn't know what in the hell she was talking about. It had to be explained to me later on; the whole business of two policemen disappearing in one of those bereft little copper towns in South Australia and their bodies being found later in a mine shaft. Two local men were arrested and sentenced to hang and, when there was some outcry against the State government, the Labor caucus in that parliament supported a vote of confidence in the Premier.

Johnny had that bland Celtic unpigmented skin and when Mah cried out I saw his cheeks take on colour. 'Fair go, Mah!' he told her. 'You know how caucus operates.'

It seemed a reasonable excuse; a political one but a fair one. *I voted against the hanging in caucus but party rules made me vote with the bulk of my party in the House.*

Mah said, 'Yes, all you jokers hide behind caucus.' She put on a whining voice. '*I voted with the others for the sake of party solidarity.* Very few of you buggers go through the business of getting any seat in any parliament in this country without ending up with souls like grocers.'

'I don't know what state my soul's in,' Johnny told her, 'but I don't need to hide behind caucus or any other bloody thing. Especially not from you, Mah.'

I could hear that peculiar breathy quiver in the voice that tells you a person's temper is about to go. I can remember looking at my hands. For she was treating him too rawly.

I heard her say, 'Clean conscience, eh, Johnny?'

'Government is government. Even the Labor Party's got to respect the law of the land . . .'

'You didn't always talk like that,' she said. And for the rest of his visit she would not speak of him. You just had to look at him to see how much her judgment weighed with him even then. He got more and more silent. So did the other men in that kitchen.

We left about four o'clock, all together. I remember a veteran of Vimy Ridge coughing and gagging in the dark hall on the way out, as if we had just been in battle; and other men standing back for me and helping me by the shoulder. We ended the day in the saloon of Lonrigan's Excelsior Hotel, where as Lonrigan's

Labor Party friends we were permitted to drink illegally behind closed doors, in the shadow of the Cross and of Mah Grant's verdict. Johnny had trouble with the demon in those days and Lonrigan ended up having to find a bed for him upstairs.

Of such potency were my memories of Mah Grant!

Fifteen years later, I could tell that it was going to be Good Friday again. But Johnny was so far delighted by the visit, swapping family talk with Dimp and Pen on the far side of the table, both benign Grant girls asking for news of McLeod and of the Japanese, not knowing what noises the irreducible Mah made to me by the dresser.

I said to Mah, 'Don't make a scene about it.'

'I don't make scenes.'

'I can remember a few.'

'I worry about him, that's all.'

'So do I.'

'Someone has to remind him. About what he's supposed to stand for.'

'Give me a look at you,' she yelled all at once at Johnny. Her two sisters were silenced. Johnny stood in front of her, revealing himself, grinning in his abashed manner. 'Well,' Mah said, '*you* look well enough.'

'And you, Mah.'

She nodded in a way that said, yes, it's all right for us, but there are others. Her nod could have implied the world of sufferers beyond the darkening kitchen window, could also have taken in Ada Mulhall on her mid-winter beach.

'Arthur Thorn,' she said then, 'tells me you intend to bring in a new conscription law.'

As written it is a graceless, a flaccid sentence. It brought the kitchen to a stop in fact. Its power took the breath out of the two younger sisters and out of Johnny. As young things, nearly children, nearly adults, they had marched and spoken, pamphleteered and spread leaflets against conscription. Conscription was the anti-Christ and anti-conscription meant youth, the flowing of sap, tender political infatuations, admiration for some of the speakers on the Yarra Bank, admiration for Johnny himself.

Conviction that stirred the base of the young womb, that moved in the loins, that raised the fine down on the backs of necks.

Pen had been pouring water into the kettle and now turned the tap half-off, so that its noise would not impinge on the question's echo. I noticed this out of lowered eyes. I saw that *she* wanted an answer, too.

In my folly, I tried to mediate, to reduce the ancient power of the word. I said, 'Well . . . isn't there conscription already, Mah?'

Mah snorted at that. 'I don't mean the militia. The militia's fair enough.' Conscripted militia did not foul the history of her young womanhood, or so it seemed.

She said, 'Artie reckons you're going to send them beyond the limits, Johnny. To remote places, you know . . . to distant capitalist battles. All that. Everything you used to condemn. That's what he reckons.'

Poor wasted Dimp Grant said, 'Artie Thorn is so damn righteous. A prig. That's him exactly. A prig.'

She turned her eyes to Johnny. They seemed to be dragging inwards towards each other with the pain of her disease. I could see that she wanted to know perhaps more than anyone. The dying have this fear that their friends will change before they themselves are safely vanished and oblivious.

'Let me be frank,' Johnny said. 'If it was the truth, Mah, Artie'd be the last person to know.'

Mah looked at her sister Pen, shook her head, snorted again from her large resonant nose. 'That's what he calls an answer, I think.'

Johnny advanced on Mah. 'Do you know what I think?' he said. 'McLeod's Americans are conscripts . . . and liable to be sent anywhere . . .'

'Which suits their interests. Their imperial interests . . . I've said before today, Johnny, your Irish boyhood gives you the idea that the only empire you need to suspect is the British. You've got too much respect for those Yanks.'

Johnny shook his head again, grinned at me, tried to involve me in a male joke, a sign that he might have been struggling.

'D'you think I'm a naïve bugger, Mah? Is that it? Liable to be swayed because I don't understand what history is?'

I smiled loyally with him but felt blank. I could see how solemn the two quiet sisters were. Mah did not answer. Johnny said, 'All right, I won't lie about what I think. I think our boys should be sent into the islands. Just like the Americans. Not just the volunteers. Conscripts too. That's what I think, Mah. An individual opinion.'

Mah closed her eyes and lowered her head with an immense, cavernous, compelling sigh.

Penny said, 'But I remember the old campaigns in the first war.' She meant against conscription. She reminded me of a relative trying to explain the origins of a family crime, the sin against orthodoxy. 'On Yarra Bank, thousands of people. There was you and Burdett and Eddie Hilton and Frank Bryant . . . every two sentences the crowd was cheering . . .'

She was invoking the old Melbourne saints; she was saying, don't repeal the cheers of that vanished crowd.

Johnny muttered, 'A different world, Pen.' He reached out his fingers and touched her wrist. 'A different world.'

'I think you're right,' Dimp told him in a loud voice, stress on each word. 'I think new times demand new measures.'

Mah said, 'What I think is that he's become a politician since Yarra Bank. In those days he didn't have to please the Press or Roosevelt or McLeod. He was himself. His own man.'

Pen turned her head away, looked fiercely at the wall and began to weep. 'Waterworks,' the big sister muttered in a noncommittal way. The kettle screamed and sick Dimp had to get up and turn it off. The quiet stammer of Pen's sobs could still be heard.

'I'm only talking about personal ideas,' said Johnny, distressed for Pen's sake. 'I made that clear. Maybe we should go now, Paper.'

'No,' Pen told us, gagging a bit more. 'I don't know what it is. I just remembered the crowds we used to get there . . . it *is* different, Johnny. I don't like it any more. I'm sorry.'

Mah laid one finger along the wood of the table and began

to wield it like a slow axe. 'You'll split your boys up, Johnny. Eddie Hoare won't take it. Others won't either. Artie Thorn would rather die . . .'

Johnny got desperate and raised his voice. 'For the third time, it's a private opinion.'

So then there was a different silence and, at its close, Mah said, 'The private opinion of the Czar is a whip for the backs of peasants.'

At last Johnny and I escaped into our Commonwealth car. He had grown a tougher skin since '26 and though he was pretty thoughtful, he didn't seem as hurt as he'd been that Good Friday. It was just as well. Today he could not have recourse to Lonrigan's pub. I waited until we were two blocks away from Mah Grant's kitchen. Then I said, 'You're going to do it. Aren't you, Johnny?'

'If I can get away with it, Paper. Of course I am.'

With an edge he could hear, I said, 'And why, I wonder? To convince the Press you're respectable . . .? Or do you want to butter up the Americans?'

'You're as bad as Mah,' he told me.

We travelled in black streets, we could see mute housefronts if we squinted out under the brims of our hats. But in the back of our taxpayers' limousine, we picked up nothing of the healthy passion of the kitchen conspiracies, the hallway despairs, the bedroom exaltations. We were two bloodless old men (that's what it seemed to me), whistling up the deaths of young ones.

He kept quiet. He did not beg for understanding.

I said, 'I'd heard the rumours this might be on. But I thought the Party wouldn't stand it.'

'The Party's got to,' he said. He even yawned. 'If the Party can't . . . there's no chance for the Party anyhow.'

That yawn outraged me. I'd seen him spend the sap of his forties mediating the Party back into some sort of unit, racing down to Sydney to argue with the dissidents from New South Wales in the basement of the Trades and Labour Council, preaching reconciliation to the Left in the years when the Melbourne Catholic push in the Victorian branch tossed up motions, concerning Spain and Ethiopia, designed not to offend the Holy Father.

In a way I understood that the yawn was not a yawn of ennui. It was the yawn of someone who has some time to wait before the sky-high wave breaks, the profound earth splits. I understood this but felt personally hurt at the same time – the sort of hurt Pen Grant had shown and tried to explain away. I was determined to pretend the yawn had been callous.

I said, 'Jesus, what a country! There's Tony Hamish. His old mum felt the bloody Hamish seed was so precious that Tony couldn't be spared to go into the trenches. And then there's you, a pacifist with second bloody thoughts. And neither of you know what it's bloody like!' I slapped my thigh as a rough sketch of what it *was* like, the knees shot inside out, the brain's mathematics spilt out over an uncomprehending landscape, the dead lusts of young men afloat on foreign tides. And all the rest.

He nodded, 'Come on, Paper. I'd never send a boy to a place like the one you were sent to.'

We kept silence for a while and I wondered if this was what democracy was; rulers sitting in a kitchen to be chastised by tough mammies like Mah, to be washed in the tears of the just ones. Rulers sitting beside cripples in cars and taking their – *my* – hard reproaches.

We were nearly to the hotel before we spoke again. I said, 'They know about Mrs Masson. Though they didn't mention it. They found out from Artie.'

He nodded again, taking account.

'Artie's in this sheepskins for Russia committee,' I said, making the link.

He sounded serene, 'She wouldn't gossip.'

'She might've said things like "my good friend Johnny Mulhall" and everyone would know what that meant. You ought to talk to her, Johnny.'

He chuckled. 'She wants the partisans to be warm. From what I've read of Russian winters it seems an excellent cause, Paper. It doesn't need any interference from me.'

'She ought to give that committee away,' I told him. I thought how the Press could, if ever they needed to, kill him for his sheepskin darling.

He said, like a private man, 'It's got bugger-all to do with me, Paper. See, if I bullied her into giving up sheepskins, I wouldn't be much different to General Masson, would I? He tried that approach.' He grinned again. 'He hasn't exactly been forgiven for it.'

The car came to a stop in front of the steps to the hotel but we did not get out straight away. His voice was somnolent. 'Pamela . . . I haven't mentioned anything to her . . . on that subject. But she's said . . . off her own bat . . . you know . . . that we ought to face up to the responsibilities of a modern State. Don't you think that's funny, Paper? In view of Mah's attitude?'

'Oh,' I said, 'the Reds will be all for it. Russia, according to rumour, is a Pacific nation, Johnny. There's supposed to be a place called Vladivostok . . .'

He chuckled lazily at this irony. 'Pamela isn't a Red. You know she isn't. She's a party of one.'

My mood was so vicious now that I messed about with the idea of asking him whether she'd in fact latched on to his willingness to conscript, whether it made her more grateful in the hay. Of course it would have altered everything if I had asked him. He'd never, after that, tell me more than I needed to know. I think that what I did say was more telling in the end. 'It's not new friends who are going to act up. It's the old ones.'

If it had been a public debate, he would have said something oratorical. He would have mentioned that this war wasn't a distant business of the northern hemisphere. He would have said that the Japanese were in Lae and Salamaua, that they were hauling field pieces up the passes in the Owen Stanleys. But in the backs of cars he was prosaic, elliptical, man-to-man, half asleep.

'Listen, Paper,' he murmured. 'I wouldn't mind Utopia any more than you would. But the place has to be preserved first. Do you want to have a bite of dinner with me, or am I too much of a bloody pariah?'

So he jollied me into having a quick meal. But I think he could tell that it would take me some days before I could give him my usual support.

Chapter Three

In those cold days I got a cheque from *Harpers* equivalent to about two-thirds of my normal yearly income, in payment for the article on McLeod. The latter appeared first of all in that journal and then everywhere else, even in my own newspaper.

I had presumed that Zimmer, the General's Press Officer, would sit on it because of its level, unadoring tone. But it seemed that McLeod was pleased exactly by its air of detachment. He had been deified without remission all that year. Now – perhaps like Zeus on holiday – he liked to see his humanity restated. I had mentioned, for example, the business of young McLeod and the toy ambulance and, according to Zimmer, the General had liked that. No one had thought before of portraying him as a soft-touch daddy.

Zimmer told me that in the penthouse at Lennon's my name was being touted as a fair ideal of the honest journalist.

About the time of our return from the Grants, Johnny also began to look on me in those terms, as a journalist as much as an unbuttoned late night friend. It had always been an unspoken clause in our friendship that he did not use me, in direct terms, to plant favourable copy and I did not use him as a source for what I could not discover by my normal diligence, questioning and recourse to sources. Now, at the start of my era of travels, this arrangement was repealed almost without either of us waking up to the fact, certainly without a word.

In the matter of conscripting youth to do battle under McLeod and Starkey and Masson I had an unspoken but concise task. It was to let it be known on the quiet that conscription was a goer, a not-so-dark horse. That Johnny Mulhall was not intractable, that the Press should not keep on beating Johnny's ears on the issue.

This new set-up gave me some spiritual unease. It wasn't because I hadn't got over my temperamental dislike of conscripting. It *was* because I did not like being in the realm of quid pro quo.

One of the journeys which fell due under this new arrangement was Johnny's excursion to the Hunter coalfields. We travelled by rail down through the half-rustic western suburbs of Sydney, where a coalfields special awaited us at Strathfield. Someone had heard about Johnny's journey, for a party of small schoolchildren in State school grey and Roman Catholic blue stood on Normanhurst station. They wore little white linen pouches which contained all that the State considered necessary – two halves of a tennis ball for use as ear stoppers, a gas mask, a tin of salve and a bandage – in the event of air bombardment.

Seeing them, I remembered that someone had told me how infants in the convent schools prayed for good Mr Mulhall; that he would return to the faith of his fathers after his temporary lapse. There was no doubt that the small Catholics waved with a ritual fervour and in better order than the more anarchic State school brats, the Tykes thereby winning this small replay of the Reformation.

In our carriage Eddie Hoare, the orchestrator of this journey to Cessnock, leaned his head back beneath framed photographs of Murwillumbah and the beautiful Tweed Valley. 'It's not the Reds,' he told Johnny. 'They can see something for their labour – knock out a nugget for Stalin, you know. It's the ordinary bloke you've got to watch. His old man's probably got dusted lungs. One of his uncles probably got crushed. He's the one who thinks there's no profit for him in any of it.'

Johnny nodded, half asleep. Eddie wanted from him one of those furious inspirational speeches but Johnny lolled back, eyes half closed, cigarette holder idle in his slack hands, Savanarola between house calls. 'And,' said Eddie, as if stung by Johnny's posture, 'they're still all pretty cranky about what happened last Christmas.'

'Last Christmas?' asked Johnny in a dream.

'When you wouldn't talk to them, John. When you wouldn't talk to them.'

They'd come to Canberra in December, Hunter River miners in cack-brown suits with baggy cuffs. And Johnny had refused to receive them because they were on strike. I remember the state he was in in those months, before Singapore went down and Mrs Masson turned up. That continent which he had constructed in his brain from boyhood, whose shores were sculpted by the wash of his cerebral waters, that country, the generals kept telling him, could not be kept. Those bloody miners, shaking the bush, arguing terms and conditions, seemed in his great panic something like a sideshow.

You didn't have to have much of an ear to hear the reproach in the way Eddie Hoare reminded Johnny of that unfortunate month. I wondered what Eddie would say if he knew Johnny had it in his moral range to conscript. I felt a mischievous and forsaken urge to let him in on the news.

Cessnock is one of those universal mining towns which, like perhaps half its natives, seemed to suffer some organic disease associated with the extraction of coal. A blue-black affliction of coal dust showed up in the stone and bricks of civic buildings, seemed to have got at the yellow porcelain of the tiled pubs, to have penetrated between the mercury and the glass in the mirrors in the Greek cafés. It was one of those places which, even before the European, must have looked like pasture land, its ancient forests deep under the ground, carbonized. The European genius had transformed it in eighty years from a tribal place of totems to a cattle-grazing duchy to a mining slum.

The official party had dined at the Hotel Wollombi. We had

got up from the dining table – from our half-eaten apple crumble – convivial. As we moved down the main street we got more chastened. For you felt that some link with the ancient hygiene of the earth had been lost here. In front of the Catholic Church a few old miners, sidelined by years of lung troubles, waited for a St Vincent de Paul meeting to begin. They turned their eyes on our group with a profound lack of expectancy and a few spat into balled handkerchiefs. 'Victims of the bad days, eh?' Johnny muttered. 'Poor old buggers.'

There were risks, of course, in saying that sort of thing in front of Eddie. Risks in admitting that, from a corner of Hunter Street, Cessnock, the war and all the high questions of destiny which bit at Johnny looked different.

Light and miners spilled out the doors and windows of the meeting place. Men from Greta, Aberdare Extended, from the Bellbird colliery famed for explosions. From Rothbury, where they'd had those riots and the police had shot a man, just as if this were Wales or Pennsylvania.

We neared the steps, under the Britannic façade of the old building all painted in awful yellow and fouled with soot. The Cessnock constables made a way for us up the steps and I saw two other men with them, in suits and pork-pie hats, who must have been Commonwealth policemen assigned here by someone who had doubts about the miners' welcome for Johnny.

When we came into the lobby the scatter of clapping that had begun on the steps filled out to become a solid noise. It was just before the applause grew total that a voice from the direction of a portrait labelled 'James Campbell, Scottish Pioneer' cried, 'John Mulhall, strike-breaker!'

Accusing voices from the floor could hurt Johnny harder than they did any other political being I ever met. A man like Tony Hamish could dismiss the interjector. To Tony, a voice from the floor was always the voice of the oaf, the flatulent grounding full of minced meat and beer. Johnny, however, couldn't overlook the chance that a raised voice was a divine reminder.

Anyhow, whatever contusions *this* voice left were salved away by the handclapping, the whistling, the considerable cheering as we got into the aisle of the hall itself. Some men stood up on their chairs to see Johnny and yell approval. He got his astigmatic look of brotherhood on his face and waved to them.

Eddie Hoare walked crab-wise wanting to protect Johnny. It was an uncharacteristic and affecting posture. He shouted at me, more or less in an Irish whisper, as we went forward. 'The ones who are cheering are probably the bloody Reds. The buggers wanted to put up Soviet flags on the walls. Jonesy wouldn't permit it.'

At last I found myself in a seat at the front of the hall, beside Jim Cowan.

The applause continued and I could see Jim was gratified by it. Perhaps he had expected something worse than this. I was not as easy about it. Ordinary people will – I'm sure it's true – applaud a man whom they've seen only in newsreels and Press photographs for corresponding to the photographs, for showing in the flesh a good likeness to the little they know of him.

Jonesy, the Federal member, was in the chair. He had drunk more beer than any two of us at dinner and his face, under the lights and in this crowded air, had gone a hue of pink. The noise began to die after Johnny had reached the platform and shaken hands with him. Men whistled equably at Jonesy, as if they were used to seeing him a bit purple-faced on the platform and forgave him for it. I expected him to embarrass us when he tried to speak but he knew what he was doing. There was barely a slur as he introduced his guest in a way that showed he knew the audience suspected Johnny.

Johnny, he said, had spent a lifetime battling for the working man. He had a fighting name from his days as Executive Secretary with the Railway Clerks' Union. In his post as editor of the *South Australian Worker*, he had shown himself beholden to no clique. The Press lords might try to spread the word that he did not have the welfare of the working class close to his heart. Anyone who was willing to believe such misrepresentations, such downright (Jonesy mistakenly said 'damn-right') lies, he had just to ask himself what John Mulhall was doing in Cessnock tonight, concerning himself with miners and their happiness at a time of such great peril to the nation?

But first, Mr Eddie Hoare.

I realize that speeches have little dramatic value and so can fall back on my old journalistic training to report what Eddie said. The objectives of the Labor Party were (said Eddie) the same as they had ever been. But what chance had those objectives of being attained if the Australia they knew was swept away? There were those who said Mulhall's Government was duping the people by putting on them restrictions they would not have accepted from a conservative government. (Cries of 'It's happening, Eddie!' and 'I'm one of them!') This was the same sort of lie Mr Jones had mentioned earlier.

Relying on the goodwill of the mining towns, the Government had promised the US fleet and army that they could depend on Australian coal to fuel their efforts in the South-West Pacific zone and as for the Australian forces – they had a right to expect coal from their kinsmen.

There was something he could promise them, the miners there tonight. It was something he had not got Mr Mulhall's express approval for, because he knew Mr Mulhall approved of it, he knew that any Labor prime minister would and John Mulhall in particular. He promised that when this danger passed, any sacrifice in terms and conditions they had made in the present would be recompensed in full. As well as that, a special coal board would be set up to deal with disputes and work for the peace and well-being of miners. (All interjections drowned by applause.) Among the broad powers of this board would be the task of stimulating and supervising the business of coal and (long pause) it would emphatically have the right to establish and acquire coal mines. (Hectic acclamation, whistles, stamping.)

Jim Cowan leaned close to my ear and whispered, 'Half the buggers think he's promising them judgment day. He sucks up to them and they don't respect him for it. He should be telling them to get their thumbs out and bloody well produce some coal.'

I nodded, as if agreeing. The noise was too great for subtle debate.

When Johnny's turn came, he began as ingratiatingly as Eddie had, repeating the lessons Eddie had preached at him in the express train from Sydney.

'I know,' he said in his heavy, emphatic style that was, for mysterious reasons, so successful, 'that no outsider could understand the bitterness that has prevailed in your industry. In the '20s and '30s a miner could be pleased if he got two days' coal cutting in the week. I remember how miners went to the Railways Commission in this State and to other authorities, asking them to spread their contracts over the year so that men could get at least two days work in a week. Nobody cared, though, if miners lived or perished, earned or went on the dole, and no one cared what scattered and pitiable little mining towns they had to live in without benefit of civilized amenities . . .'

At my side, Jim Cowan did not wear on his face any of the cumbrous disgust he'd shown when Eddie spoke. Yet he still disapproved of the soft-soap. He kept his lips set, ventriloquist-fashion, when he spoke to me. 'Everyone talks to them like they were bloody Irishmen.'

Johnny had got on to the miners who used to rise in the morning and wait at their kitchen tables for the whistle to blow, only then knowing if there might be likelihood of work that day . . . He was stirring the wells of their historic griefs, he was turning to them the mirror surfaces of their myths. The applause showed it. Then, having forged a sword out of their lore and pointed it at his own heart, he turned the point on them. He, John Mulhall less than anyone, would not ask any miner to forget the grievous history of the industry. But as Mr Hoare had said, that history could only be amended and redeemed if Australia remained.

When I say he'd thrown a spell on them I don't want to claim too much for that power, any more than I did earlier for the applause. But he was certainly talking to their deeps and using words that carried a sort of freight of holiness with them, words that had been holy in the miners' Catholic and Methodist childhoods, words holy in the miners' political present, such words as 'redeemed history.' And he had the capacity to intone the nation's name in that old-fashioned way of the Gilmores, Lawsons and Bernard O'Dowds, as if it were the name that stood for the only continent *capable* of redemption, the one nation chosen as sweet distant Cosmo and Utopia in the benign South

136

Seas, the one place at whose fall the gods would despair, it being the gods' sweet acre, potential Eden, experimental garden.

Now Johnny could say what he wanted. Was it just for American conscripts in the Solomons to have to suffer or perish for the sad history of coal cutting in Australia? Was it just that Australians who had never been near Cessnock, Maitland, the western coalfields, should have to suffer or perish? And since what happened here in the Hunter could make its mark on what happened in the furthest north Pacific, was it fair that the Soviet Union, already so hard beset on one front, should be assaulted on its Pacific shore because the harsh story of Australian coal cutting deprived, here in August, '42, the American fleet of the coal it needed in the south Pacific?

So, as usual, he preached at people and got away with it. Some of them might have been privately dissenting – the Northern Lodge would go out before the end of the year. But any interjection would have stood out that night as mean as hell against the bulk of his oration.

We left the hall on a tide of acclaim. Jim Cowan's face was radiant but Johnny looked dazed, like a man who had just been through an accident.

Chapter Four

Then there were refreshments at Jonesy's. Mine wives sat on Mrs Jones' *petit-point* lounge under a wedding photograph which showed a Jonesy straight and slick-haired, before the grog got him. From the midst of a crush of people in the hallway, Johnny grinned at me, an earnest middle-aged miner talking at him and making points with a finger against the palm of a hand. I could tell Johnny was happy, that he thought it was a night of reconciliation. Perhaps it was.

'Keg's on in the kitchen,' someone told me.

I found Eddie out there, watching through his thick glasses the tapping of the keg which stood on the kitchen table. Young miners with brilliantined hair, who looked more or less like Jonesy in his wedding picture, stood around with empty glasses in their hands, waiting for the ale to flow. When it began to, there was a cheer and whistling. Eddie did not join the queue, did not hold a glass in his hand. He, too, was a frugal man. The logistics diverted him, that was all. He winked at me. 'This is Jonesy's kingdom,' he said. 'Up here. Imagine being able to get a keg these days!'

Johnny crushed in for a while. The keg was the centre of the ceremony and could not be ignored. He was cheered and offered a brimming schooner-glass. He looked at it crookedly but with whimsy, as if it did *not* hold his death. 'If you'll excuse me,' he said, 'I'll wait for the tea to brew.'

He and Eddie nodded to each other, as if meeting for the first time that night. They looked naked there in their better suits, wrapped each in his separate specialness, without liquor in his hand.

Two women began to push into the kitchen. They wore twin-sets, carried empty glasses and wanted to break up the all-male rite. One was tall; one short, sweet, plump.

This little one was the rowdy one. She said the normal things – 'Are mere women permitted to drink out here?' Middle-aged miners hinted it might require a payoff at some undisclosed time. From these exchanges I learned the little one's name was Glenda.

Apart from the ground around the keg, there was a separate and more solemn party of men in the corner by the gas stove. They talked in level tones. They weren't willing to celebrate or pretend that Johnny had changed history. Their laughter, when they laughed, was performed with a taut upper lip; they nodded as if they'd come to Cessnock Council Chambers and to Jonesy's just for the sake of having their suspicions borne out.

For some reason I was attracted by their aloofness. I made a fairly fluid progress across the kitchen linoleum, on a tangent that would bring me near them. On this course I could hear what was being said. 'One-sided bloody appeals. I mean to say, when's he going to go and put it to the bosses like he did to us? Tell 'em to forget the bloody history of their avarice? I mean, when you read it in the papers . . . you just read it there. You'll see he's talked to us like bloody kids. And the stupid buggers were all his way . . .'

The group had that method of staring down at their beer as if it held pretty dismal portents.

'One-legged bloody policies,' they intoned, making more or less the same speech, one after another. 'Get down on us and everyone's happy. Mention a capitalist might have to take a smaller cut and the papers yell bloody socialism . . . Whipping boys, us!'

Then, 'D'you see he's got this cripple travelling round with him? Bloody living and breathing omen, that bugger. Sign of Mulhall's bloody one-sided attitudes . . .'

The man who'd said it had his back to me but my resentment at being written off as a cartoon of government policy wouldn't be stopped by small legalisms like that. I tapped the man on the shoulder. Turning, he showed me a florid face, a bit like Jimmy Pointer's but some years younger.

I said, 'I'm the bloody sign, mate. And the sign has a name. Paperboy Tyson is the name . . .'

'Sorry,' he said. 'Didn't see you there.' But he spoke as if the imagery he'd used still stood.

I made a silly speech about how I'd been crippled and he kept waving his hand at me, apologizing, but as if the whole business of the Turkish machine-gun in Anzac Cove was a private frivolity of mine with which he wouldn't choose to argue. Of course, I see now that only part of my anger was really for him; the other part was for Johnny, for conscripting me like this to serve in the coalfields.

The girl called Glenda came up. Her glass brimmed, she was fresh from the keg. 'Don't argue with that crowd,' she told me. They called friendly abuse back to her; they asked her where her husband was tonight.

'I've already apologized,' the florid boy continued telling her. 'But he keeps dragging his legs into the bloody argument.'

Glenda jinked her pretty little head. 'Come on,' she said to me. 'There's better people than these to talk to, eh.'

I went on arguing but found somehow she'd led me out on to a verandah closed off from the sharp night by striped canvas blinds. There she smiled and shook her head at me and leaned a haunch against a blue-painted table. Her heels kicked by accident at a bucket of pegs. That was how members like Jonesy kept their seats against challenges from brighter and younger men – by not renouncing the buckets of clothes pegs on their back verandahs, by sticking to their striped awnings, by running chooks in the backyard. I could hear the birds murmur and cackle in their sleep somewhere out in the dark.

'That crowd slinging off at you . . . they just got tossed out

140

of the Aberdare Lodge, eh. They thought they had a bloody life membership. They got pretty bitter when the election went the other way. That was six weeks back.'

'Bastards!' I uttered between my teeth but I laughed and raised the glass I found I had carried with me, all unwitting, between the thumb and forefinger of my right hand.

'You're good at that,' she said. 'The way you can carry a glass, eh.' Her non-interrogative *eh* diverted me, as much as my trick with the crutch and the glass kept her entertained. I wondered where she came from. North coast New South Wales, perhaps. Grafton, Lismore. A sweet dumpling of the rich mud flats of the Tweed.

'I can only do it when I'm angry,' I told her. 'If I tried to do it sober, everyone'd have to wear a raincoat.'

We introduced each other. Her name was Glenda Casey, she said. Her husband was one of the men who'd got the coup together at the Aberdare Lodge. He was the new union treasurer. 'He's a Labor man. I'm Labor, too. Whatever Labor is, eh!'

Trying not to sound like an enforcer of orthodoxy, I wondered out loud what she meant by that.

She began to frown. She had seen me with John Mulhall. I rushed in to tell her, 'No, I'm just interested. I never belonged to any party. Too much of a bloody infidel, that's me.'

She grinned at me. She seemed a bit wary still. But there was a maternal content to the smile. The honest mother, dressed in a twin-set whose skirt didn't quite accord at the waistline with the subtleties of her hips.

She said, 'Well, you heard that bloke . . . the one who ribbed you. Just like he's always saying. Your friend Mulhall quick enough conscripts workers, you can't deny that. But when does he conscript wealth, eh?'

'No one ever conscripts wealth,' I told her. But I laughed. Tonight it was a light matter to me.

'I know that all right,' she assured me. 'I've got this sister works for some bloody nob in Vaucluse, eh. Live-in-maid, you know. Well, see it this way. Your friend Mulhall, who gives a lovely spiff, I don't deny that . . .'

I interrupted.

'You're a Queenslander, aren't you?'

She frowned. I'd demeaned her coherence on the poor grounds that I was enchanted by her. 'Queenslanders call speeches *spiffs*,' I told her.

'That's it,' she said, impatient, wagging her head. 'Marburg.'

'Ah!' I pretended I was privy to all the nuances of Marburg.

'What I was saying, your mate John Mulhall tells us he needs help. Without stint, eh. No bugger holding back. And then there's Mrs Robinson in Vaucluse. Who does damn all except keep the gin industry going. Can't even get dressed without my sister. When do you think the manpower blokes will get round to sorting that one out, eh?' She sent me her maternal smile. 'Well, you're probably right, Paper, they never will. They won't even make Mrs Robinson iron her own bloody bloomers. It's what Churchill calls total war. But it's more total for some than for others.'

She drained her glass and made an impatient little gesture, using only the last two fingers of her right hand. 'Give me yours and I'll get another.'

I waited for her, my hip against the table. Very happy in a temporary sort of way. It was cold out there but only on the surface of the hands. As she came out again, frowning a little, juggling the two glasses, I heard them call after her, 'Don't get any chilblains out there, Glends!'

After she gave me the glass I put my free arm on her shoulder. She didn't pull away and, in spite of the crutch that sloped between us, I found it a sweet contact. Did she believe that the wealthy could somehow be perfected by legislation? I asked, sipping beer and moving the crutch away, so that I could feel her radiant thigh against mine. *I* didn't believe wealth could be overthrown even by revolution. Wealth was the original sin, it could not be rooted out.

She said, 'But you've got to try, eh. You've got to try. Paper. A man is meant to . . .'

I kissed her jaw where a small crop of blonde furze ran out from behind her ear. 'Johnny will only be allowed to save the country within limits. The limits are that Mrs Robinson won't

142

lose your sister. I'm sorry for your disappointments, Glenda. But would you rather Tony Hamish were running the show?'

She looked straight ahead, ignoring my lips. 'No, I wouldn't, Paper, but there's this. If Tony Hamish were urging us along and not urging the rich, I wouldn't feel so disappointed. It'd be what I'd expect of the bugger.'

And she began to stare at her beer in that augurer's way I'd seen inside by the stove.

'He's a good man,' I said. 'Honest, Glenda, the genuine product. I like him better than any of the other buggers who whizz in and out – and I've seen most of them.'

She was still depressed. Given her name was Casey, she was no doubt any old Catholic. Perhaps to waver in faith pained her. 'They're all good blokes. They've all got loads of mates,' she said.

I could see people in the kitchen beginning to make moves, as if they'd come out here. It was a strange thing that a private argument on a back verandah, on a night when frost is on the cards, was capable of dragging others towards it, setting up its own field of force.

I kissed Glenda full on the mouth, she kissed me back. There was a familiarity about the whole thing, even to the taste of her saliva, as if she were that forgotten love who goes on waiting there, just beyond the corner of memory.

And s te had the grace, in responding, not to give a damn about the crutches and whether I could retain my balance. She left the question of balance to me.

'Where's your husband?' I said.

'Home,' she said. 'Flu, eh!'

'Listen,' I said. I told her that I occupied Room 19 at the Wollombi. She made a *tch* and shook her head. 'Oh, Paper,' she said. 'See, one of the kids has a temperature. I couldn't spend any time . . '

'But maybe a little time,' I said. 'A speck of time for an old digger, eh.'

The first miner to give in to his bladder appeared at the kitchen door, grunting, already working at the buttons of his waistline, embedded as they were deep in gut-fat. 'Lovely night for it,' he called ambiguous but without malice, as he passed us.

Not for the first time, I used my old wounds as a moral lever. I whispered. 'If you're worried about . . .' I nodded towards my shortened limbs '. . . it wouldn't shock you or anything.'

She raised her chin, almost looking down on me. I hung limp on the crutch pads.

'I wouldn't be worried by a thing like that,' she said. 'It's the kiddie with the fever.'

'Does Jonesy have a back gate?' I asked.

She went with me. I forget now the precise stratagems by which we entered the hotel in such a way that her name and that of John Mulhall's entourage wouldn't suffer damage. I suppose I went in by the main door while she used the lane in the old stable-yard, where the cars of the Commonwealth and of various business travellers stood, some high as a haystack with those new gas bladders atop their roofs. Through their plentiful shadow, she got up to me by the back steps.

It doesn't work for a cripple to be passion's slave. I admit I thought, after she'd rushed away a little after midnight, that I might let myself slide into the infatuation. If Johnny wanted me to travel, I'd travel on a regular basis to the coalfields. I don't have to tell you that was idiot stuff. Millie's sweet companionship could be had where it was needed, in our gimcrack capital of which I was a founding denizen. That, I confess, admitting now the meanness of the thought, decided me. I never saw little Glenda again. I wonder how the great strike of '49 left her honest mothering soul.

Jim Cowan told me that that night Johnny, who tended to tears anyhow, wept as he said goodnight to Jonesy. He did not know, of course, what doubts girls in twin-sets had uttered on his host's back verandah.

Chapter Five

Zimmer was Mephistopheles. He made his second bid for my soul with the suggestion that I might go to Moresby. 'I know you'd have special problems in that climate,' he said. 'Prickly heat and all the rest.'

Prickly heat seemed, at the time, a remote risk. The invitation came to me by telephone on the winter's worst night. Sleet from Black Mountain tickled the panes. As you considered the timbre of the wind, you knew that out along the pastures of the Cotter sheep were perishing in the teeth of the blast.

Zimmer pitched the invitation as a sort of reward for my earlier work and, as soon as I heard it, I wanted to take it up. Yet I felt a kind of humiliation, too; the offer smelt to me of usage. It didn't matter so much if Zimmer was the user. What worried me most was whether Johnny was a party.

I called Johnny as soon as I could. I could tell it was fresh news to him, not so much by what he said but by the tone of his laughter. He thought, in a word, that the project was mad.

'What if I *did* go?' I asked.

'Seriously?' he said.

'Would you have any objection?'

'You don't work for *me*, Paper.'

Then he laughed again, unsure, as if he'd lost track of me.

'You *hate* generals. You hate the whole bloody military genus.'

But at last he said, 'As long as you didn't stay too long.'

'What's *too long?*'

'You know what I mean. For the whole damned siege.'

I told Millie as we sat together in her kitchen in Reid. Millie was one of those people who get disturbed by a high wind. So she was already frowning, one ear raised to her shuddering eaves in an instinctive fear that the roof would fly away.

She said, 'You? A disabled man?'

'Well, you know . . . Journalistic thirst, eh?'

'You had a thirst to see what things were like in 1915. And look what happened.'

I kissed her ear. 'This would be different. Scotch in the administrator's villa, houseboys, gin on a tray with a spray of bougainvillea . . .'

Sniffing out my own earlier suspicions, she asked, 'Has Johnny anything to do with this?'

'No,' I insisted. 'No. He laughed.'

'He laughed? He's your best friend. What was he doing laughing?' Her eyes looked bruised in that light, under the harsh argument of the west wind. 'Johnny's changed,' she told me, stating it as a principle.

I got peevish at that. 'Why do you always have to bring up Johnny? *Zimmer's* the man who gave the invite.'

On the day I set out a car from the US Embassy was to take me from the Branch Office to Goulburn. Before it left the capital it had to collect Millie and even before it had reached her gate the ghost gums of Constitution Avenue shivered in the strong windy light with a sort of final look to them, as if my travels would be long in content if not in time.

Pam Masson emerged from the door of Millie's bungalow at the same time as Millie herself. When I saw her advancing down the path, one shoulder dipped slightly, the wind flaying her beige coat, the mad idea came to me – Johnny had sent her. For Johnny knew something. If he came to say goodbye, I'd wonder why. Does the king emerge in mid-winter to wave the minstrel off? Like hell. But if the king has consented that an ambush be laid down the road for the minstrel, he might send a courtier to wish the victim well, to soothe him, to mislead. I saw her raise her head, though, the eyes narrowed against the weather, and smile at me in that broad intemperate way that headmistresses would have beaten out of her if her old man had sent her to school. And with the smile, my lunatic suspicion vanished.

Millie was still kicking against the idea of the journey. But she seemed more sanguine about it at least, settling herself squarely on the seat beside me and smiling at me like a jolly aunt. 'Pam tells me,' she murmured, 'Moresby hasn't been bombed since the 17th.'

Mrs Masson had taken her seat on the far side of Millie. I wished I'd struggled, this cold uncertain day, to the centre of the seat, to have the comfort of being flanked by them. The odd undistinguished number seventeen gave the bombing a substance it had not had until now. But for Millie's sake I pretended to take comfort from it.

'Who tells you these things, Pamela?' I asked. 'Do you get letters from the General?'

'Notes,' she said. 'That's all.' She looked out at the bungalows of Northbourne Avenue. 'Jimmy Pointer keeps me posted. He tells me McLeod's not happy with Dick's progress.'

'Not happy? The poor sod's been there only three weeks.' I remembered what he had said in Lennon's about the general of the first battle. After ten seconds thought for him, I found it necessary to remind myself that the anguish of generals wasn't such big cheese. Beyond the torments of the careers of officers stood the pits of unambitious dead. It was for them I was supposed to keep my torch burning.

Mrs Masson reached across Millie and took my right wrist. Because her arm was so long, the action didn't cramp the back seat, didn't crush Millie between us as a sort of neglected third party. She said, 'Listen to me, Paper. Jimmy can prove the Japanese won't take Moresby. He can show you on a map and it sounds convincing at the time. Just the same, if everything goes bad, make sure you catch one of the early planes. I mean, don't hang around out of curiosity or professional ethics.' She remained like that, stroking my wrist, identifying my fear.

'Will I pass on the same instructions to Dick?' I asked her.

Biting her forefinger, she stared away down the Goulburn Road at the lanky, loutish trees crowding up to its verge. 'Dick knows the conditions of the game,' she said. 'Even if he wanted to get out, he knows he'd be an unwelcome escapee.'

It sounded like she was condemning or – what was the same – explaining him.

Chapter Six

It was hard travel. There was endless cyclonic bouncing and I fouled three heavy-duty sickbags between Brisbane and the coasts of Papua. I thought that I might be rewarded, as the DC-3 banked above the Coral Sea, with a picture of an ideal tropic port, a town-space cut out of – and hard-pressed by – a sort of equatorial lushness. But Moresby looked municipal, like one of those ordinary Queensland coastal towns on a flat Tuesday. The familiar tourist blues struck me; had I come all that damn way for this poor vista?

We flew around the mountain on the western side of town, a double-circling like the fidgets of homing bees, a pattern of flight designed to prove our friendliness to the gunners down there. I could see the tin warehouses, some with fire-marked holes in their roofs where the emperor's bombs had gone in. A host of cargo ships sat in the grey, still, hazy harbour. I saw a few Somerset Maugham hotels and unroofed bungalows in the lower part of town behind the docks and then, on the two hills on either side of the port, more desirable bungalows and residences among scrubby trees. From my window they seemed very like the trees of my childhood, the same old flora, as bad a return for all that journeying as the view itself had been.

Tucking in my chin and pressing my forehead to the glass I could see the faces of naked soldiers raised towards me from the gunpits 500 feet below. Even at that remove they resembled faces of infants. They produced in me a strange mental ache, like the ache in the iris of the eye when you walk out of shade into strong light. I thought, there *is* a war, it is *not* a fiction dreamed up in sundry capitals. To those child faces it is as real as Millie's breast is to me. And, of course, once the war became substantial in my brain, it was Millie who grew into a dream and a rumour.

We began to drop. I saw sago palms, native huts, a dawdling native family on the edge of the road, lifting their faces. I saw kunai thickets in Gordian clumps. Afternoon rain was falling in the hills behind the port. This, I thought, is more like what a tourist wants from the tropics.

When we landed, a young American crewman helped me down the steps and told me to remember my Atebrin. Another American adolescent met me at ground level and took my kit.

Before I'd reached the jeep, my correspondent's fatigues were filling with sweat. I felt trapped in that dense, adhesive air. Pity the tropic cripple, I thought.

On the road towards Masson's headquarters the child chauffeur drove with flair, showing off to me, and we saw the sights you'd expect – trucks going to the head of the short road, unwitting rows of indentured black labour on the way to the start of the inland track, where they would heft supplies up mountain sides for the sake of John Mulhall's holy continent.

We were well down the road and I was admiring at ground level the palms and the native gardens of taro when a jeep, weaving out from the direction of the coast, put itself in our path and began to honk. Two American soldiers jumped out. They told me they were official US photographers and Colonel Zimmer had ordered them to photograph me. As they blustered me towards a cane brake I remarked that it was pretty whimsical of McLeod to send American army photographers here before he'd sent any American infantry. 'This is the bottom of the world, sir,' one of the photographers told me, squinting through his viewfinder. 'Everything's back to front here.'

The other one began directing me. 'There's a column of Aussie infantry coming along, we'll use them as background. *That's* right, lean kind of casual like that on your crutches. Yeah, that's it.'

We waited a while for the warriors. Great blue butterflies jerked and yawed among the trees and large gobs of hot rain fell out of a sunny sky on to my bare arms. The infantry appeared, single file, from beyond the screen of bamboo stalks, some of Dick Masson's veterans from the desert. They looked young, too, but in a different sense; they *moved* with the economy of older animals. Without too much intensity they wondered who the cripple was, sweating and blushing in the middle of the road, being snapped there by American non-combatants. An advertisement for an ancient war, one of the once-young whose pain had turned to a fossil, a museum-piece. Only their eyes pivoted and once each man was past I got no backward glance.

An advertisement for an ancient war – or for McLeod?

Beyond the mosquito netting at the front of the big tent, the females of the anopheles species ranted. They wanted the intimate blood of Paperboy Tyson. A medical orderly in Brisbane had explained to me that they needed it for the production of fertile eggs. Sometimes I would jerk awake to find one in its long-legged stance making a love-meal of my wrist.

I believed Masson was making me wait, letting me ponder whether I ought to be here or not, the properness of it. Even the half bottle of Scotch he had sent me seemed like an ironic echo of our interview in Brisbane. And in that wallowing air, Scotch was no elixir.

In this tent there were other cots, rolled blankets on them. If they were the cots of the Press contingent then it meant I'd been excluded from something they were in on. The activities of some of Masson's signallers out in the compound, the numb drill of a headquarters company, the becalmed stances of gunners in their pits this evening of no raids, put me further into the megrims. I asked an orderly who brought me a meal what he did about prickly heat? 'Medicated powder, sir. Do you have any?'

I shook my head. 'It's the crutch that's the worst.'

He looked at the crutches leaning against my bed.

'No, I don't mean those.'

He told me that all those blankets lying around were not for journalists. A party of Americans was coming the next day. I asked him why the blankets were needed. He said they were necessary in case of malarial fever. 'If you get it, sir, one wouldn't be enough.'

I asked him did he think the Japanese would take the port. 'No fear,' he told me. 'They're eating some of our blokes. That's how hard up they are.'

Night fell in the expected equatorial manner, like the descent of an axe. The orderly lit the storm lanterns for me.

At length a truck rolled into the central area among the tents. I could identify it not by its unlit shape but by the busyness of the voices and the feet that got down from it. There was a sharp conversation, men talking in well-formed sentences as if they were not going to bed but back to their desks. They sounded in fact like voices in a more temperate climate. As they faded, Masson appeared beyond the netting at the front of the tent. He undid the cleats and entered.

'Don't try to get up, Paper,' he told me. In the small light I could see the difference in him. Away from the disordered world of taxis, half-porters, adulteries and politicians, there was a directness to him and an added toning, not just sunburn, in the skin of his face.

He sat, grunting a little at the comfort of the hard chair, and stared at me. I didn't like it. When I met him at the Lodge and in Lennon's he had been just another suppliant soldier. Now he disputed the kingship of Papua with a Japanese called Tomitaro Horii. His stature was sharp-defined; he stood out even in the dim light with keen, unqualified edges. He said, 'What in Christ's name brought you here, Paper?' He'd been more ceremonial than that in the parlour of Lennon's.

'Zimmer asked me,' I told him.

'Oh,' he said. He looked at his hand, first the palm, then the top. 'Up here – when I've had the time – I've often thought it was pretty stupid to ask you to carry a message to Mulhall. You see things clearer in a zone of battle, clearer than you do in the fairly confused circumstances of Brisbane. It was one of those tactical errors, I suppose, trying to enlist you. But then, the uncertainty of the time and place . . .'

I said, 'Look mate, the set-up worries me, too . . .'

But he waved that aside. He put his hat down crown-first on the table. I could see sweat gleaming on the band. 'If you're here to observe me, Tyson . . . I'll put it harder than that . . . If you're here to spy on me . . . I wouldn't be very amused . . .'

I got angry, of course. But anger's a physical hazard in that climate and my head began to waver and ache.

'Do I look qualified to turn out a report on a general?' I asked him. 'Do you think Johnny's such a bloody fool as to give me a job like that?' I got a scathing itch on my thigh. I began to scratch it with wide, raking motions of the hand. 'Jesus,' I told him, 'I'm already sorry I came.'

Masson smiled. 'You have no responsibility to a uniform. You can get around in a bathrobe if you want it.'

'I'd frighten the bloody native bearers.'

He laughed at that. He even laughed with more authority in an area of combat.

I passed on the message from Pam, and Masson told me to tell her that everything was working well.

'Even for the general in the first battle?' I asked him.

'Even for him,' he said.

When he got up to go, I found I didn't want him to leave. I was not ready in mind to lie in the saturated dark in the midst of empty cots. I delayed him a while by asking how he slept in this climate. His answer was no comfort. 'Like a just man, Paper,' he said, grinning, abandoning me to the questionable night.

He was out beyond the mosquito netting when he remembered something. 'Oh, I'm flying to Milne Bay tomorrow, Paper. You're welcome to join the party.'

'But there's a bloody pitched battle there!' I protested.

'Well,' he said whimsically, as if someone had told him of my prejudice against generals or he'd somehow pick it up. 'A general's got to pretend to be interested in these things.'

I didn't doubt for a second that he was putting me on trial.

* * * *

153

As we fell again down the opaque funnels of cloud, the mountings of my seat gave way. I could see from the new position I thus took up, my false leg poking crookedly at the roof. I saw, too, the inner fuselage above my head streaming with moisture, as if there were no division at all between the tempest beyond the bomber's skin and the tempest we suffered inside it. Yet in this unchosen beetle-like position, I felt instantly happier. While seated upright I'd had to take the jolts in the belly, the buttocks, the non-existent calves of my legs. The hardy medium of the spine I now lay on was better suited to deal with the shocks of tropical flying. On my back I was calm enough to wave to the co-pilot who was leaving his seat to set me upright. 'Don't bother. It snapped but the screws are holding.' The co-pilot turned his eyes back to the blunt faces of the clouds. They were what I wanted him to apply himself to.

I waved, too, to Masson and his aide, making soothing movements with my hands. I'd found a posture in which I was willing to risk a crash. I didn't want any kindly person dragging me up into a posture in which the idea was hard to bear.

The child-pilot decided he could not get below the cloud. He began to haul his machine up the cloud-faces yet again, looking for a window, a vista of earth or water, of some medium appropriate to man.

The sweat of my body froze on me once more. I could see, on a handrest above the aisle, the open, easy left hand of the General. There was no violet tension in the knuckles. Like Johnny, I thought. When they were babies, when they were secret princes in their mothers' wombs, someone had whispered to them about destiny. That they would not have inconsequential deaths in a column of mist while in transit. If they were to die at all, a noxious fairy told them, it would be on a summit, at a terminus, a point of arrival.

I was pleased we were climbing. I knew there were mountains hereabout, against which unambitious infants like Paperboy Tyson had *no* immunity. Yet we reached such a height, without getting one damn glimpse of the substantial world, that I had to beat at my upper arms with my fists because of the cold. My jaw hung agape, shuddering. The General sat up straight, chafing his own arms with his hands. Once he leaned forward and spoke to his aide, who got up and stumbled forward along the canting deck towards the pilot. Then he tottered back, spoke to the General, knelt by me and screamed in my ear. 'Going back . . . five minutes . . . unless we find a break.'

As he spoke, sunlight entered the windows. I saw it fall on the side of Masson's face first, then I felt it reach the fabric of my pants above the knee and I saw the two pilots nodding and grinning sideways at each other. By struggling up I could see a wide bay beset by hills, divided by peninsulas. If there was a battle on, the jungle shut out all view of it. Only the jungle was aggressive, edging its mangroves forward into the slate waters of the bay. We spun inland then, to the safest airfield.

Our landing threw up whorls of dust. There were jeeps waiting there but the path to them was across steel matting. The tips of my crutches slipped in the perforations. Beneath the matting, the wavering soil of Milne Bay smelled of the memory of the mangroves it had nurtured until two months back. Down a rutted track the vehicles took us past batteries of working artillery. The noise, of course, brought to me the flavour of another morning, the nausea of old wounds.

Headquarters for the defending force was a circle of tents just like Dick Masson's own headquarters near Moresby. Once perhaps, and for generations, the clearing had been a native taro plot; roots had grown in its mud under the tutelage of gods and ancestors. Men had sung incantations here and cajoled, bullied, chided and flattered the alligator gods and the dead whose memory of taro was still strong. Now all it yielded was last night's rain, rising in vapour.

My journalistic instincts kept me close to Masson's left shoulder as he approached the commander of Milne Bay. There was relative quiet in this grove; the gunners in this sector must have been sleeping. Dick Masson said to the man, 'I thought I'd come and see you, Bernie. McLeod doesn't like our crisp despatches, old boy. He wants us to write a daily novel. That's the sort of thing those Yanks go in for, my friend. An expanded bloody prose style . . .'

The commander let his pipe drag his mouth crooked. He

resembled a Mallee farmer about to discuss wheat prices. 'Bugger-all to tell him,' he said, very low and moist.

'Which matches the bugger-all he knows about New Guinea, Bernard. But I believe we must try to become more effusive.'

They disappeared into the shadow of a vast tent, the Huguenot and the farmer, and the aide and I were diverted to a side tent, set up with trestle tables and a rostrum and blackboards. 'A bloody mission school,' I told the aide, who started to laugh. Since my flat-on-the-back act in the plane, he'd decided I was a character and that it was all right by the General if he condoned me.

A young officer arrived at our sides, sat us down and told us what was happening. There was every chance, he said, that the Japanese would make further landings, especially if weather grounded the P-40s. If you moved troops in this swampy ground, round to the south of the bay to deal with possible assaults there, you would never be sure that you could get them back quickly through all that mud. So it was hard to take up fixed positions until landings occurred.

The enemy did not fit the European caricature of the Japanese, he told us. They were big buggers, marines; they were inventive and careless of their lives. At first dark they chanted – no one knew if it was a religious or a military chant but it was very beautiful, hundreds of voices at a time. Then they'd climb trees and call out the usual challenges. 'Aussie, I f. . . your wife.' The major attacks, the many infiltrations, came at night. Daytime was all artillery, patrolling, sniping and raids by the P-40s. The Australians, he said, had just won back a mission station called KB, on the northern arm of the bay. And so on.

I made my notes. It was all solid stuff. Something to show for my excursion.

After tea in a mess tent, the farmer and Masson rode off in jeeps, taking all their retinue, leaving me sitting under the torrid canvas with a mess orderly who had hay fever. Noon was past. Frequent tea cooled my sweat. A vast thundery cumulus threw a shadow halfway across the headquarters and I began to feel neglected and querulous. In this time messengers arrived and left, lean runners from the forward units, an occasional officer in a jeep. One of them, a captain of artillery, arrived in a pillar of dust, rushed into the tented office – where I could see him conferring and nodding with the duty officer – and hurried out again. I was waiting for him by his mudguard.

'Where are you going?'

'KB,' he said, briefly, as if I were an habituary of the cursed bay. He did not seem to see my crutches, my age and other definite signs that I was a tourist. I hurried the accreditation papers out of my breast pocket. I said, 'General Masson tells me I'm allowed up to KB. If I can find a lift.'

He shook his head, he blinked his set eyes. I was one detail too many to absorb into the furious equatorial day. 'I don't know if I can get back in time. Once it rains on these roads . . .' he shook his head again. 'All right,' he said, 'I'll see you get back.'

The track he drove was an impossible thoroughfare. He took it single-minded and unblinking in the dust, he didn't give a damn for the chassis and suspension. There was none of the average bravado of a young man showing his older passenger what could be done with a recent model. He stayed sullen. He showed as small an interest in me as he did in the youths who slept on ground sheets among the roots and the trees, right up against the edge of the track. The fixity of their sleep echoed exactly the way he drove. The track worsened. Rain had cut cross-wise courses in it. But our progress continued among sleepers and, half across our narrow path, a tall Japanese sniper lay, his legs tangled in the fronds of a felled palm tree.

'Far now?' I called, sweating from something more fearful and internal than the mere jungle noon.

'No,' he said. But he gave no details. He had driven over the tall corpse's wrist, which I took as another sign of his inelastic nature.

To me the road now seemed just wide enough to admit laden carriers in single file, but with the blunt nose of his vehicle my driver seemed to force more generous dimensions out of it. We sprang from one stable patch of sand to another, across corrugations of baked mud.

So we got at last to a clearing where soldiers sat smoking and drinking tea in the shade of tall kunai. He stopped near them and climbed out, not inviting me to dismount. He asked them some question. The soldiers pointed over their shoulders with their thumbs, or directly across country with a slack, crooked index finger. Still sitting up in the jeep's passenger seat, I began to be distracted by a stench I remembered from the hospital ship.

My driver came back and we made another 100 yards in the jeep before he decided the track would not be challenged any further.

'You be all right?' He asked me, looking for a second at the instrument panel, just like a man let down my machinery. 'You be all right getting along?'

I said of course. I was a bit slow climbing out and he waited for me but it was a struggle for him. He wanted to move faster. Looking up after my first few crutch-strides, I noted the ruins of some simple buildings of fibro and roofing iron and palm-frond. A cross still stood atop one of the walls. In the shadows were some broad-backed black corpses, one of them in the rags of a mission dress.

My guide had given in to an impulse to be quick and I raced to keep up. 'You don't have to come any further,' he said.

I told him not to worry, that I could keep up. He gave a little sort of maimed grin with the corner of his mouth. It wasn't *keeping up* that he'd been talking about.

In the shade of the palm grove we saw men digging graves and the candidates for the graves lay all about under blankets. I suppose there were a few dozen, though as soon as I saw them I was no longer in any state for making dispassionate tallies. We walked in among them. Swamp water pooled in the shallow bottoms of these holes. A small man appeared, another officer, wearing the medical corps badge. 'You're . . .' he said, pointing at my driver and clicking his thumbs for the name.

'They thought I could identify Lieutenant . . . ,' said the driver but I couldn't get the name. He had a rigid lower jaw, my jeep-mate, that didn't allow for so much refinement of sound. The medical man nodded and led us in among the blankets. 'Happened yesterday,' he told us. 'How long since we lost KB? Yes, yesterday. We couldn't find any tags.'

This doctor was as indifferent to the specific pains I had taken to get here as the driver had been and even among these reeking mounds I was childishly resentful.

We stopped by one of the blankets. 'Listen mate,' said the doctor. 'They did tell you there'd been, ah . . . torture?'

The taciturn boy nodded.

A medical orderly pulled back the blanket, his fingers blessedly long and feminine, raising a false supposition that the remains would be delicate. I took no more than a glimpse. I noticed that the body was naked except for stained army shorts. I noticed the damage to the arm nearer to me. I did not look beyond that.

'That's the birthmark,' said my captain. 'No doubt in my mind. The arms . . . what about the arms?'

'I won't tell lies,' the doctor said. He began then to give details of the death. 'Listen,' he said, 'I give you my professional word. He wouldn't have felt much towards the end. Would've been in shock from the wounds in the arms. I'm sure you understand that.'

My friend nodded. He wasn't going to argue with the doctor. 'It's him, though,' he said. 'All that battalion wear shorts like that. It's their . . . you know . . . it's their trade mark.'

I wondered, what if Johnny had a picture of this? War was abstract to Johnny. He talked about it in the same tones of theological horror as he spoke of capitalism. War and capitalism were tableaux in an Eight Hour Day street parade. He kept his mind intact because he lacked the mental habits that could bring him to an image like that of this boy, who was now taking his wounds with him into the swamp.

The doctor said, 'There's a minister coming up to do the burials. Would you like to stay?'

My friend's eye wandered all over the clearing. I could tell he didn't want to stay for the burial. I could tell he was searching out a pretext. His eyes took grateful cognizance of me. 'I've got to get my friend here back. Has to catch the plane before it rains.' Thunder from the west supported his argument.

We left in a hurry. I looked at the roadside soldiers still

sleeping under the daily bombast of the thunder and pitied them in advance for the jet dark of four hours' time, when the lovely chanters would start up, and the mutual barbarities.

I called above the noise of thunder and cannon and the considerable racket of the jeep itself. 'Mate of yours?'

'Ah,' he said, looking about him as if he didn't know of whom I spoke; 'Ah,' just like he'd forgotten the exact connection. 'Ah, brother. He's my brother.'

I don't have to say that the tenor of the trip we'd made became clear to me. When he dropped me back among the headquarters' tents, the conversation of both of us had been reduced to grunts and pieces of sentences. He said, 'If you write up any of that, you won't be using names . . .'

'Don't know any,' I said.

'That's right.'

Masson's aide was waiting there for me. He seemed peevish, asked me was I ready.

The gravid rain of the tropics fell on us before we were half-way to the airfield. We had to wait a while on the seeping metal framework of the strip and Masson shunted up to me in streaming oilskins.

'Paper,' he said, 'I don't want you going off on expeditions without reference to anyone.'

'Well,' I said, feeling that the tour of KB gave me *some* moral rights, 'I don't bloody well like being left round a tea tent for hours. Without a word from anyone.'

He considered me for a while, the rain that half-blinded me not blinding him at all. 'The Americans are arranging your transport?'

'So they reckon.'

He nodded. 'Paper, I've shown you Milne Bay. I want to treat you fair. Through no fault of your own you need a lot of attention from the orderly. I think you should tell the Americans you're going home on Thursday.'

Our bomber was rolling towards us, propellers dicing the air, sound falling in great blocks upon us. My voice was quelled by the propellers. But not his.

'Don't go thinking it's a matter of personalities. Paper!' He moved his hand in a small, benign chopping motion. Then, not even trying to read the clouds that threatened our flight path eastwards, he climbed the steps into the belly of the plane.

Chapter Seven

That night the great marquee of which I'd had sole use was full of members of McLeod's advance party. They sat on cots in their combat boots, shirts pulled out at the waist for the sake of coolness. They drank bourbon from enamel mugs. The ones who faced the tent flap took some interest in me as I busied my way to my own bunk and swung my body on it.

While I moved my shoulders in complaint on the hot mattress, I saw some of the Americans pointing me out to a heavy-set man in a different uniform. This man stood, turned and approached me. Through migrainous blots of colour, I saw him to be Jimmy Pointer. I laughed in a way that had almost a begging sound to it, a plea to be left alone.

The wild flight back had been full of vertical movement and sideways jerking. My seat had been repaired and I'd had to take it all sitting up. It was cruel to reach my cot and find a talkative friend approaching it.

He stood over me. 'Want any of the invader's barbarous liquor?' he asked me.

'No, no,' I closed my eyes, smiling politely all the while. For my head's sake I hoped he wasn't going to start talking about the war beyond the war, the war against those pleasant, boyish, subtle men at the other end of the tent. I asked him about his plane flight, hoping to get him going on the nature of his journey instead of its purpose. He made the jump anyhow. He got on to *purpose* within ten seconds.

'. . . to act as a buffer between those jokers and Dick Masson,' he told me. He touched the side of his nose like a tout. 'Those upholders of manifest bloody destiny up there, at *that* end of the tent . . . them and more so their boss. They want the whole bloody lot, Paper, I assure you, old son. They want *us* in their bloody pockets.' He dropped his voice lower still, '*McLeod*, Paper . . . *McLeod* is trying to panic Johnny.'

'Oh,' I said. I must have been tired. I didn't even want to hear the General explained away.

'I went to dinner with them all,' he told me nonetheless. 'In Brisbane last night. Johnny arranged it. He chose a temperance hotel called the *Canberra*! Guests to gather at six o'clock in the evening. A good working-class hour if ever I saw one!'

'Well,' I told him, in a fraudulently sleepy voice, 'Johnny's pretty unworldly.'

'It was a damn awful evening,' Jimmy said.

'I can believe you,' I agreed.

The Premier of Queensland and his missus had come (said Jimmy) and there'd been McLeod and his wife. There was also an American officer who, Jimmy suspected, had the same peculiar kind of research and planning job Jimmy himself had – that is, planning to vanquish your allies rather than your enemies. Then there'd been dear old Jim Cowan, the Press man. 'The meal was beef broth, mutton and three veg. And, Paper – I don't lie – custard tart. A bottled-in-bond State banquet. And for drinks they served Mynor fruit cup!'

The two bullies at table, said Jimmy, had been the Premier of Queensland, a barbed-wire Scot who'd never liked Johnny, and McLeod. The Premier had kept on demanding hard liquor in the most boorish terms, sending for the manager who, in his turn, said he couldn't serve liquor because it was against the law. The Premier had roared, 'I make the damn laws in this State.' The manager, a real Methodist bush lawyer according to Jimmy, went on telling him with respect that was not true, that the legislature of the State made the laws and there'd be no Scotch.

Mrs McLeod spoke up about then in her sweet, mediating,

twangy voice, saying it did not matter, the General and she didn't need anything other than this delicious *punch*. ' "Punch", she called it,' Jimmy reiterated. 'Such suavity, Paper, such *savoir*-bloody-*faire*.'

But while she tried to mitigate the effects of the Premier of Queensland on Johnny, no one was mitigating what McLeod was pouring in his ear. 'He kept saying, you know, the whole set-up in Papua isn't working, that if methods aren't improved Moresby will go . . . to the Japanese bush-hiking club! He wasn't talking about from the sea, either. He was talking about Moresby falling to Horii in his bloody crampons and haversack! Starkey ought to go up to Moresby, McLeod kept saying, and he ought to *energize* the situation. The very word he used, Paper, three bloody times over. Starkey should *energize*!'

The word sounded grotesque to me for I was of an innocent race who at that time had not caught the argot of Madison Avenue.

'Something for your friend there, Jimmy?' one of the Americans called to us. I waved a hand in limp refusal and they left us alone.

'Can't you see the plot, Paper?' Jimmy whispered. 'He gets Starkey off the mainland, out of Victoria Barracks and into a tent. Into a tent like this, on the edge of a jungle. Starkey can't bring his staff with him – it'd take a month to set them up in a place like this. Starkey becomes a commander in the field, a tactical bloody clerk, Paper, and there is no one to oppose McLeod's all-consuming intent. That's the picture, Paper. What do you bloody think of it?'

He wiped his nose and took a sad sip of the alien distillation, the conqueror's potion, but did not wait for my answer. 'Honest, it sometimes looks to me, Paper, that we couldn't do without someone to prove to us that we don't count. We're the lost peasants of the South Pacific looking for a propèr backside to kiss. Too many bloody peasants in our nation, old friend, literal peasants. Where'd your family come from?'

Mark Twain had once said that Australian history read like wonderful fiction, but the fictions of the origins of the Tysons did not *energize* me that night.

'I don't know, Jimmy. Scotland somewhere. Grandfather used to talk about Dundee ... I don't know.'

Jimmy dropped his voice even further. I had to lip-read half the sentence, since it was smothered by the scream of a night-bird, a sound coming to me like a fragment of the singing and terror of Milne Bay. He had lost all interest, if he ever had any, in the question of the immigration of the Tysons.

He made a tiny masked gesture with his thumb towards the men further up the tent. 'They'll whinge when McLeod tells them to. They'll make the faces McLeod prescribes. They'll ask the questions for him. Quite a study they'll be, Paper, quite a study.'

He drifted away then, a beatific grin on his face. The beatitude of a man who knows his terms of reference.

I was not as sanguine as he was. For a start, I still had to get to the latrines across the compound.

Later, I asked him to douse the storm lantern at my end of the tent. This permitted me to unstrap my false leg with the appropriate modesty. But Jimmy returned, as if to tuck me in. 'Do you have malaria, do you reckon, old dig?' he asked me, sitting on the end of my cot.

I slept as suddenly as if hit, with the military seer still casting his shadow across me.

'If the Japanese took this roadhead,' an American staff officer posited, 'it seems that with their capacity to outflank, even in jungle conditions, they'd take that port within a day.'

We were standing in a square of dried mud among eucalyptus trees and spear grass and dusty native fields. Trucks came all the time, unloaded, wheeled and left. Above us the track travelled in switchback towards a hazy crest, and on it moved lines of natives in coarse linen skirts, travelling in pairs, each with his walking staff, a box-load of supplies slung from a pole carried between each pair. Their bed-rolls cosseted the ends of the poles, the part that went on their shoulders.

From a distance it was an aesthetic sight. You thought of Nubians hauling limestone up the ramps of a pyramid. For the Nubians themselves it would not be so pleasing. Yet they seemed to ratify, those firm-shouldered slave figures, the story Masson's staff officer now began pitching the Americans. The Japanese could not take the roadhead, he said. It was a theoretic contingency. Their line of supply would be stretched so thin across the mountains, and our line so short and easily serviced, that there was no reason why the ridge could not be held and become a springboard . . .

I watched a polemic smile on the face of a US colonel standing there. Looking at the man you'd nearly be justified in believing, as Jimmy did, that saving the port meant less to him than saving the argument.

'But there's no reason,' he said, 'why the same formula would not apply to us. If we force them back across the Owen Stanleys we'll get to the same stage, where our line of supply is thin and theirs is, so to speak, short, broad, healthy. And so, sir, do you envisage we shall yo-yo back and forth on our respective supply strings for the remainder of the year?'

Masson's officer almost closed his eyes and so, with his New Guinea tan, took on a look of mahogany rationality. 'That could happen,' he said, 'only if these events took place in a vacuum.'

Jimmy had, of course, been listening to such exchanges all morning. He stood in the dust, his eyes lowered, his ear lifted. He reminded me of a man at a tennis match who listens only for the plunk of the ball against cat-gut.

'There is friction in war,' Masson's staff officer expounded. 'Crossing the mountains is no mechanical process. Men are worn away by it. The enemy's supply situation can likewise be affected by events elsewhere . . .'

In that heat I lost track of the debate. At last we were given some tea and Jimmy and I went looking among the stands of bamboo and around the store sheds for colour, for infantrymen with stories, for a closer sight of native carriers. We found only storemen with sheets in hands and pencils behind their ears and a few mechanics reaching deep into the engine of a truck.

Jimmy himself was sluggish, even though his enemies, our allies, had gone to so much trouble to prove his judgment of them.

'Well, Jimmy,' I said. 'Speak to the General?'

'Bloody Masson,' he said. 'He just looked at me in that murderous bloody polite way of his, Paper. Then he said, listen, Jimmy, a general has too much to do to start giving ear to gossip from home. I stared at him, Paper, I couldn't believe it. I bring him the graph of his bloody future and he calls it gossip.'

'But he worries about it, Jimmy,' I assured him. Jimmy was like me, a sort of joke at court, but he'd always given good stuff and now deserved some in return. 'He worries about the gossip from home and what it means. He knows war's a branch of politics and more so if . . .'

Under the stifling sun Jimmy watched the mechanics with one eye closed. '. . . if your missus is in the Prime Minister's bed,' he said. 'More so then. What's that noise, Paper?'

We both had been noticing for a little while a sort of rhythmic splash of air somewhere behind the sheds, and once a voice had risen, a call of pain or authority. We went behind the sheds, searching in an idle way for the source of the noise. Jimmy Pointer said it was a threshing machine; but did they need a thresher up here? I said a generator with a loose belt.

We came out of the turquoise shade of the warehouses to see a wire compound ahead and a barracks inside it. It was an old compound, older than this young war, perhaps as old as the last. Inside it some sort of parade ground had been cleared, and across this space three native policemen rolled a forty-gallon drum, a fourth policeman carrying a bundle of sticks over his shoulder. A white man in khaki oversaw the work they did. The noise had stopped.

In another direction, four of the race I'd just been thinking of idly as Nubians were being escorted by an armed guard through a gate into a further stockade within the compound. In there, in spite of a banyan that grew in the middle, the sun dominated. A few iron-roofed huts, which would have been murder at this hour of the day, stood about. This was an old colonial prison, such as I had – until then – seen only in Hollywood films about darkest Africa. There were some thirty natives there, most of them standing or tensed on their haunches. All of them were intent on the four newcomers.

'Well, I'll be damned, Paper old boy,' Jimmy told me. 'I think we just missed a flogging.'

Nearer, we could see that the gate of the prison cage stood ajar. The four new prisoners passed inside it and native policemen stood back bare-footed, holding their rifles athwart their thighs.

Next we noticed a white man there, inside the cage, someone we had not seen until now, a small man in khaki. He scooped goanna oil or lard or balm from a jar and with a tentative second finger applied it to the fresh white bruises and the slashes on the backs of the four.

'Oh, Jesus,' I said. I felt again a pulse of that migraine from which I didn't suffer in more temperate places. I even gagged a second, so that Jimmy Pointer was distracted from watching the colonial drama and asked me if I was all right.

'They put them over the drum, it's traditional you see, Paper,' Jimmy told me. 'It's a rite that native labour understands. In some places they light a fire in the drum. I mean, a Melanesian doesn't have any reason to carry supplies for our fair Commonwealth, you know. They don't have the same affections as you or I do.'

'Does Johnny know?' I asked him all at once, a childish, unworldly question. Of course he did not answer it. The white man in the prison had just about finished with his goanna oil and the other Melanesian carriers stared at the backs of those who had recently been punished and nodded their heads and made comments. As the small man raised his arms and began preaching in pidgin, I could see the marks of the Salvation Army on his collar.

I am not proficient in pidgin; there were usages I did not catch. But the man's homily went this way, at least as far as I can remember it. He said, 'Brothers, Harris cries plenty for him black brothers and Christ cries plenty plenty too.'

He talked with emphasis, mourning the stripes on their backs. He began to weep fraternally with them and the Lord. 'Christ him catch on quick quick black boys believe Jap feller he spirit of ancestor come back in Japanee skin. Christ want Harris tellim black brother that soul of dead he no come back in Japanee skin. Soul of dead he belong of Jesus, not in Japanee skin. Japanee soldier belongim Japanee skin, Harris promise you plenty. And Japanee soldier in Japanee skin plenty plenty cruel to Harris black brother. Japanee soldier work Harris black brother plenty plenty hard. Aussie boss easy easy. Japanee boss hard. Harris black brother carry load along Japanee, Japanee cutim throat, shootim, stickim. Harris tell you true. Jesus wantim black brother carry load along Aussie feller. Jesus say Aussie feller plenty good for Harris black brother. Japanee no bringim black brother no cargo. Japanee him bad spirit. Harris tell you. Black brother better believe Harris plenty . . .'

They all nodded in such deep agreement that they could have been doing obeisances. Harris noticed us beyond the wire; he raised his eyes to us. They were not the eyes of a fool. His eyes said: this is the kind of work I do, making plain the ways of the Lord.

We turned away and walked into the gaps between the stores and the garages. To show we were passing from one picture of the world to another, a chain of lightning crackled in the sunlit air above us. We came back from the place where the invaders were ancestors incarnate bearing sweet cargo, to the patch of dust where Yankee staff men flourished their gifts of tactical thinking.

Jimmy Pointer said, 'There'll be a big shake-up here when this war ends. Those chaps in the stockade there . . . their not-yet-conceived bloody offspring will hear about it. It's folly to treat native peoples that way . . . yet, of course, at the moment, there's this desperate supply problem . . . you can't drive a bloody truck over the Owen Stanleys . . . and so you can't have your native carriers buggering off for primitive reasons . . .'

Jimmy laughed then and slapped my shoulder. There was some friendliness in the slap but a kind of patronizing pressure as well. 'My dear Paper, I do believe you're shaken. Are you just an ingenuous boy, after all?'

That night Dick Masson put on a frugal banquet for his guests. The meal was taken on trestle tables among an avenue of smouldering mosquito coils. Their pungency undermined the taste of the canned ham and vegetables, the tinned peaches and the ice-cream from the ice-cream machine which McLeod had consigned as a gift to his front-line general.

Masson sat at the head of the table with McLeod's chief-of-staff, their faces both conformable but shut-in, like churches on a Monday morning. There was a rumour that they had not got on together. Jimmy and I were placed far down the table. Jimmy seemed hurt about it. He said nothing. But I could tell that after the warnings he'd given Dick Masson he felt that he should have been up there somewhere on the General's left, giving off some sort of crafty influence, a real Renaissance cardinal.

I left the table early. The younger men of both McLeod's and Masson's staffs were talking about batting on with Scotch and bourbon and beer in someone's tent. This seemed to be against the wills of their generals, who were itching to leave the feast so that they could write reports on each other's shortcomings, states of soul, blindnesses.

When the orderly came into the tent and asked me if I needed help, I was seated on my cot, undressing. I asked him to help me into my bathrobe, a gift from dear Millie, towelling, black and white stripes. She'd got it from an expensive Sydney garment house and it was the only thing I could wear with any comfort in this barbarous port.

He helped me into it, I sat back on the mattress and saw out the edge of my eye the black and white sash lying on the bed. As I reached for it, I was confused by a yell from the boy. In that same instant, the sash reared and scalded the knotty veins on the front of my hand. The orderly seized a book I'd brought with me, a pre-war volume, heavy-covered, thick of page, and began beating the sash with it.

I had noticed as I fell off the cot that the sash had – like Pharaoh's rod – turned into a black-and-white banded serpent. Because of the pliancy of the cot the orderly was finding it hard to kill the snake with a book. He hit it fair behind the head but it squirmed with all the usual serpentine magnificence and lashed sideways at the novel. Then the boy reached for Jimmy Pointer's swagger-stick at the foot of that officer's bed and at last broke the thing's neck with it. By this time, I felt the first panic tingling in my fingers and my vanished feet, the first icing of the lungs, and I wondered why the boy honoured the snake with so much attention.

When he'd finished off the snake he flung it on the floor where it lay differently, still a fine clear black and white but all the venomous electricity of its body quenched. He picked up one of my discarded army socks, bent to me where I half lay on the floor, having slid from the bed, and tied the socks as firm as he could around my middle arm, using the swagger-stick to tighten it. He told me to lie still. He'd go and fetch the MO. I begged him to wait. I did not want to choke alone on the venom. I could feel my windpipe begin to clench.

The first soul to come back was one of the Americans. His accent was broad and, just as in a Western, he poured liquor on a bushknife he took from his belt, picked up my swelling hand, argued for a second with Jimmy, who'd also come in, about whether it would be better to lift me on to the cot, and then cut open my hand. Beside the radiant pain of the snake the needle pain of the bushknife counted for little.

The American began to suck my blood and spit it on to the floor. I watched his scarlet mouth rising from the wound but I felt little gratitude. I observed him in the way a man about to hang watches a sweeper in the execution yard. I resented him for the normality of his actions, the bobbing of his head, the cool intake of my blood through his lips. I was sure that for me all bobbings, all mouths, were about to be cancelled, the mouths of fraternity and solace and desire, Johnny's, Millie's, Pam Masson's.

I called out bits of messages to Jimmy – he was to take them back to Canberra with him. I don't know what they were, I'd become drunken. I might have asked him to order Johnny to give up Pam Masson or to cleave to her above everything. I can't remember. I know, however, that Pam Masson came in for mention. I can remember, too, General Masson's medical chief-of-staff turning up, swabbing the wound with Condy's crystals and then injecting me with something. And the terror-stricken fall into a sleep for which someone was to blame – though I didn't know who it was. The surgeon or the snake.

Chapter Nine

It took fourteen days before I regained a clear head. After the bite, four days passed before I even surfaced. I woke beneath a mosquito net, in the same fury of fear in which I'd passed out. If I dreamed in those four days I can remember none of it. But I remember the dreams that came after that, in the fevered chaos of my recuperation. In that time I would get fits of anxiety and retract my body into the centre of the small cot. I suffered a lot of fever. I slept shallow, the sort of sleep in which phantasms proliferate. I believe that all this - the onsets of fear, the huddling of the body and the dreams of the animal itself - are the usual results of snake bite.

The image of the snake was in all the dreams. I ought to say *in the dream*, because whenever I fell off to sleep, the dream started again. Not as precisely as a novel; but at least the setting was continuous and the snake always had the most to say.

The dreams always proceeded in my childhood village of Nottingham or its environs. The village slept in its yellow weatherboards among holy Aboriginal hills of conical shape. It was a place so quiet, so far up an ancient snaky river that on most week days the victim and his snake could carry on a debate in the main street without any fear of traffic.

If the venue was not the main street itself it might, for example, be the public bar of the Riverview Hotel. In this dream a bullock team always stood beyond the door, attached to a long shaft of red cedar from up river. There was no bullocky in the bar and no barmaid. But this accorded with the realities of Nottingham – the bullocky would be in the outhouse or visiting a lady, the barmaid stayed in the parlour knitting until your end-of-drink loud voice brought her back out.

Through a further door into the hallway of the dream I could see the postcard photographs of Nottingham boys who attended the Great War. I was there (I am there to this day) full-length, skinny-necked, calf-eyed, wearing my cap at the tilt, one foot raised and placed on a stool, one hand hussar-style on the hip.

In the dream this picture always took the snake's eyes as well as mine and he'd begin to nag me.

'Oh yes, the boy from the bush. I know all about it, don't you worry. I *know*. Kempsey down river, the biggest town you've seen. Three thousand souls in the high season. And all at once there it is: the archduke dies and gives you the chance to travel, the liberation from cow-cockydom, eh? I know. I *know*.'

The snake would say, 'Fancy yourself in Paris, eh, with a bob in your kick? Fancy yourself among the mosques and the whores with a quid or two? Fancy yourself at last off the margin of things, eh? Slap in the middle of the world? Eh? Eh?'

'I know, I know,' he'd say. 'You never got off the margin, did you? You never got off the edge, see. You never got into the middle. Never. You had your chance to enter the tribe, land in the centre, you know that. But never got yourself as far as the beach. Still in the surf and your eyes – I *know* – your eyes were darting, bloody darting, looking for the right place to put your-self so you'd collect the Turkish tickets, the Turkish exemption, old dig. So you wouldn't need to cross the circumference, so you could stick to the fringe, so you could watch and be the watcher. I know . . .'

I can remember radiating my anger towards him for he didn't know what the pains of the process were, the process I'd gone through to exempt myself from a landing on the beach. But I think that what worried me most was I could see the direction his argument would take, that he would stretch the debate – if it was a debate – to cover Johnny and Mrs Masson.

So he kept nagging me, in my long-running dream, about how I'd chosen the bullets in the kneecaps rather than risk the solid earth beneath my boots. When I objected, he would raise his voice. 'I went to no little trouble,' he'd tell me, 'to pass on the message, friend. Dying under Jimmy Pointer's swagger-stick just to give you the good oil, old dig. Do you think this is pub talk, what I'm telling you? Do you think it's bloody kitchen gossip? Is that the sort you think I am?'

In the same way that he kept coming back to my behaviour at Gallipoli, once he got on to Johnny he kept circling back to him, too, during all those days of fitful harassment beneath the mosquito net. We sat on the front verandah of the farm at Nulla, on my mother's old lounge suite that had more innate right to be where it was than the Vatican had to sit on its hill or the Parthenon on its. We could smell the pregnant clouds of mid-afternoon. Opposite us stood the peak of that hill without a name. In it dwelt the spirits of the ancestors of Charcoal Doyle, the half-caste horseman and drunk my old man employed now and then.

I can remember now the stillness of the continuing dream, the stillness of my eternal childhood, the elastic quietude of those seconds, between crow-call and cow-moo, on Nulla Creek. It could be stretched like a decent tarpaulin fair across human history so that plagues and trade, pyramids, fights and councils could all be subsumed in the immense smoke-blue melancholy of Nulla.

If the damn snake would stop hammering me.

He said, 'So you're a watcher, I know. You watch a man with a wall-eye, say, old dig. You watch a chap with soft lips. You watch a bloke whose hands aren't firm. They play with a holder and they aren't firm. You watch that sort of bloke. You watch him make the edicts. A bloke with a wall-eye! You think, if I had legs I could wallop him. I could surpass that bugger. You think, I could take his girl. Right out of his floppy hands. If I had the kneecaps. No risk, no risk, you think. You know what I think of that argument, don't you, old dig?'

In his view, it came to that: Gallipoli and Pam Masson were some sort of connected inheritance that I had side-stepped (and the irony of that last word isn't lost on me, either). Smart people will line up to say that the snake was me and that I told myself, while poisoned, the things I wasn't game to give space to while healthy. But that sort of nonsense reduces dreams to a sort of mathematics, which they have never been. I go with the Red Indians and with the sorcerers of the Pharaohs in believing that snakes are autonomous fauna in dreams.

While the snake berated me those two weeks, Dick Masson's militia was drawing down jungle tracks back from the village of Isurava. Veterans going forward to join them found the dry lake of Myola, where supplies were meant to have been dropped, understocked. While the snake yammered away, Myola was abandoned, men wept at night for blankets and whimpered in the heat of day. The singers of Dai Nippon knew how to penetrate a perimeter from the rear; they could get within your elbow room and the mutual strange cries went up as you held the body of your enemy closer than any brother. The dead were buried in holes shovelled out with helmets, hewn with machetes. You sucked the rainwater held in pockets of fungus on trees, you slept on seeping inclines. Pneumonia was epidemic. Feet rotted in the drenched air.

I know from official histories how Johnny took the news from up the track and the reactions of McLeod and Starkey and Dick Masson himself. Dick amended his early mistakes with supplies. I know a sentence like that sounds as if the young did not die for the errors. But whenever you speak of generals you end up using terms that are like the ones cricket commentators employ to explain why a test match is lost.

So I say again, Dick got over his mistakes. He had the Americans dropping material at pin-points, learning greater accuracy as they went. He arranged his reserves, he covered the remote tracks by which the Japanese might outflank the town. He wrote clear, sharp-edged reports to Starkey and McLeod in which words such as *energize* had no place.

But from Brisbane, McLeod harried John Mulhall. It was Malaya all over again, he told Johnny. And, out of tact for his own past, avoided mention of the Philippines. Starkey should be sent, he said. In the Cabinet, one of Johnny's ministers said that Moresby would fall and Starkey should go up there and fall with it. Even as I slept and heard the browbeating serpent it was all coming out the way the remarkable Jimmy Pointer had foretold it.

Having woken from the snake I was reading a Dorothy Sayers novel in my cot, a sodden sheet over my waist. While Lord Peter Wimsey pranced his cool way around a murder in the Kentish countryside, Maurice Tyson would at points in the unremitting tropical afternoon break into an extra sweat of terror, terror without cause, a cold sweat on top of the hot one in which I already lay.

Above the roof transport planes wheeled – the red cross on the roof, marking the location of my terror and of the wounds of younger men, being a sort of point of reference for them. One of those planes coming from Brisbane with a few platoons of infantry carried Jimmy Pointer once more to Port Moresby. He had chivvied a seat for himself and so was returning to the front line of his struggle with the Americans.

He visited me first. I suppose I wasn't as busy as Dick Masson. He sat beyond my mosquito net, his swagger-stick that had slaughtered the snake clamped beneath his armpit. He had a gift for me, a half bottle of Scotch which he put on the floor by my bed. Then he took an envelope from his right breast pocket and passed it to me under the net.

'Now, Paper, old horse, this may explain why you were invited here,' he told me.

I opened the envelope and took out a cutting from a glossy magazine. Someone had written '*Life* Magazine September 5, 1942,' across the top of the cutting. It was that photograph of me against the background of unfocused infantry, the one the Americans had taken on the day I got to Moresby. Jimmy – I'm sure it was Jimmy – had underlined some of the caption. It read: 'Maurice Tyson, wounded veteran of World War I, is said to be General McLeod's most favoured journalist. Invited to accompany the General in his inspections of the front, he did not allow his handicap to stand in his way. Here he is seen near

177

Ower's Corner at the beginning of the notorious Kokoda Trail. Behind him allied infantrymen move to reinforce the embattled battalions far up the mountain track.'

The thing aggrieved me so much I couldn't stand having it in my hands. I crushed it, holding it in a wad in my fist. I didn't want it to run around biting my friends, amusing my enemies, doing McLeod's work for him.

Jimmy said, 'It's like one of those pictures in *Cole's Funny Picture Book*. You know. There are seven animals hidden in this picture. Can you spot them? Spot the seven bloody fabrications in that picture. Eh? Eh?'

And in case I'd missed them he began enumerating. Since I was at the beginning of the 'notorious Kokoda Trail,' McLeod must be. By the word *allied*, Zimmer implied, for the sake of the American public, that by miracles of training the General had made his conscript infantry ready for the jungle. And so on. I didn't really listen to anything Jimmy said. I was appalled at what McLeod's apparatus had done with me. Already I was embarked on rehearsals of furious speeches McLeod and Zimmer would cop as soon as I was plane-worthy enough to reach Brisbane.

Yet, in a way, my anger was just a side issue. Worse was that the clipping from *Life* came to me as a rider to the snake's argument. If we had still been on talking terms the serpent would have said, there you are, a digit in the lies of a general, a bloody grace-note, a brush stroke on the edge of the picture, an advertisement for other men. On the edge again, a beast of margin. I know, he'd say, I know.

As I lay listening to Jimmy, I could smell in my sweat the foetid wisdom of the snake.

Jimmy was my source of news and from him I learned that the enemy had taken Iorabaiwa, a native village not thirty miles from the place where I was recuperating. Yet in the evenings Major Pointer would nag me not about the enemy but about the Americans. 'Dick Masson,' said Jimmy, a sweat of approbation along his jawline, 'keeps telling people the right thing. No matter how many troops the Japanese have, every one of them has had to walk from Buna. In a word he believes they've finished themselves. Iorabaiwa's a hollow victory for a hungry army, the way Moscow was for the Corsican. He's twigged the military meaning of it all, the old Dick. What he doesn't understand is the politics. There's a mad streak in the bugger. It explains how he came to marry the most unsuitable girl he could bloody-well find. Well, he's going to have to be bit more flexible than that if Starkey turns up.'

It was curious the way the Japanese counted with Jimmy only in so far as they were a pressure on Johnny's brain and McLeod's and Starkey's. The fall of cities and the savaging of populations were footnotes to Jimmy, or he talked as if they were.

When I left the hospital, they put me in a tent with him, a different tent from the marquee where the snake had found me. I pounded my cot each time before I lay on it, often just so that I could break into Jimmy's stream of agonizing about the Yanks.

Yet I wasn't ready for my escape from the place. The doctor was worried by my nausea and giddiness. Plane travel, he said, was ill-advised. So I hung around and watched younger, sicker men loaded aboard the transports.

On the day Starkey came to Port Moresby, I was sitting behind the netting flap of the tent reading a borrowed novel. I saw Starkey's jeep pull up in the midst of Dick Masson's staff tents and Starkey himself got out, wearing a bush jacket, infantryman's shorts, socks to the knees. He looked exactly like Falstaff doing purgatory as a scoutmaster. There was a sort of antheap scurry among Masson's officers, some emerging from tents, some disappearing into them, all in a manner that appealed to my anti-military warp.

Dick Masson himself did not take part in this flurry, however. Starkey was left standing, blinking around him in the sunlight, waiting for the proper greeting; but Dick Masson did not appear. I saw Starkey lean and say something to the two aides he'd brought with him but still Dick Masson failed to show up. I knew he was in his operations tent and I began to think of going myself to fetch him, just to snap this hiatus.

When it had gone on for the time specified by Masson's sense of grievance, he emerged from his tent without any flinch of surprise and walked without a smile on his face towards Starkey, to whom it was left to reach out a hand.

I could hear fragments of Starkey's sentences and I know from later histories what was said there. 'You got my letter all right, Dick? . . . Big timers thought I ought to come . . . for a time . . . military ignorance . . . simple-minded politicians . . . panic. All they can see . . . the lines on the map . . . always got on, Dick, you and me . . . can make it work all right . . . no lack of confidence in you . . .'

Starkey went on, taking conciliatory pains. A nod, at least a nod, was required from Dick Masson. He did not nod, he did not seem to yield himself to whatever arrangement Mulhall, McLeod and Starkey had arrived at. When he began to talk you could tell he wasn't making any reply to the matters Starkey had raised. He was talking about nothing except domestic arrangements – where Starkey would sleep, dine and wash himself.

Masson pointed to three tents, each about as big as the one Jimmy Pointer shared with me. They had been pitched on a little rise just beyond the staff encampment. I had not noticed them going up this morning, yet they showed me Masson had forewarning of this visit and that his inelastic welcome was a matter of plan, not of impulse. The tents were placed pleasantly against a palm grove – it wasn't their location that made Dick Masson's behaviour look so grudging. It was in part the way he pointed them out, his hand palm up, both the index and the third finger jabbed towards them in an inexact gesture, the way a publican, doing too much profitable business for his own good, points out the closet at the back of the house to the one guest too many.

Night fell before I saw Jimmy Pointer again but I knew he'd be inconsolable. I met him in the mess tent. He was prodding at an army goulash with his fork. 'Paper,' he said, 'the bastard's done it.' He meant McLeod, of course.

'What?' I asked.

'He's expelled poor bloody Starkey from his own country. Moresby, Paper, Moresby's obviously going to be the Capri of McLeod's Roman bloody Empire.' He went on stirring the lees of his dinner with his fork, as if he could read in the gravy the whole sad outcome. 'Have you seen Dick?'

'No.' I had avoided him, in case he thought I'd just been Starkey's forerunner.

Jimmy leaned closer to me and muttered in my ear. 'He thinks Starkey's let him down. He thinks in a word Starkey should have told Johnny and McLeod to go to hell. He thinks Starkey should have said, I trust Dick Masson. He thinks Starkey owes him that. He's got these views about what people owe him – it isn't much he wants. He just wants every bugger to be chivalrous.' Jimmy scalded his mouth with black tea and winced from the painful fragrance of it. 'Jesus, I hope he wakes up to what he's doing to the old bloke.'

Even later, when we were both on our cots, Jimmy kept worrying it out. 'Two bloody generals and only one staff between 'em. Two bloody generals and only one battle to whack up. And the old bloke turning up with just two retainers. Hardly enough to carry his whisky, Paper, and his bloody suppositories.'

I met Dick Masson only once in the next few days. We stumbled on each other in the midst of the compound and he considered me for a while, weighing me, then decided that in this present impasse, this shackling of him and Starkey together, I did not count. 'Feeling better, Maurice?' he asked, but without any smile. I said I was.

'Then you must be looking forward to your escape,' he suggested.

The third morning I woke to see, beyond the mosquito screen, Starkey and Masson confabulating together in the middle of the compound, out in the open, with the brassy morning sun shining in the old man's eyes. As Jimmy had suggested earlier, they *did* have the look of two men squashed together into one role, the two ends of a vaudeville horse. They soon broke up the conference but Starkey went away looking sun-struck, pink and angry.

In that uneasy phase, while Masson and Starkey occupied the same crowded skin, I would see Starkey's aide come down from the hill and ask for this document or that and request that the General be put on the distribution list for all sorts of reports. I would see him go back up the hill with envelopes in his hands, which might be reports or might be complaints from Masson. I'd begun to wonder myself how long Starkey would tolerate being the dowager in the west wing and how long he'd stand the vague discourtesies of the domestic staff. I had a seat on a transport plane to Brisbane for the following Wednesday. I began to think kindly of the horsepowers that would lift me out of all the grievances and niggling in that palm clearing.

Dick Masson must have gone on working all that time. If the work of generals has anything to do with the dirty labours of the children up the track, then Dick must have functioned with passion those five days. The line held on a ridge called Imita. Large patrols went out from there and what a later generation called body-counts were published each night. As the snake said I had, the enemy – at the limit of his impossible line of march – ran willingly to the bullet.

Some time in that deadlock period, Jimmy Pointer and I took the path up the hill to visit Starkey's little encampment. Jimmy, who had been asked up there for a drink, kept insisting I ought to go with him. I don't know why. Perhaps it was friendship. Perhaps he had political reasons for wanting me to be there.

I remember standing outside the lantern range, outside the mosquito flap, while Jimmy went inside to tell the General he'd taken it on himself to bring me. I heard the General say, 'For Jesus' sake, Jimmy. A journalist!'

'I'm sorry,' Jimmy said. 'I thought it was a social visit.'

'It is but . . . we'll talk about larger matters. It's not all going to be women and golf, for Christ's sake.' While the mosquitoes went for my blood, I could hear the old man's aides arranging glasses and bottles.

'What's his name?'

Jimmy told him.

His tone lightened. 'Johnny Mulhall's mate?'

Jimmy told him that was right.

'The snake-bite victim?'

Jimmy admitted that, too. So I was bidden in from the dark. A baize table set with drinks stood under the lantern. There was a generator somewhere that provided electricity for Dick Masson's staff tent but General Starkey had been excluded from its blessings.

The General's aide passed me a Scotch with water in it. 'Wait,' said Starkey, before I could tighten my hold, 'I consider that any man who drinks with me does so in confidence.'

'You don't have to worry about that,' I told him.

So I was given the drink. He kept saying that he knew I treated Johnny Mulhall on the level and he wanted the same. His talk was full of all kinds of old-fashioned, four-square, clubbish phrases like 'on the level.' Meanwhile he drank wildly and stayed sober. Behind his squat, grey moustache there was, most of the time, a knowing, tough, all-forgiving grin. I could see he was a man who set no limits, who devised no tests which, if other people failed them, wrote them off. He was different from Masson. He knew about politics.

He liked Johnny. He said of him, 'Mulhall put it to me straight.'

I was finding out again what I knew already – that Scotch did not go well in the tropics; created, in fact, a kind of internal humidity to match that of the drenched night.

'Do you know Masson?' the General asked me when I was almost asleep.

'A little bit,' I admitted.

'He's a difficult bastard to know, of course,' the General said, pushing his moustache forward, helping me out.

'I know his wife better,' I said.

He laughed at that – a laugh that was meant to be evil and sounded innocent. 'You bloody devil! You and half the stud bulls from Brisbane to Melbourne know the lady.'

In that distempered, toned-down light, just bright enough for me to see the brown dregs of my drink and the major facts of the others' faces, Jimmy winked at me. The General became confused at my lack of a reply. His moustache fluttered again. 'I hope she isn't a close friend of yours,' he murmured. Old Jimmy settled in for some more facial semaphoring. But even I could tell from all this that Starkey knew nothing about Pam Masson and Johnny. The facts had reached East Melbourne, the

Grant girls' muggy kitchen. It was old socialist gossip. It was McLeod's gossip, too. Yet, by some amazing means, it was not yet the talk of Victoria Barracks or of the grand bourgeoisie of Toorak.

'She's beautiful,' Starkey murmured. 'But quite strange. Bit of a red-ragger. So I'm told.'

After they'd got into the second bottle of gin, Jimmy had the chance to pretend he was emboldened by booze to speak out for fraternal reasons, for brother Starkey's sake.

'What I'd do, sir,' he told the General, 'if you'll forgive me ... what I'd do and I'd do it bloody quick, too ... is get your staff up here.'

Starkey said, 'Why in the hell? All that crowd?'

Jimmy put on a sort of filial face. 'You know,' he said, sketching military hierarchies with his hand in the damp air. 'So you won't end up reduced to just another general in the field, Ted ... I can call you Ted?'

I saw the venous purple of the General's upper cheeks spread down past his mouth. 'Masson said something like that today, by letter, mark you, not face to face. I hope to Christ, Jimmy, you aren't Masson's bloody runner, Masson's bum-boy, eh? Eh?'

Jimmy closed one eye, 'I'm nobody's runner, general.'

The General puffed a bit, diffusing his rage, his blood returning to its proper channels, 'This is pro tem, Jimmy.' He waved towards the canvassed darkness. 'This is a visit. The politicians ... other people, too ... they'll get over their bloody spasms. All they need is an advance to restore their souls. They'll bloody well get an advance, soon enough.'

His tongue flicked out over his lower lip, on it the complex savour of Melbourne, the city where his wife and headquarters waited for him, the city where women and waiters favoured him. He turned to me, believing somehow I *was* a friend of Masson's. 'Doesn't he understand I had to come? I'll tell you this, there's no more pathetic being than a general sacked in mid-conflict. He drags off home to his wife and you can see in the poor sod's eyes the sentences that are going to go in his memoirs. Which no bastard will read, anyhow, because no one reads books by blokes who get the sack! But you can see the compositors are

184

already typesetting the sentences in his bloody brain, the accusations. He'll say that later generals succeeded because of *his* planning. And he's probably halfway right. But what does it bloody well matter? He's a leper. Well, I don't intend to go that way. No fear I don't, Paper. And someone ought to warn Masson against doing so.'

He coughed then, shifted his buttocks and so shifted to a higher key of anger. 'At the moment I wouldn't mind being what my friend Jimmy calls "just another general in the bloody field". But even if I wanted to sink so low, I couldn't. I don't get any operational reports from Masson. I send Les here' (he pointed to an aide) 'down the hill like a bloody message boy from the Water Board to remind them to put me on the distribution list. But I've been given nothing. Not yesterday's situation report. Not today's battle order.' He chewed wildly at the linings of his jaws. 'He must know I'll have to do something. Is he obdurate? Eh Tyson, is he obdurate?'

He sat back and eased the rancour with a mouthful of gin. 'At least,' he said, holding up a stubby fist, 'he's not bloody stupid. He knows I'm staying *this* - my hand.'

I covered my eyes, some of the old snake-bite panic arising in me. 'I can't talk to him. It wouldn't work.'

'Oh? It's just I heard people say you influence John Mulhall.'

'No, no. That's just gossip.' I wondered would the snake come in my sleep and chastise me for denying it.

I heard the old man sigh. 'All right. It's all up to my own bloody wisdom.'

I came to my last Moresby dawn as sweetly as a schoolboy wakes to the last morning of term. It was the clamour of jungle birds that woke me at an hour when beyond the mosquito flap, the trucks in the mauve dust looked like honest, grazing beasts.

Struggling up I saw Jimmy Pointer seated on the end of his bed, in uniform except for gaiters and boots, fingering a webbing belt. His shirt was marred with patches of sweat. He looked to me as if he'd been perched there, watchful, all the night.

Though he didn't look at me, he could tell I'd woken. As soon as I'd stretched, he began talking. 'Starkey's aide turned up . . .' He looked at his watch. '. . . Hour and a quarter ago now. Had a wireless operator with him, not one of Masson's boys, another one he must have found somewhere. They were in the radio tent a bloody age.' He turned his eyes on me. The pleasant, florid, world-beating face had taken on creases from keeping watch over generals. The seams of his face glittered with sweat.

'What does it mean, Paper?' he asked me. 'They've got a meeting at nine. And Starkey nicks down here and sends off transmissions before the sparrows are up. What does it mean?'

I said it might be business, that Starkey had interests in companies.

At breakfast Jimmy played with his food again, chewing papaya and drinking tea - no proper breakfast for a big man.

We watched Masson's aides putting documents and water on a table in the midst of the clearing. A banyan tree standing there threw shade and dropped pods across the table top. We saw Starkey arrive, walking at a measured pace lest he arrive before Masson. We saw Masson emerge from his tent and adjust his stride so that he reached his chair, putting a hand on it, the instant Starkey claimed his. It all looked like an Asian ritual to do with 'face.' I was reminded of the prisoners Jimmy and I had seen emerge from the track and group at the road head just yesterday. Ancient young Asian faces with overgrown hair, knights who had failed to become corpses. Cramped with dysentery, walking with the dandy gait of cruel dengue. They would have understood a ceremony like this.

Jimmy and I stuck in the mess-tent, pretending to watch the tan surface of our tea but spectating in fact. Masson handed the old General a folder; it was put aside without being looked at. Starkey joined his hands and settled himself into a kind of straight-talking pose, the sort of posture that reminded me he'd begun life as a schoolmaster. I could hear nothing and lost interest but Jimmy kept watching, gauging the gestures, his own lips moving sometimes like a lip-reader's.

Then he grabbed my wrist. 'Oh Jesus, Paper,' he said. 'It's a serious business.'

'Well?' I said.

'Greece,' said Jimmy, not taking his eyes off the game. 'Dick's ripping into Starkey about Greece. You know. About the fact they fled. It's lunacy. He should never, never bring that up. Not here . . .'

'You've just got to dramatize, Jimmy,' I told him. 'No bloody help for it, is there?'

Jimmy said, 'He'd only raise the matter if he'd done his lolly, old dig, lost his composure . . .'

I studied Masson more. He didn't seem to me to be uncontrolled. He was throwing in a little emphasis, yes, but there was no sign of temper. I began to laugh.

'You know everything about those buggers, don't you? They're like racehorses to you, Jimmy; they're like greyhounds are to a Redfern boilermaker . . .'

But though I spoke to him the way you talk to any *aficionado*, to those people, for example, who won't let you forget they know the first words the tenor utters in the second act of *Cosi Fan Tutte*, he did not laugh with me. He stopped wincing, sat up straight, drained his tea.

'That's it, Paper,' he told me. 'That's the issue.'

'What issue?'

He stared at me. 'Dick Masson's just got sacked.'

I looked at the table again. Was the banyan shade such a filter that it had leached out the anger of the scene? The two generals kept talking together, like two sober men working in tandem.

'No,' I said.

'I'm not going to argue with you,' he told me loudly, like a man speaking up once the curtain's come down. 'McLeod's won, Starkey's stuck here, Masson's finished. We're behind, Paper. *Behind*!' He meant in some race. He stood up from the table and I could not ignore the unusual resignation on his face.

I was glad to get away from him. I went back to my tent, sat on the cot beside my luggage, my old portmanteau with its bulging strap. I would be taken to the airport at noon. A sated tourist, I did not even want to look out at the balmy scene beyond the flaps. Jimmy Pointer joined me, saying nothing, throwing his gear into a kit bag. 'I went and saw the transport officer. There'll be plenty of room on the plane back to Brisbane. The others' (he meant the Americans) 'are no doubt flying up a few companies of ice-cream machine mechanics to celebrate their victory.' He yawned. 'There'll be room to stretch out on the way home.'

'You're going home?' I asked him.

'It's all over here.'

'Are you serious?'

'Step out into the sunlight, Mr Tyson,' he suggested. 'Ask the operations officer what his new orders are. He'll tell you. Starkey's taken over. Dick's history. Bloody sad.'

He was not fully packed when Masson turned up in the tent without announcing himself. I was pleased he did not look at me. He watched Jimmy Pointer, who ignored him. 'Suppose you heard, Jimmy?' said Masson.

'Bloody tragic,' Jimmy mumbled. 'But of course, foreseen. By some of us anyhow.'

'Huh,' said Masson and shook his head. 'He'll take over my staff. A good staff, that crowd.'

Jimmy said nothing. He squeezed this morning's moisture out of his shaving brush and pushed it into his kit. Then he cleaned the subtle blade of his razor. Dick Masson bunched his lips, considering the blade from a distance. 'You're just about the only person here who's got any real influence, Jimmy,' he muttered. He was going to say, you're welcome to go and mediate with the old man.

But Jimmy wouldn't let him get that far. 'I want to keep the influence I've got, Dick,' he murmured. 'You'd understand that.'

I kept averting my eyes but I was fascinated by Jimmy most of all. To know where people get it from – that infallible sense of when to abandon the dying beast, the doomed meat.

Anyhow, Masson nodded. His right hand fluttered on the upper leg of his trousers, as if in memory of some piano phrase, more Chopin than ragtime. As doomed meat, I thought, he knew how to perish with some grandeur. I could see he was going to discomfit Johnny's ministers, and probably Johnny himself, and they would all cringe when they knew he was waiting in their ante-rooms.

It was Masson's calmness that really seemed to get Jimmy going. He said, 'Starkey tells me he didn't get any intelligence reports. Not until one o'clock in the bloody morning. One o'clock, Dick, it's a bloody despicable hour . . .'

In an off-handed way, Dick Masson explained himself. His intelligence men had had a crowd of prisoners to interview, he said. Even from those mute faces, it seemed, they got more news than could be fitted into the usual daily report. He himself had not received the document until after midnight. 'Not that the report's a reason, Jimmy,' he said. 'The report's no reason . . .!'

'No,' Jimmy said. 'But it's a bloody bottler of a pretext, old friend. Did you, for example, send anyone up the hill to tell the old bugger not to wait up? Did you let him know the thing would be waiting by his cot-side with his morning tea? Did you bother to do that?'

There was an unyielding half-cough down in Masson's throat. 'It isn't my job to explain small operational delays,' he said.

'You don't *have* any job. Starkey's been squeezed into your job. We are all being smothered by the Monroe bloody Doctrine, mate, colonized, emasculated, euchred. Don't talk to me about what your bloody job is!'

Masson showed his teeth, the fiercest gesture of anger he'd been guilty of all morning. He said, 'Don't you believe, Jimmy, for a second that it's all over. It would be a mistake, my friend, to go over to Starkey once and for all.'

'I've got no personal preferences, you know that,' Jimmy told him. 'But a man has to be living before you can form an alliance with him, mate. A man's got to be kicking . . .'

The deposed General's tongue lashed about against his lips, a demonstration of animate existence. 'I wanted to remind you that John Mulhall has to be spoken to yet,' he said.

I thought of the ring-in operator transmitting Starkey's condemnation of Masson out into the silken tropic night. I imagined the volley of censure arching up over Queensland, dropping down towards Johnny's mute senses, embayed as they might then have been in the arms of Mrs Masson. If the idea of that drained Jimmy's petulance a little and made me flinch, it didn't seem to give Masson any pain.

He turned to the door, still looking like a proprietor, a man with rights in the staff, in the battle, certainly in this modest bit of tenting. I was as pleased to see him go as people sometimes are when a cripple removes himself. Yet he did not go the whole way. He turned in the door, a hand lightly on the pole. 'Could you squeeze up a bit, Paper, d'you think, and make room for me on the plane?'

'Too right,' I said in a hurry. 'I hear it's going back pretty well empty.'

'No, it's not.' Masson shook his head. 'It'll be full of the wounded.'

Part Three/Chapter One

'The Colonel will speak to you, Mr Tyson,' a corporal told me.
He extended the telephone towards my grasp. I took it without
thanks.

'Hello,' I said into it. 'Is that Zimmer? Good. I wanted to pro-
test in the strongest terms about the lie that went under my
photograph. You know what photograph. You know what lie.
The lie that the General was ever in New Guinea.'

The corporal took no notice of me, went on with his paper-
work. Behind me, officers traversed the lobby with praetorian
tread. They took no notice of me, either. This was McLeod's
headquarters. Queen St, Brisbane, an insurance building and,
aptly enough, confidence radiated from the sixth or seventh floor
– whichever the General occupied – down to the ground floor
juniors who moved around me in nifty uniforms – files and
attaché cases carried under arm – and waited for the lift to the
higher levels.

I, however, lacking their certainty, their crispness, had not got
beyond this corporal just inside the front door.

'Lies?' said Zimmer, as if the word were a piece of confusing
colonial dialect. 'Listen, I wish I could invite you up to talk
about it. *Lies*. I mean, Mr Tyson, you're a working journalist.'
It was the first time I'd ever heard *that* little exotic. 'You know

I'm not responsible if some caption-writer – Stateside you understand – incorporates some fanciful data in his copy.'

'You could get him to print a retraction,' I said.

'Would such a thing be in the public interest, Tyson? You tell me?' There was a pause but I couldn't frame the words. For I knew I should myself have used his phrase, 'fanciful data'. Primitive words like 'lies' had no purchase on his copywriter's sensitivities. I have seen them tread over my horizon since, the euphemizing front-men who window-dress the dirty work of governments and corporations. I imagine them all as spawned without sex, atmospherically, by Zimmer.

He said, 'You might like to know, Tyson. Response to the picture itself has been excellent.'

'Whose response?' I asked.

'The Republican Party's in the first instance.'

'But he told me he doesn't covet the throne.'

'If you mean the presidency, Tyson . . . well, neither he does. It doesn't mean that various party wheels don't try to contact the General through me . . .'

I rocked on my crutches, grinding the tips into the linoleum beside the desk. Many floors above me, Zimmer seemed surprised by my vehemence. I said, 'If I let everyone know about this lie of yours . . . what would the Republican bloody Party think then, eh? How do you bloody dare to use me as a stage prop? I was bitten by a snake, I could have died. For the sake of gilding McLeod's bloody lily.'

'Um,' he said. You could just about hear the exact nodding of his head. 'We heard about your snake bite. Let me say this. The General was very pleased to hear you'd come out of your coma.'

The corporal at the desk had now raised his eyes to me. I was getting out of order and fingers whose click would bring armed guards were poised. But my affliction inhibited him.

'I want to see the General,' I told Zimmer.

'Not today, Tyson, not possible, much as I'm sure he'd like the chance to meet you again.'

'I want to see him, Zimmer, for Christ's sake!'

'But he has to debrief General Masson. You know. The one who's failed to optimize the Moresby situation . . . '

I gave it up and returned to Canberra, slowly, as the doctors had suggested, by train. My hand was raised to caress the air as I dismounted from my carriage in the late afternoon. Winds still blew from the Alps as they had when I left but carried on their breath now the redolence of spores, of spring sap. There was no one to meet me, no limousine from the American Embassy. It seemed I'd fulfilled my task by McLeod.

At the Senate entrance, though, one of the parliamentary attendants was waiting and the hot flushes of homecoming swept over me. At once I wanted to reach Millie. But Mr Mulhall, the attendant said, wished to know as soon as I got home. I was helped to my office. In the light of my concluded journey, of the lecturings, of the snake, of Jimmy Pointer's visions, the furniture and fittings in that room – once the lights were switched on – looked naïve, the way the bedroom you had as a boy does when you return to it a man. But it was not so much the office that had altered. It was the furniture of my eye, the appurtenances of the seeing orb, that had changed.

I called Millie and felt disappointed when we agreed – because of the hour – to meet the next morning. Her voice was full of that terrible liquid chastisement, as if she believed as the snake did that I went looking for my disasters.

I sat around. Johnny didn't come in till late. I was all at once so pleased to see him that I failed to do a comparison job on him, the way I had with my office and its contents. Within twenty seconds his lanky, strolling shape, his lips and hands with their bright-boy-of-the-family softness, his askew eyes, had all grown familiar again, elements taken as read. I found with relief that in spite of all the whisperings of the snake I liked the bugger.

He quizzed me about the bite, the coma, my resultant health. But it was his own colour that looked poor.

When I mentioned it, he touched his chest negligently with two fingers. 'No. A few twinges, Paper. The last couple of days.'

193

'What sort of twinges?' I asked.

'Ah,' he said, pretending to have forgotten the name of his disease in the exact tone that gunnery captain at Milne Bay had pretended to forget the name of his relationship to the dead. 'Ah,' he said, 'bit of angina. You know. Bugger of a thing. Sins of my youth, eh, Paper?'

Masson lay at the bottom of all our talk and in the end broke the surface.

'Flew back with him?' Johnny asked all at once.

'Yes.'

'Didn't waste time leaving the scene, did he?'

'No. He didn't.'

'Roaring and ranting, eh?'

'No. Cool. And bloody intractable.'

'Oh, hell,' said Johnny.

For a while he became quiet, a burst of acid from his rushed dinner soured his lips. He said, 'Paper, I want to enunciate a principle. Between you and me. No apology. Just a principle. Apart, of course, from the damn principle that I've got power anyhow over Starkey and Masson. The principle is that I refuse to get rid of a commander-in-chief at the height of the battle. Flat!'

'Battle,' I repeated, nodding, tasting the novelty of the word. The idea of the battle was a different thing here, in the gumnut capital, than it had been up there. Up at Masson's late headquarters it had been a manageable enterprise proceeding with some sweat and danger up the track but certain to return dividends. Here in the Senate wing it was a larger beast, less definable, less amenable to human intention than it had seemed to be in the clearing in the kunai.

'And there's the corollary to that principle,' Johnny told me. 'If the commander-in-chief sacks someone at the height of the said battle, in circumstances where I have to choose between the commander-in-chief *and* the someone, then I go with the commander-in-chief, I stick with Starkey.'

The axiom out, Johnny sat on my desk in the accustomed unrestful way. 'Of course,' he told me, 'if he was going to sack anyone . . .'

Unlike Major Pointer, Johnny did not see McLeod as a wilful party to the tragedy. He talked as if Masson's fall was an act of God, set up by unthinking forces. I could see the gritty weariness of his eyes. It wasn't a time to start telling him of plots.

Then he murmured, 'I haven't heard from Pam yet.' He yawned. 'I wouldn't be the full quid if I didn't expect some trouble from that quarter.' He loked fair at me, in a way he generally reserved only for audiences. 'You know, Paper, even in a marriage that's been declared dead, you get old loyalties resurrecting themselves. Sour marriages have a pretty good track record over sweet affairs . . .' He coughed and switched off his gaze. 'By the way,' he said, as if proving his theorem, 'Ada's coming over from Adelaide on Tuesday.'

He didn't tell me more than that before he went. Whether she'd travel on the basis of information received, to mend her fences, or whether she meant to make another dutiful stab at performing the duties of a prime minister's wife (whatever these might be), Johnny left me to consider. The usual delicacy of our friendship, as well, prevented me from asking questions like that.

One afternoon, soon after my return, Artie Thorn ambushed me in a corridor of the Branch Office. It was while I was still full of the flatulence of homecoming, of finding that not even those close to me were interested – at the pitch I expected – in my travels. I had been passing along the hallway on the Opposition side of the Branch Office. At the doorway of the parliamentary library I heard a wheeze, a hand came down on my shoulder. 'Maurice,' I heard.

I saw his old-fashioned legal suit, the large, pale, well-made face, a sort of dried froth on the lower lip, product of his heart trouble, of his uneven breathing. 'Maurice, I hear you were *bitten!*'

I told him about it in the usual terms. In regard to snake bite, I had towards outsiders the initiate's contempt for the layman. But I knew he'd been stricken, too. While I was away in

Moresby his wife had died. He had the bereft look of the survivor of a long marriage.

When I offered my sympathy, there was a smirk of pain on his lips. 'Come,' he said, 'come in here.'

He began dragging me through the varnished library doors, putting his own large shoulder to the heavy hardwood frame. The force he put into it, in spite of his low ration of breath, reminded me by contrast of the time we had shared a car to Goulburn and he'd sat up straight in his straight collar and kept his fist on the door handle all the time. I'd mentioned to him the danger that he'd slip the lock and spill himself out across the red gravel. 'Maurice,' he'd told me, 'I wasn't made for this age. The idea of an impact. At this speed . . .'

Inside the library he led me to one of the semi-circular bays of red reference books. He fussed me into a seat. He looked to left and right, checking on the insulation provided by old leather, old documents. Even stooping, he towered over me.

He said, 'Maurice, it was a painful business. A bowel growth.' He was speaking of his wife. 'In the end there wasn't anything for it but large doses of morphia. When you consider how sharp and true her mind was . . .' He gave a little snort of grief. 'I remember the last afternoon I had a good talk with her. She was talking about John Mulhall. She remembered him. You know. From the days of the Yarra Bank, the great fight against Hughes. Johnny was a fairly romantic figure, you know. A sort of young Lochinvar of the anti-conscriptionists . . .'

'I know,' I told him. The Grant girls had made that clear.

'These days,' he said, '. . . well, she wasn't encouraged by his recent behaviour. Neither, I have to say, am I.'

He showed me now that the loss of his wife hadn't slowed down his courtroom reflexes. He reached for a bound copy of *Hansard*, finding it just about as readily as if he'd placed it before he met me and had practised the movement. He pushed it in front of my eyes. It was opened to a 1940 debate on conscription. 'Read that,' he told me.

He joined his hands, a courtroom gesture.

I could just about – in spite of his recent loss – have reached out and dragged his hands apart, the mannerism – on top of having *Hansard* forced on me – was so annoying. Artie niggled at everyone, even Tony Hamish. 'It's the middle class who get socialism in it's deadliest form,' Tony had said once. 'It's not so much the bloody workers, not incurable cases like Johnny or Eddie Hoare. It's buggers like Artie Thorn.'

Artie had had the same good education as Tony Hamish – Melbourne Grammar, Arts and Law at the university. Maybe it was the fact that his mother had to give singing lessons to pay his school fees that had acted as the trigger. Maybe the airy remark made by a squatter's son – 'Thorn's old lady gives music lessons!' – made him into what Tony thought of as a class traitor. The trouble was that among his Labor colleagues he never behaved like a class traitor. He always wore his university regalia, whenever he could, embarrassing his un-degreed brothers in processions or on visits to bush high schools. I think some of them had even come to resent his parliamentary uniform, too: the dark suits and vests and butterfly collars. Seen from the Press Gallery, among other parliamentarians he looked like an English remittance man wandered into the House without warning and given second-class seating on the back-benches of the proletarian party, among people with whom he had nothing in common.

The year before, the good Irish Catholics of the Party Executive in Victoria had expelled him from the Labor Party for going to meetings of a body called the Australia-Russia Friendship Society, the group which – in another city and another State – Mrs Masson favoured. Artie had at the time put on the plumage of martyrs. 'If it is a choice between the Party and the Society, I must choose the Society,' he'd told the Melbourne Press. In private, he told people he trusted – the Grants in East Melbourne, perhaps even John Mulhall in Canberra – that the Irish Catholics in Victoria, with their bent towards forgiving such a good friend of the Pope as Franco, were sending the Party away from its natural friends into the arms of its natural enemies.

Though he was an independent now he sat in the midst of his old Party. His speeches were rich with phrases implying his solitary posture. 'If it were my last act as a Member of this Parliament, I would oppose . . .' 'It is my profoundest conviction . . .'

197

'I would defend this principle against all the expediency of party, all the malice of special interest . . .'

Artie was, therefore, the voice of conscience lost, the ghost at Johnny's feast, and he'd have been all the more numinous a presence if you hadn't been able to see him straining a bit at the role.

Having got me riled, he all at once slumped, his breath escaped him, his eyes filled. 'She said to me, the last afternoon she was clear . . . she said, you know, Arthur, we've lost him.'

'Lost him?' I said. 'Who owns him, then? The girl? Eh? The girl?'

'No.' He shook his head and waved a hand. 'I know the girl. She's been in the chair the dozen times or more that I've spoken to the Society in Sydney.' He wanted to get off the question of Mrs Masson; she didn't touch the true nature of Johnny's bondage.

He said, 'The truth is, Maurice, the scales have fallen from my eyes since that was said. Since she said, we've lost him, Arthur. I read the signs now I did not dare read in the past. If you'll just look at this debate . . .' He urged the open *Hansard* on me again. 'Tony Hamish argues herein to conscript youth for the northern hemisphere. Johnny speaks against it. But on what grounds? He says there aren't the means to train them. He says that soldier's pay isn't enough. That the soldier's wife gets three bob a day, which doesn't pay the rent, and the soldier's child, he gets a shilling a day, which is the rate the State fixes for the upkeep of indigent children. You see, Maurice, he argues like a trade union official. He doesn't argue for principle . . . he argues over relative justice, over crusts of bread, Maurice, not even the whole loaf . . . Once, Paper, once . . . he wanted the whole loaf.'

I made a half-yawning remark about how arguments like that sometimes do better on the floor of the House. He didn't seem to hear me. I was reminded of the Browning poem we had beaten into us at Nottingham Public, all the children of Nulla, five to thirteen years, hammering it out in a rhythm like that of a north coast mail train. The poem that goes, 'Just for a handful of silver he left us/Just for a riband to stick in his coat.' And that ends with the type of murderous forgiveness Artie would have been only too pleased to extend to Johnny. 'Then let him receive the new knowledge and wait us/Pardoned in heaven, the first by the throne.'

Artie said, 'I remember the day in 1916. When old Billy Hughes said the time had come to conscript the young. For that obscene war, Maurice. There was Johnny and Hilder and Davis and myself, and we all went walking in Fitzroy Gardens, arguing about what should be done. Davis is dead now, so you only have *my* word. It was dusk, I remember. Poor Johnny had just been released from a drying-out hospital called Lara and this idea of Billy Hughes seemed to put him into a profound depression. Well, perhaps we could normally have brought him round by sitting with him in a pub. But that was out of the question that evening, with Johnny. What I noticed then, Maurice, was how supine he was. We had to argue him round. And his despair – it was very strange. He said he was going to volunteer in the morning, he hoped to Christ they'd take him, even though he was a reformed drunkard. He kept on saying such things as, it's no good, the country can't be separated from its pernicious origins, the nation isn't perfectible.

'Davis and Hilder and I had to stay out in the park with him till three o'clock in the morning. And me with a full day of court the next day. We had to remind him of such things as the Easter uprising in Dublin. Could he countenance the Australian conscripts be used to put down people's honest uprisings and just reactions? Did he really, in despair at the world's evil, accept the idea of himself, Private John Mulhall, in an imperialist army, compelling his cousins in the streets of Dublin, his fellow workers in other streets, in other cities?

'And that's how he became a leader in the fight against Billy Hughes, Maurice. You see, to bolster him, we founded the anticonscription congress right there, on a park bench, and we made him the secretary. And then we took him to a Melbourne teashop at dawn, and his blood was screaming for whisky, but he had a reason not to take any – he was secretary of the cause which we'd just about imposed on him. So you see, Maurice, it's just like this.' He tapped the copy of *Hansard*. 'It wasn't principle so much. It was a sort of drying-out cure. Mind you, I hate to talk like this . . .'

I considered my hands, whether to lose my temper with the righteous old bugger, in spite of his impaired breathing and the death of his missus.

I said, 'I think that's the difference between Johnny and you, Artie. Johnny's the practical politician . . .'

'And what am I?'

'Well, you know Artie. You're the prophet Moses.'

He closed his eyes. He didn't like my saying that.

'I would rather a man *did* kill himself with grog,' he told me, 'than make a present to McLeod of this nation's youth . . .'

Once more he checked the walls of our bunker of old *Hansards* and *Commonwealth Year Books*. 'I don't say these things to everyone. I'd like to see John Mulhall go back to old principles. And that's all I want.'

'And what about me?' I asked. 'Do you want me to remind him of his boyhood, do you? Of his whisky youth, eh? Is that it?'

He surprised me by closing his eyes, by going soft, his chest seeming to collapse. He said, 'I think you could do worse, Maurice. Much worse, son.'

'How did you find out?' I asked him. 'About the girl and Johnny?'

'The Society. It's one of those items that are passed around. Carefully. As something that has to be kept quiet. Not as gossip.'

'Oh, no,' I said. 'Not as gossip!'

He explained there was a housewife Pamela Masson was pretty close to in the Society. That might have been the source. But again the shaking of the head – he wasn't very interested in the question. Yet he'd taken the trouble to inform the Grants.

As he put the *Hansard* away on its shelf, I dreaded that he'd give me trouble, set to recruiting me in earnest. Instead he just thanked me for my time, nodded, and moved down the length of the library like a scholar looking for more solid provender.

Oh, Artie, I just about muttered. You'll see the coming of the anti-Christ all right. And soon. And then it'll all be over for you. Wife. Cause. The works.

Chapter Two

I said nothing to Johnny about Artie Thorn's concern for his soul. It must have been a foul enough week for Johnny, even without appeals of conscience from old friends. On a sharp spring day, Masson arrived at the Branch Office and, as my diary says, 'talked *in camera* to the War Cabinet.' But Pam Masson did not appear, did not arrive, at a time of her choosing, on the Sydney train and lead a quiet, waiting life in Millie's back room.

None of us in the Press Gallery heard any hard news about this *in camera* meeting, my diary notes. Even in his memoirs years later – memoirs marked by the tone Starkey had predicted – all Masson says is that Johnny had assured him that day that another command would be found for him. An air of pained discretion hung over the event.

But, in a more intimate sense, I already knew something of that meeting. Johnny, flanked by his War Cabinet, by Eddie Hoare, by McHenry, Darcey and the others, a tribe of ill-assorted Celts, and – on the far side of the table – Masson the patrician General. And Johnny hampered, wanting to ask after the man's wife, wondering whether there was a gloss of marital triumph in the sheen of Masson's Sam Browne belt, in the wronged composure of the man's green eyes.

General Masson went home to Sydney without, of course, visiting me over in the Senate wing and giving me any word.

Then, in the Press that weekend, there appeared a picture of the General and his wife rigging a dinghy on a beach at Middle Harbour. It was a picture which the censor should not have passed. The paper knew what it was doing in wilfully printing it. It wanted to push Johnny into making the sacking of the General public. This General has been reduced to rigging dinghies on a Sydney beach! That's what the winsome snap really meant.

The Saturday paper originated in Melbourne and was therefore not thrown on to Millie's front garden until dawn on Sunday morning. Millie found the picture first. No fool, she understood at once why the paper would go to the trouble of getting from another city a photograph of the Massons.

But that wasn't as important to her as the picture's human meaning. She said, 'Our girl's gone back to him.'

'No.' I said. 'She can't live with Masson. What's happened is, she's left Johnny.'

I should have been pleased, the snake would have desired me to be. She's wide open now. I could have decided, she's not one man's or another's. But I grew depressed instead. Abandoning Johnny, she was abandoning me.

Millie was bathing herself when Johnny rang. I knew it was Johnny. His driver, Reg Whelan, would have brought the papers with him when he collected Johnny at the Lodge. Johnny always scanned those papers at a hectic rate on the way to the House, the way old journalists get used to doing, no slow rustle, the pages being whipped back, the eye moving at a rate you could believe would smudge the ink. Then, late in the paper, he would have come to the handsome picture and Reg would have glanced in the mirror and wondered why that noise - like a Greek wrapping fish - had ceased.

After that there would be no one Johnny could speak to except Millie and me.

I don't know why I wanted to forestall Millie from answering the phone. But I strained upwards on my false leg, I lunged for my crutches. I called, 'Don't worry, I can get it,' and so on, just to prevent Millie rising in the bath water. I won the uncontested race to the telephone. Her bathroom door stayed shut.

'Paper.'

'Johnny.'

'Seen the Melbourne rag?'

'Ah, yes.'

'They . . . ah . . . they look pretty conjugal, don't they?'

'People do. If you can't look conjugal for a bloody photographer, what *can* you manage?'

He laughed in a sapless way. His voice was thin, desperate but staunchly conversational. 'Well, what's happening, Paper, eh? What's the word, eh? On that woman?'

'I don't know, Johnny.' I found I was choking down the brotherly urge to offer to find out.

'Does Millie hear from her? Could I speak with Millie?'

'No, no, Johnny. Millie's heard nothing.'

'I can tell,' he said, 'it's no use pushing a woman like that. With Ada, I could pull out the stops, rush things, I could play intellectual bloody games in my letters, you know, Paper. Blinding the poor bloody girl with science. You can't do that sort of thing with this one. Not with Pamela. Christ, no.'

I heard the sound of Millie shifting in her bath and shifting again and then settling. The sweet lapping of the settling water.

Johnny said, 'D'you think Millie could call her? A bugger to get through to Sydney, I admit that! But I thought that perhaps she could call from the shop – it's Monday, you know. No do's on Monday, eh? Especially not under John Mulhall's Cromwellian government. Therefore no one to buy dresses. On a Monday.' He laughed at the image of himself as a killjoy. 'I don't want to put Millie on the level of a spy . . .'

Ada Mulhall's train would have left Adelaide about dawn. By now it would be dawdling towards Bordertown. Australia Felix would lie ahead of her. She might have a compartment of her own in which to think, though for a few bob conductors always let tired soldiers into the first-class corridors, and she would hear young militiamen talking, belching and dossing beyond the door. So Ada might ask them in, grow motherly with them, thinking of Kevin. And the thousand villages and pastures standing between her and the capital would fly by in quick order.

It came down to this. Johnny needed to know about Pam Masson. So that he could get together a face to present to Ada at the door of the Lodge.

'It's all right, Johnny,' I told him. 'Millie wouldn't mind.'

I didn't know whether to be angry or flattered that he thought news could pass from Pam Masson to Millie to me without any distortion. Did he have the right to believe I wouldn't bend or break or subvert the tidings, that I wouldn't at least put spin on the ball?

Millie came out at last, her face pink from the humidity of the bath. I told her the truth, that it had been Johnny, that he hadn't even seen the picture as an assault on Starkey and the politicians who stood behind Starkey. All he'd talked about, I said, was what in the hell Pam Masson was signalling as she put one long hand around a shroud and smiled her broad, unschooled smile for the camera.

When I suggested that Millie might care to ring Pam Masson today, she got peevish.

'I've got my tax, Maurice, and a pile of ticketing.' She flinched at the idea of the sharp ticketing pins. She was always waving her hand about and swearing when they went into the pad of her thumb. 'You need hours, Maurice, hanging on, listening to all those howls and whistles on the line.' She frowned. 'And in the end, she's just as likely to be out.'

'Even if she is,' I said, 'that's some sort of message.'

Through the parlous morning, Millie drove me towards the Branch Office in her Austin. Snow wind from Cooma blurred the ghost gums, yet there was a bite to the sun through the window glass. I thought, the old capital's come through another season.

I knew that the singers had been expelled from Milne Bay. Some sources in the Army Department had told me that in the weeping forests, strewn among stinking lilies, the profuse dead of the enemy held up Starkey's vanguard at the approaches to Nauro, halfway over the mountains. I did not know – because

McLeod sat on the knowledge – of the ships sunk in the Solomons or of what you could only call the panache of General Hyakutake's ideas on Guadalcanal.

To my ignorant eyes, our pastoral city shone with a sort of permanence in the light of early spring. And at the least Johnny need never return to that quiet grinning panic he'd let me see on Singapore night, and from which McLeod and Mrs Masson had lifted him.

Anyhow, Millie let me off at the Branch Office and drove away, maintaining her silence, thinking of tax and credit and the Sydney supply houses.

She'd overstated the hardships of calling Sydney. I waited not much more than half an hour to be connected to Pam Masson's number. I heard the operator tell her it was Canberra calling. She must have believed it was Johnny.

'Paper,' I told her, as soon as the operator had got out of the way.

She asked how I was, being exhaustive about it. She believed I'd had all kinds of adventures. She would have talked about snakes and liana vines through three expensive minutes if I had let her.

I said, 'Listen, love. Johnny's wondering what's going on. So am I, in my way. And Millie.'

'So you're calling for him,' she stated.

There was that imputation in her voice that reminded me of the snake. I said, 'I'm calling on my own bat, Pamela.'

All the risk of such an intrepid statement went for nothing, all the perverse courage. She got angry all at once but even that was independent of me. 'I suppose the question is whether I'll ever go to bed with Johnny Mulhall again? Is it?'

'I suppose it is.'

'Paper, never fall in love with anyone who has any power. You and Millie are so damn lucky.'

'Oh yeah,' I said. 'Because we have no power. Because we're on the bloody margin.' I was, of course, quoting my old serpentine mate. His pernicious talk had coloured everything. I said, 'You never had anything to do in your life with any bloke who wasn't at the centre or bloody heading for it. For a girl who never got the Leaving Certificate, you've done pretty well with the blokes you've picked . . .'

She said, 'Don't try that rot with me, Paper. Do beautiful women go for important men or do important men go for beautiful women? And if we knew the answer, what would we know?'

Meanly, I inquired, 'So we accept we're beautiful, then?'

'I mightn't have been to a good school,' she told me. 'But I can tell if I'm beautiful or not.'

'Yes,' I nodded. 'You're beautiful. So let's get off the subject.'

'Paper,' she whispered, 'we're a pair of idiots, eh?' She'd picked up the Australian intonation since her English girlhood. 'But does he want me there, arguing with him half the night? Because I tell you, Paper, it'd be Kilkenny cats.' She kept a silence that was in fact full of a sort of projected brawl with Johnny. 'I can't tell you how angry I am, Paper. A man of John's stature . . . just giving way to McLeod like that. Well, it could be excused as military ignorance. But then Starkey . . . Assassination, Paper. Do you realise it was assassination you witnessed in Moresby, the favourite assassination that old men carry out, the assassination of the talented young? You were there, after all. What did *you* think you were seeing?'

I said, 'It was hard to see it as a straight-out knife job. From the second Starkey turned up . . . your bloke was hurt, then he went on hurting himself. Honest, Pamela. If it was assassination, it was bloody subtle.'

I told her about Jimmy Pointer, how Jimmy saw it all as a tragedy arranged by McLeod, of whom Starkey was a victim too. 'But at the risk of sounding callous,' I pursued, 'there's other tragedies. Up the track you have twenty-year-olds getting killed. It isn't the finish for Dick. He can speak to Johnny, to the War Cabinet. The Army Minister can promise him a new command. For Christ's sake, Pamela, it's the dead who find it hard to get their cases reviewed.'

'Are you implying I don't grieve for them, Paper? They're just not the subject of this argument, that's all.'

She was, of course, right. 'Very well,' I said, 'All right. Don't let the bugger drag you down into a state of brooding over this whole mess, Pamela. He's just not pliant, not . . . you know . . . not elastic. That's all.'

She thought of that a while. Her silence showed she understood the danger I spoke of.

'What else could Johnny have done but back Starkey?' I asked. 'Dick Masson's a man of merit. But he's not Jesus Christ.'

For some reason, she said, 'Dear old Paper!' as if I were a dog, not so fast on the uptake, but worth a place by her fire. I could taste at the roots of my tongue a kind of acid of rejection, a eunuch bile.

She said, 'Tell him to be patient. You see, Dick and I – we had at least this in common . . . the struggle with Fascism. When we talked about Hitler, when we talked about the Japanese in China, we were on safe ground. Now there's nothing in common. Dick thinks he's outside history, when all along he thought he'd be right in it, with his foot on the throttle. So you can explain that to Johnny, too . . .'

The operator interposed. 'War economy measures required that no trunk call should exceed nine minutes unless . . .' Her honest Southern Slopes voice showed her unease at having to read out a bureaucratic declaration like that. I was reminded at once of another plain and readily confused woman, whose mooching train had by now reached the wheat fields of Wimmera.

'His wife's coming tomorrow . . .' I told Pamela.

'Does she know?' she rattled out. We were both talking in shorthand, under the edict of the operator.

I said, 'Artie Thorn knows. And some of his old socialist mates in Melbourne. It was one of your friends in the sheepskin society who passed the news.'

'No, that's impossible,' she said, just as the operator cut our connection. I sat for some twenty seconds, listening to the apologetic nullity of the line.

Johnny's Monday Press Conference was held in a room in the House of Representatives wing. I made heavy weather of getting there, even though it was a journey I'd made often before. While

I progressed, feeling the pain in my vanished knees more than was usual even for the first day of the week, I held to the idea that I could, if I chose, subvert the message I would pass on to Johnny. I could say, shaking my head, 'She's very angry.' And that was the truth. I could say, 'They both think a great historic wrong has been done and it binds them together.' I could make it sound like a final judgment.

It was spacious room where the Press met Johnny, different from the closet fitted with camp stools where Tony Hamish, during his pontificate, greeted us to rare conferences. Johnny treated the Press like an alternative cabinet, and an excellent mahogany table and plush chairs were provided for us. I could see Jim Cowan, acting as usher, holding the door ajar for the late-comers and glancing at his watch.

I passed in. Johnny sat at the head of the table, inside the door. He was talking to the others but his eyes slewed towards me and he raised his left ear. My colleagues might have been jealous at that quick effect of my arrival but they went on talking among themselves like gentlemen, perhaps because that was the way Johnny cast them. I bent to his ear as best I could. I still didn't know what I had in my hand – or so I fancied. The assassin's knife or the sweet despatch.

It might have been of panic that I delivered the latter. I said, 'She's pretty angry about it all, Johnny. But she's staying away for your sake as much as hers. What I suggest is, get him away. You know, give him a command . . . soon as you can.'

He muttered, 'Not easy, Paper. Starkey's a great hater . . .' But his face was suffused. I couldn't help putting my hand out and squeezing his shoulder, feeling with surprise the muscular fibre there, the residual firmness of the young socialist, the Brunswick first-grader.

'It's money in the bank she'll be back,' I promised him. Then I went and sat in my place.

He had always treated us to more news than he gave most of his junior ministers, more news than the censors would let us print. The reason was not all *bonhomie*. Through us, he made the Press magnates feel they were in his confidence and that they ought to act as people do in a confidential arrangement. Today,

208

though, he seemed to treat us with special liberality. He began with Rumanian oilfields and ended with the thatched village of Menari on the Trail.

He told us that the US surface navy had not yet sunk a ship. He told us how many young had perished when the ship named after our modest capital was torn open in the Java Sea. The list of the dead was an exact tithe of the population of our slumbrous town.

Millie stood by her mirror and powdered her ivory thighs, the slight marbling of honourable forty-four-year-old fat there. She said, 'That's why I had a bath. We owe it to Ada to go. She'd be insulted if we didn't . . .'

I burrowed with my backside, seeking a deeper, more permanent connection with the chair. And my shirt sleeves were rolled slovenly, a declaration that I was not likely to be forced out tonight. I said, staring liverishly at the liver-shaped map of Guadalcanal in the morning paper, 'It's for people she feels at ease with, Johnny told me. He lifted an eyebrow when he passed on the invitation. I can tell he doesn't want us there . . .'

She was feeling her way into a slip now, doing without a corset. 'It's not his party,' she said. 'How dare he.'

'For Christ's sake, you have to look at what we did, Millie. What we did was procure a girl for him.'

'I won't have you speak like that,' she said. She turned adamantly towards a spring frock, borrowed from stock, that hung from a coathanger behind her door. Her firm, faintly dimpled hands took it by both shoulders. 'Men do what they want, anyhow. Why should we be forced to take sides? Or feel ashamed?'

I saw with disquiet the dress go on over her head. It was a signal that she wouldn't be moved now. Only at rare times, times of moment, did she take something expensive out of stock, risk the stains, take the chance that she'd have to sell it whisky-marked or gravy-tainted at a big discount.

I told her, 'You look very nice, Millie. But I'm still not bloody coming.'

She stared at me straight on, from her fairly large, halfway Asiatic eyes. I could imagine her as a mother, a child could get feelings of safety out of a potent gaze like that. But not so much a grown man. 'They're going to be mixed up good and properly,' she told me, 'if I turn up and you don't.'

It was the truth. They would both be puzzling out meanings if Millie arrived without me. Johnny, who'd seen me hale that day, wouldn't believe I was sick. 'Oh, hell!' I called out, throwing Guadalcanal from me, starting to tighten up the tie which had been lolling like a resting lizard down the slant of my chest.

I was silent in the car, amusing myself with thoughts of the last time we'd visited the Lodge and how the shops of Civic, the poplared road over the Molonglo, the bungalows of Yarralumla had all had that aspect you could only call 'surreal', of something that's about to know the hoofs of the four horsemen. And how the walls of the Lodge had been tainted with the light of distant fires.

There were other touches of the old *déjà-vu* - Weeksie was again at the drinks table just inside the parlour door, handing out drinks in the same grudging manner people had got used to in the parliamentary bar. I would have liked to pause there, to take thought and receive a Scotch out of Weeksie's hand, but Millie had swept on towards the middle of the room to give her four-square respects to Mr and Mrs Mulhall. And I, devoid of policies of my own, was swept along by her purpose.

It was, as Millie had said, people shy Ada trusted. Johnny's Treasurer (whose name I don't mention since he himself became king in time and the evocations of his name would distract from Johnny). And Johnny's Treasurer's wife.

The Army Minister and his. And one of the staff from the British High Commission who'd spent time with Ada once at a party. People like that.

As we approached the Mulhalls I crouched down over my

crutches, as if begging some immunity for cripples that night. I noticed how much all these like-thinking people were enjoying themselves. There was no Tony Hamish, no Jimmy Pointer, no saturnine departmental secretaries. You could see the unfeigned width of the smiles and hear the louder-than-usual voices of raconteurs. The Treasurer, who came from a good Catholic electorate, the Catholic Army Minister and his missus and all the rest of them, seemed of a celebratory mind. I don't know how many of them knew about Pam Masson. But if some of them did, her absence and Ada's presence probably gave them the idea that the world was at last swinging back towards its old rightness.

By her man, Ada stood bright-eyed and a little round-shouldered, wearing her dismayed yet all-powerful grin. Her hair was flattened back on her forehead, swept back behind her ears. It was an adventurous hairdo – the hairdresser had taken her by surprise – but she had tried to comb it down into something more accustomed.

'You know these two!' Johnny said as we steamed up, coming out with it so loud that the parliamentary heads and their wives who'd been talking to the Mulhalls until then took it as their marching order and went away to tell Weeksie what they wanted to drink.

Ada, too, had heard I'd been in New Guinea. It was notorious news which she seemed pleased to fall back on. She quizzed me about everything that had happened to me there. I noticed her hands, joined over her thighs, and the fingers, even in this benign company, worrying at the flesh of the palm.

Millie asked if her own journey had been comfortable. Johnny (I think) and I got the comforting idea that we could go on just talking about journeys all night.

Ada said that she'd let into her compartment two boys from a battalion posted to Moresby. They'd slept on the luggage racks above her head, even though she offered them the couch opposite hers. It seemed that luggage racks were the ordained place for soldiers. They were so young and they'd been with their families and girlfriends in Adelaide, eating, going to the pictures, courting. They slept on the wire as deeply as if the wire were eiderdown, said Ada. They'd been perfect gentlemen . . .

212

'Did they know who you were?' I asked, diverted by the story in spite of myself.

'No,' said Ada, 'and I didn't tell them. They would have tried to get promises out of me . . .'

Johnny blinked. His grin was now gentle and less bogus. 'Promises? What kind of promises, eh, Ada?'

She reached out and slapped his wrist, as if he'd said something improper. 'They would have said, you ought to get your husband to pass this or that. You ought to get him to legislate about the black market, or about leave, or shorter hours in the raincoat industry. Anything. People stop me in the grocer's and ask me things like that. They want more butter or prunes.' She laughed and shook her head. 'It's no joke.'

Indeed, the idea of Ada Mulhall being stopped outside the chemist's by women who idly wanted the earth changed wasn't one that gave us comfort and from Millie's throat and Johnny's came two reflex groans of compassion. It was luck, I suppose, that one didn't come from mine. That she could have been in Canberra all that time and got her shopping done by the servants of the Government didn't enter into our response.

Now she was confused. She had been telling us a funny story and we had failed to laugh. 'Yes . . . well,' she said.

At last Millie and I got away, liberated by the arrival of later guests. When I reached Weeksie I demanded – in spite of his puritan visage – a double measure of Scotch. Millie and I spent the next hour talking to the Treasurer. He was an engine driver who'd taught himself John Stuart Mill in the railway barracks, who'd learned *Rerum Novarum* by heart. This self-education had served him well enough to get him appointed, while still young, to the Banking Commission. He enchanted us tonight with his financial talk. We were happy to spend time enthralled with his long, sad, homely face. I saw that the Mulhalls had separated and were entertaining different parties in different corners of the room. Johnny rolled out sentences at his group and Ada listened to hers.

The Treasurer was no permanent haven – others wanted to speak to him too. We had just got another drink, Millie and me, and had taken up our stance by a painting of a bullock team plodding into a dusk beneath red gums, and we were letting the Scotch wash some of the sweet luminosity of that painting's dusk into our brains – or I was, anyhow – when Mrs Mulhall veered across the room and cornered us deftly.

She began speaking quickly for her. She said, 'I wanted to talk to you both. Do you have the time? I'm glad you do. When I got the letter I thought of you two as people I could speak to ... I got a letter from friends, you know, saying there's a woman. Maybe I shouldn't be surprised about that, eh, Paper?'

I shrugged as hard as I could, to show it was permissible for her to suffer surprise. I flinched from the special mention I was getting. 'I suppose I'm not a good wife,' she went on. 'I suppose I'm negligent. But I think you both understand how things are. There are lots of things I really can't do. Canberra ...' She shut her soft brown eyes and shook her head.

'You ought to speak to your husband, Ada,' Millie told her. 'The woman's a friend of mine. I don't mean to imply for a second that that makes it all right by me ... But John's the one you ought to talk to.'

Mrs Mulhall shifted her mouth round in a tormented way. The subtle craft of their marriage couldn't stand that sort of shock.

'I understand how you'd feel loyal to Johnny,' she told us.

'No more than to you,' said the relentless Millie.

I got into a sort of panic of truthfulness – in that direction lay the only means of escape from these two terrible women. 'There's a girl,' I said. I should have kept quiet then but I found I said, 'It isn't going to last, though.'

Millie made a long, calm survey of me. I thought, the bitch is going to argue with me about *that*.

'What's her name?' Ada said.

'Didn't the letter say?' Millie asked.

Mrs Mulhall shrugged but there was something very tough about the movement of her shoulders. 'I wanted to be sure. That it was the right name.'

Millie said, 'If it was from old friends, it was probably right.'

'Pamela Masson,' said Ada.

We said nothing.

Ada said, 'I'll go home again next week.'

'Why? Why go home?' Millie asked her. 'This is your home. According to the voters. You've got every right to call *this* home.'

Ada said, 'If I stayed, people would know why. We couldn't take that. I couldn't and Johnny couldn't. No, I'll go home next week. And come back for his birthday. That's in December. You say it won't last, Paper?'

She *would* hound me on that. Something I'd never thought before I said it aloud. But Ada and Johnny were credible partners and credibility, most times, romps home at short odds. I coughed. 'These things generally don't last, do they, Ada?'

'I don't know,' she said. 'I suppose I'm showing weakness.' But her passivity was tougher than armies.

Now Johnny saw us all together there, by the painting, and came and retrieved Ada to take her towards a late arriving guest. At the same time he managed to compel Millie across the room, on the same sort of pretext. I could see him making frantic introductions between Millie and the newcomer and leading them into absorbing lines of talk. In two minutes he got back to me, where I stood immobilized by the painting.

'Well, does she know?' he said. My blood crept, the way they talked through me.

I barked, nearly loud enough for Weeksie to hear. 'Of course she bloody knows. Why don't you ask her? Why can't you speak up to each other? Of course she bloody knows.'

He made a sound with his teeth. 'But she can't say anything to me,' he said. I was mellowed a bit by the disappointment in his voice. Otherwise I was furious enough to have said anything – in fact, I had it in mind to say, 'Was she always as limp as this, was she limp as a girl when you went to bed?'

'Don't use me as a clearing station, Johnny,' I told him. 'I never wanted to be a party to any of it.'

Johnny said, 'Thing is, Paper, I don't like being with someone who knows I'm a liar.'

He meant Ada. It was all right to be with me, no matter what his sins. I was his father bloody confessor. 'Oh, well,' I went on puffing. 'Oh, well, I knew I shouldn't have come to this bloody shebang. I knew you'd both get me in bloody corners.'

215

He laughed at that and straight away became the wary, social Johnny Mulhall with the oblique eyes and the bent grin. 'Masson,' he told me. 'I think we've got poor old Dick fixed up with something. Not so much a command . . . a military mission, Paper. To Russia.' He shook his head broodingly as if over the idea of the steppes. 'It ought to be fascinating for him. He'll lead it with the rank of major-general. Might come back as pink as Pamela, eh? It'll take some steam out – the generals are already taking sides, half the buggers for Starkey, the other half for Masson. No greater pain in the neck than that. Oh Paper, Paper!' It was a general lament for the confused times.

I didn't intend, though, to let him off so light. 'I don't think a military mission will satisfy Pam much,' I said. 'Not when she thinks he's Alexander the bloody Great.'

But Johnny understood I was being peevish and just grinned again, or else flinched with one corner of his mouth, and shook his head.

Within the hour I got away from them. It would have been sooner if I'd been able to walk abroad and didn't have to depend on Millie's little Austin. The Prime Minister and his missus were, of course, left behind in that house so alien to their spirits. I could have imagined with a bit of accuracy the edgy kindness they showed each other before they fell asleep, each in separate territory, lying as correctly as the subjects of State burial either side of that bed. Where at least Tony and Mrs Hamish had roiled and moiled in their time.

216

Chapter Four

She went home, Ada Mulhall. Though she thought she was weak, it was something the strong couldn't do. By the Southern Ocean she would sit down and wait for Johnny's birthday, just like that. She had more faith in the clock of the season than most other people did that year.

The clock whirred though. It took no heed of Artie Thorn in his iron-principled wing-collar, frowning in the government corridor, head sideways, ear lofted to overhear the unholy word, the word that ended his world. It was not impeded by Johnny's slow expectation of Pam Masson, that she would arrive on the Sydney train at mid afternoon and join the queue for the capital's few cabs. The clock whirred, and a white pollen fell on the bonnets of black government cars, and Mount Ainslie bounced the light back from its slopes with a proper summer brazenness.

Jimmy Pointer was back at his desk for a while. According to him, McLeod was planning to move to Moresby soon. Therefore Jimmy believed he himself had to be ready to leave for the front, to keep pace with the devil. He'd had time, though, to discover that Dick Masson had been given a sort of 'informal office' in a building in Sydney and a secretary to help him organize his mission. Masson was happy again, said Jimmy. Already writing to the Russians. Like his office, his letters were informal and a bit speculative. For Starkey hadn't yet been told, either about the mission or who would lead it. Johnny and the Minister for the Army were allowing Starkey to mellow before they broke it to him.

With her husband off all day writing letters to Muscovites, no longer needing her as a hand to rig his dinghy, there was nothing to stop Pam Masson coming up to the capital to look at Johnny again.

She turned up at Millie's on the first day of November. I remember the date because on the way to Millie's by taxi I saw women, the wives of Catholic public servants perhaps, emerging from the Catholic Church in Manuka, standing on the steps a while, then turning sober as widows back inside. The taxi driver told me that if you visited a church and said certain prayers on that magic eve, you got a soul out of the torments of purgatory. But to liberate more than one, you had to leave your pew after each such exercise, sniff the outer unredeemed air a while, then return to repeat the rite. A failed Protestant ought to have smiled at exercises like that but I was touched by the sad, level energy of those women, by their air of efficiency as they worked to free their ancestors and succour a quotient of the world's dead children.

When I got to Millie's I found the table set for three. The flavour of the expiatory acts of those women in Manuka was still with me and I wondered for a mad second if she'd set the extra plate in memory of her dead young husband. So I was pleased to see her pottering around the place in an unceremonial way and with a faint smirk on her face. 'We've got a visitor,' she told me.

Pam Masson manifested herself then, in the doorway from the hall. She bore the obvious marks of what had taken her so long to get here. She was in a uniform.

There's something pathetic about a young throat sticking up out of a coarse military collar. It made Pam Masson appear childlike, an aspect by which I wasn't used to viewing her. She'd spent two weeks in a suburban camp doing her basic training, being equipped with a battle-dress meant for a woman as tall but broader, bunning her hair up to fit her hat. I went up to her and hugged her strenuously, the way a father would. I joined

218

in the laughter that was bubbling out of both of them, reunion laughter and laughter also at the idea of Private Masson.

She said, 'I'm having a uniform tailored.'

And I said, 'Tractor-Driver First-Class Masson.'

Johnny had been summoned. He arrived about nine o'clock. The way an aunt would who is, say, putting her nephew through university. Pam offered her jawline to him. I heard him brush his dry lips over the area of skin she proferred. Her gestures were large but her general manner was shy. She sat in a single chair, as if there were some risk he wouldn't keep his hands off her.

He threw himself in a corner of the three-seater and Millie went to make him tea, while I was left in my accustomed single-seater to watch the two of them. Johnny seemed so transported he couldn't smile at her. He would pat his knee and smile at it and sometimes he would turn to me and smile.

'I'll have to talk to the Minister of Supply,' he murmured. 'The jacket is nothing less than a crime.'

I said, 'The Minister of Supply tries to fit out average women perfectly. He isn't used to fitting out perfect women averagely.'

Mrs Masson laughed at this *mot* of mine. She told us that a fat quartermaster sergeant had told her she *was* an oddity. After a time, and before Millie got back with the tea, she got up and came to the empty space beside Johnny, putting her hand to the back of his neck. Then she pushed herself, by medium of the crass, creased jacket, against him, while he just went on talking about war and politics.

I did not want that hand for myself. I thought that what I'd seen was simply the sweetest, most plenitudinous thing I'd seen happen to any man. And I rejoiced, at least for a time, without question.

A day and a half later she went back to her camp. I imagined her lying in a barracks hut after lights out, her hands across her belly. Other recruits whispering of men. I wondered if there was that sort of sexual steaminess in a women's barracks after dark, just as in a men's; if Johnny's name was ever spoken in complaint by other girls, the political comment coinciding with her private barrack-room desire.

*　*　*　*

Before too many more souls had been freed from torment, I heard from Jimmy Pointer that the Russian mission would not travel. Starkey had been told of it at last and had objected in the fiercest terms. A man who'd just been disciplined, he said, should not be offered a plum. He spoke about 'votes of no confidence in myself,' a phrase that carried innate in it the threat of his own resignation.

Jimmy said, 'Johnny's put his money on the old bugger and has to see the race through.'

Millie and I weren't aware of any pause in the Mulhall-Masson affair. At the end of her training she became an instant corporal and went to work in some cipher office in a bunker in the sandstone ledges of Middle Harbour. She came to Canberra every second weekend that Johnny was there.

Whenever I saw her I asked her about Dick and she'd say always, 'He's waiting, he's waiting. But he'll be all right.' She had become wistful about him. But there wasn't any more talk about his rage, even if he had some; and I don't see how he could have missed out. The thwarting of the Russian mission didn't mean as much to her as the sacking in Moresby; she knew this time that Johnny and the minister were straining to find him a post that didn't demean him.

In the meantime, the old man in Moresby was doing well enough, sitting in Masson's camp-chair and running Masson's staff. His battalions were over the main range now. The valleys widened and the earth did not stink here, nor the forests seep so much. Native bearers returning along the track wore yellow flowers in their brushy hair. The young men were still hungry but could live in these plentiful high valleys on yams, taro, paw-paw, sweet potato. Though at the main dressing stations the wounded had to build their own shelters and lie on the comfortless ground, none of us knew it except the doctors and the youths themselves. In the large world, and everywhere except in McLeod's sycophantic headquarters, it was thought Starkey had been doing pretty well so far from restaurants and women in rainy Moresby.

Chapter Five

That month there was a special party conference called in Melbourne. Johnny set out to catch the train straight from his office in the House, wearing the suit he had worn all day. His car waited for him downstairs, but he raced round to the Senate wing to visit me before he left.

He was very direct. He said, 'If Pam turns up on Saturday, will you and Millie mind her?'

I told him that of course we would.

'There's a bomber flying up from Melbourne on Saturday night. I'll come on that.'

'It won't be comfortable, Johnny.'

He waved the question of comfort aside. Yet he still did not leave me. Cars and trains awaited him, but he wanted to talk.

I knew, because it was my business, the matters that would be raised at that conference behind the locked doors of Trades Hall, among the brotherhood. Proposals about party structure. About the admission of women as delegates. There were thirteen ideas about changing the constitution so that society after the war could be edged closer towards Utopia. (All the ideas would be tossed out by the people later, in referenda; for people would go for Johnny's view of the war but not his view of the millennium.)

Anyhow, there was no need for him to tell me where he was

going or what his intentions were. But he hung round just the same, squinting and having a yawn.

He said at last, 'I want to raise something at this conference. And it won't be too popular with the Grant girls, Paper. In fact they might never have me in for tea again. You understand me?'

I nodded, then I shook my head. I couldn't say much.

He said, 'I'm going to raise it in conference first, see. Not in the House. Not in front of Tony Hamish and all the other silver-tails. But in the family, as it were.'

I felt an instant personal fear, a kind of grief like that which had brought tears from Pen Grant the day we visited her. As if the old Johnny was changing himself, wilfully and without cause, into another creature.

'Have you warned anyone else?' I asked him.

He mentioned the Treasurer, the good engine driver, the reader of Mills, Keynes and *Rerum Novarum*.

'And what did he say?' I asked.

'He thinks I'll get away with it.' He yawned as he had once before, in the car, returning from Mah Grant's harsh judgments. 'He thinks I should give it a go. He thinks we'll grease it through . . .'

I could not help continuing to shake my head but this time for more specific and political reasons. For I still suspected the Party would devour its own flesh – devour him, that is, and hand rule back to Hamish – before it broke its old canons.

'You don't think it's as easy as I say?' he asked me.

'No,' I said. 'I don't know. It's just a political opinion.'

Johnny said, 'All I want is the 110th meridian across to the 159th. And just up as far as the Equator.' It was a preposterous sentence. 'That's the limit I want to send people to, Paper. I'm not sending them to put down workers' revolts in Belfast. I don't want to suppress the Chinese. It's just our backyard, Paper . . .'

I stared at him and saw a loose-limbed man with a half-embarrassed smile, and beyond him saw the machine that gave him his kingly breath, the machine of his Party. I did not see, within, the frantic man – none of us adverted to *that* man enough. The man upon whom the omnipotent, all-owning, all-producing Yanks placed their weights. Roosevelt holding planes

222

and soldiers from Johnny Mulhall's sacred continent because John Mulhall and his Party would not send conscripts afield. Reading the correspondence now, I see Johnny pleading that half his eligible men are under arms, pleading the 50 000 who are still in another hemisphere, pleading his 40 000 dead or lost or maimed children. Through source books, through letters printed in books by strangers, I see the man bleeding within those loose limbs hitched on my desk.

He said, 'If I do it while Eddie Hoare's in the bog ... if I don't use the dread words ... you know, Paper, the names of the anti-Christ. If I grease its flanks and spring it on them ... we can slip it through between lunch and tea-time.'

Millie and Corporal Masson and I picnicked on Black Mountains on the day of the conference. While Johnny, quick as an assassin, dropped the measure unannounced into the agenda, Pam Masson lay on a rug, sleeping neatly on her back, a tailored jacket beneath her head, her fine calves mocked by her clodhopper army shoes, her feet aimed towards the dreaming suburb of Yarralumla. The shade of an alpine gum fell over her face.

A journo who waited in the entrance to Trades Hall in Melbourne that day, kicking at the masonry for very boredom, told me later how Eddie Hoare appeared through the doors from the conference hall, pointed a livid face towards the half-dozen journalists standing about and said, 'He's done it. The bugger's done it. Not a word to his Cabinet beforehand. At least we know now. Where we bloody stand!'

The journalists understood how rare it was for Eddie to vent himself to the capitalist Press. They took it as a sign that in that moment Eddie Hoare had chosen to destroy his leader rather than put up with heresies. Then they could see him think the better of it. He considered their faces, smiled, nodded his head, as if seeing behind them the sinister ambiences of the Press barons. And so he turned back indoors.

Back in the hall, a back-bencher had fought off Johnny's proposals and moved that the matter be put to each of the State Executives. Maybe the young man hoped Johnny would oppose this idea and display the mental habits of an absolute monarch who deserved the knife. And so there would be revolt and schism and a season of that internecine frenzy which to some Labor men was dearer than winning votes.

Johnny did not oppose the motion; he voted for it. From what I know now, I think he believed that afternoon that he could carry each of the States. Not the Queenslanders maybe, not the Victorians, not those two thorny races. But the rest of us.

Whenever I saw Johnny in public in those days, even if he was moving down the corridor from his office, his eyes seemed near-closed to shut out the embarrassing condolences of friends. The Victorian Executive had rejected his proposals by five votes, the Queenslanders by seven. The small Tasmanian Executive had accepted them by one vote. Old friends and one or two of his ministers were running him down in the *Worker* and the *Labor Call*, in both of which he had once been a darling. He was up late every night talking to the party powers in Perth and Adelaide and Sydney. He was a man under visible assault and the sight pleased the Press barons, all of whom ran editorials with an indecent glow of anticipation to them, asking if the Party would split again and consume its own parts.

On the day of the Executive vote in Sydney, I was ordered down to the city by my boss. I would travel first class and have a suite at the Australia. He wanted my by-line, he said, for the story. The story was that if the Sydney boys went against Johnny, the Press would make a feast of it. The barons could at the same time rant against the Party's sense of honour and rejoice at Johnny's political distress.

I travelled in a crowded first-class compartment. Group captains and public servants sat up all around me like tailors' dummies, and only my one empty pants leg and my leaning crutches detracted from the untoward masculine excellence of the carriage. I was pleased when Jim Cowan turned up and told me Johnny was on the same train and wanted to know if I'd like to have a cup of tea with him.

In fact Johnny's compartment was just a few yards down the

aisle. As soon as I was clear of my own and had gathered breath, I could see two of Johnny's back-benchers sliding its door open. They, too, were arriving by invitation, it seemed. So I knew that this was not going to be a quiet, confessional session. I clapped on speed so that I could enter just behind the two politicians.

I caught up just as the second back-bencher was about to shut the door. He was a square-faced man of my own age, the sleeves of his suit too short for him, so that he reminded me of a pub bouncer. He spoke with no smile. 'I didn't know the representative of the Sydney Press would be here,' he called over his shoulder towards Johnny.

From behind his bulk, I could hear Johnny. 'Come on, Reg, Paper is here as a friend.'

Reg stood back and I squeezed by sideways on my crutches, no part of my clothing touching his. Then he slid the door shut behind us and came himself and took up a seat beside his colleague.

Johnny spoke to me first. Perhaps it was crafty of him to have me there, for it showed he wasn't going to crawl to them. None of the stuff he said was worth recording; it was all Millie's health and how he didn't see me any more except at Press conferences. Reg gave a little slap to an upholstered armrest and looked at the ceiling. He had been a member of one of the fragments left over in Sydney from past party disasters. He had come back into the main body less than a year back. Now Johnny had sprung these foul proposals on him. In their shadow, mention of Millie's health must have seemed a provocation.

The collapsible table was up and the NSW Government Railways silver service lay on it. Johnny started dishing out the tea, taking account of our individual quirks of taste. He always made a point of the pouring and dispensing; perhaps the ritual was a further buffer for him against his old whisky urges.

I could tell nothing serious would be said until he'd had his first deep draught of the tea, and Reg and his friends observed the decency of that. But once they had their cups in their hands, they could all drink it so bloody hot! I sat listening to the noise of their gullets.

'Finished your brew?' Johnny asked.

'Finished,' one of them said, but with suspicion.

Then Johnny said, 'Reg, Sid. Look, it's got to happen. There are strict limits where the young can be sent. It's not like last time. They're not being sent to France. They're not being sent to Italy. Not to the bloody Tigris or Euphrates . . .'

Reg held up his hand. 'It's no good, Johnny. Save your argument. I went to the bloody foreign wars when I was a boy. My own son's been rejected from this one, thank Christ. I'm not going to send other sons against their wills.'

Johnny stared out of the window of the carriage and saw – perhaps without understanding – yet another afternoon herd of dairy cows making away from the train towards their milk shed up on the hill. It was possible that all the dairy herds from Goulburn to Picton let the wail of the evening train dictate the time they traipsed along for milking. And the farmers sipping tea in their kitchens likewise let the Sydney Mail, even in drought and under the weight of letters from bank managers, compel them out of doors from the afternoon session in the shed. Johnny knew little of this. He had never been a country boy.

'I respect that, Reg,' he said. But he was still looking out the window, as if he was talking about the strange, twice daily eternal business of milking.'

Reg said, 'I used to respect you too, Johnny.'

'Oh,' said Johnny, 'not any more? Well . . .' He swallowed the rest of his tea. 'You've been with us long enough, Reg, to know there's a difference between principles you hold on the backbench and principles as they translate on to the front bench. You know that . . .'

'Yeah,' Reg told him. 'I think Lord Acton called it "power corrupts . . ." '

'In subtle ways, Reg, in subtle ways.' The Americans say: our conscripts are campaigning in places close to your shores, places you won't send your conscripts to. *You'd* say, a bloody good thing, too. And so would I, Reg, if we look on the whole business as a sort of absolute moral matter.'

Johnny, tea finished, had a cigarette in one hand and his ebony holder in the other and was using them as he always did, in the nature of expository aids. 'But it's not just a moral matter, it's a political matter. I used to think they were the same thing. They're not. It's no use telling our old mate FDR that we're delighted with ourselves for our moral attitude to the whole business. That won't make him reward us with ships and squadrons.' He had held up both hands to ward off the arguments he himself had used when young. 'I know, I know. It *suits* their government for them to come and die.'

Reg smiled. 'Woken up to that one, eh, Johnny? Woken up to the American empire, old son?'

Johnny smiled; you'd call it a disarming smile. 'They're not as bad as the British, Reg. And they're more efficient.'

'They're all as bad as each bloody other,' said Reg.

'But who can live for long,' Johnny said . . .

'In a euphoric dream:
Out of the mirror they stare,
Imperialism's face
And the international wrong.'

We stared at him. The verse was unfamiliar. It was probably Pam Masson who had given him Auden's poem about September 1, 1939.

Johnny got diffident about it. 'I just remembered those lines,' he said. 'Imperialism's face and the international wrong . . .'

Reg said, 'Exactly.'

Johnny said, 'The proposal covers a sane area, Reg, Sid. The nation's front door. What any sane man would call the nation's front door. It isn't immoral even if in my private heart I'd want it otherwise.'

'Huh!' Reg murmured, shaking his head. 'If I'd thought this was on, I'd never have been seduced back into this Party.'

'I won't be moved from this, gentlemen,' said Johnny.

Reg said, 'Is that a threat, Johnny? Or are you going to start weeping soon the way you do in caucus.'

Johnny laughed, genuinely tickled. 'I don't weep in caucus, Reg.'

'Bloody buckets, that's all. Gloria bloody Swanson.'

Johnny started choking from laughter and tobacco smoke. He proffered a dish of digestive biscuits. 'Here, have an arrowroot, Reg, and give me a rest.'

Then, 'Sid?' he asked the other one.

Sid kept his eyes off Johnny. He was a smaller man. He had a shyer, more honest, more painstaking look than his brother politician. I found out later, when he reached the Cabinet, that that was the extent of his talents. When Johnny spoke to him, however, he put on the face of a man who is trying out all the earth's balances in his head, painfully, behind his eyes.

'I'm a bit embarrassed to get called to the tea table like this, Johnny,' he said, in his quiet and falsely delicate voice, 'and to find Paper here. I know Paper's absolutely trustworthy. But as a higher authority says, no man can serve two masters.'

'I despise the other,' I told Sid, completing the quotation, 'I despise the other master.'

'But he pays your wages, Paper,' Sid pointed out. 'And shunts you round first class.'

'More fool him,' I said. But of course this coy back-bencher had reminded me most painfully of my bifurcated existence.

Johnny ignored all this chat about my employer, the conditions of my labour. 'What about it, Sid? Do you know what you're going to do?'

Sid raised his awesome, bland face. 'I'm voting against you, Johnny. You know that, you've already sent someone round to ask me.' He named one of Johnny's emissaries, a senator from New South Wales.

'And beyond that?' Johnny asked, looking him straight in the face, a pretty rare and always deranging Mulhall device. 'Will it be civil war, Sid?'

Sid said, 'First of all, we'll see if you win tonight, Johnny.'

Reg took up the running. 'You're going to be deadlocked, old son. The three biggest States against you. The three tiddlers for.' He whistled. 'I'd hate to have to push a barrow with all that against me.'

Johnny closed his eyes. Behind the steel-rimmed lenses I could see the pallor of the eye pouches reach down all the way to the corners of his mouth. I wished he could have managed to look a bit more commanding in front of these two parliamentary hacks. The hacks looked at each other while Johnny's eyes stood shut. Shallow hope raised Reg's eyebrows, there was smooth-faced and obsequious contempt in Sid. They rattled me, those two.

I said, 'You ought to be careful what you say and do. There's only one bloke who can win an election for you next year. You know who it is.'

That made them start working on their ironic replies but Johnny forestalled them. 'For Christ's sake, Paper!' Then he laughed his ricketty laugh. We were eking up a hill and the evening sun hung over a field of green wheat and redeemed half of Johnny's face from the sickly blue light in which the rest of us sat. His cigarette holder pointed at me, sharp end first. 'They already think I'm your boss's nominee.'

Reg had enough amity in him to smile. 'Not quite as bad as that, Johnny.'

The train was late into Central and I had to share a taxi with the back-benchers to get to Trades Hall in time. The cab let us out in Liverpool Street. On the pavement and steps, rank and file cuffed Reg's shoulders and Sid's as the two of them forced their way indoors. Voices called, 'Don't stand for it, Sid! Don't stand for it, Reg!' When Johnny's car pulled up in Goulburn Street, someone called from the steps, 'Here comes a traitor to his class!' Johnny loped forth from the back seat wearing a sort of Richard II grin, the rictus of a weak king. Yet I knew how the crowd would contract from him as he climbed the steps, I knew this person was safe.

Supporters and dissenters massed around him and carried him up the steps and indoors. Following, I crossed the lobby and found all the seats in the hall already taken. My Digger's badge, as well as the badge of my disability, soon earned me the offer of one. From it I could see Eddie Hoare on the platform, laughing with some of the faithful and counting off emphatic points with his fingers. But Johnny climbed to the rostrum as a dazed presence, gusted along by catcalls and applause.

He made one of his worst speeches, one of his most desultory. He made no argument that I had not heard before. What, say, could we expect to have in the Pacific, he asked, in the world after the war, if we did so little there now? Eddie Hoare wriggled

229

in his seat, grinning a polemic grin, sensing that Johnny was disordered, sniffing out the moral and rhetorical advantages. When Johnny had finished, he received what you'd call substantial but merely well-mannered applause.

Eddie began with the story of Johnny's work against conscription in another war. It was a speech about Johnny's fall from grace. 'How can a man change so diametrically?' Eddie asked. 'From being the champion of one thing to being the apostle of its opposite? When John Mulhall was a young man, he lived under the guidance of some of the spiritual elders of the movement. Artie Thorn had been a friend. Hilton counselled him. They kept the young Mulhall out of temptation.'

As if Artie Thorn had been speaking to him recently, Eddie told the story of the night in Fitzroy Gardens when young Johnny wrestled all night with angels. 'This man has forgotten his origins, has outgrown the benign influences of his early years. Now his friends are the Press barons, he seeks and receives his political fuel from them, not from his own honest rank and file! And now John Mulhall is willing to send our young compatriots by force to die in fields which will become of less and less value to the nation as the conflict progresses.'

It was then that, for reasons I can't judge, Eddie lost control of his measured, acid speech. I'd seen it happen in the House, the pallor and the fixity of the pupil. And there was that uncomfortable tremble in the voice that made people turn their eyes aside. He said, 'So what do we say to the proposals of a man who has forgotten his traditional support? Who has forgotten the working class and sees them only as an audience to whom he preaches austerity, yet who possesses – and it's the truth, believe me, brothers – who possesses strange luxurious friendships. Let me tell you something of this advocate of austerity.'

Eddie himself knew he was at the brink now but the hysterical machine of his oration had him by the ears. Supporters of Johnny were hissing him, standing on seats, making hushing motions at him with their hands. I think they knew nothing of Pam Masson and considered that the words 'luxurious friendships' were mere puritan malice.

Whatever the nature of their noise, they brought Eddie back

230

to the simpler planes of the debate. It seemed he greeted them almost with gratitude. 'You are right, my friends,' he called. 'There is no need to descend to personalities at the possible cost of failing to show how the Prime Minister's case falls by the weight of its own contradictions . . .'

I saw Johnny on the platform sit back and caress with his long fingers the side of his jaw. In the end he was cheered out of the hall. It was neither his speech nor Eddie's that accounted for the applause. It reminded me of something I would never have known just by living in Canberra – that people believed in Johnny's integrity, that the idea was an intimate one, even with some of those who were against the evening's proposals. When it was attacked by Eddie Hoare they felt a personal insult.

The Executive would meet later in the evening for their vote, after the faithful and not so faithful had gone away. The result would be telephoned through to Johnny. So we went back to the Australia, at least I met him there, downstairs in a parlour where he was soothing himself with still more tea. Jim Cowan sat with him. When Johnny saw me come in through the lobby he laughed – it was the sort of greeting you utter when, all confused in a foreign city, you spot your cousin. 'Sit down, Paper,' he called, 'sit down.' And when I had, he leaned towards me. 'Jesus, that Eddie. Close to the bone, eh? Of course he's hurt, Paper. You've got to watch out for a fellow who's genuinely hurt.'

I said, 'I reckon the crowd was with you, two to one. As much as that.'

He winked. 'Don't be so surprised, Paper.'

Jim Cowan dragged a tea-leaf from the sweet beige surface of his cup. 'We've got the numbers on the Executive, too,' he said. 'In just about those proportions. No worries, no worries about it.'

But I did not believe that.

At last the night manager walked in and asked Johnny where he'd like to answer the telephone call that had just come. Johnny went off, sauntering, to the man's office.

I watched Jim Cowan clash his cup against the rim of his saucer, put them both down, join the hands. There was a mist of sweat on the venous right hand.

'All right, Jim, I said. 'What *is* going to happen?'

He shook his head. 'Oh, we've got the numbers. I mean it. We've got them.'

'But if you haven't . . .?'

'It'd be the end of him, you know. It'd split the Party. Eddie Hoare . . . Eddie would lead the rebels. You know that, Paper. You don't have to be told.'

'That's right,' I said.

'But it won't be happening. Unless . . . you know . . . unless he gets ratted on in a truly monumental style.'

Johnny reappeared, sauntering, the same tired lope he'd gone out with. He stood by the tea table, blew some air through his lips and chuckled. 'They went *our* way. Twenty-seven in favour. Thirteen a'gin. Your mathematics came out all right, Jim.'

I thought, it's on, he's really going to send them. I thought of Pen Grant weeping over her sink. I felt a short-lived regret akin to hers. But, 'That's settled then,' I said. 'Now you can get some sleep.' I remembered that was a futile promise I'd been making Johnny for months.

Johnny said, 'Jim can sleep . . . you need it, Jim. I have to go out for a little while.'

Staggering across the lobby, he vanished down the stairs towards his Commonwealth car and its driver. I looked at Jim across the tea things and shook my head and made an amused and indulgent noise. But Jim would not be amused and indulgent with me. He said, 'He has to go and thank his supporters. You know, in the Executive.' It was probably the truth but we both knew that later, with only the moon violating the black-out, he might go to that street above the harbour and beg tea and other comforts.

The next morning Jim told me that McLeod sent a telegram from Moresby praising Johnny for a step that transcended (according to the cable) narrow party limitations.

Chapter Six

Consider, then, a characteristic December day in the capital. Ada, returned to the Lodge to celebrate Johnny's fifty-fourth birthday privately with her husband, sits before an electric fan and sends out a few invitations to *real* friends to come to Boxing Day lunch. The same fretful west wind that plagues her pushes red dust, some poor cow-cocky's flown-away farm, against the pores of the Branch Office. A sober mind can just about manage to hold on to a line of argument. Those who have lunched too well stick to their offices, fans beating the dense air towards them, their shirts unbuttoned, their chests pink with heat.

I myself was sitting doing damn-all, with my own heat-pink chest bared, when one of my colleagues raced into my office and told me that Eddie Hoare was on his feet in a debate then in progress on the Industrial Regulation Provisions Bill, and accusing Tony Hamish and Hamish's past government of treason.

We rushed along to the Press Gallery, I myself taking great swinging strides on my crutches. In the narrow back row we took seats. There were only a few other correspondents there, most of them young, posted as sentries by their office chiefs on the off-chance that something would happen.

Below us maybe one-fifth of the members of the House of Representatives were in the chamber, yet those who were resounded like gold merchants on a bourse. On Tony Hamish's side of the House, some half dozen spokesmen of the Tory way stood in their places shouting; Mr Hamish KC himself, with a white fist clamped around his watch-chain and a genuine suffusion of blood across his jaws. Others shouted from their seats or sat side-on, shaking their heads. It was known for members to use such gestures for theatrical reasons but you couldn't mistake the acrimony of these shouts nor the genuine colour on the faces.

Old Jack Niell, the Speaker, sweating beneath his wig, was frightened by what was happening and dealt short, jolting blows with his gavel at the bench.

Things were not so disordered on the Government side of the House. Some back-benchers laughed at Tony Hamish's fury. It was Johnny's aspect that puzzled me. He sat only inches from Eddie Hoare, yet his eyes were fixed on the papers in his place, his mouth bunched in a speculative manner. They looked a strange pair, for Eddie's short-sighted eyes didn't seem to be part of the scene either and were directed, unfocused, towards the gallery. He was calling, 'Table documents? The Opposition, Mr Speaker, pretend they want me to table documents. It is but a pretence. They'd be red-faced if I tabled the documents at this stage, Mr Speaker. Red-faced. Caught like a schoolboy in a melon paddy.'

This didn't seem a very exalted image with which to hit an old silver-tongue like Tony Hamish. Yet it touched off a new chorus of rage in the Opposition benches. 'Lying Marxist dingo!' I heard among the rest. Eddie heard it, too.

'Oh yes, oh yes,' he roared. 'Smear a man's politics. Anyone who throws doubt on the Melbourne silvertails' capacity to rule, Mr Speaker, is a dangerous radical. Well, what is the word, Mr Speaker, that is the epithet for men like the former prime minister there? In his Savile Row suit once so admired, according to the mindless scribes of social papers, by Lady Beaverbrook . . . I want to know . . . wait for it, wait for it . . .'

For they were all screaming and poor Jack Niell punished his bench and begged for orderly debate.

'What word is there,' asked Eddie again, 'for that man who

approved a certain plan, a plan to abandon two-thirds of this continent to its enemies? What word would the Queenslanders have had for him if they had known that in his grand strategy they would have been written off? What word would the West Australians apply, or the people of Adelaide, who were all cut off in two neat paragraphs in a plan *that* man there, Lady Beaverbrook's tailor's dummy, signed during his unhappy period in power?'

The rumour that such a plan existed had been around for a year or more. It had infected ordinary people and not just journalists. The rumour said that, should the Japanese arrive, the military intended to draw a line, Brisbane to Melbourne, which would be held. The vaster, vacanter portion of the land mass would be flung away. The Brisbane line fell across people's grey matter as one of those grand, persecuting, weirdly nourishing myths that humankind suck on for perverse reinforcement. Like the bunyip, which infests all swamps but no specific one, it was known as a fact. Yet as with that mythic beast, no one man with one name or one trade had a scratch to show for his encounter with it. My friend and I in the Press Gallery looked at each other, knowing what Eddie was doing. He was taking the beast down off the plane of fable and accusing Tony Hamish of having a hand in its begetting.

I noticed back-benchers on both sides rushing out to fetch reinforcements from the offices and library and bar. It had become an afternoon of high party significance. The torrid west wind and a man's intimate sweat and discomforts would now fall beneath notice.

Meanwhile, Eddie once more rubbed in the principal items of his story. He named the general who devised the plan and drew the line, he named the dates on which it was presented to Tony's government, he dated what he called 'the craven speed' at which they'd approved it. The present Government, he said, taking his eyes from the apogee of that chamber's roof and nodding towards Johnny as towards a brother in a seamless fraternity, the present Government would not have a bar of it, pledged itself to the defence of the entire continent. People in the west and the north of the nation were aware of this firm intention, had seen the nation's defenders turn up in those areas and take up position.

Eddie then made the comparison between Johnny's brave appreciation of the real world, of the Pacific latencies, and Tony Hamish's rusty view of events.

Johnny seemed to shy from these compliments, rarely raising his eyes above the level of the table where the parliamentary clerks worked. He abstained, or so it appeared, from this mean partisan brawl.

Eddie gave a Press conference at dusk. It made, of course, a lovely story, a gift. There was that in it which would give the ordinary reader not only homely rage but also a vertigo thrill that men armed only with oddments of strategic jargon and a few fountain pens could slice off two-thirds of the nation's geographic and mystical flesh. The next day the matter was revived through questions from Johnny's back-benchers. Eddie spoke again with his fixed, raised eyes. Hamish rose and grew livid. Johnny again sat there silent and demure as any employee of the Parliament.

Next morning a note from Tony's secretary waited on my desk, asking me if I could come to his office about ten. I believed it must be a general invitation to Pressmen but when I got to his ante-room, there was just his secretary present to lead me through into the office which had once been Johnny's. Hamish was more of an interior decorator than Johnny. He went in for pictures of himself shoulder-to-shoulder with monarchs and prominent British Tories. But he had not hung so many photographs in *this* room, a sign that he considered himself to be in temporary exile.

He looked up for an instant from his papers. His full lower lip, which gave him at an early age a fatherly look, was tucked in now. He stabbed a blunt, well-tended hand towards a seat. 'Take that, Tyson, and Keith, help him.'

That 'Keith, help him' aroused me. If he thought me such a cripple, he should have come around to my office.

I told the secretary, 'I can sit myself down, Keith, I'm not bloody helpless.'

The secretary nodded and went back to the ante-room. Tony

Hamish put on the unnecessary stunt of holding his eyes to the papers of State on his desk. 'Come on, Tony,' I said, 'If I'd thought you wanted to bloody read, I wouldn't have been so punctual.'

Cat-quick, he switched his gaze from the desk to me. 'All right. Tell me. What's happening to your friend Mulhall? Is he flying to bits? He sits there like the creation of a brain surgeon.'

I asked him if he could be more definite about what he wanted to know.

'This Brisbane line business,' he said. 'He knows I signed it as a plan to be followed only *in extremis*. A matter of last resort. He has it on his own files in those terms. For all I know you may have it in yours . . .'

I said nothing.

He beat the desk with his hand. 'More than by Eddie Hoare's Red ranting, I am offended by John Mulhall's silence! He'd better get over it, Paper, that's all. You ought to tell him that. He'd just better admit that every cabinet must have a plan like that, a plan for its back pocket, a plan to operate on short lines of communication . . . he *knows*, the bugger *knows* . . .'

I'd rarely seen him come down from Olympus like this and show a sort of lumpen anger. I remembered that even when his own party worked at his downfall, his pain had had a patrician air to it; he moved in the corridors like a spurned tribune going home to open his veins in a warm bath.

'So I think *you* ought to tell him to recover from his silence,' he told me as a threat.

'He'd be a fool to do that, Tony. He has an election to fight next year . . .'

'I, too, Paper, have something to use in elections. The John Wesley of wartime austerity, the tender of the ascetic flame! Who visits his woman in Commonwealth vehicles. Mr Tyson! A Red slut and a general's wife!' He made it sound like two separate women. 'I've had my wild days, too, Paper, as you would be the first to point out. But then I never pretended I was strong on self-denial. I am known to like dinners, wine, conversation.'

He drew in those full lips. There was a slight blue whisker-shadow on his jaws. The Hoare offensive was narrowing him down, taking the shine off his elegance. He said, 'I can feed a back-bencher the right questions, Paper. I can make some young member's name. He has simply to ask whether the close friendship between John Mulhall and Mrs Masson had any bearing on the New Guinea business. And as you know, I have a few boys on that back-bench who share my faith, who'd go to hell for a smile from me. Boys who believe I'm coming back, Paper!'

I was tempted to laugh but an instinct told me not to write off a man of Tony's gifts. I think, later, he always remembered that though I did him many a disservice, I never laughed at the idea of his comeback.

'Tell him,' said Hamish, 'tell him to stop Eddie or he can expect a sharp response.'

I began struggling with my crutches. 'I'm not a bloody messenger boy,' I told him, as I had to tell everyone that year. I managed to get erect, I said, 'You know, Tony, people are going to believe this whole Brisbane line business of you. They'll say that's like the Hamish we know, the old Sahib of Toorak. Eddie might tell the lie. But you're the one who makes it credible, Tony. Because you're the one they saw licking the wrong arses before this whole mess began.'

I'm sure I left his office like a man who's faced up to a single hard option. I believe Hamish was shamed a little by the thud of the crutches and the drag of the false bakelite foot. He called after me, 'This isn't my normal method of dealing with problems, Paper. But for God's sake, it's so unfair . . .'

He may have imagined, during the next hour, that I was in Johnny's office, telling him the picnic was over, that he must curb his radical friend. He may have eaten lunch in expectation of an easy afternoon's session.

In fact, while he still would have been at the table, I'd already made a rush by taxi to the airfield and was bouncing down to Sydney in a DC-3, my arrangements so swiftly made, my serpentine strategies marked down. From the window I watched the valley of Burragorang – in whose green deeps I'd spent the sweetest fortnight of my childhood – reduced by haze and height now to a ditch on the landscape.

Chapter Seven

We swept in over the heads of the fishermen out on Botany Bay, and so got down. The orderly who helped me out of the plane pointed to a requisitioned aero club shed, where I could ring for a taxi. Inside this structure I found wall ordnance maps, chairs, tables, sugar bowls and, behind a counter, a girl in khaki to pour tea and butter the toast. She had just the two customers at the moment, both of them notorious, occupying the table furthest from me. General Starkey and Jimmy Pointer. I hoped they mightn't see me. I had a mind only for the telephone, for a fast drive into town.

But it was Starkey who got up from his chair and claimed me. 'My God!' he yelled. I remembered again his schooly past, and this experience of his rushing up to meet me was like a return to your old school, when a teacher who once beat you until the veins stood out on your wrist now treats you as a friend. I remembered the grudging welcome he'd given me in his tent outside Moresby and tried to fit with it his present warm greeting.

The old soldier looked younger, thinner but still stout, and yellowed with Atebrin. 'I was just talking about you with young Pointer here,' he said. I looked at Jimmy's face, expecting to see on it a mocking reflection of the unlikely claim Starkey had just made. I saw nothing in Jimmy's features, though. The blue eyes were immobile. He just nodded. His smile was an honest social smile.

'Come, come,' said Starkey, bullying me by the shoulder, 'Is there time for another cuppa here, Jimmy?'

Jimmy squinted at his wrist watch. I noticed then he was wearing an extra pip on his shoulder; he was Colonel Pointer now. I thought I could see the cause of it in all the fatherly grinning Starkey was directing at him. Starkey, it seemed, had discovered him.

I said I had appointments in Sydney, that I would need at once to order a cab. 'No, no,' the General roared. 'You can travel in my car - expecting it any minute. Tell me about how you are. What was the outcome of the fangs, eh, eh?'

I told the easy lie, that I was good as new. I congratulated him on his New Guinea triumphs.

He said, 'Let me tell you, Paper, it's hard enough dealing with the bloody Nip . . . But that bugger McLeod!'

He shook his head but then smiled again, his cheeks two perfect yellow apples. 'You need to have some smart chaps on tap if you hope to deal with McLeod. And speaking of smart chaps . . . you might have noticed an old friend of yours has been promoted.'

I offered Jimmy my best wishes. My mind was still taken up with my destination. I wished they'd let me try for a taxi.

The General pointed to Jimmy's shoulder straps. 'A reward for being able to read the future, as if it were written history,' he said, a bloom of brandy showing up behind the yellow cheeks.

'Whose future, sir?' I asked.

The General stretched out his hand. I could see a few tropic sores on the flesh, dusted with some medical powder. 'The future of that fringe of islands, Paper. Do you think that this is the last time they'll be fought over? I tell you, we'll see the Chinese make a bid and the bloody comrades, too. It's always been a dream of those buggers. And the Americans, the Americans will want to go on controlling the whole bloody circus for at least half a century yet. That's the future, Paper, the way we read it . . .'

He sounded as if he'd spent an intense session with Jimmy.

I winked at Colonel Pointer, who lowered his eyes and let a slight coy amusement affect the corners of his mouth.

At last the old man's army car turned up outside the tea-house door. At the time Starkey had been leaning forward about to prod my coat sleeve with his finger tips, a signal that I was going to be given something in confidence. Inside the vehicle he kept his conspiratorial manner, talking to the driver in clipped, breathy sentences.

I found out they were on their way to the Australia. They'd flown from New Guinea the day before and spent the afternoon in Brisbane. There, Starkey told me, they'd made a social call at the penthouse at Lennon's, where Mrs McLeod – 'Poor bitch,' said Starkey – was still imprisoned.

Jimmy winked at me broadly now and, to stifle my laughter, I had to grunt a bit and pretend to cough. In other company I would have laughed out loud at the idea of Starkey calling on Mrs McLeod to look her over for seduction. I imagined the Asian contempt with which Missy Ah must have moved during his visit, I imagined the bright little Sergeant of Malinta questioning him with immense seraphic eyes, half catching his purpose (for the little bloke was no idiot), half at a loss.

'We took them for a ride,' said Starkey. 'Down to Southport. You know they've never been to the beach, all that time they've been stuck in that penthouse. The little bugger was carsick in Jimmy's lap.'

Yet all this talk was a parenthesis until we were properly settled in our seats and the driver had reached third gear and a straight length of road. Jimmy faced me from the dicky seat. Starkey, with his broad arse, took up half the back seat and I had the other half to myself. The General glanced out of the back window at the homely streets of Mascot, just like a syndicate head in a gangster picture. Then he placed a hand near my false knee.

'No bugger told me about Johnny and Pam Masson.' It sounded like an apology. 'No one. I suppose somebody knew, but no one passed it on to me until Jimmy came up to Moresby the other day and put me right . . .'

I said 'They've been as secretive as they can be.'

'I needn't tell you I'm amazed, Paper. The old bugger!' And he uttered his earthy laugh. 'What I mean is, I find the man's support of me even more breathtaking. I understand the girl's stuck to her husband. Loyal, I mean.'

'She felt he'd been badly done by,' I said. 'She believes he's one of those great commanders.'

'There aren't any great commanders any more,' he told me. 'Of course, I've met the girl. In the past, I mean. I've ... I've seen her ... a beautiful woman. That man Mulhall ... I'm amazed by his integrity.' The chuckles began again. 'Jesus, I might myself sack my best friend for a go at that one!'

I kept straight-faced but Jimmy forced one short, contemptuous hiss of laughter through his closed lips. It seemed he could still get away with being his own man.

Starkey composed himself. 'Is it still on?' he asked.

I wasn't going to tell him all the truth. 'It's different now,' I said. 'She's taken the shilling.'

'Joined the bloody army?' he asked me.

'That's right.'

That, too, amused him in a fleeting way. I explained, 'I think it was to get away from her husband.'

He clucked his tongue and, with a fake solemnity, lowered his big jaws against his throat. It was hard to dislike him. 'I know, I know. He's such a righteous bastard.'

'I think she's a bit guilty about him, you see.'

The old man had now joined his hands, which gave him even more the look of a bogus penitent. 'In view of Mulhall's loyalty to me, I would never knowingly embarrass him. I want you to tell him that. That I just didn't bloody-well know.'

The old request to pass on word! I had come to Sydney on my own account, neither tipping off Johnny nor asking my boss's leave. The afternoon session would be news, with Eddie Hoare still rampant. I would have to compose my copy at second hand – the exercise of a freelancer, a man who makes his own time and chooses his place. I was enjoying travelling, that is, as my own agent. But now Starkey reduced me again to the role of staff runner.

I said I would certainly pass on his sentiments to Johnny.

He nodded, he was content. He said, 'There's a posting in the Middle East. Commanding troops in transit. Exchanging prisoners of war. So on. I think it just about warrants the rank of major-general.' A stutter of merriment rose again to his Santa Claus features. 'With her husband as far away as all that . . . well, the lady isn't likely to be distracted from dear old John Mulhall.'

They let me out at a corner in King Street. I baffled the servile driver by springing up through use of my indomitable wrists, employing my false leg as a pivot. The unowned Colonel Pointer left the limousine and accompanied me to the door I was seeking. I saw him advert to the fact that it was the entrance to a club. He whispered to me, 'Starkey's going to perform one of his boring adulteries tonight. A forty-five-year-old from Point Piper. He's been going troppo up there in Moresby. I surprised him chatting to a Melanesian housemaid.'

I leaned on my crutches. 'I hope he's lined up someone for you,' I told Jimmy.

He said, 'Even if he does, I shan't be available, old Paper. I'm having dinner with a Supreme Court judge. This war will end one day.'

He saluted me with his swagger-stick, the one which had broken the serpent's back.

As the car turned away, I saw the old man grinning at me from the car's back window and I understood it was a grin that had to be transmitted in its turn. In the sense that it was meant to be passed on to John Mulhall.

In a private room upstairs, at a table set with heavy starched table linen of plain design, sat the barrister I'd come to meet. I was surprised to see the state of the man who got up from his chair to grab my hand. I had last seen him two years back, when he was a member in the Branch Office. He had been one of that gang of Sydney Tories who'd detested Tony Hamish. Even so, when Hamish got to power at Easter '39 this man had expected a place in the ministry and his friends in the New South Wales machine had expected it for him because of his known gifts. He had not got it. Hamish would never be known to make appointments according to merit, for all his life he feared vipers at his breast. My friend had then lost his seat in the election of '40 by a gross or so of votes. At the time he told me that he could have held his electorate had he been a minister and it would not take me long today to find out that this opinion had become an article of faith with him.

I abominate at most times these little delineations of political rancour and apologize for setting one down here. It might go to explain, though, why the man had taken to wearing an old-fashioned alpaca coat like the ones ancient law clerks wear, and how the eating of the bread of hate had blurred his features and thickened his body by a good two stone.

It was while I looked at him in his ancient cloth that I noticed it was as hot as a tomb in that private room.

We ordered. He wanted a full-scale roast dinner with a bottle of Murray River mud. I thought a salad would sit well during my flight back to the capital. After the waiter went and we began to talk, the subject-matter put him off his food; he left a good third of the beef to stiffen in its gravy. He punished the claret, though.

He said, 'I've always wondered what to do with this, how to exploit it.' He patted a manila envelope by his plate. 'I mean, when to use it to best effect against that pompous bastard. I'm glad you called me, Paper, you can consider yourself the catalyst, my friend.'

I shook my head. I must have been shocked by his willingness to traduce Hamish. And all at once I became scrupulous. I said, 'This might not, of course, be used in the House, publicly. It might be used just to hold him still while Eddie Hoare pins him to the wall with this Brisbane line thing. Does that suit you?'

The man pecked at his claret. 'I've never seen Eddie Hoare as the sword of justice. But as you will, Paper. I want my country and my party rid of Hamish. I know that in strict terms the Brisbane line business is unjust. But people are going to believe it of him. It's what they expect of the craven bugger.'

I heard my friend's teeth make another snap at the glass, sufficient almost to break the rim. 'I say get him coming and going,' he told me. 'I am happy enough for John Mulhall to win the next election, as long as Hamish is shaken loose from the tree.'

244

'You admire Johnny?' I asked him.

'I think he would be dangerous only in the peace. I expect to be Attorney-General by then, under a prime minister from Sydney. I won't name names. But would you like more beer, Paper?'

I said no, that I'd like to read the affidavit he had in the envelope by his elbow. That made him at least put down his glass, so that he could pass me the document two-handed.

As I opened it, he briefed me.

In 1938 (he told me), in our winter but the summer of Europe, Hamish had made a side trip to Germany during a visit to Britain. Tony had been Attorney-General the year of Munich. My friend reminded me this hot day that the *Sunday Times* had named Tony among the half-dozen best orators in the British Empire – counting in all the niggers as well, said my acrid luncheon companion. In London the social columns that fatuous season got excited by his urbanity, that he wasn't the usual uninvitable colonial. With people such as the Beaverbrooks and Lord Salisbury he'd become a prized dinner guest.

It was at these dinner tables that a Tory fringe began to whisper to him that there'd always be a House of Commons seat for him 'over here' if ever his countrymen gave him the push.

Anyhow, he had taken a week off from his conquests in the West End and gone to have a look at the new Germany. His travelling companions on this excursion had been a colleague – a fellow minister – and the minister's wife. They were both Sydney people, my friend said, as if that were in their favour. They had both been shocked, it seemed, by the demeanour Hamish had shown the Nazis. The minister's wife had, before her recent death and while Tony was still in power, been so haunted by it that she'd made this affidavit in her final illness and authorized my friend to exercise his discretionary use of it.

The woman's affidavit said that Hamish, her husband and herself had stayed in the lavish British Embassy in Wilhelmstrasse. The minister and the wife had always been inquiring sorts of tourists and went off on unaccompanied shopping trips. They had noticed the marked Jewish shopkeepers, they saw the storm troopers shopping in Jewish establishments, making loud jokes about Semites, breaking fixtures as if by accident, playing butterfingers with pottery, casually staining fabric, scratching the surfaces of paintings.

Meanwhile, Tony Hamish stuck to the embassy round with the ambassador. In his company, Tony was invited to address a dinner given by the head of the Reich Words Ministerium. At table he swapped anecdotes with charming German officials and then got up to praise the evidence of good order, economic thrust and human fulfilment that were apparent in the nation. In those days there was no shortage of ratbag luminaries praising national socialism at ministry dinners in Berlin. News of Tony's speech did not reach either the British or the Australian Press.

Two days later the three Australian tourists visited the great works at Siemenstadt, where Hamish once more found the degree of technological excellence so astonishing that he went to further excesses of admiration. He spoke of the thorny individualism that marred industrial life in Australia. Perhaps many nations, he suggested, could look for salutary influences to the superb orderliness of German industrial activity. The minister's wife said in her affidavit that she was horrified the more by this speech because she had been told by an American journalist – the affidavit named him – that a section of the works was run on the unwilling labour of communists, Catholics and other enemies of the State.

The deceased lady stated further in her deposition that she and her husband had been able to explain this behaviour to each other only in terms of a sort of mental over-excitement Hamish had shown at thinking he'd seen the political salvation of a nation, at having had it apparently demonstrated to him that society was perfectible. Anyhow, he'd gone on to tell his gratified audience that he was sure those lies which were the work of international Marxism would never achieve a break in the peaceful connection between the German people and their British cousins. He dragged Australia into this statement of consanguineous harmony. When he sat down, the lady could see that he believed he'd performed a service to international peace and afterwards, in their car zooming back to Berlin on the Arvus, he made a few half-bashful remarks that tipped her off to the fact that that had been his purpose.

246

On that reflection, the statement ended. I heard my luncheon companion stirring the lees of the claret in the bottle, pouring them out, taking them in with his quick swallow.

'Get him with the one or the other,' he said. The words came with a wince of flatulence to his lips. 'I have two other copies. If the viper should ever again raise his head high.'

I thanked him and was pleased to have to leave in a hurry, since the Douglas was to return to the capital by dusk. My leave-taking was half-shameful. I think I could sense the poor sod's coming dissolution; I think even then, in my rush for a cab to Mascot, the alpaca coat looked like something that hangs behind a door in an old man's death room. The sight of his empty bottle and murky glass abashed me.

He did not have much more than two months to live, anyhow, and dropped dead in the midst of a briefing in an equity case. It would have been a good one for a future attorney-general to have had under his belt.

'Where've you been?' Tony asked me that evening, when I called his office. I knew from my colleagues that there'd been no lifting of Eddie Hoare's privileged libels that afternoon. 'Question Time was a bloody circus,' Hamish told me. 'So what do you want? Because I won't postpone retaliation one more day. Tell me what you choose, Paper. A massacre or a settlement?'

I told him that the workers of Siemenstadt sent their best wishes.

'What?'

I repeated it.

He said, 'I think you'd better come to my office and spit out whatever bloody nonsense you've hit on to my face.'

'Why shouldn't you come to mine?' I asked him. 'When it's all said and done I'm the resident cripple.'

'But I'm not John Mulhall. I don't go creeping round among the Press after dark.'

I got to his office, taking my time, the affidavit nested in my breast pocket. Telling him there were copies, I let him read the thing. He said, 'Do you expect me to quail in front of this . . . this fiction . . . this fiction of an hysterical bitch?'

'A late hysterical bitch,' I said. 'A bitch who can't be reached, appealed to or subjected to party discipline.'

He let the affidavit fall on the desk and a small movement of air from the window of his office pushed it towards me. 'Her motivation must be entirely transparent to you, Paper. Her husband wasn't asked to speak. And, if he had been, he would have proved the normal antipodean embarrassment.'

'It doesn't matter what in the hell I think her motivation is. It's what Johnny could do with this if it were tabled in the House.'

He pushed his jaw forward and frowned at me and I felt a sort of insidious sympathy. I said softly, 'This'll put an axe in Eddie Hoare's left hand, to go with the one he's wielding in his right.'

I picked up the document that Tony had let fall and put it back in my suit pocket, in case he decided he'd rather tear it up than let it flutter.

'Nothing more to say?' I said.

I got up to go and he called to me when I was at the door. 'So you think I'm a Nazi, Paper, eh?' His voice had just a little whimsy in it.

'I don't know, Tony. You're a bit of a bloody chameleon, if you ask me.'

He said, very evenly, 'Paper, when I'm in power again, expect to be turfed out of your cosy billet round there.'

'That's a risk I'm game for,' I told him, my lack of animus matching his.

For I thought I could see his future, the blunting of the face, the premature alpaca, the hiring of private ill-ventilated rooms, the drinking of sour wine, all that I'd left behind at two o'clock that afternoon in Sydney.

I was as wrong as you can be. But that's another story.

Chapter Eight

Pam Masson turned up early and without warning at our door on the morning after Christmas. The capital she reached lay sated with the festival, becalmed among motionless trees. She had ridden in the cabin of an army truck all the way from Sydney and hadn't slept much because of the driver, who'd kept her awake with indecent suggestions in spite of the difference in their rank. For I noticed she now wore the single pip of a second lieutenant.

Even allowing for the rigours of the journey and the speed of her promotion, I could see that the woman who sat in Millie's kitchen had altered, had taken on a mood and a posture outside her normal range. She drank her tea with both hands, staring through the steam like a refugee. When she walked there was a jerkiness. Her feet, in her army shoes, struck the ground vertically, instead of on a horizontal glide, as was intended by the institutional cobbler. She could have been wearing high heels.

'I feel as if I've been down a mine,' she told us. 'Do you think I could have a bath?' Millie made off, going to look for bath-heater wood in the back garden.

'No, no.' Mrs Masson jumped up and grabbed Millie's shoulder, panicked by the idea of any friend of hers having to ply a tomahawk in the breathless yard. 'I just want cold, I just want cold water. Honestly.'

Millie pursued her all the way to the bathroom saying, 'Are you sure? It's no trouble.'

I was pleased when the girl was locked away in the bath. Even without the surprise visitor and her surprising state of soul, I was pretty petulant. Our austere Christmas had not been austere enough to assure me an unclouded brain. When Millie got back to the living room, I turned on her.

'Now what do we do?' I demanded. 'Go and have Boxing Day lunch with Johnny and Ada? Fill up on pineapple ham? While the girl's here?'

'Of course,' said Millie. 'We agreed we would.'

I came up with my normal accusations – that she'd do anything to lunch with the Prime Minister. But she would not be stung on this morning.

'I wouldn't do that to friends,' she told me, holding on to the rules of thumb of friendly etiquette. 'Say I was coming to lunch and then make excuses at the last . . .'

Mrs Masson emerged from the bathroom, her face a little marbled and blurred, I thought, a little blue from the cold water. She wore her army shirt, the sleeves unrolled and dangling, and her skirt. Her white legs were bare, and her feet. I sat in an easy chair, by an open window, wanting a draught, blaming the sunlight for the temperature of my liver. I looked away from her because of my own ugliness. But from what I could tell, she was still sullen, or busy with thought.

·I said, 'Where did you eat your Christmas dinner?'

'I worked,' she told me, the way a person does who is glad to have avoided the feast. She stretched and smiled. 'I held the fort when no one else wanted to.'

'See Dick?' I asked.

'He sailed four days ago. Pleased to be out of it by Christmas, I think. Aren't people amazing, the things they can talk themselves into. He's just about decided the Pacific is a sideshow anyhow. He's sure he can work himself into a big staff job with the British. I know they think a lot of him. More than they think of Starkey . . .'

We spoke of drought, we spoke of her army work, at least about the temperament of her sister and brother officers. By an instinct we avoided the mention of Johnny. Yet, yawning, she gave us a hint; she said, 'I might put in for a transfer.'

'Where to?' I asked, at once alarmed.

She inclined her head towards me. 'Well, not as far as Dick, anyhow.' She yawned again and stretched, grinning, showing her upper teeth. 'Darwin's always appealed to me. Not as an army posting. But I mean, as a place to live. If you're going to live in Australia, you might as well live somewhere like Darwin. An authentic sort of place . . .'

But, I thought, prime-ministerial visits to Darwin are a bit far between.

She sprawled in abandon, one leg forward, one back behind the back leg of her chair, her arms thrown out wide and her trunk reduced by exhaustion to its usual open, unclaimed look. 'Would you mind if I slept the morning away?'

Millie looked at her with what I think of as Millie's pernicious directness. 'We'll be away at lunch-time.'

'Please, I'm sure I'll still be asleep.'

'It's at the Lodge,' said Millie.

Pam Masson nodded. 'His wife there?'

'Yes. She's been there since December the twelfth.'

I wanted to punish Millie for being so scrupulous about dates. Lieutenant Masson said, 'I'd like to see him if he's got time.'

Her voice seemed only half-conscious. There was none of that trowel irony you get in the speech of women who have been hurt by all the usual contradictions of being someone's girlfriend on the quiet. By such usual contradictions as being the last person who gets an invitation to lunch at the Lodge.

She just yawned again. Millie was left staring and puzzling. I remember the alarm I felt. We had become, without knowing it, a foursome. Maybe it's too much to say that we were like planets held in balance.

Anyhow, it was hard to imagine, that morning, how Millie and I would stand towards each other if the substance or, worse still, the idea of Mrs Masson was taken away. Harder still to think of Johnny and me alone, out of the girl's magnetic field.

* * * *

251

Ada was a literal-minded woman. She'd said she would invite only her friends to this lunch and she'd been literal about that. There were just eight of us, seated in the dappled shade among the rose trellises to one side of the Lodge.

Johnny was late. But it didn't seem to put anyone off their talk and Ada smiled from one to the other of us, trusting us, taking pleasure in our loquacity. She would listen to people for a while, then spring up to run in and fetch plates of nuts or canapés. The Commonwealth would have permitted a maid for such work but I think a maid might have scared her, might have broken the rule of friends only.

Returning from her excursions to the kitchen, she would alight in a seat beside a different guest each time. By these means I found her at my side at last, turning her murderous grin on me, her hands joined.

'John shouldn't be too long,' she assured me privately, as if she believed I couldn't enjoy myself until he turned up.

'Oh, no,' I said. I was in the exact panic that I thought – beforehand – I'd get into if she started talking to me alone. 'It doesn't matter, Ada. I came to see you, too, you know.'

I heard her soft laugh at my elbow; she absolved me from my well-meaning lie. 'I think,' she said, explaining the delay, 'things are coming to a head at Buna. You know, I said to John last night, I said, at least Kevin was saved that. At least he was saved having to spend Christmas in one of those terrible jungle situations . . .'

I could, of course, without too much mental strain, taste the sort of Christmas evening the Mulhalls had had, under the scalding westerly, under the churning fans of the Lodge. While Johnny's juices were still involved with the sombre duty of digesting the heavy dinner she'd got ready with her own hands, she'd probably raise two deadly topics in one sentence: Kevin, the dead son, and Buna, the Japanese beach-head that wouldn't fall.

But I agreed with her, anyhow, and started talking about what I'd seen and heard of the Japanese, about how tall they were, how crafty, how fierce. I was very pleased to get on to subjects like that. I expatiated. And she seemed to take some comfort from my chatter; she went on smiling a broad, innocent smile.

Then, in the midst of all my New Guinea talk, she said, 'Has Johnny ever spoken to you about wanting another son?'

Later I could reflect that that was the trouble with shy people – they were like kids, they didn't understand the limits of polite talk, they broke the fences. 'No,' I said in a rush. 'No. We never talk about . . . such things. We just talk about politics.'

Her voice was low and she put her hand on my wrist for a second, as if to indemnify me for the way I was suffering. 'I just thought, Paper . . . I don't know what men talk about to each other when they're on their own . . . I thought about how he always talks about the troops, you know, as if they were his boys . . . and sons are so important to a man . . . it might be the reason for this other woman. Or part of the problem. You know. All other problems aside . . .'

I couldn't speak to her. I had never even thought of Mrs Masson as a bearer, a suckler, hanging baby napkins on her hill at Double Bay. Ah, it could be said, he never saw her as a whole woman! And of course I didn't. The whole business of being obsessed has damn all to do with seeing people as integers.

I was still muttering at Ada when we heard the dry crackling of the river gravel on the Lodge drive and saw Johnny's car arriving. Almost at once Johnny himself appeared – like a shy stranger at some other person's party – in the parlour door, dragging his driver Reg Whelan with him.

Ada got up to greet Johnny and to make Reg welcome. I was aware of the stirring of the shoulders in the nice man from the British High Commission over this serious incorporation of a driver into the official party. If the nice man had been watching me, he would also have seen a stirring of the shoulders, as of a man delivered from a burden.

We ate some cold cuts. Millie brought me mine, set it on my lap with a thud, just like an aunt letting her nephew understand she expects his good manners to extend right through the afternoon.

Johnny galloped through his lunch. I was placing my own plate, with its fragments of meat, at the leg of the chair when he came up to me. He tamped his lips with the butt of a fist to suppress the wind he'd got from eating his lunch too fast, in too

253

taut a mood. I resented his edgy grin a bit; it was too much on top of all the edgy grins of his spouse.

He said, 'Millie told me, in her disapproving manner. Pam's there.'

'She's sleeping, Johnny.'

He said, 'She told me there wasn't a chance till New Year. Couldn't get leave . . .'

'She must have juggled it with someone.'

I watched Ada laughing with Whelan over a funny story about Whelan's four-year-old. 'She says she'd like to see you, if you have the time,' I told Johnny.

He whistled through the cigarette holder. At first I thought the noise was some sort of comment but I looked up to see that he was merely clearing it of any impurities. 'That's a bloody funny message,' he told me, without any obvious concern.

I was half drunk and too grateful when Millie took me home at three. The day did not come to a dazed end, though, the way a day after a festival – a day of cold meats and the last of the wine – could be expected to. Pam Masson had rested and was sitting at the kitchen table reading a new copy of Graham Greene's *Brighton Rock*. The book had the look of a Christmas present. I wondered for a second who the donor was. I noticed the sharp way her eyes moved, the good hold she kept of the binding, the crisp turning of the pages.

Millie, and more so I, found all this unrestful. Mrs Masson wasn't behaving like a soldier on leave, like a girl in a heatwave, at the butt end of a holiday. She drank nothing but tea. From out of the sun-mad core of the country, over there westward, a great silence overcame us. Millie and I could make no dent in it, just with our half-shaped sentences. I would have liked to go to bed but at any hour there was still the chance of a visitor. Johnny.

When he turned up at the door we knew who it was, both by the odd hour and the rhythm of the knocking. Millie was towelling a few plates in the kitchen. I had noticed her yawning. In her dress shop she'd suffered a Christmas rush from which members of the Press Gallery and intelligence filing clerks were exempt. Because of her location now, at the back of the house, she was free to exercise a rare cowardice and ask Pam Masson to answer the door.

In my customary chair, I could see the two of them filing back down the hall, Pam with her arms folded across her breasts, the way women fold them in the cold, and Johnny muttering away with a half-smile on his face. I noticed at once, though, the separateness of the two of them. The girl looked inert, there was no cogency between them.

We talked a while. I made a few poor jokes about the state of my liver. I was just about to announce that I'd better go to wash myself and prepare for my sulphurous summer sleep when Millie called to me from the kitchen the way she had the first night Johnny and the girl had met here. But this time she wanted me to run the water for her while she looked beneath the sink. She claimed there was a blockage. Both Johnny and Pam offered to help us but - again, as last time - knew they'd be refused, knew that the crisis was a fraud.

In fact the water was running true in the kitchen pipes. I did not even bother to glance at them. I sat at the kitchen table, whence I could hear them both talking, the blurred but complete sound of each word through the brick wall. Millie had by now done everything she needed to, had wiped the benches twice, had wrapped the last of the Christmas ham in a tea towel and stuck it in her ice chest. She surveyed her immaculate kitchen with true aggression, wanting it to provide a task.

I got up and switched on the mantel radio that stood on a ledge by the window. The idea was to enable the two in the other room to talk up. In fact the radio's voice screened us, left us free to listen in to the voices next door.

An ABC journalist was broadcasting from Buna. In a little time, he said, he'd be speaking to three soldiers but first he wanted to tell us what Christmas Day had been like at Buna. It had rained all night and the earth gave off vapour all day. Yet in spite of the stink of the soil, the heat rashes, the flesh rot, all the boys were in picnic spirits. An Aboriginal infantryman had won the Military Medal on Christmas Day, an outcome full of handy symbolisms. The commentator milked most of them. Artillery observation had risen to such an art on this swampy coast that an observer had been able to direct a round to the midriff of a Japanese officer who had stood up on a mud parapet to command his men.

Half-listening, I became depressed for everyone up there in those foetid bogs. Even for the commentator, who had to say just about what he was saying.

And the alternative programme impinged from next door. At first the talk between Johnny and Pam Masson seemed like a political argument. I wondered if they talked politics a lot when they were alone. They were speaking now about an early election, it seemed. There had been rumours that Johnny, once he'd got the conscription laws through both Houses, would call one.

At first I thought she was discussing it in straight political terms – whether a '43 election was ill-advised, whether it was too opportune to call one just after you've done something of which the Press barons approved.

But she quickly got more emotional than that. I heard her say, 'The hacks in the Victorian Executive . . . Soft-headed opportunists . . . Deciding to kill off a better man . . .' And then I knew what she was talking about. The Victorian Executive of the Labor Party had named someone to run against Artie Thorn in the next election. I had seen a report of this in the Melbourne Press. It was a vindictive action but I knew that party machines were greased with animus. No one should have been surprised. I wasn't. Artie Thorn least of all. But Pam Masson was.

She kept saying, 'Does it matter if he votes against you on this issue or that? Is he such a threat, then, for God's sake? Do they have to obliterate the poor old fellow? Do you think for a moment he'd go over to Hamish?'

Johnny said of course Artie Thorn wouldn't do that. He spoke as level and lazy as he could, reducing the matter to its dimensions, a piece of marginalia even in a marginal kingdom. 'That's not the issue,' he told her, 'you know it's not the issue.'

She said, of course, that she'd like to hear what Johnny's idea of the issue was.

'Political parties,' Johnny told her, his voice full of that same

Christmas weariness that weighed on Millie and me, 'simply like to expand. Coburg happens to be a sure-fire seat for us. That's the issue. Very simple. The issue is Artie is now an independent, love, and parties abhor independents. To people like that Melbourne clique he's nothing but a bloody vacuum they can fill with a man of their own making. That's a fair picture of what the issue is, Pamela, if you ask me.'

I could hear a grunt of disgust from the girl. 'You could stop them. You could tell them to just leave him in peace.'

'Peace,' he said very low, though still I could hear that, too. He laughed a little and there was some desperation in the sound. 'He's never given me much peace. I didn't get much peace from him in the past few months.'

'The poor old chap's just lost his wife,' she said, as if that explained Artie's political toughness. Then, 'He loved *his*,' she added.

'Come on,' said Johnny. 'Fair crack, love . . .'

'And so you won't stop them? All those awful Melbourne hacks? All those devotees of Franco? Those backyard fascists who used to think Il Duce had his good points? You won't stop them for a man of genuine conscience, a man out of the same stable as you, Johnny . . .?'

'Jesus . . . stablemates? I wouldn't go as far as that, Pam.' His laughter was just like a plea for leniency. He said, 'I'm not supposed to tell that Melbourne mob what to do. I have enough trouble with them. You see, what grounds . . . what *political* grounds . . . would I have for interfering? I need the buggers, love, every one of those twisted Irish souls. I need their assent, Pam, you know I do. A sight more than I need Artie Thorn, putting on the agony on the back-bench, behaving like a prisoner of the bloody Inquisition.'

I thought I could hear him weep for a little time and, as Eddie Hoare kept saying, weeping wasn't foreign to him. He said, 'Pamela, I didn't expect to have to come here tonight and argue about Artie Thorn. I grieved for his wife – I used to know her well in the old days and I believe the death was terrible. But it doesn't alter things.'

There was now an amnesty between them of nearly a minute.

The radio commentator was talking with a nineteen-year-old called Private Sankey of Proserpine, Queensland. Sankey sounded like an articulate boy. He had had a number of verses, the commentator said, published in the army magazine, *Salt*. I hoped his high school education would not be annulled by a bullet.

Pam Masson broke into Sankey's greetings to his family. 'There's his health,' she said. 'Cardiac asthma. You want to be practical and political. Then why don't you let him be re-elected? He'll be dead in three years, he knows that. Then you pick up the seat in any case. Isn't *that* callous enough for your bloody Victorian Executive?'

'No,' Johnny muttered. 'No. They want to punish him. They want to cast poor Artie out. I can't help that.'

She got very loud now. 'So if you spoke to them about it, they'd ignore you; they'd ignore the Prime Minister of Australia?'

'They wouldn't ignore me. They'd remember I interfered. Elephantine bloody memories, love. Artie . . . you have to understand Artie . . . he begs to be exiled. He's been in bloody exile all his life. He wouldn't feel justified in his conscience if he was smiled on by a party, by any party. When you go round begging to be outlawed, people are only too bloody happy to oblige.'

I found I was holding my breath. His voice, I thought, will fall away to fragments. He himself seemed aware of the danger. So, to prevent it, he reached for a mean, harried sentiment. 'If his cardiac asthma's so bloody bad,' he said, 'why does he have to go from city to city forming committees against me? If he's doomed, why doesn't the bugger rest?'

It sounded as bloody-minded as any of the questions that Melbourne gang had asked themselves and answered to their satisfaction. I am sure he regretted it as soon as it was out, but there was no chance of cancelling it.

Pam Masson went quiet now, that quietness that comes once a person decides there's no profit in ranting. 'I don't know what's happened to you, John,' she told him. 'How long have I known you? It seems sometimes each decision you make, you change into a different man. A lesser one. That's ... that's how it seems ...'

I could certainly hear crying now. I could see as acutely as if I were in there with them the tears coming down the blue beginnings of tomorrow's beard, out of his ill-assorted eyes. His colleagues in caucus, whose lacrimatory glands had become just so much sinew, thought his tears were a stunt. But whatever his tears meant meant when they fell in the Party's secret counsels, they sounded like weariness tonight, like a man begging off. I looked at Millie on the other side of the table. She tucked in her lips and nodded at me. I could tell she expected now that Mrs Masson would begin comforting the poor weary bugger.

Instead we heard her level voice, just tilted a little bit by desperation of her own. 'I must go for a walk Johnny ... John ... I must just ... End of question, I suppose ... I find your attitude ... Hell's bells. I don't know ... Can't see any way around it ...'

I heard her in her half-stampede to the door, I heard it close after her. Soon she'd be lost in the shrubs of the suburb or stampeding across the pastures towards the War Memorial and the slopes of Ainslie. I found myself up on my crutches, heading down the hall to divert her, to bring her back from among the prunus shrubs. But I was sidetracked by Johnny, who stood in the living room door. Our eyes coincided for once in such a way that he had no doubt about whether I'd heard, whether I was a party. I was, of course, held up. I couldn't leave a man who wept like that, without excuse or concealment, without raising a hand to his eyes.

He said to me, 'It's all a mystery. Who'd think she'd worry about an old fart like Arthur Thorn?'

I said, 'She'll be back, Johnny. It's no big issue.' We went to the kitchen, Millie and I competing to say that the girl would return. Millie poured tea into him. I switched off the voices of his children in Buna and we talked directly to each other, like brothers brought together by a family funeral, in the shadow of Millie's small kitchen mercies.

But we were both scared that he'd killed the alliance with one peevish sentiment. Years later you begin to wonder if the *casus belli*, the reason given for the split, really is the one stated. Years

259

later you might wonder if the woman – without knowing herself what she was doing – had grabbed on to Artie Thorn as to an instrument of salvation. No such reasoning – very little reasoning at all – operated in Millie's kitchen that evening. I see Millie's breasts enlarged by shadow or instinct as she leans over the blinded king.

After a while, it came to us that she couldn't stay out on Ainslie all night. The jacket of her uniform, her kitbag, her copy of *Brighton Rock* all waited for her in Millie's spare room. We would see her at breakfast, we promised ourselves, as Johnny left for the Lodge and we at last took our rest.

She came back while we were both sound asleep. The note she left thanked us for putting her up and said she thought she ought to find an early lift back to Sydney rather than risk not finding a late one. Sure that army trucks always go somewhere at dawn, whether or not there was much sense to their journeys, she must have hiked the three miles to the transport depot. I have no doubt it was a frightful hike for her. Nor that the militia boy on sentry-go must have been astounded at his post to see her appear, all bleak-eyed, out of the scrub.

Millie, who had not latched on to the feelings of finality with which Johnny and I were afflicted, never forgave her properly for clearing off like that, for deciding she'd had enough of the hospitality of the house while the hostess was still asleep.

Millie was lucky to be able to entertain herself with this grievance. For Johnny and me, the catastrophe was pretty close to absolute.

Chapter Nine

I knew that the Prime Minister and Ada would not celebrate the New Year with any of their friends. But I did not find out until the holiday was over that Johnny had vanished on Hogmanay without telling either Ada or Jim Cowan, his Press Secretary, where he was going.

Reg Whelan, Johnny's driver, admitted taking him to the airfield; the transport manager in the House knew that Johnny had gone to Sydney in a Mitchell bomber. According to Jim Cowan, he had not booked into the Australia, nor was he there at the moment. He had contacted none of his colleagues. Jim had had to call Eddie Hoare in his little terrace in Redfern but Eddie had not seen the Prime Minister. Mrs Masson's telephone did not answer, and the Army Minister, who could have found out where she was, had taken his large family camping at Noosa Heads and was beyond reach of the telephone. Such was government in a small kingdom, among such boys as us!

It seemed, then, that Johnny had cleared out on some sort of anonymous holiday.

I knew nothing of this myself until Jim Cowan came to my room in the Branch Office two days after the New Year. By then the public servants from Treasury were, according to Jim, whingeing about the accumulation of papers needing signature on Johnny's desk and implying by movements of the eyes that they'd always been afraid this sort of delay would sooner or later beset them under a Labor prime minister.

Jim Cowan told me, 'Ada doesn't want the police brought in – she realizes that'd make it a political event. Or a public one anyhow. She doesn't want Johnny embarrassed ... She's a bloody fine woman, that one. A brick.'

I don't think he'd ever liked Pamela Masson.

'Ada understands what it means?' I asked him.

'Sort of,' said Jim. 'She'd been with him long enough and she'd seen it happen before – after Johnny lost his place in the House in the election of '31. He'd also cleared out without asking anyone's pardon a week after Kevin Mulhall's death. She reckons,' Cowan told me, 'that it's always been a matter of his hitting the grog, too. They'd telephone her from the hospital, or the police would. Of course, in those days he wasn't as well-known ...'

'And he didn't have angina, either,' I mentioned.

Poor Jim Cowan said, with that tick of real apology everyone liked him for, 'I know you hate travel, Paper. But d'you reckon you could come to Sydney with me?'

There were no bombers for us. We took the slow afternoon train down through the eroded pastures to Sydney. That, I remember, was the last summer of a drought that seemed, like any old tyrant close to death, to keep eternal state in the land. The following year the pastures would grow vernal, Lake George would bubble out of the earth's bowels, a decade of floods would commence. They cast no foreshadow on us. It was hot in our carriage. The line seemed to have been designed to keep the sun in the passengers' laps.

For my own soul's sake, more than for Jim's, I mentioned that I knew a few colonels at the Darlinghurst barracks. We'd soon bloody-well find out where Mrs Masson was, I promised him.

But by the time the train ground into Central Station, it was too late to pester colonels. We took an age getting through the throng on the platform. A troop train was leaving for Brisbane and it must have been a Sydney battalion, because there were so many women and young children. Half the latter slumped sleeping across the arms of young wives. We joined the long, ill-tempered taxi queue and whistles and cat-calls rose from the citizens in the line when drivers ignored civilians and opened their doors to high-tipping American officers.

Some time after ten, in the darkened city, we found a small room to share at the Criterion. By bribery, and by co-opting the driver's better nature with my tottery display on the crutches, we managed to retain the taxi, giving the cabman Pam Masson's address in Double Bay. It was one of those ferocious Sydney nights, before the southerly turns up. On the way to Pam's place I saw the young whores fanning themselves in doorways and complaining about the tardiness of the sea breeze. Smooth-cheeked American sailors, their hair shining with the evening's sweat or with grease, blundered in front of the cab, whistled it, waved plenteous money at the driver. But he was doing well enough from us. 'I don't know why they pay those buggers so much,' he growled. 'Don't know the bloody value of money . . .'

Beyond the Cross, Sydney grew properly dark and became suburbs. The masts of old wooden yachts tilted by starlight on Rushcutters Bay. Jim Cowan murmured, 'The water would be lovely tonight.'

'Like a bloody caress,' said the driver.

Getting him at a soft word, I said, 'Are you going to wait for us at Double Bay?'

I heard him make a dubious noise with his lips.

'We'd pay you half again of what's on the meter,' I told him.

He laughed then. 'Mate! I can't have you travelling on your crutches all the way back into town.'

We reached the address; we could just about see the harbour's smooth reaches below us. Behind its black-out curtains, Pam Masson's house was dark. I stood on the porch, tapping the stained glass panel in the door, and Jim Cowan went to hammer on side doors or windows. The driver came in to help me after a time, as if a multiplication of knuckles would conjure up someone inside to open up to us.

'Are you blokes coppers?' he asked us.

'Well, at least the way we're paying you,' I told him, 'you can tell we're probably spending some other bugger's money.'

Jim returned to us. He said, 'I wonder if something's happened. If she's . . . you know, sick, inside.'

I went through a few seconds' idiot panic at the thought of Pam Masson dead inside the house, even at the idea of Johnny murdering in passion.

'No.' I said, 'No. The army would have sent someone to look for her.'

On the way back to the cab, as if to justify the journey, Jim Cowan opened the letterbox. It was two-thirds full of letters. He held them up to the starlight, one at a time, looking for some enlightenment from the calligraphy. 'Forlorn bloody hope, Jim,' I told him. The cab driver stared up and down the street, perhaps for more desirable passengers. Yet I noticed one of the items Jim picked up one-handed and dropped again, and I reached into the box myself and retrieved it. It was a newsletter, folded duplicating paper. The mail wrapper round it was marked *Australia-Russia Friendship Society*. Everyone's morale was so low I tried to make much of this. 'We could get the names of the Executive out of here. I mean, Jim, some of them are Johnny's friends from the Yarra Bank days.'

Back in our room we lay on our beds, the window open to the static air, our bodies naked except for linen briefs.

I had nothing to read and turned to the sheepskin push's newsletter. Under 'Members in Uniform' it listed Pam Masson, wishing her well in the ranks. I noticed the committee had arranged an afternoon tea for its supporters, set for a Saturday early in January, since members of the armed forces on week-end leave would be able to attend. I did not immediately understand that the date set was for the following day.

As the telephone at my side pealed again, I could see Jim Cowan's mute, broad face beyond the glass of the booth. His back was to the street door where a dazzling Sydney morning washed across Hyde Park and lapped the steps. He looked so fretful that I waved to him before I picked up the receiver.

It was one of the Victoria Barracks colonels I'd promised Jim yesterday. He sounded in a hurry – he could feel the oppor-

tunities a sweet day like this offered in a maritime city. He probably had a sailing date at noon. He hadn't budgeted that I'd call
him, drive him to make inquiries.

This time he had hard news for me. 'Whoever gave you the
whisper she was transferred was quite right, Paper. First of all,
I was able to find out it was Moresby. Well, that isn't anything
out of the ordinary; they're sending women up there now.'

I said, 'Moresby.' My calmness astounded me, even though
I knew I would never visit that port again. I acknowledged with
a quiet mind that that was just about the end of the exercises
of passion for Paperboy Tyson. Even my friendship with Johnny
would be hollower now, simpler. If ever we found the bugger!

The soldier thought it was geography that had confused me.
'You know, Port Moresby. You should know. You're a bloody
journalist, aren't you?'

I said, 'My boss believes I am.'

He returned to the business of Mrs Masson. 'The reason your
mate couldn't discover much – she's been sent to McLeod's
headquarters there, in the vice-regal bungalow no bloody less.
Fair enough job, eh? I don't know how she managed it. I've
heard all these rumours about her and a politician . . . well, you'd
know more about that than me. But maybe Dick Masson set it
up before he left, to keep her away from Canberra. McLeod
saving a marriage while he saves the world! Listen, cobber, none
of this is going to turn up in the *Sunday Truth*, is it?'

I repeated all my ethical assurances. I had an image of light
in my mind, the light of last St Patrick's day, a village swept
by a light of a different ilk than the blue coastal daylight behind
Jim Cowan's head in Pitt Street. Light in which Pam Masson
walked along in red dust, laughing with McLeod's G-3, chief-
of-operations.

I asked the colonel when she was leaving. I heard him grunt.
I'd stuck another plea between him and the fierce sweet Saturday. He told me he'd call me back with that. Her transport would
probably be arranged by the Americans themselves.

I hung up, left the booth and joined Jim Cowan. It was a dismal conference in that hallway. The door to the bar stood open,
an alcoholic cellarman swabbing the floor. A cold ammonia

smell stained the air. There was nothing more we could do at this hour. Jim had called all the old Sydney friends on a list drawn up by Ada. He knew that if they were old *family* friends Johnny would not be with them, but the list had to be put to use. You felt it was only after you'd done your duty by a list like that that you'd earn the real flashes of information, the genuine oil. And so Jim had been through it.

He had also snaffled another cab and been around all the main hotels, identifying himself. But none of them had Johnny on their registers.

My friend the colonel called again. My crutches felt tenuous as I rushed back into the booth to answer him. She'd left on Thursday for Brisbane, he told me.

'It's not possible,' I said. 'She left her letterbox full of mail.'

There was a pause while he checked some other movement order. He said, 'Listen, Paper, while we're speaking she's flying out over the Coral Sea. Well on her way . . .'

I said, 'More like fleeing. Who'll stop the letters overflowing all across her bloody garden . . .?'

'She's probably made arrangements,' he said.

'It can't be right.'

He said, 'I spoke to the chap who put her on the plane. She's gone all right.'

I took this from him equably, as I had earlier news. But I felt a terrible acceptance in my gut, as if the vitals had opted for a mute old age and the end of things, the dispassion of death.

I emerged to Jim Cowan yet again and put a hand on his shoulder. Like anyone bereaved I wanted a Scotch. But the bar was full of murk and the stink of the mop. Old Jim Cowan said, once he'd been told, 'Well, we know where he hasn't been. He hasn't been with her.'

He was ready to go on to new possibilities. I suppose I was lucky to have him as a companion.

Chapter Ten

The Australia-Russia Friendship Society's tea-party couldn't be ignored. Jim Cowan and I entered the venue, a hall in Campbell Street, through a mob of children, all rampaging, ducking, swerving, tripping on the steps which gave on to the pavement. In the doorway we came to young conscripts talking to girls in white blouses. Beyond I could see older people; it was – in a small way – like advancing through the seven ages of man.

Within the hall itself an art competition for children had been arranged. There were Ginger Meggses by the dozen, a few Disneys, many houses and gumtrees and horses and cows. Gummed stars sat on some of the entries. The judge had already been around, the winners were known. At the end of the floor, under a stage, a table was set with big teapots, sponge cake and fairy bread as yet ignored by the children. Most of the adults in the room were around this table but halfway up the hall sat Johnny, attended like an invalid member of the party by a couple of about his own age. He was the first to notice us, for he was familiar with our shapes and, using crutches, I could hardly steal up on anyone.

I heard him say, low and off-handed, so that he did not panic the hall in general, only the couple who sat with him, 'Here comes the bloody Commonwealth Police.' Johnny's two friends, the man and the woman, turned their narrowed eyes on us, surveying me in my fedora and crutches and Jim Cowan in his Homburg. We were at least out of place and over-dressed and therefore under suspicion of being cops.

As we arrived before Johnny, he said, 'You two bastards would have to turn up.'

'Oh, for Christ sake,' I told him 'It took two days to find you, Johnny. We could have sent journalists after you.'

'Aren't you a journalist, Paper?'

'So are you. But you're meant to be a prime minister, too!'

I could tell that the couple were baffled by his presence in the first place and now by our arrival. They watched Jim Cowan and me as if there was some danger they'd be judged negligent in their care of him.

When Jim began talking earnestly to Johnny, the man drew me aside a little. 'We didn't know what to do, he said he needed three days' rest. But we had to take him to the local quack. He had these chest pains and he hadn't brought any pills with him.'

'Just as well you did it.' I told the man. 'He's had this heart problem . . .'

Johnny interrupted; he mistrusted the idea of his friend and me conversing out of his hearing. 'Clive lent me one of his shirts,' he said. He touched the clean collar. Yet he had not had this morning's shave.

Clive got closer to my ear. 'He's a remarkable chap. Under other circumstances we'd be flattered to have him in the house. But the missus and me . . . we've felt pretty responsible . . . He's just not so well.'

I said, 'It's all right. Jim's his Press Secretary. We're both used to him. All his ways. We'll look after him now.'

Clive and his wife excused themselves then. Nearing the table, they spoke to some of the crush there, the men and women of the Society, who kept glancing over their shoulders and registering the presence of John Mulhall. I was aware that we had muddied their expectations, their sense of the special grace of the event, by turning up in our flying squad hats; but I could see Clive explaining to some of the men that we were not from the Attorney-General's, that the Australia-Russia Friendship Society was safe from scrutiny.

I said, 'Did you know she's gone, Johnny?'

He stared at me as I expected, all the confusion of his crooked eye. 'Where?' he asked.

'Moresby,' I told him.

'Ah,' he said. 'I didn't know that.' Then, 'Why?' he asked. 'Why did she go to Moresby? To a place like that?'

I said, 'I wish I knew, Johnny.'

'Once,' he told me. 'I would've thought a prime minister had the power to stop people. You know. Going to places like that . . .'

'Didn't you check up with the army?' I asked him.

'No,' he said. He looked bemused. He hadn't made any of the inquiries we had, his journey hadn't been on that level. It had been a private man's journey. In a daze he'd gone to her house every day and every evening. It was as if he had forgotten his power to single out her location. The darkness of her house had foxed him, he said. His friends the Gibbs had told him she'd come to the social, that she was reliable about meetings.

'So,' he said, some kind of lump of laughter turning far down in his throat, 'I was sitting here expecting someone, Paper, and in *you* walk. You're not very pretty buggers, are you?'

Jim ascertained that the Gibbs were people he'd met years before in Tasmania, while he was down there helping in the organization of the Railway Workers' Union. That would have been before he married Ada, and so Clive and his wife had not had a place on Ada's list. They had one on his, though.

Jim Cowan had fallen back towards the door now, waiting for Johnny to say what ought to be done, whether tea should be taken, whether we ought to leave at once. Pam Masson had never been Jim's business, nor did he want a bar of her and her benevolent society.

I said, 'Well, you can write to her, Johnny. It's just that . . . I don't know.'

I didn't, either. I remembered the gorged letterbox. You couldn't argue against something like that. It was like a personal assurance from the girl that she was finished with the lot of us.

'Moresby, eh?' he whispered. 'It's a bloody long way.' He stood up in a rush, leaving his own Homburg at his feet. Jim

Cowan came in and retrieved it. It was clear the Prime Minister wanted to go for a walk. The Gibbs did not follow us when we walked off with him - they were saved from further quandaries. At the door, Johnny turned to me. 'Pubs open yet?' he asked. 'No, Johnny', I said. I could speak because I was the boozer, Jim Cowan the abstainer.

'What about if we hit the bombo together. Eh, Paper?'

'The women wouldn't forgive me,' I told him. By the women I meant the accustomed women, Millie and Ada. He could tell that. He could tell from that sentence that Pam Masson had been taken off the register in my brain.

He put his fingertips against his sternum and pressed. 'A few flutters,' he told us. 'I might see a quack.'

In the streets, even in Campbell Street with its light traffic, the early afternoon papers were advertising the fall of Buna. No one could have said any more that the continent of Johnny's cerebrum was subject to real invasion. Johnny paused with us, beyond the children, the fierce pavements bouncing heat in our faces. He withdrew his holder from his pocket; it was the old tool that permitted him some measure of gesture. He was immobilized, though, by the dimensions of that instant and his hand hung by another pocket, the one where he could find a cigarette to slot into the thing. Then he moved off, unstrung at the knees, not having eaten enough of the food that Clive's wife had, you could bet, pressed on him.

Across the bitumen of his newly delivered kingdom, his progress was that of a drunk.